HIS MOUTH HOVERED JUST ABOVE HERS,

less than a breath away, the heat and scent of him invading her senses like potent wine. She felt him everywhere. In the thunder of her heartbeat, in the accelerated rhythm of her pulse, in the fluttering pit of her stomach. Her own breath came fast, mingling with his, making her light-headed with anxiety and something more.

Something indefinable.

She made a sound. Not a sound she had heard from her own lips before, not a feeling she had ever felt.

He leaned into her, his body heavy and warm, disarming in its comfort. She felt almost as if he shielded her in the same instant he ravished her.

"What are you doing?" she accused, but the words were less forceful, full of breathless curiosity.

His head lowered fully and his mouth captured hers, drowning out her startled cry. Harsh and warm, he smothered her, taking what she would not willingly give, devouring her like a ravenous beast . . .

Also by Libby Sydes

STOLEN DREAMS
UNTIL SPRING
THE LION'S ANGEL
BAYOU DREAMS

Libby Sydes

Annalise

A Dell Book

Published by
Dell Publishing
a division of
Bantam Doubleday Dell Publishing Group, Inc.
1540 Broadway
New York, New York 10036

The trademark Dell® is registered in the U.S. Patent and Trademark Office.

ISBN: 0-440-22232-X

Printed in the United States of America

Published simultaneously in Canada

February 1997

10 9 8 7 6 5 4 3 2 1

RAD

*For my husband, Rick, to whom I vowed I would never
dedicate a book. This one is not for you.
All my love.*

ACKNOWLEDGMENT

To my editor, Laura Cifelli, for her patience and amazing sense of humor and encouragement in the midst of missed deadlines and temperamental opinions.

Chapter 1

CASTLE MARCHFIELD WAS GROWING COLD WITH twilight, and colder still with the chill of death. It permeated the stone walls like wisps of damp fog that hovered over the heather and gorse on the distant moors. Servants moved like specters from duty to duty, their voices hushed to escape the notice of their mistress. Grief had its sting, but it did not consume the duchess. Her son's passing only proved what she had spouted these many years past: Marchfield was a cursed place.

With a wail that had sounded as evil as many claimed her to be, Eleanor had sent her lesser servants fleeing from the room in terror. Only a trusted few remained, hardened souls accustomed to both the wild rantings and blade-sharp intellect of their mistress. From the head butler to the lowest scullery maid, they knew clearly that Lady Eleanor was not demented, more the pity, just unpredictably volatile and exquisitely cunning.

Robed in a gown of deep crimson velvet, she paced the chamber, purpose beneath each embroidered slipper. The death of her sixteen-year-old son was a grievous detriment to her plans, but she was not undone. She would get around this as she had all else in this damned keep.

She pulled a cashmere shawl tight around her shoulders and turned a resentful glance on the shriveled bedclothes. Young Richard's shrunken body lay beneath, still now, at peace from the six-night struggle that had finally claimed him. She would not give in now. Had she a weaker constitution, she would have collapsed decades ago.

She must think, must plan. This latest tragedy would be her downfall if she did not. Soon a message would arrive from the king, a sickeningly warm condolence on her latest misfortune, tinged with an underlying note of triumph. Then an offer for protection.

Marchfield stood on the blood of its ancestors, and Eleanor would not hand it over. Using truth or trickery or whatever means necessary, she would hold her lands a little longer, fight the relentless tide of time a little more strongly, until there was no fight left in her. She would die herself before allowing everything she possessed to revert back to the Crown simply because Fate had seen fit to take every male of value from her.

She spun away from the deathbed, repulsed. Weak, all of them! All the Marchfield men had proven to be weak from the cradle. Ten offspring she had carried within her body in wretched agony only to bring eight babes to full birth. One she had lost to a frail constitution before his seventh birthday, two to mishaps the year they were sent away for schooling, and three just on the verge of adulthood. One other—the one for which she'd harbored the most hope—had managed to survive the raging fever of his eighteenth year only to recover as an idiot. And now even this last child had played her false, gone in his prime before securing legitimate male issue.

She stood on the brink of collapse, straddling the razor-sharp dividing line between truth and treason. Tied by birth to France and by marriage to England, she found herself bound to neither. With Napoleon rising to power and the king and queen imprisoned in revolutionary France, she could not chance a return to her birthland, but with her son's death, reversion of her English lands was automatic.

Napoleon wanted her Bourbon blood. The King of England wanted her Catholic soul. Mad George felt the Revolution was Divine Punishment of the House of Bourbon for its unnatural support of the rebels in the Thirteen Colonies. He would like nothing better than to marry a Bourbon descendant off to one of his landless favorites in order to control her possessions.

With Richard's demise, there was no one to save Eleanor now. No one save herself.

She snatched up her ornamental walking stick and marched to the bedchamber door. Her steps were sure, the cane with its carved and gilded lion's head a symbol of the power she still narrowly wielded.

Bedamn the English king his false protection and Napoleon his heresy. Both might want her holdings, but they would not get them, not while the Duchess of Marchfield had breath in her body to plot a course trickier than the rulers' own to assassinate her last healthy child.

She flung open the chamber door. "Max," she demanded in a deceptively mild voice. "To me."

A spare man of distinguished bearing slid from the shadowy end of the corridor and regarded his mistress coolly. He hated death, would not be in its presence, and was grateful she had allowed him to remain in the hall. With equal portions, Maximilien de Chastenay both despised and admired Eleanor. Without question, he feared her.

He moved toward her calmly, an illusion of attending her command while keeping his distance. Even in her fiftieth year, her beauty was unsurpassed, rivaled only by her wealth in terms of a woman's worth. Long before she married the Duke of Marchfield, she had been a woman of independent means, a countess in her own right with the exquisite beauty to accompany her bloodlines. Now, even in advancing years, her body was lush and graceful, the lines on her face few. Though her eyes told a haunted story, the rest of her remained untouched by the tragedy her life had become.

In years past Max had lusted after her, an utterly beguiled young secretary in the throes of overripe lasciviousness for his master's wife. To his moral condemnation, his passion for her lingered still, long after he discovered that he could never trust her.

"Your Grace," he said, and bowed his obeisance.

"Attend me," she repeated and strolled from the room.

The library at Castle Marchfield was as fine as any on the continent. Semicircular and almost cavernous in size, it was stocked from floor to ceiling with writings both common and rare. But its valuable collections were coated in dust and cobwebs now and its hearths had long grown cold. Heavy velvet draperies, rotting with age, covered several nooks and embrasures where children had once curled upon tapestried cushions to read in the sunlight that poured in through costly stained-glass windows.

Eleanor paused before the door, the briefest moment of uncharacteristic hesitancy, but telling in the extreme. Max hung back, appalled by her uncertainty, then stole forward to open the door as if he but performed an expected courtesy. With a harsh breath, Eleanor swept inside like an empress, stirring fine puffs of dust in her wake.

No one attended this room; no one was allowed. It had been closed since the old duke's death, forbidden to all who might have learned from its many treasures. She stopped before a desk of neoclassical style and rested her palm upon its unpolished surface. For a single moment, so fleeting and unrecognizable, her look changed.

"I should have let Elbert do it," she whispered bitterly. "His bastard was conceived before we were wed."

Max grimaced. That she should bring up such now, when it was too late, was a sign of her unparalleled strain. Eleanor was a woman of action, not one to contemplate useless should-have-beens. He wondered at her sudden melancholy over her dead husband's indiscretions.

"He kept the boy's birth a secret until that whore of a mother showed up one day with the child on her hip. Elbert could have legitimized the whelp, taken him from her that very day to raise. He wanted to, you know. Elbert was always such a theatrical sentimentalist." Her brows drew together. "Wed less than a year and *enceinte* with our first child, I had too much pride to allow it." She looked back over her shoulder with a cold smile. "Dear Max, what a delicate, wilting violet I must have appeared to act so betrayed, as if I truly believed Elbert as virginal as I was on the marriage bed."

She smiled, flushed with the memory. "He had been much too experienced for that, too good with a green girl to be green himself. I certainly didn't suffer from his past experiences, save my misbegotten pride and jealousy." Her smile turned to ice. "Marchfield would not stand in peril now if I had agreed to let him legitimize the brat. The price for arrogance is high, Max."

Too high, he thought. What was left of his own father's family had been sent to "sneeze in the basket," as the French peasants called the decapitation death. His brother was working for the private factions supporting Napoleon's movement. But Max knew how quickly the tide could turn and the betrayers could become the betrayed.

Eleanor ran her hand along the finely crafted desk, a gift for her husband on the anniversary of their betrothal. She'd had it designed by the Adam's Brothers to match the many bookcases lining the wall. It now stood as coated in neglect as the rest of the chamber. She lifted a ring of keys from her waist and unlocked the desk.

"I should have let him do it," she finished savagely. "The boy was schooled at Oxford and made barrister, not an ignorant puss. He married well and has a cottage full of healthy children, while I am left with this more wretched course. I would change it all if I could!"

Max smiled cynically but kept his own council. What a hypocrite she had become in her grief even to think to lie to him at this late date. At different points in their lives, they had been friends, enemies, and lovers. It was only herself that she deceived by such nonsense. Eleanor Angelique de Bourbon-Conde had met John Elbert le Fort, Duke of Marchfield, on a trip abroad. Despite criticism from both families, she had married him within the year. The Duchess of Marchfield would never have let another woman's misbegotten son have more claim on her holdings than her own blood kin.

On the desktop lay books and manuscripts, sketches of bold new ideas, foreign texts left untranslated. They were scattered like plucked lilies, well used and appreciated in their time but dried up now, forgotten. Elbert had been dead for sixteen years, gone swiftly, suspiciously, like most of his offspring. The desk and its contents were once a part of the Duke's daily pleasure, as necessary to his personal satisfaction as his beautiful wife.

The contents lay in Eleanor's way. She swept the worst of the mess aside with her forearm, spilling priceless documents to the floor, and uncovered a long flat drawer. Taking another key, she unlocked it and pulled out one thin sheet of vellum.

She turned to Max, her voice strained but final. "Fetch him."

For the first time in nearly a decade, Max's wit failed. He looked at his mistress one heartbeat too long before recovering with a gracious nod. "But of course."

"You don't approve," she purred.

"On the contrary," he countered smoothly. "I

approve of everything you do, Your Grace. I merely don't understand."

"Worthless as he may be, Bryson is the only legitimate heir left. We must return him to Marchfield and marry him off quickly, before the king learns of Richard's death. If we can get a child of him, there is nothing the king can do."

Calmly, carefully, Max tilted his head in inquiry. "How is this possible?"

Her eyes flashed with heat. "Think you that I cannot carry it to fruition?" She ran the back of one sharp nail down the side of his face. "Even mindless animals mate, Max."

He ignored her cruelty and the rush of dark lust threading through him. "When the king finds out, he will investigate."

"If we get an heir of the boy beforehand it won't matter." She took up a quill but found no ink. The pots were turned on their sides, the ink dried to powder. She spun back and shook the document at Max, her reserve starting to crumble. "Can your brother smuggle him out?"

Max stiffened. "These days it is impossible. Etienne cannot even get himself out. I think you must send English men. It will be safer."

"Very well, then send two whom you can trust to go alone and keep their tongue. You yourself must go to the village and find a girl."

His arms and chest grew clammy beneath his fine linen shirt. "What would you have me say?"

Her face flushed in angry hauteur. "That you should

have to tell the young women of the village anything is an affront! Whether directly or indirectly, every morsel of food that goes into their mouths can be counted back to my generosity."

Max waited quietly, knowing she would come about. She was too keen not to have considered every angle before embarking on this course.

"Very well," she conceded. "Tell them that with Richard's death, Bryson is giving up his calling and will be returning from a monastery to take his rightful place here."

She began to pace as her mind ticked off the possibilities, considering every snare. "Tell them that since joining the order, he feels estranged from the ladies of his station and prefers a common lass from among his own village."

She paused, eyes alight with her own skill. "Oh, how they will love that rubbish! Tell them he has no desire to join his house with another of influence, only to serve those who have served his family these many years in his absence."

Max breathed deeply. "The ton will never accept her."

Eleanor's eyes were sharp and piercing when she turned to him. "Will they not, my dear Max?"

He felt it then, the first stirring of triumph, the thrilling rush of moving beyond the impossible. His body quickened with old yearning. She would accomplish it. The indomitable Duchess of Marchfield would return her idiot son, marry him to some biddable village girl she could manipulate, and have the ton groveling at her feet to accept the chit. Eleanor would keep her illusive enemies at bay awhile longer, perhaps permanently. Hadn't it taken over a decade to best her this last time?

Max shivered at the wicked delight in her eyes and lowered his own lest she see the admiration and desire there. She would toss it back at him at some moment most opportune for her, most disastrous for him.

Brilliant, cold bitch, she would stop at nothing to get what she wanted.

Eleanor hated Napoleon and had no respect for English monarchy. Nothing bound her but loyalty to Marchfield. With each child's death, she had grown harder, colder, smarter. Max had no doubt that she was nearly as deadly now as her unknown attackers.

"Which girl do you have in mind, Your Grace?"

Her eyes narrowed. "Choose the apothecary's daughter. She is of marriageable age and will have been raised to respect a submissive attitude. Her father is a God-fearing man, revered in the village. If he is not influenced by greed, he is certain to be impressed by the thought of marrying off his only child to a former man of God."

The blood drained from Max's face. He knew of the apothecary's daughter, a lively, too-inquisitive young girl with a sweet temperament to match her fresh beauty. He swallowed hard and tried to smile. "But Bryson hasn't been in a monastery, Your Grace."

Eleanor glared at him with a silken warning. "Of course he has, Max. Who will say differently?"

Chapter 2

Nothing will be impossible for you.
MATTHEW 17:21

Annalise Weatherly knelt in the garden behind her small cottage and let the rich soil sift through her fingers. Her father's voice drifted on the cool breeze, his idle ballads a balm to her soul. She packed dirt around the struggling flower, then sat back on her heels to survey her handiwork. Columbine and daisies struggled in neat rows, the scent teasing her with the freshness of new life. She loved gardening. The feel, the taste, the very smell of grass and flowers, herbs and dirt lifted her spirits to soaring heights of imagination and contemplation.

Her brow knitted in resignation. Unfortunately, she had no talent for it. No matter how lofty her sights, her abilities lay somewhere far below desirable. Beneath her incapable hands, weeds and ivy seemed to thrive best in the small patch of ground. She worked hard to keep the flowers, herbs, and vegetables from being overtaken.

Mistress Crocker downhill, now there was a woman with the Lord's own blessing for making things grow. Annalise, on the other hand, seemed to have a knack for making them wilt. She smiled wryly and dusted off her apron as she rose to her feet. There was no use lamenting her shortcomings when she had plenty of other things to accomplish.

She had the agreeable task of delivering a cough elixir for Mistress Ackermann's youngest son, then the more unpleasant chore of helping Gerty Rukin with her weekly bread baking. Such simple tasks were like to go undone since Mr. Rukin's death, as if Gerty would fret herself right into the grave alongside him. Annalise knew it was the pain of loss that made the widow so churlish these days, so she kept a close eye out for Gerty's needs, though it tested her generosity more than any other self-imposed duty. She would stop by the bakery and coax her cousin Mary Greer to accompany her, making the task more bearable.

Picking up her basket, she left the embarrassing little garden behind and headed for the fenced pasture behind her cottage. She would steal a few coveted moments with Silvaticus before completing her chores. He grazed near, a noble steed awaiting her attention with bored indifference. She knew he enjoyed her visits no matter how he liked to kick and prance as if bothered.

Named for his savage nature, he had not calmed much over the year since the blacksmith had acquired him from an abusive owner. No one could yet ride him, but Annalise had faith that he was a worthy horse despite his bad temperament.

She fished in her apron pocket for the stump of a carrot, then held it out. "Come, Silva, I've no time to coax you today." The horse sniffed the air and quivered with expectancy but did not approach. Annalise knew patience was her only hope but she could not afford to indulge a leisurely half-hour. On a sigh, she tossed the carrot over the fence.

She made her way back across the rutted lane to the rear entrance of her father's study. It was only a small room attached to his shop, but he referred to it fondly as his place of great thinking. He had, in fact, begun to submit papers of his work, but as yet no one in the scientific community had taken notice of James Everest Weatherly. Annalise thought him a brilliant man who sadly lacked the knowhow for self-promotion.

She slipped quietly through the back door. He would be immersed in planning his next talk and would forget to take time for refreshment. Annalise wouldn't let him go too long, lest he become overtired. She placed her basket on the floor and washed up at the bowl.

"Papa," she called, peeking her head around the door. "Are you and Aunt Mellie ready for tea?"

He glanced up from several scattered sheets and smiled. "Annalise, come in. Look, child, Mistress Crocker has brought us a whole basket of vegetables."

Stifling the urge to poke her tongue out childishly, Annalise walked over and sifted through the offering. "It is a good thing she thinks so highly of you, Papa, else we would starve."

He chuckled lightly. "It's not as bad as all that." He opened one arm for her to take comfort under and squeezed when she moved into the familiar spot. Tucking a strand of hair behind her ear, he smoothed his hand across her brow as if to wipe away the creases there. "What is your discontent this day?" he asked.

She glanced up, surprised. "I have none. Why would you think it?"

A frown, a sigh, a creased brow across her lovely forehead. There had been only the two of them for so many years, it wasn't hard to know. Only to fix.

"Has Master Walter been a bother again?"

"Silly Walter?" Annalise smoothed her father's wrinkled coat, a familiar though useless gesture she took pleasure in repeating each day. He had a smell she liked to call ink and dignity that would always mean love to her. "Walter is always a bother," she teased, "but he is pestering Sarah Beck now." She peered over at Aunt Mellie dozing in the rocker. Bundled from neck to heel in layers of quilted goosedown, she looked like a wizened little elf hiding among bedclothes.

Annalise slipped from beneath her father's arm and walked over to place a kiss upon the old woman's frail cheek. The papery-thin skin was cool and incredibly smooth, as delicate as a baby's. Blue veins showed right through, both fascinating and saddening. Time was rushing on without Aunt Mellie, stealing away her last flickers of strength. At ninety-seven, Mellie had outlived everyone in her family save her youngest nephew and had come to stay with Everest out of necessity two years past.

Annalise counted every second of it a sort of bittersweet joy. "Aunt Mellie?"

The elderly woman stirred, then smiled. "Child, did you see what Mistress Crocker brought?"

"Like salt in a wound," Annalise replied, "good and painful for me."

Aunt Mellie patted Annalise's hand. "What mischief have you been about this day?"

"I've not found trouble once," Annalise answered proudly.

"But has it found you?"

Annalise grimaced. "Not yet, but the day's only half over."

Mellie cackled. "You'll do, child." She squeezed her great-niece's hand, then drifted back to sleep.

Annalise left her to her nap and began to tidy up her father's desk when an unusual sheet of paper caught her eye. It was not their common stock but expensive linen, no doubt imported from Spain. She picked up the sheet and turned.

"What is this, Papa?" she began before the words written there registered. "Oh." Pity softened her brow. "What a cross the Duchess Eleanor has had to bear."

Everest nodded and concern etched a deep groove in his brow. "The duchess has buried so many children, Annalise, I fear it has hardened her heart."

Annalise took note of her father's troubled tone. "Are you concerned for her physical well-being?"

"More her spiritual, though I have not counseled with her. She sends for neither my medicines nor my advice anymore."

"Ah." Her heart squeezed at her father's tone. "After what she has suffered, Papa, it would be easy for her to think man is inept and God has abandoned her."

"I suppose." He straightened the papers he had been

laboring over into neat, consecutive sheets and wondered if he should pay his respects at the death of yet another Marchfield child. He had not know the sixteen-year-old boy; few in the village did. The occupants of the castle had kept to themselves these many years since the old lord's death. "Rumors will be rampant in the village, Annalise."

His foreboding tone set her nerves on edge. He was fussy about nothing, serious about everything, and he never lent an ear for gossip. "Rumors, Papa? That's not like you."

"No, not me. But the village—"

A sudden commotion in the street had the neighbor's dogs yapping. Annalise heard several astonished exclamations and rushed over to peer out the window. She found an extravagant carriage pulled by a team of four matched horses rolling to stop in front of the shop. A coachman sat at attention in a plumed hat and rich red jacket. His face was expressionless, his eyes focused straight ahead. It was as if he hadn't a clue that he'd just turned a whole village street into chaos.

Annalise motioned to her father. "Come quickly. It must be from Marchfield; it bears the le Fort crest."

A thin, elegant man alighted from the carriage. His clothing was foreign and too fancy for village folk, yet Annalise sensed he was not royalty or even nobility. He had the look of a refined and very important servant. She jumped when he began walking toward them.

"Papa, hurry."

Everest made slow progress to the window, his joints stiff and uncooperative. He peered out the window and sighed. "Lady Eleanor's man." He glanced over at Mellie and motioned Annalise to the front room. "I pray no one else has taken ill."

Annalise watched the servant approach. He had a sober countenance, but his eyes were oddly watchful as he took in all surrounding him with sharp, darting glances. She could not imagine what he thought to find lurking behind her boxed hedges and holly trees. Nothing more exciting than a stray cat or wares peddler ever showed up unaccounted for in Marchfield Glen.

Strangely unsettled by his behavior, she turned from the window and followed her father. "I'll make tea," she offered.

She returned in little more than a quarter hour to find the visitor comfortably seated in their parlor. Though he looked content enough on her mother's floral settee, Annalise's father had a pinched look about his mouth.

The man rose as she entered and nodded formally. "Miss Weatherly, your humble servant."

"Sir," she answered. She set the tea tray down, then poured, all the while aware of the man's assessing eyes on her. She felt inspected but was not discomfited. His gaze was neither leering nor lewd, just studious, as if she were a riddle due much contemplation. It was her father's look that concerned her. His brow was knitted, his mouth pinched. An odd mixture of anger and alarm shone clearly in his eyes.

"Annalise," Everest said gravely, "Max has come from Lady Eleanor with a request."

One would have expected her father to be elated. It was an answer to prayer, the blessing of a lifetime, the fulfillment of every village girl's dream. Instead, Everest paced by the hearth, his arthritic limp more pronounced than ever.

"It is not fitting," he said for the third time. "Lady Eleanor should seek to join her son with another of his own class. Has she given no thought to the unrest it will cause?"

Annalise sat on the edge of her chair, her hands folded tensely in her lap. "Master de Chastenay explained all that, Papa."

He spun toward her, mild terror in his eyes. "Do you actually want to do this, Annalise? Marry a man you have never met, one you know nothing about?"

Her chin came up swiftly. Soft curls escaped her bonnet to bounce around her cheeks, and her eyes sparked with mild frustration. "No, not the way you say it. But if he is everything Lady Eleanor's servant claims, he is what I have prayed for." She lowered her gaze to her hands, lest her father see the terrible, confusing mixture of fear and elation in her eyes. "A wealthy and titled man of God," she said softly. "How can I not want to?"

Everest knew his daughter well. She was strong-willed and determined when she set her mind to something, but a gentle heart beat within her breast, one free from avarice or guile, free from the machinations of a corrupt world. Marchfield Glen was small and isolated, not the sort of place to give a young woman much of an education in worldly matters, certainly not a place to prepare her to move from village life to castle and court, even if she had the blooded ties to support it.

Which Annalise did not.

Her heart beat the most common mixture of generations of English scientists with a dollop of Viking explorer somewhere far in the past. It was preposterous even to consider the idea of marrying a simple country lass to the Duke of Marchfield, as if the alliance were nothing more than unconventional. To subject his well-accepted daughter to the possibility of becoming a social pariah was unthinkable for the father who had spent his life nurturing and protecting her.

"We have only the word of a servant, Annalise. You do not know this man, no one in the village does. He was sent off years ago. Many noble sons are dedicated to the church, but that does not make them men of God." Frustration underscored his rising worry. "Six years, de Chastenay said. Why in God's name has he stayed away so long?"

Annalise smiled suddenly, impishly. "Waiting for me?" She could see her father was not amused and softened her tone. "Is it so hard to imagine that perhaps his destiny has been here all this time?" When her father did not answer, she asked quietly, "Do you have another choice for husband in mind?"

Everest pushed a shock of thick gray hair back from his brow and shook his head. "You know I do not. I have always determined to let you choose, as was your mother's wish. My desire is to guide you only."

"And you have guided well, Papa." She touched his hand in reassurance. "I promise not to make a hasty decision. I will spend whatever time necessary in prayer and contemplation until I have an answer."

But she knew already. It was an assurance deep down, unexplainable even to herself. A simple knowing that this was the path her life would take. Anticipation thumped with her heartbeat, drowning out the whispers of uncertainty. If she set upon this plan there would be no turning back.

Ah, but the things she could accomplish as duchess would mean so much to the village. Her mind could not even take hold of all the possibilities.

"I see the determination on your face, daughter," he said, growing a bit desperate. "But the rumors!"

Annalise looked up sharply. "I have heard the stories, mean words meant to scare little children into good behavior. You cannot even consider that they are real!"

Everest shook his head. "I fear they could be all too real. What do we really know of Lady Eleanor?"

"We know that she would not murder her own children!"

A faint blush tinted his cheeks, but still he persevered. "How do we know that?"

A disbelieving smile touched Annalise's lips before the seriousness of her father's expression filtered past her naive instincts to automatically deny such an accusation. Aghast, her expression darkened and she shook her head. "Papa!"

"See?" he responded, "You cannot even conceive of such an abomination, yet horrible things happen all the time outside the fields of Marchfield Glen. Annalise, you do not know the corrupt world that awaits you across that dividing line."

He wandered back to the window and braced his gnarled hand on the ledge, looking out at the village that had sheltered his child so closely over the years. Joseph Gordon's dog, an ugly spotted cur with a crippled hind leg, had gotten loose and was chasing Jimmy Lamb down the lane. The dog was harmless, but little Jimmy didn't know that as he ran, wailing at the top of his lungs. Big Jim caught the boy up in one arm and laughed jovially, setting his son's small world to rights once again.

So simple to smooth out the rough spots with a young one. More difficult now that the years counted Annalise a woman.

"We don't know the true intent of any man or woman," Everest said. "Only what we see on the surface. And what I see is a woman who no longer asks for medicines when someone in her house is ill, a woman who no longer attends Sunday services."

"Perhaps she sent to London for a physician," she said quietly.

"Perhaps." He turned away from the ordinary, predictable sights of a village at midday to face his daughter. "Somewhere I failed her."

"No." Annalise rose swiftly and went to him. "You did a fine job, Papa, but that did not make you responsible for every soul in the village—" She stopped immediately at his stern glance. " 'Man has a free will to do as he pleases, whether it pleases God or not.' "

"You quote my words well, Annalise." He smiled sadly. "This goes beyond missing services, child."

Annalise noted his concern, but she was her father's daughter. She had never been taught impossibilities by this man. Hard work, dedication, committing her works to the Lord—those had been the foundation for achievement preached to her from the cradle. She knew no other way but to set a course and go forward. Raised within the secure confines of a devoutly Christian household, she had never found a need to question the validity of her beliefs or the power they wielded. Her father lived what he preached to her every day of his life, and in eighteen years of working and learning beside him, she had found no reason to doubt the truth he espoused.

The very lessons he had taught now empowered her with their truth. With God's help nothing was impossible to her. It was a thing she felt as keenly as she knew it, a knowledge deeper than intellect. Her faith was the beacon that guided her life, her comfort in troubled times, her stabilizing conscience during bouts of rebellion.

Nothing was impossible to her—even marriage to a duke.

"I must consider this offer," she said softly.

Everest studied the young face so like her mother's at that age. The sweet smile, the stubborn chin, the bright eyes. Annalise was so precious to him, but he could hold her no longer. At eighteen, she must marry soon. He knew this no matter how he liked to set the knowledge aside for later consideration. The village boys had been interested for several years and were growing more bold in their flirtation. There had even been several offers.

Everest had so little time left as the sole man in her life, the one she looked to for guidance. He could no more let her go willingly than he could stop the normal progression from child to woman.

"Annalise," he beseeched softly.

"All will be well, Papa," she cajoled sweetly. "You'll see."

Chapter 3

For all was blank, and bleak, and gray;
It was not night, it was not day;
It was not even the dungeon light,
So hateful to my heavy sight,
But vacancy absorbing space,
And fixedness without a place;
There were no stars, no earth, no time,
No check, no change, no good, no crime—
But silence, and a stirless breath
Which neither was of life nor death
                                    LORD BYRON

THE CRIES OF THE WRETCHED ECHOED ALONG THE stone passage, a constant dissonance whose only variations were pitch and intensity and intent. Silence never fell within the hidden catacombs of St. Bertram's Priory. Rats scurried across the dirt floor, scrabbling for bits of old cheese and stale bread. The quickest, smartest and strongest took the prize. The weak died. They scattered small tufts of fetid straw in a thin stream toward a crack in the corner wall. Frigid winds howled through that one small fissure, as if it alone were the gaping entrance to a sort of contra-Hades where eternal cold was the penance for remaining alive.

Bryson le Fort waited for Delphi's inevitable screech, subconsciously bracing himself against the piercing abomination of her voice. He crouched in a dark corner away from the distorted glow of a rushlight and clasped his hands over his ears. Raymond would return soon to take the torch, but for now it cast wavering shadows along the dank walls, illuminating Delphi's grotesque face.

Madness was evident in her twisted features and vacant eyes. From time to time clarity would come upon her expression and she would peer at Bryson in wounded accusation, as if he were to blame for her incarceration. Those moments were the worst, the brief instances when she knew but didn't understand, when sanity revealed the horror of her circumstances. Those seconds of painful coherence were fleeting, the only blessing in this God-forsaken place.

Delphi remained unusually silent; she hadn't noticed the rats. Bryson slid up the wall slowly so as not to startle her and tucked his shoulder into a small crevice of uneven stones. That they had been put together was his fault, a little altercation with Father d'Eglantine. Peaceful behavior was rewarded with anonymity; bad behavior with Delphi. His muscles burned from the previous cramped position, and he flexed each limb slowly, carefully. The knuckles of his right hand were bruised, but Father d'Eglantine would move his jaw even more gingerly for several days at meal time.

Bryson closed his eyes against the wailing cramp in his

belly. Chances were he wouldn't be allowed food at all—a little extra purgatory within the bowels of Hell.

Delphi curled up into a tight ball against the wall and began shivering. Bryson closed his eyes briefly. *Pathetic idiot*, she had rolled up near the Hades hole. Her clothing offered no comfort, hardly more than threadbare rags that she picked constantly. Until she stopped the destructive little ritual, they wouldn't give her better from the charity sack. Bryson ignored a twinge of guilt. He wouldn't move her, couldn't bare the smell of her. In truth, if he attempted to share his own meager body warmth as some were inclined, she would howl like a rabid animal. He folded his arms over his chest and waited in apathetic silence while she rocked and shivered and rocked to some internal cadence.

He drew a sigh of relief when she tucked her head under the crook of her arm and began humming an ancient French dirge. She would go for hours. He closed his eyes and set the rhythm of his breathing by her chant.

And proposed to ignore the hunger and cold and stench.

A sudden movement sent the room spinning. The distortion was brief, only long enough to make Bryson feel as if the world were dropping off beneath him. He grappled with the wall a second, then realized Raymond had merely lifted the torch from the wall sconce. Voices accompanied the action, low-pitched words from featureless faces. Three or four men stood in the darkness beyond the cell and murmured among themselves without a care for their words, as if the idiots in the cages were all deaf as well as insane.

Bryson understood only bits and pieces of what they said, as his command of spoken language was rudimentary. There were many things he remembered clearly from before, many more he did not. Most of his past recollections were shadowy images, vague like his dreams. Language was like that. Clear in his head, but murky and difficult-sounding when spoken aloud by others.

The presence of strangers threw him into chaos, and his palms broke out in a chilling sweat. Scientists and doctors came and went, men of pain and torment. Raymond's key grated in the lock and Bryson pressed back against the wall, his heart slamming sickeningly against his ribs.

He'd had no warning, wasn't prepared. It wasn't possible to remain docile without warning. His nails bit into the stone behind him. He shut his eyes tightly against the rushlight and prayed they had come for Delphi.

"Bryson le Fort. Marchfield?"

No, no, no. He tossed his head back and forth as a succession of titles were rattled off too rapidly for him to grasp their meaning.

Lord Anglin.

Viscount Ridgestone.

Your Grace?

He would not hear them. One breath, two. Think of the past. Remember the lake, its clear cool surface, its green banks, a time when he was free. Perhaps those days were not real, merely the tortured fantasies of a young lunatic, but he clung to them.

Delphi screeched suddenly, and Bryson wanted to weep in selfish relief. They hadn't come for him after all. He had been mistaken, the titles merely a taunt. The pity he could command for Delphi was naught compared to the remission of terror within himself. His entire body shuddered then seemed to dissolve as he sank into the wall. *Take her, take her.* Her screeching filled the cell in decibels that pierced his ears, his conscience. *God's sake, take her quickly!*

Someone touched his arm.

He rose up like the maniac he was and began fighting, twisting and writhing and bucking. He knew it was useless but he wasn't prepared, hadn't been warned. He couldn't get past that fact. Delphi began tearing at her matted hair and squealing louder. She banged her head against the wall in a rhythmic *thud, thud, thud,* her wails picking up volume. It took two men to contain her; three to subdue Bryson. By the time they dragged him down the corridor, the entire hall was screaming.

The first plunge into the tank was always the worst. The cold hit him like a slap in the frigid depths, sucking the strength from his limbs. He could never get his bearings when thrown in, and struggling only increased his disorientation. His arms thrashed for purchase; his lungs burned. He kicked out frantically and felt for the bottom of the tub. His left foot connected with something solid and he thrust to push his body up. His breath wheezed in and out like great sucking bellows when his head resurfaced from the liquid blackness.

Raymond slapped a collar around his neck. Two other men grabbed his wrists. *Ah, God.* Bryson fought until the continuous friction of leather against skin bloodied his flesh, until they cut off his air. He could feel himself slipping into a greater darkness than the dank ugly room, going limp despite his will to remain strong. It was futile, always futile, but he had to fight back. It preserved some piece of him, kept some small sense of dignity alive, some recognition of himself as human intact. He was terrified of a day when he lost the will to fight.

"*M'sieu* Bryson."

Father Armand's voice.

Bryson went perfectly still and focused on that voice, the cool clear accent, the soft diction. An involuntary shudder rippled through him as his frantic gaze searched for and found the small, elderly priest just to the left of Raymond. Bryson's knees and elbows were jelly, his eyes misty with relief. He made a sound, so pathetic and small it embarrassed him. He looked crazed and knew it, with his wild eyes and unstable breathing, but the fear was receding bit by bit. Father Armand would recognize that. Bryson would have himself under control in a moment, if he could keep the priest in his line of vision. Whatever sadistic plans the others had in mind, they couldn't carry them out with Father Armand present.

Someone put soap in his hair. He flinched when it mixed with the water and ran into his eyes, but he would not close them and risk losing sight of the priest.

He could endure the sting, could revel even in the soap's new smell and abrasive cleansing power. It was rare, a small treat like fresh bread, and he wondered what tortured price he would pay for the luxury.

They scrubbed weeks' worth of matted grime and vermin from his scalp. He would not look at what floated atop the water when they dunked him and began again. Face, neck, arms, chest. The harsh soap stung the cuts and raw places on his skin, but he didn't care. Not yet. There would be plenty of time later to care about the reason they were washing him.

They hauled him from the water onto a wooden ledge to finish his extremities. It was degrading to be exposed so, but their scouring would get rid of the lice and fleas until they sent him back into the filth.

Father Armand made a *tsk*ing sound with his tongue, belittling those around him with nothing more than a saint's concerned eyes and the gentle chastising sound. "Can you not take that cruel strap from his neck?"

Raymond offered an apologetic look but set his jaw. "He's killed too many guards already, Father. You know I won't take the chance."

The elderly priest scoffed. "A misunderstanding perhaps. He's killed no one. Rumors are the Devil's work, Raymond."

"I buried Henri myself," he told the priest. "I know what the lunatic is capable of."

Bryson stared hard at the priest. No matter which way they shifted or turned him, it was essential to keep Father Armand in his line of vision. Finally they pushed him back into the water for another rinse.

He came up sputtering and searched calmly, meticulously at first, then frantically. Father Armand was gone; Bryson found nothing but a yawning, empty dimness where the priest had been standing. He jerked his head to the side, sending pain shooting down through his neck and shoulder. Raymond snarled something vile and shoved him back around. Two more brutes helped pull him out of the tub completely and stood him on the stone floor, naked and dripping and shivering.

"Here," came the voice of Heaven, "he will catch his death."

Bryson wilted immediately at Father Armand's voice. He found the priest emerging from the shadows with a pile of folded cloth. He let his arms hang limp and submissive while the men began drying him with rough linen sheets, then proceeded to dress him in unfamiliar clothing. He had never seen the waistcoat of red brocade or the hunting coat of yellow buckskin, both stitched with intricate patterns woven along the edges. The fabrics were foreign in this hellish place, brilliant to look upon and exquisitely soft. When each exceptional piece had been tugged into place, they covered the whole with a monk's robe. Bryson began to tremble anew.

Father Armand moved forward quickly. Bryson reached out and grabbed the priest's hands, his fingers spasming in a hard grasp.

"Here now!" Raymond cuffed him soundly on the side of the head.

Bryson ducked to deflect the force of the blow but did nothing in retaliation. Unlike some of the guards, Raymond was neither reprobate nor deliberately cruel.

Each man bore a healthy if unfriendly respect for the other.

"No," Father Armand reprimanded. "Leave him be." He squeezed Bryson's hands in return.

The priest's flesh was thin and delicate, his fingertips permanently ink-stained. Bryson cursed himself for the strained sound in his throat and tried to lessen his tight hold on the priest's palms.

"No, do not worry," Father Armand said gently. "I have news for you. Very good news."

"He can't hear you, Father," Raymond growled. "I don't know why you bother talking to these lunatics like they can understand."

"Hearing need not be perfect if understanding is clear," the priest chided.

Disgruntled, Raymond shook his head. "He does not understand, you know that."

"Do I?" Father Armand smiled. His eyes were weak with age but wisdom shone from the cloudy depths. He looked fully at Bryson and spoke with precise diction. "These men are from England, from Marchfield Castle."

Bryson only stared back at him.

"They have come to take you home." His brow softened in compassion. "They say you cannot hear me, Bryson, but I think you *will* not. Harken to my meaning this day."

He had long suspected the young man understood much more than he let on, and he allowed Bryson his subterfuge. The priory at St. Bertram was admired for many things, but its housing of the insane was not one that inspired merit. Paris was much better, more forward-thinking in its approach, but the heart of France was no place for a noble son these days. Poor souls were delivered to St. Bertram's when there was no room elsewhere for them, or no one cared to find better. The priory did what it could to serve the Lord's work in their wretched lives, but it was never enough to assuage Father Armand's feelings of inadequacy.

Bryson had been sent to them six years earlier after a serious illness, a tall and striking young man with no more physical responses than a beautiful, exotic plant that lived and grew but had no soul. Away from the eyes and ears of his distraught mother, he had been sent to die. Instead he had lingered, then slowly improved, then very slowly thrived. But he had never recovered. Bryson le Fort had reached manhood in the "corridor of the damned" as hopelessly lost as the wretched beings surrounding him.

"Marchfield," the priest repeated. "Do you remember? Do you understand?"

Bryson only stared back, dead to everything but the sudden roaring in his head.

"Forget it, Father," Raymond snapped. "We'll get the chains on him, *oui*? He'll understand soon enough."

Bryson did not move when they pushed aside his monk's robe and exquisite clothing, nor when they manacled his wrists. Other than the fresh raw patches, his flesh beneath the iron bracelets was scarred over and numb. The rest of him was covered in a cold sweat beneath the double layers of cloth. He shivered hard and slid Father Armand an accusing stare, then looked forward into nowhere.

He did not understand why, after all these years, the old priest had betrayed him.

Annalise stared in awe at the luxurious barouche. Brass lamps and trimmings glittered sedately in the late afternoon sun. Inside, the seats were a dark burgundy velvet, more elegant than anything she had seen in a conveyance. Pelisse in hand, she hurried toward it before the entire village turned out in curiosity. The carriage itself would cause a stir. The fact that Annalise was climbing aboard with her luggage would start a gossiping riot. She hid a mischievous smile and slid over to make room for her cousin and dearest friend, Mary Greer O'Malley.

"Poor Father will be bombarded by more questions than he has answers." Her smile faded swiftly and she swallowed. "What do you think, Greer?"

A puff of timid indecision followed as Mary Greer placed her portmanteau beside Annalise's. "I think you are so courageous." She dropped to a whisper. "Rose says you best thank the Almighty you were home the day Maximilien de Chastaney came around, else he might have picked another girl."

Though not much older than Annalise, Greer's sister Rose was married and fancied herself possessed of the world's wisdom on every subject. Annalise sent her cousin a disgruntled frown. "Rose makes it sound as if he were after livestock." She raised her hand with mock flourish. "If this girl won't do, choose another. How about this strong beauty with the golden pelt?"

Mary Greer dropped her gaze sheepishly. "How do you see it?"

It had never been said in Marchfield Glen that Annalise Weatherly was a girl to mince words. "Not much better."

With a cry, Constance O'Malley ran out to the carriage, a large basket in hand, its contents covered with her best linen. Her round face shone as she shoved it inside. "I still can't believe it," she whispered, wiping away a tear with the corner of her apron. "It's a miracle. You mind my words, Annalise. It's a miracle from God for all of us. Your dear mama would be so proud."

Annalise wasn't convinced her proper mama would have thought it anything but feckless. "Check on Papa and Aunt Mellie," she pleaded as the coachman stepped up. Though not openly rude, he gave Greer's mother a pointed look and waited for her to move aside.

"A miracle," Constance repeated, drifting back. "You remember, Annalise."

Too soon the carriage lurched forward and Annalise's stomach suffered a nervous drop. The village sped away beneath them at a pace and comfort she had not hither-tofore imagined existed. She was used to brisk walks and an occasional bumpy wagon ride. Never had she ridden in anything so elaborate or commodious.

Nervous excitement sang through her, heightening the color in her cheeks. She smoothed her gown of white and pink muslin over a deep green satin skirt and marveled at the fine, sleek fabric. Of far superior quality than anything she had owned until now, it fell perfectly over the tips of her new black kid shoes. The neck was daringly low, and she touched the white fichu loosely draped and tied at her bodice to make certain she was adequately covered. She looked straight ahead and acted as if she were not a bit more impressed with the feel of her delicate new clothing compared to the linens and woolens she usually wore.

Gazing out the carriage window, she took in the ordinary sights of village life, the everyday occurrences she had always taken for granted. Something urged her to store them away, to keep them safe and locked inside.

Smoke from peat fires curled out chimneytops, many a good husband's supper kept warming. Children played along the lane, their voices shrill and sweet in the late afternoon quiet. Dusk always fell on the glen with a soft hush from the grueling day. Bodies were tired, minds ready for rest. Mothers called their wee ones inside like hens gathering chicks to the nest. It was time to rest and reflect and ready oneself for the morrow.

Annalise glanced over at her cousin. There was a stirring inside her, as if she faced a perilous voyage, leaving all behind with no turning back. Fear and excitement raced through her with equal portions.

"Oh, Greer, it's all so astonishing. I can hardly credit it."

Mary Greer simply looked afraid. "A miracle, as Mama said."

Both girls had the love and respect of the village, but there the similarities ended. Where Mary Greer maintained a submissive attitude and bent toward intellectually retiring, Annalise was mischievous enough to stay on the very edge of trouble. Constance O'Malley pleaded continually with both girls to conduct themselves with the proper comportment of gently raised young ladies, which they did—most of the time.

Mary Greer, too bashful to push the boundaries, thrilled to experience life vicariously through Annalise's impulsive bravery, and Annalise was only too willing to indulge her.

Fair-haired, Annalise seemed to capture sunshine in each curl, which was fortunate, since her coiffure came undone more often than it should and fell in heavy flaxen waves to her waist. There was a vibrant urgency in the blue eyes that gazed out the carriage window and watched the village go by.

Mary Greer, darker by comparison, with rich nut-brown curls always perfectly placed, was a nice contrast for Annalise's fairness. The girls were known to cause quite a stir on market day when strolling arm in arm down the lane, baskets bumping against slender hips, warm smiles on their faces.

The carriage hit a deep rut and nearly tossed the girls to the floor. Mary Greer grabbed the leather strap. "Perhaps he's driving a bit fast," she said nervously.

Annalise rapped importantly on the roof. "My good man, slow this thing down at once!"

The carriage slowed suddenly, drastically, and the girls exchanged wide-eyed, startled glances that spontaneously dissolved into a fit of giggles when they realized they were merely rounding a sharp curve. Sufficiently quelled for the moment, Annalise folded her hands tightly in her lap, determined to behave.

Quaint shops and cottages gave way to green pastures dotted with livestock, then deep brown forests. Unlike many parts of England, hunting was permitted on certain days in the woodlands around Marchfield Glen and the castle park. Most, save the butcher, thought the dowager a benevolent duchess for allowing it after her husband's death.

Annalise pulled her gaze away from the pretty countryside. Twining her gloved hands together, she finally admitted to the unsettled feelings in her heart. "Father's not pleased, you know, and now I'm having second thoughts."

Mary Greer had never seen Annalise so apprehensive. She made a consoling sound and patted her cousin's hand. "To quote your own words, 'For a chance to marry a duke, I wouldn't have a blink of indecision, much less a second thought.' "

"I lied." Annalise smiled weakly and settled back against the velvet cushion. "I'm a ninny for feeling a bit of cowardice when I've already given my word to the duchess through her man, but . . . well, there it sits. I'm feeling as if I rushed my decision a bit." She took a deep, fortifying breath. "Thank you for coming with me, Greer. I couldn't have done this alone."

"Bother," Mary Greer said softly. "I'm frightened of my own shadow. But thank you for the opportunity. I've always wanted to be a lady's maid."

"Companion, you goose. Father must stay with Aunt Mellie, and I needed a companion."

Mary Greer blushed delicately. "A chaperone, you

mean. As if I could ever stop His Grace from stealing a kiss. I'd probably swoon before you did."

Annalise's stomach suffered another drop that had nothing to do with the carriage ride. "Oh, Greer."

Mary Greer noted her friend's pale cheeks and the tight hands fisted in her lap. "Dear Annalise, I'm sorry. It's just that I've imagined him so often as a sort of handsome prince. I forgot entirely that he might be . . . otherwise."

" 'Otherwise,' " Annalise echoed. "You mean an ugly ogre with a bulbous nose, crooked body, scaly skin, unsightly warts—"

She collapsed suddenly onto Mary Greer's lap with a combination of nervous giggles and downright terror. "God in Heaven, Greer, what have I done?" she cried from the depths of her cousin's skirts. "It seemed such a grand idea when Max was in our modest cottage. It seems perfectly horrid now."

"There, there." Mary Greer patted Annalise's shoulder. "It's not as if you must go through with it. Surely you may change your mind if things are . . . well, too deplorable."

"May I?" Annalise sat back up and hugged her knees to her chest, as if no more than four years old and venturing away from home for the first time.

But there was something in the air, a new wind, prodigious change. She sensed it the day Master de Chastenay visited her house, she felt it even more keenly now. There was no turning back, no matter what lay ahead, no matter how she tried to reassure herself otherwise. That, perhaps, was the most fearful thing of all.

"It all sounded so important a week ago," she

whispered. "I had such noble thoughts of all the things I might do for the village and for Papa's research. I even thought of Widow Rukin, though she's always so precisely unpleasant." She rested her chin on her upraised knees. "But mostly I thought of me, Greer. Of not having to marry Master Walter or the butcher's son or any other common boy I've known all my life." She slid an honest glance at her confidante beneath thick lashes. "Do you think God will punish me for being avaricious?"

"I don't know yet," Mary Greer murmured.

"Yet?" Annalise asked in mild panic. "Just when will you know?"

"When I see His Grace."

With a groan, Annalise hid her face in her hands. "Do you know what I *really* think?"

"Oh, *please* don't say it!" Mary Greer warned, sensing what was to come, what they were both afraid to voice aloud.

But Annalise had to; she could not let her awful suspicions go without ever acknowledging them at least once.

Her voice was steady but vapor thin. "I think the Duke of Marchfield must be quite dreadful if he has to send a servant to seek a wife for him from among the village folk."

Chapter 4

"ALL IS LOST!"

Lady Eleanor stormed from the window embrasure where she had been keeping watch and rounded on Max as if he alone were to blame for the fouled plans. "Perkin and Amos should have had the boy here days ago. What is keeping them?"

Max had no answer, nor speculation. The plan had been constructed meticulously, even allowing sufficient time to formulate further options after the boy's arrival, depending on his capabilities. All had changed now.

"We should have received word if there were problems at the priory," he offered helplessly. "If there has been a mishap along the way . . ."

"A mishap?" She laughed bitterly. "Of course there has been a mishap. Napoleon has discovered my plan and had them all slaughtered at the coast, or George got there first and bored them to death." She spun away, her emerald velvet gown dragging on the pristine marble floor of her drawing room.

"Napoleon is fighting on France's northern frontier, and George cannot know yet," Max reminded quietly.

She turned an elegant glance his way. "Do you dare to underestimate any of them before me?" Her eyes narrowed dangerously. "Convince me quickly, dear Max; the chit from the village will be here any moment." She turned back to stare out the tall windows. Acres of forest and sloping fields lay before her, bisected by a thin ribbon of brown. The village road, as yet empty of travelers, wound through stubble crop plots, graceful grazing acres, and woodland parks. Gardeners, shepherds, and farmers toiled year round at their respective tasks to keep Marchfield pleasing and productive.

She flung the damask drapes aside and paced the chamber once again. "Where is he?" No answer was expected, but a demand for action lay beneath her tone.

"I will send someone to search, Your Grace."

"Do not be absurd, Max. Have you not just convinced me that no one is the wiser yet? I don't need another spy to see how he is before the girl arrives. If he's too bad off, we must needs arrange a proxy marriage before she is the wiser."

Then tie the unlucky chit to the marriage bed? If the boy was too bad off, what further issue was there? Max wondered. He was uncertain if his mistress had gone completely over the edge of reason with young Richard's death, or if she was completely sane. Did she have within her grasp the final plan to thwart George once and for all or the final downfall? He glanced back out the window to keep watch, as he had been doing the past two days. His blood surged suddenly, then drained completely from his face. He turned to regard her.

"I fear, Your Grace, the point is now moot."

Eleanor swung back to find not one but two carriages approaching the castle. The first bore the le Fort crest. The other was glaringly unmarked.

She hissed an obscenity, grabbed up her skirts, and flew from the room.

Annalise gazed in awe at the castle before her. All her life she had marveled at it from a distance, imagining herself standing on the steps to be greeted, strolling the gardens, or dancing in the ballroom. Except for one, insignificant time when she accompanied Aunt Constance to deliver pastries, she had never been farther up the winding road than the last few cottages on the very outskirts of the village.

Marchfield Castle was fondly called *La Petite Nationale*, the little nation. Originally built during the reign of William the Conqueror, it had been designed to be entirely self-sufficient during a siege. It had grown so large and spread out over the centuries that it would be impossible to protect the whole of it now, but the castle itself still could provide for itself. From brewhouse to dairy, kitchens to game larder, rickyard to storerooms, there were so many buildings beyond the enormous great hall that Marchfield did, indeed, look like a small nation.

Built of pale stone, the main hall reflected the warm peachy glow of sunset, but there its gracefulness and warmth ended. An austere magnificence held one in veneration upon arrival, but it was a cold beauty, impersonal and intimidating.

Dating back to the eleventh century, only parts of the original structure remained. Additions and renovations added regularly throughout the centuries made up the bulk of the castle's present state. Turrets rose to four spears at each corner where colorful banners snapped in the breeze. The marriage of two powerful families was represented in the ancestry of the standards. The raven stood for Maire of Ravenwood, the castle's first lady, and the shield for Bryson le Fort, its first lord, a bastard knight who had been honored with lands and title by William the Conqueror in 1066 for deeds done on the field at Hastings.

Uniformed guards patrolled the walkways, and Annalise wondered just whom or what they guarded against. The enormous outer gates swung open and the carriage clattered along a cobbled drive through vast, manicured grounds. They finally reached the castle and pulled beneath a covered archway. The carriage rocked to a complete stop, as did the breath in Annalise's chest. The coachman opened the door with grand reserve.

"M'ladies, this way please."

She grabbed Mary Greer's hand. "Wait!" There was a majestic presence to the pomp of the coachman, the parklike grounds, the castle itself. "Oh, Greer," she repeated. "What have I done?"

Mary Greer looked at the castle, then back to Annalise, giving her hand a reassuring squeeze. "Something grand, I'm certain," she whispered. She stepped carefully from the carriage. "Something *truly* grand."

Within the shadows of a ground-floor embrasure, Max stood with Lady Eleanor as she studied the girls. "The one on the right."

"Aye, Your Grace," Max answered.

"And the other whey-faced chit?"

"Mary Greer O'Malley, the baker's daughter."

Eleanor cut him an inquiring look. "A mild complication. Are we concerned?"

His neck grew hot beneath his collar but he shook his head. "Insignificant, as you suggest."

Lady Eleanor smiled. "Annalise. It has a nice, biddable sound. Will she be a nice, biddable girl, my dear Maximilien?"

She had better be, Max thought. God help them all, she had better be.

The front portal of Castle Marchfield swung open. Lady Eleanor swept through, her voluminous skirts flowing regally behind her. Her smile was brilliant for the two young women standing anxiously beside the carriage.

"My dears," she welcomed, jeweled fingers outstretched and sparkling in the late-day sun. "Come in. You must be perishing in this dust."

Annalise curtsied deeply. "Your Grace, it is an honor."

"Nonsense, child, 'tis I who am honored that you would consider my son's humble request."

Annalise's nerves contracted. She looked around in search of the duke but saw no one save Lady Eleanor and the servant who held the door. She slid a glance at

Mary Greer, who could only stare at the beautiful duchess in awe. "May I present my cousin—"

"Mary Greer, of course," the duchess intoned, "the baker's daughter." Eleanor smiled. "How good of you to accompany our dear Annalise."

Struck by the grand welcome, Mary Greer curtsied deeply, then held up the basket she had brought from home. "My mum sends her greetings and these fresh buns."

"How lovely," Lady Eleanor crooned. "How very thoughtful of your mother." The other carriage was visible now, the thud of the horses' gallop still faint but growing louder. Eleanor managed a placid if tight demeanor toward the girls.

"Please, follow Max inside. I've rooms prepared for your comfort abovestairs. My schedule is entirely too busy for me to be a proper hostess just now, but Max will see to your needs in my absence. Until dinner then, my dears."

There was no doubt that they had been summarily dismissed, but both girls had noticed the approaching carriage. Mary Greer moved closer to Annalise, alarmed that it might be *him*. She wasn't quite prepared to meet the Duke of Marchfield just yet, though they had come here for that very reason. She wanted desperately to hide behind a yew hedge and peek at him unseen. If he was truly wretched, as she secretly feared, she needed time to compose an appropriate sympathy for Annalise.

Following the servant inside was exactly what they needed to escape an impromptu introduction. Mary Greer took Annalise's arm and began a gentle tugging. But

Annalise—a pox on her curious soul—dug her heels in more firmly than Sam Blacksmith's most stubborn mule.

"Might this be His Grace?" Annalise asked in a breathless rush.

Lady Eleanor sent both girls a look so chilling it froze them in place. Then just as swiftly she softened. "It could be anyone, my dear. Go along now."

Annalise had noted Lady Eleanor's razor-sharp glance and the cajoling one that followed. Both had been used effectively. The first to stifle her, the second to confuse her into the thinking she had misread the first.

She took one last look at the approaching carriage, then complied with her cousin's infernal tugging. "I'm coming, Greer," she whispered, moving toward the front entrance. "You needn't yank my arm from its socket."

"I'm sorry," Mary Greer whispered, and released her cousin at once. "Is it he?"

"I don't know."

Mary Greer heard the underlying fear beneath her cousin's sharp retort. Deep down, she was just as frightened, perhaps more so. What happened to silly village girls who married above themselves? Mary Greer was very much afraid of losing Annalise once the marriage was done. A duke might allow his wife to hire a baker's daughter to serve in the castle, but he would never allow her to invite one in for tea.

The castle's entry hall was large, rising several stories to an ornate ceiling where saints were depicted in all the holiness and martyrdom the artist could render. Sunlight shone through high arched windows, while crystal and brass chandeliers shimmered from lighted candles. The room was dark and medieval in style, needing every ounce of added light. It smelled old and drafty, too, despite fresh flowers on the entry table.

Though meticulously kept and furnished with the finest craftsmanship each century had to offer, it lacked the warmth and homey feel of Annalise's simple cottage. She wanted to pull back the heavy draperies and throw open the windows to allow the sun and fresh air inside to dispel the gloom.

Max led the girls across the room to a warm spot in front of a massive hearth. Annalise sat, hands folded primly in her lap. And waited like docile guest. But as soon as Max excused himself to order refreshments, she jumped from her seat and ran back to a window overlooking the courtyard. Alarmed, Mary Greer followed.

The black carriage had arrived. The dust was just settling when the coachman jumped from his high seat to talk excitedly with Lady Eleanor. The door to the vehicle swung open and two more men emerged, large brutes in common clothing. They reached back inside and pulled another man out.

By the look of him, he must be a criminal. His hands were shackled behind his back, pulling his shoulders into a taut, unnatural position. His ankles, too, were bound, the short length of chain allowing nothing more than a stumbling crash to his knees from the ignominious way they hauled him from the vehicle. He righted himself quickly and faced them all with a defiant stance. His hair was long and wildly unkempt, dark golden curls that spiraled down his back and over his shoulders without even a ribband to secure them out of a face that was terrifyingly beautiful.

Even from a distance, Annalise was struck by the incongruity of his looks. His bone structure was strong and well defined but spare. A fresh cut outlined his jaw, made more vivid against flesh that held the sickly cast of one who never saw sunlight. His eyes were dark and depthless in his gaunt face. They promised vengeance as he began to struggle against the two brutes holding him.

Though surely a criminal, his clothing was noble—a buckskin coat, linen shirt, breeches with buttons at the knees. And the carriage had undoubtedly stopped at Castle Marchfield by design, not error.

Annalise watched as Lady Eleanor strolled forward to peer at the man. He had not yet seen her and fought violently against his chains, a madman gone madder still at being bound. Annalise wanted to shout at the two louts to calm the poor soul, but they only made matters worse with their inept tugging and fumbling. They had contained him by force but that was all. Annalise sensed that only the chains kept the beastly one from smashing their skulls together and fleeing their brutish strength.

Suddenly the duchess made a sharp command and the entire world seemed to pause. The madman stopped dead still. He stood like stone, only his chest heaving in and out from exertion. His shoulders were tense, every motion arrested, as if time had ceased for one small moment. Finally, slowly, he turned toward the voice.

He stared at Lady Eleanor for innumerable seconds that stretched and expanded until the very air filled with a horrible expectation. His entire body was stiff, his eyes hellish and unblinking. Time itself went motionless, absorbed by that one look.

One murderous, revengeful look before he threw his golden head back and howled like a deranged animal.

The sound shuddered through Annalise like thunder. Her gaze flew to Mary Greer but all words were trapped in her throat.

"Oh, dear," Max stated behind them. "You two were supposed to stay by the hearth."

Annalise swung around, her pulse hammering out a terrible knowing. "Who is he?"

Max smiled thinly. "Come, refreshments will be here any—"

"Who is he!"

Max closed his eyes briefly on a sigh, then regarded the young woman with frank annoyance. "The Duke of Marchfield, of course." He waited to see if she would faint or squeal like a little mouse and try to run back to her father's cottage.

She did neither. Instead, she surprised him by turning back to the window, her head erect, her shoulders braced.

"Why is he bound?" she asked in a thin, steely voice. "A man returning home from a monastery is not bound."

"There were . . . difficulties—" Max began only to be cut off.

"Is he a criminal?"

"No. Never that," he answered, then repeated passionately, "never that!" His expression grew pained, his eyes fathomless as he looked back out the window with the same fascination as the two girls. "You must understand, he was the very best Marchfield had to offer, the beautiful, favored child. Though not the firstborn son nor even the second, one always had the disturbing impression that he should have been.

"Bryson had the sharpest mind, the keenest wit, but he lacked the birthright to use either to best advantage. In truth, he reveled in his freedom rather than jealously bemoaning his brother's place. He was wild and sweet and smart, both the boon and bane of his father's existence."

His brow creased with grief. "But there was an illness, you see, in his eighteenth year . . . nothing else to be done but send him away."

"Oh." Annalise's heart plunged, stripping away all hope. "It took his mind."

The words were whispered, dull with understanding. She knew of such, of course; England's own king suffered bouts of dementia that seemed to come and go like unpredictable seasons. Annalise wanted to scream but dared not, wanted to weep but could not. She lay her forehead against the cool window glass and let all her dreams settle to dust in her heart.

Mary Greer made a sound of compassion and pity, and lay her cheek against her friend's.

"It's not as if I didn't know," Annalise said.

"Oh, but it's so unfair," Mary Greer cried.

"Unfair?" Annalise lifted her head and laughed softly, her gaze transfixed on the beautiful madman outside.

"That a simple chemist's daughter should be given the chance to marry a duke or that she should not?" Struggling hard not to cry, she turned to smile at her cousin. "But think, Greer, it was such a delightfully grand notion for a time."

Mary Greer burst into tears.

Chapter 5

Woe to him who builds a
city with bloodshed . . .

HABAKKUK 1:12

Paris, France

THE YOUNG REVOLUTIONARY WALKED QUICKLY toward the square. In barely two years, the world had turned upside down. The feudal system was gone, a constitution had been drafted, the church reformed, and local government reorganized. A new France had emerged, one characterized by a declaration of rights. The Old Regime was doomed—as doomed as the king who had once ruled by divine right and absolute sovereignty.

The new France was the work of the Enlightenment. Its influence, corrosive of the principles and practices of the Old Regime, advocated natural law instead of divine, reason against superstition, anticlericalism versus church domination.

Justice rather than privilege.

The young man smiled cynically as the prison came into view. Where was justice now? The challenging ideas had subverted the old ways and demanded new solutions to governmental and societal problems. On the surface, the ideas were the work of intellectual giants: Diderot, Montesquieu, Voltaire, and Rousseau. But beneath lurked another reason, another intelligence that operated under the cloak of darkness: a hidden society of savage, evil men bent on the total destruction of the old ways with no basis of morality to guide in the new.

Persecuted by the princes and dukes in Germany, the secret society had come to France. In the philosophy of the times and the frenzy of revolution, the "Illuminated Ones" had found a place to flourish. They were the enlightened, the light of reason, above the law. They would strip the world of superstition and govern by intellect. They existed to establish a new world, a new government, a new religion that worshipped reason and would forge a universal commonwealth.

They had brought the revolution to a feverish pitch and now a machine stood in the square, the people's favorite pastime. It wasn't enough these days to jail aristocrats for being born to a noble bloodline. They were also being slaughtered in the prisons.

The young man paused and ran his sleeve across his perspiring forehead. The machine was quiet today. Martins dipped over the stained cobbles, their cries the only natural sound breaking the stillness. There was sin here, exhausted to silence from a week of raucous bloodlust. The heat caused a hellish stench to arise from the corpses, a stench that fouled every inch of a once-graceful city and castigated its citizens for what they had done. Ashamed now, the city was quiet, inwardly awaiting a retribution that would not come in the form of man, only in their scarred souls.

The young man might have felt the pangs of remorse himself. But his soul had already been sold. Only irony touched him now, and a sense of disgust at the needless slaughter. With renewed vigor, he passed through the square, looking neither right nor left. These days keeping a moderate countenance was tantamount to keeping one's head.

He had mixed emotions about the demise of France. While he cared little for the dead aristos his heart cried out for the inevitable extinction of gentility and refinement. A ruling class of soldiers and peasants would destroy the beauty and culture they had known. The noble cries of liberty, equality, and fraternity that had incited the revolution were twisting with power, growing as rancid as the headless nobles.

He passed beneath an arched entry that stood high and imposing over open gates. His expression was as cool as a well-sculpted marble bust, as composed as a gentleman entering a fine restaurant rather than a prison. But his garments were common, carefully chosen for their plainness. There must be no hint of the aristo about him. These days it was dangerous even to appear bourgeois. Middle-class men or women who opposed the guillotine aloud would find themselves subjected to it as well.

Power had shifted. No one was immune.

He entered the death house nonchalantly, rolling and lighting a Spanish cigarette as if bored. He inhaled deeply, hoping the tobacco would override the stench. Blood filled the cells and ran in rivulets down walls and stairways and into the clogged gutters. The atrocities committed inside had become simple matters of butchery and did not bear justifying no matter how grandiose the cause.

Reaching the guard, he crushed the cigarette beneath his heel, then held out papers.

The guard ignored them. "I know you, Citizen. Go on in."

Once inside, he was greeted with a scream of pain and torment. Like waves crashing upon the shore, it seemed to have no end, just a mind-numbing constancy that beat against the walls. It broke suddenly and changed, became newer, louder, higher in pitch. It was that first moment of clarity, the shuddering realization that there was no money or title or authority strong enough to stop the massacre befalling the victim. The woman's terror increased into frenzied pleas that echoed along the dank walls in search of help.

He strolled faster, trying to outdistance the terror that followed him. He was by trade an assassin, but his kills were quick and painless, a matter of money or power. Torture was for fools. It profited nothing and lent room for error. When he reached his second-floor destination, he rapped lightly on the door.

A soldier answered, his eyes wide and light with fervor. "Ah, Citizen, you are expected."

He passed inside without showing a hint of the disgust he felt for the depraved little worm and approached Fabien d'Eglantine, cousin of Fabre d'Eglantine, the dramatist deputy, credited with having invented the revolutionary calendar. Fabien was rigged out in his monk's frock, a subtle attempt to inspire reverence. But beneath the flowing robes, he was armed with a stiletto. The young assassin thought him a villainous hypocrite who occupied his time hatching plots to discredit innocence and do away with the rich, whose fortune he secretly envied.

"Sit down," d'Eglantine said. "We have much to discuss." He pushed a coded message across the scarred desk. "They have removed him."

The young man's spine tingled, but his gaze remained lazy and uncommitted. "Yes, I know."

D'Eglantine looked up, malice in his eyes. "You will take care of this immediately."

The man shrugged casually. "*Oui.* Why was it not already done?"

"He is harmless in this state, but we thought to use him later. That plan has been ruined now that they have sent for him."

"But he is useless for their purposes."

"Is he?" Fabien folded his cuffs back, exposing thick, fleshy wrists. A small tattoo on his forearm just before his elbow branded him as one of the secret ones, beyond the law, interred even deeper beneath the *Illuminati* to another realm, another reason. A far darker place. The assassin had a similar tattoo. "We cannot be certain."

"It will be difficult if I cannot move freely across the borders."

"Tedious perhaps. Nothing is difficult for us." Fabien pushed a packet of documents across the desk. "You will be received in England without much ado, especially now when so many aristos"—he smiled cruelly—"and *near* aristos are flocking there to escape justice."

The assassin was no more loyal to the new France than

he had been to the old, but he must play their games, protect himself. He would have been in England long before
now if French soldiers were not patrolling the shores
looking for just such escapees. Being caught would con-
demn him without trial. He smiled easily. "I am at your
service, of course. The job will be done with all haste."

His gaze was pitiless as he rose from his seat and
departed the small, spare office. The screams had
changed to a low, wailing hum. He walked faster to
outrun the distaste rolling in his belly but made a wrong
turn and came face to face with the very thing he was
trying to avoid.

A woman, young and fair as winter twilight, had
already been stripped naked by two guards. No doubt
she had been discovered trying to escape France, for she
did not bear the sickly cast of one who had been incarcerated for long. One guard had her spread on the floor,
while the other thrust himself between her legs.

She would be raped until they were sated, then
probably dismembered. The assassin knew her torture
could go on for hours if the jailers took pleasure in
carving her piece by piece.

He tried to move, to escape without notice, but his
motion caught her thrashing focus and her desperate
eyes pierced him, a split second of recognition that
chilled his blood.

"*Mon Dieu!*" she screamed. "*M'sieu*, please, it is I,
Juliana. You must save me!"

The guard thrusting into her paused. The one holding her arms looked up. "You know her?" the second
asked with sadistic warning.

Her once-pale breasts were bloody and tooth-marked from savage bites, her gaze stark and frantic as a rabid animal's. His expression closed over. "I might have worked in her stables a time or two. Saddled her horse, helped her mount." He met the guard's gaze straight on and smiled. "She rides well, I see."

The guards laughed uproariously. "You want a turn when I am done, *mon ami*? Look, her skin is white as milk and soft as silk. You may never get another chance at an aristo this young and fetching."

"Later, perhaps. I have business now with a smuggler." Smiling, he backed out of the room, then walked away from the sound of the woman's renewed pleas. She called his name in swells, alternately cursing and begging.

Long after he left the prison tonight, he would hear the sounds of Juliana's death, see her pleading eyes. It would be that way for days, his dreams swimming with images the color of blood and cries that mocked him as craven. He would do nothing, of course. He had papers now, unimpeded passage out of France. He had freedom.

He stepped from the gray stench of the prison into blinding sunlight. He would take care of his nasty little business across the channel, then be done with the *Illuminati* and its deeper secrets. The indelicacy of their coarse bloodlust and the rape of refinement had finally left him cold.

When the "illuminated ones" infiltrated England in full power, as they soon would, he would go elsewhere, perhaps to America. There would be no reason to overthrow a government already made up of people as common as the dust beneath his feet.

Chapter 6

Marchfield Castle, England

IF BRYSON'S HANDS HAD NOT BEEN MANACLED BEHIND his back, he would have strangled the woman before him. All these years he had thought her dead, thought them all dead, and mourned grievously in those first lucid months while he lay in his own filth, unable to move or speak or understand why his life had been stolen. Why else would he have been sent to the hell-hole to rot if not for the fact that his home and family had been destroyed?

The sun beat down upon his head and shoulders, warm despite the chill of approaching evening. He wanted to turn his face up, to capture each dying ray, but he dared not take his eyes off his mother. The soul-searing anguish of betrayal overwhelmed him. The desire for revenge poured through his bloodstream, hot and thick—ugly as the love he'd once had for the beautiful, faithless bitch observing him with a mixture of emotions so complex he could not completely unravel them.

Disbelief, horror, triumph. All showed beneath the cool veneer of her expression, as if he were an amazing but degrading curiosity from the traveling freak show they'd seen in London when he was young. He remembered twisted faces and limbs, grotesquely misshapen bodies. They haunted his nightmares still.

The smell of dry summer grass wafted on the breeze, a brittle starchy scent. The horses shifted, feeling the tension, shying from the fear in the coachman's grip. Bryson wanted to go to them, to calm them, to bury his face into the strong necks of healthy horseflesh. But his feet were shackled and he could not move his hands.

Panic shivered within him, waiting, waiting. It would erupt any moment and he would be helpless against it. Bound and helpless and raving. He clenched his jaw. He would remain calm; he must. He wanted to strangle Eleanor. He wanted to grovel at her feet for bringing him home.

Colors flooded him, too many to absorb at once after years of endless gray. The hard, crisp green of the tended lawns, the flat, dusty yellow of the rolling fields in the distance. The crimson elegance of his mother's gown. Scents astonished his senses, rolling over him on the wind, not one of them foul or fetid. His eyes hurt from the radiance but he basked in the sun's rays, just stood in the fall of light and sound and color, and tried to absorb it into his skin.

Marchfield Castle loomed before him, rising bluntly against an azure sky, too severe to be elegant but inspiring nonetheless. It welcomed him, if she did not, this place where he had laughed and wept and played as a child. The place where he had thought himself safe.

Panic crept closer again, insidious as a demon, but he

would not do battle with mind terrors when reality surrounded him in a splash of vibrant color.

His gaze took in as much as he dared while keeping his mother in sight. He would not look away fully but hazarded a glimpse and a glance of whatever he could. At the window stood Max, dark and exotic-looking, little changed in the passing years. A man of many talents who had served his father as secretary, advisor, servant— a man Bryson had known all his life, who now stared as if he had risen from the dead. Come and welcome me, Bryson wanted to cry, but Max stayed, transfixed and shielded, staring with the same terrified awe as the two fresh-cheeked girls by his side.

Bryson glanced briefly at the girls with their huge eyes and stricken expressions. They had none of the look of his sisters, at least he did not think so. But too much time had passed to know for certain. He felt as if he moved in a fog, groping for a clarity that would not emerge even in bright sunshine. He tried to recall names—his sisters' faces were so clear—but only syllables came to him, the shortened nicknames of his teasing.

Gwen and Gabby, the two little ones with smiles like angels and eyes the color of rain. And the older one who was more serious and liked to scold him, for all that she loved him as much as he did her.

There were others, too, older and younger, not as vague as the rest of his past. Where were Luke and William, the brothers whose names he could spell before he could his own from spying on them during lessons? And the smallest, Richard, who had taken to following him like a shadow sewn to his backside? Had his mother sent them away, as well, to suffer for sins he could not fathom?

There were others he could no longer even picture in his mind but knew somehow they existed . . . or had.

Large spaces of time were missing from his memory, gaping holes full of black pain and nothingness. Confusion was like a swirling mist that went round and round in his head, making it pound so fiercely he thought he might be ill. He took one deep breath, then another in an effort to stabilize the panic in his belly. He didn't know which aspect of his life was more frightening now: the reason he had been sent away or the reason he had been returned.

The clamor in his head intensified, a thousand crazed souls crying for freedom, but all around him the world was as still as an indrawn breath.

Birdsong pierced the silence, one melodious warble from a distant tree that must seem so ordinary to those around him. The breeze was cooling. Bryson felt the evening bite on his cheeks and neck and longed to hold the day at bay. His mother was talking again, uttering fierce, rapid words he couldn't quite understand but sensed he should be able to. His panic intensified but he controlled it by listening intently, concentrating on the sounds. He became frightened by the familiar way the words rolled carelessly in his mind when it had been so long since he had easily understood.

Slowly they took a cadence and form he recognized, and he allowed his mind to take hold of them instead of disregarding the confusion they caused. Like mist swept from a pond surface, things began to clear. It occurred to him finally that he had not heard his native language spoken since he had been sent away.

English words and accents and inflections filled the scented air, as familiar and welcoming as Marchfield. He wanted to weep, to embrace the treasonous woman before him with the language he knew, but all he could do was stand in his chains and wonder what was happening to him.

She pointed one clean, manicured finger at his feet and flung words at the keepers beside him, who shook their heads defiantly. More demands were thrown out in the sound of outrage he remembered hearing only rarely as a child.

Amos eyed the idiot Duke of Marchfield and wrung his thick hands, then crossed himself for protection. "If it pleases Your Grace," he begged, "he's already escaped once. It took us two days of hunting marsh and moor to find him."

Eleanor's eyes narrowed. Bryson was pale as death. The planes of his face were sharp and angular—his eyes were dark with pain. "What are you saying?"

"He's strong, God help us, strong as the demons that possess his mind."

"Speak another word like that aloud and it will be your last," Eleanor hissed. "He cannot move properly in those chains. Remove them. He must be able to walk into the castle with some semblance of dignity. His future bride awaits him there."

Amos offered her a pleading look. " 'Haps we could tie a rope to him before taking the chains off?"

"Imbecile," Eleanor snapped, "you are as bad off as he is! I must have him looking presentable when he walks through yon door, not led around like a mongrel dog. His bound hands we can hide beneath a cloak, but his feet must be free."

Amos nodded in obedience and bent to one knee. After taking a key from his pouch, he unlocked first one side, then glanced over at Perkin. "Watch him," he warned as he finished the task.

But Bryson did not move. There was no flight or flee left in him. For interminable spans of time that stretched beyond the mere counting of minutes, days, or years, he had existed in the corridor of the damned with only one hope keeping him alive: the chance to return home. To return to Marchfield Castle and his family.

"Fools," Eleanor hissed. "Look at him. He is as docile as a lamb. Hand me the cloak."

She swung the heavy woolen garment over Bryson's shoulders, then took him by the upper arm. "Can you understand me?"

He stared at her, a murderous promise in his eyes.

Her sharp nails bit into his arm. "Heed my words well if you are able, Bryson. You will walk into this keep as if you are its master, for if you do not, you will never see the light of day again."

She took one step forward.

He followed.

❧

Annalise stood frozen at the window, the urge to stare at the man heading for the entrance overriding even the staggering need to flee. She'd seen everything: his shackled feet and hands, the worried look on the coachman's face, Lady Eleanor slinging the cloak over his shoulders. He was a lunatic, of course, not fit for decent company, certainly not for the blue-veined daughter of a nobleman. Why else would the duchess have sought marriage with a simple village girl?

Mary Greer's hand crept into her own, and her cousin's voice was low and urgent near her ear. "We'll go. Soon as we are able, we'll go home and forget this horrible injustice."

Annalise shook her head once. Furiously she fought the tears that welled in her eyes. "No," she said. "We'll not run away. It's what they will expect now that I've seen him. I'll not be a timid milquetoast and give them the satisfaction."

"But you cannot think to stay!" Mary Greer cried anxiously.

"I cannot think at all just now," Annalise whispered back. "But I'll not run." She couldn't run back home in disgrace to a father who had tried to warn her with words gentler than she deserved so as not to hurt her feelings. She would, instead, seek the chamber the duchess had offered earlier until she had time to sort through the tangle of outrage and hurt reeling in her mind. "Do you remember which room Lady Eleanor said was to be ours?"

"No," Mary Greer said in near panic. "You can't mean to stay here!"

Annalise turned to look for Max but he had disappeared. She grabbed her cousin's sleeve and headed for the wide staircase. "We'll find it ourselves, then." With Mary Greer in tow she mounted the stairs as if her life depended upon it, every step a weighted taunt that whispered her foolishness. They had barely reached midway when the front door opened below.

Lady Eleanor searched the room coolly, then glanced over at Max, who had reappeared at her side. "Where are they?"

Mary Greer tugged frantically at Annalise's sleeve in an effort to keep her moving up the stairs, but Annalise stood still as stone, neither hiding nor announcing her presence. Her heart beat like a captured bird in her breast but her expression was flawlessly fixed.

The madman stood below in profile. Tall and wide at the shoulders, he was much larger than he had seemed through the glass. He stood rigid, his shoulders braced as if to defy the world. The cloak slipped to one side and hung like a broken drape, revealing his shackled wrists. What Annalise could see of his face was expressionless but his hands were clenched into tight, violent fists, as if he but waited upon his freedom to unleash the fury inside him. A trickle of blood ran across his knuckles.

His head did not turn a whit, but his eyes searched, absorbed, and catalogued every inch of the room. The cloak slid the remainder of the way to the floor and puddled at his feet, revealing dirt and muddied patches on his clothing. As if the observer sensed himself being observed, he turned slightly and lifted his chin to look up.

Annalise gasped aloud, then spun around and fled the rest of the way up the stairs.

She had caught nothing more than the faintest glimpse of his pallid features, but she had seen into his heart, seen the black, undiluted rage that lay there.

The quiet was startling. Bryson did not know how to immerse himself in the peace and tranquility of it. He turned slowly around the large room abovestairs where they had taken him, pulling hard at his memory, but the recollection eluded him. For longer than he could recall, he had retreated into himself from the constant clamor and discourse in the nether realms of the priory. He didn't know how to go on without the noise now, how to be in this place of too much quiet and sweet, buttery warmth.

Light poured in from the setting sun, deep golden rays that spilled across everything in its path. He moved silently to the tallest window and stood, letting it flow over him. His wrists ached and he rubbed them. careful of the raw places. They had removed his shackles, removed them as if he could be trusted. His breath struggled for a normal rhythm but he was overwhelmed by the tiny freedom.

He searched his surroundings but found nothing common to him. He had not occupied this room; he was almost certain of it. He had only left the nursery floor by a handful of years before being sent into the bowels of Hades. This was a man's room, his older brother's perhaps. But the plague had taken Stephen, he remembered that, and a sister whose name he still could not recall.

But he could see her face clearly, not ashen as it had been in death, but fresh and smiling down at him from the leafy boughs of a tree in full bloom. They had gone to gather wildflowers, grumbling the entire way because the little ones had been allowed to tag behind and they would have to keep watch until Nanna caught up.

Madaline.

The name came to him in a whisper, soft and painfully empty of life. Her name was Madaline and she had been much older and contracted to marry the Earl of Devonshire in the spring. It had been a powerful alliance. He remembered how his mother had been pleased, smiling in a secret, satisfied way that she made look humble when around friends. Then the plague had come, stripping away Madaline and Stephen so fast they had all reeled from the impact. He recalled the friendly camaraderie of the earl weeks before the plague, then the cold, impersonal way Devonshire had stared down with clenched jaw at Madaline's grave before mounting his blooded mare and riding for France.

Bryson's fingers curled into a fist and he held a tight grip on his emotions. Memories were flooding back, so fast he could hardly contain them, but they were foggy and disjointed, and he could not be certain what was real.

He tore himself away from the painful past and stared at the door leading into the hall. His hands began to tremble. No one had come to greet him.

He searched the silent room and realized he'd been waiting. He could not think where his brothers and sisters might be or how to find out. Had his mother sent them all away to suffer for some nameless crime, or had it just been him? What had he done, what sin could he have committed so unforgivable? His palms grew clammy and he forced himself to relax, to inhale the clean, fresh scent of the breeze. He took it deep into his lungs and held it there as long as he could, held it until his chest hurt, as if it might be stolen away otherwise.

Idiot! Lunatic! To hoard the very air he breathed.

He exhaled slowly and turned his attention to inspecting the room, searching it out from his faulty memory, but there was nothing that he recognized.

A massive bed dominated one wall, its wood heavy and intricately carved. The covers looked so soft and inviting he wanted to lie down and bury his face in them. He was weary unto death, exhaustion bearing down upon his shoulders until he could hardly stand. But he feared—more than anything he had feared in his life—sleep. He could not be certain where or to what he would awaken.

Was this moment real or some sick delusion of his mind, a hallucination from which he would arise only to find himself back with Delphi and the others in the living nightmare? He shuddered violently at the thought and stayed clear of the bed.

He wandered the room silently, touching things, pulling them to his nose to breathe the cleanness of them, as if there were not enough freshness in the entire world to fill the void. A low fire burned in the hearth, beckoning. He paused before it and held his hands out until his fingertips burned, then curled them inward to hold the heat in his palms as he paced the room again.

It had been a long time since he had felt the brand of fear that made his mouth dry and his knees tremble. But he felt it now as he paced, yearning within so deeply that it terrified him to want anything so badly. They would come any moment to drag him away. His coming home had been a horrible trick, a cruel punishment, an insane mistake. His pacing grew more frantic, as if he must absorb every inch of the room before it was stripped away.

He finally came to a mirror atop a washstand and stopped. Staring back at him, he found a stranger with wild golden hair, ashen cheeks, and sunken eyes. He stood for a moment, transfixed, then backed away slowly and found the bed. He lay on his stomach with his face buried in the covers.

Let him awake if he must to the bowels of St. Bertram's Priory. The hideous creature in the mirror dared not live elsewhere.

The chamber was richly appointed. Annalise paced it without regard for the imported damask that draped the windows and tabletops, the intricate needlework of the tapestried footstool or the hand-painted porcelain basin. Anger and anxiety marked each step. How could this duchess think to play such a sorry game upon her? *How could Annalise herself have been such a fool?*

"I think we should return home at once," Mary Greer pleaded for the third time. "Please! It'll be dark soon, Annalise. I'd not like to be walking the path after the sun sets."

Annalise turned from her pacing and sat on a long cushioned seat beneath the window. "We're not prisoners, Greer."

As if her words conjured the deed, a sudden *click* sounded at the door. Mary Greer's face paled; Annalise's flushed crimson. She leaped up and crossed the room in a thrice, but her fears went unfounded. The door opened easily to reveal the duchess.

Eleanor stepped inside and glanced at the baker's daughter. "Would you excuse us for a moment, my dear? Max has refreshments awaiting you in your own chamber down the hall."

Mary Greer did not mistake the request for anything but the demand that it was. Her face drained of color and she hesitated, torn between her loyalty to Annalise and her fear of the duchess. "Begging your pardon, Your Grace, but——"

Annalise shook her head. "It's all right, Greer. I'll be along soon."

Mary Greer's relief showed on her face as she bobbed a quick curtsey and hastened from the room.

Lady Eleanor's immediate questions were answered. Annalise knew about Bryson, she could see it in the girl's eyes. Resentment hovered in the pale young face along with hurt feelings . . . and curiosity. "Ask what you will," she said. "I know you have questions."

"What is wrong with His Grace?"

Eleanor admired the girl's bluntness and courage. Whether it would serve either of them well in the months to come was yet to be seen. "Six years ago he became ill unto death and was sent away to a hospital of sorts. He recovered, a shock to us all, I assure you."

"Is he a lunatic?"

Eleanor decided against lying or pacifying. "I don't know."

"Is he dangerous?"

"I don't know that, either."

Annalise's eyes sparked with resentment and frustration. "But you expect me to marry him, not knowing, as well."

"Guard your tongue," Eleanor warned. "Even with his great imperfections, he is a better match than any a chemist's daughter could make in the village."

Annalise cringed at the mercenary words, but her voice was strong with conviction. "Only if I am shallow-minded enough that title and gain are the only things of value to me."

"Oh, don't be a silly girl." Eleanor laughed softly. "If you were hungry for a love match, you would be wed by now. Many a village boy has drooled in his nightly ale at the sight of you, but you have turned them all away."

Annalise flushed hotly but had little rebuttal in the face of the duchess's stinging truth. "Because I have not yet found my young man."

"Because your destiny lies here!"

The words gave Annalise pause. It was, perhaps, what she feared most, what she had felt from the onset. The giddy, frightening, inevitable intuition that she had been called to do this.

"Why have you chosen me?" she asked. "There are those in the village who would be much more easily swayed and impressed than I am by all that marriage to the Duke of Marchfield has to offer."

"Common girls, all of them."

"I am the same stock."

"Perhaps." Eleanor smiled. "Perhaps not. Your great-aunt's lineage is questionably adequate, if one must count that sort of thing. I am aware that she spent time at court in her day." Her eyes narrowed. "Of a certain you are common enough with your sharp tongue. But you are sharp-minded, as well, and you'll need that over the months to come." She strolled gracefully across the room to the mantel and picked up an exquisite vase. With one, negligent flick of her wrist, it shattered into a hundred pieces on the floor.

"A king's ransom to replace it. I will never miss the funds." Her smile was brittle. "You, on the other hand, bartered for better fabric from the squire's wife so as not to appear too shabbily attired when you arrived here, then made the dress yourself because there were no funds for a London seamstress. You copied current fashion perfectly and sedately, so as not to draw attention but to fit in. In a word, you wanted to impress."

Annalise had promised a month's worth of tutoring the squire's lazy daughter in exchange for the fabric only to have it thrown back at her. "No, I wanted *not* to embarrass."

"Even better," Eleanor commended. "I need someone who will not succumb to a fit of vapors at the first sign of trouble, and you have not."

Perhaps not, Annalise thought, but she wanted to with every breath she took. "I cannot pledge myself to your son without further consideration," she said quietly.

"You have *already* pledged yourself to my son," Eleanor warned. "I have the letter of intent with your signature. The contract is as binding as a proxy marriage should I take it before a magistrate for judgment."

The color drained from Annalise's face. "I merely promised to consider . . ." But the wording came back to her, as clear and precise as Max's voice the day he had stated the terms of the letter to her. "But he said, your servant assured me—"

"You are smart and beautiful, but entirely too trusting," Eleanor said. "The first and foremost lesson you will learn as a duchess is to trust no one. Beyond that you may keep the other qualities that brought you here."

"Deception brought me here," she retaliated.

"Dear Annalise, you are not ignorant of what the Marchfield money and prestige can do for you. Do not ruin your life by reconsidering."

The words were a warning, silkily spoken but dire nonetheless. Annalise felt the first quiver of alarm crawl down her spine. "What are you implying?"

"Simply this: If you leave here before exchanging vows with my son, you leave ruined. You will never make a decent marriage, in this village or any other." She walked to the door and smiled thinly. "I am certain your father will also be turned out when the town hears of his daughter's unseemly behavior."

Confusion strangled whatever words Annalise hoped

to say when the duchess strolled briskly through the door. She paused at the threshold and glanced back over her shoulder, smiling like a cat. "I suppose we will know for certain if he is dangerous by morning."

The door shut with a click of finality that let Annalise know it had been locked. She hurried over to test it and found her assessment accurate. She spun back to look for another means of escape and found a door set into an interior wall. She ran for it, then heard a sound that stopped her cold. A scraping came from the other side. She moved toward the door more slowly, wondering where it led, what the sound could be.

Creeping closer, she pressed her ear against the wood. Naught but the sound of her own breathing pounded in her ears. The noise came again, a grating indistinguishable at first, then obvious. Her heart racing madly, she jerked back and stared down with morbid fascination as the knob began to turn.

Bryson lifted his head slowly. He heard voices like a distant echo that seemed to draw closer the harder he listened. They did not come from the hallway but seemed to center in the distant wall. He noted a door near the hearth, more like another panel of the wall at first glance, but it was set with a brass knob and keyhole. The voices, muted but definitive, seemed to come from the other side.

He slid from the bed and stood, poised to run or fight. He was not given to startled responses and waited, impatient but curious, for something else to occur. The conversation continued, rising in pitch from time to time, then fading into murmured responses. He heard his name and moved toward the panel, wondering who plotted against him. He already knew the door to the main corridor was locked, the windows too high to afford escape. He had not tried this panel and had no idea where it led or even if he would leave this room given the chance.

He stood poised before the door until the voices stopped and only muted footsteps were heard. Then he waited longer. Finally, he grabbed the knob and turned.

Chapter 7

Teach me half the gladness
That thy brain must know,
Such harmonious madness
From my lips would flow
The world should listen then—
as I am listening now.
                    —PERCY BYSSHE SHELLEY

THE CONNECTING DOOR SWUNG OPEN.

Their gazes locked.

His eyes were ice blue and implacable, challenging
her from a face that was inherently beautiful despite its
deathly paleness. He looked nothing like she had imagined after the first meeting with Eleanor's secretary—not
pious or circumspect or ordinary—and not grotesque, as
she had secretly feared.

Instead she found a combination of incongruities.
Beauty and fierceness, strength and pallor. He was wide
at the shoulders yet thin at the waist. His clothing,
though ill-fitting, still managed to look graceful on him
or he in them, giving one the impression that he would
look lordly in any manner of dress. A small, thin cut ran
along his jaw, a wicked and common sight more

apropos to street toughs and tavern brawlers, certainly a vast contradiction to his wild, too-pretty hair and aristocratic bone structure.

He towered over Annalise. Lean and well formed, he appeared an uncivilized nobleman dressed out like a prince. His eyes were wild yet guarded, his expression intense. She swallowed and tried to find her voice, but it had fled along with her courage.

Shock propelled her back a step on legs that trembled unforgivably. "Good sir," she began before remembering her place and his title. "Your Grace." The words were weak, a petition for mercy and humanity and whatever else she might need from his crazed soul.

He did not move, only stared at her with eyes too blue for a madman, too depthless to be sane. They were fire and ice, blue as an Arctic sea, hooded eyes that reflected back at her only a guarded glimpse of the soul that lay beneath, that haunted place black as pitch he fought to conceal.

He was not bound. His arms hung freely at his sides, though his shoulders were stiff and alert. He stood in his finery, a misplaced nobleman in tailored clothing not quite tailored for him. The shoulders were broad enough, but his ruffled cuffs lay a mite too long on his hands, his trouser pants in the same disarray. The ensemble had been meant for a taller, lankier man.

Unfathomably dark destruction lay in his gaze, a murky cavern of bottomless cruelties. Yet he seemed to have no intention of coming after Annalise in a fit of uncontrollable rage.

She lifted her chin and stared back at him with

renewed bravery, then wished she had not. His eyes narrowed savagely, and she saw the glaring and dangerous threat there, so obvious now that they stood face to face.

She had called him a madman, but she could not be further from the truth. There was sanity there, murderously bright and intelligent. His eyes burned with it.

She backed up quickly before he reduced her to cinders. Her wits scattered when she bumped into the wall and realized she had neatly trapped herself. She fought back with the only things she possessed in abundance: suitable manners and forthright determination.

"Your Grace," she said with overbright candor, "it's so good to finally meet you!"

Her voice came out sharp, a disparity to the fear he read in her eyes. She dipped into a curtsey, ridiculously deep and submissive.

Bryson couldn't fathom why she did it. He had watched her scramble away, inadvertently pinning herself into a corner. Such a foolish girl with her wide, expressive gaze and cupid's mouth. Her blue eyes were imbued with more innocence than he had ever known. He watched as she pressed back against the wall.

Her cheeks were flushed, her hands clasped so tightly together her knuckles were white. She cleared her throat and tried to smile, but she was clearly afraid of him.

She should be. Silly, pretty girl. With one strike of his fist he could remove her from this capricious, deceiving world. Or worse.

He stepped back, allowing her space to dash for safety, yet she remained, poised at the edge of flight, an inquisitive captured little starling whose heart beat visibly in her pale throat.

Without warning, Bryson's pulse leaped in response, a hot throb of hunger that he had not experienced with such vigor in longer than he cared to remember. He stood perfectly still, willing it to recede, demanding mastery from the one area of his life in which he had always maintained control.

What little light was left glittered off the ends of the girl's hair in luminous radiance, an ethereal attempt to hold the day. A golden light in gathering darkness, she stood like an angelic rebel in rapt anticipation of what he would do next, unable to decide what she herself should do. Bryson's nostrils flared on one deep breath, then he turned his back on her and retreated into his excruciatingly quiet room.

"Your Grace!"

He paused. He had not expected her to follow him, not with the abundance of mistrust he read in her eyes, nor to command him with a voice now devoid of prudence. She stood just inside his chamber, uncertainty in every line of her posture but persistence in the purse of her mouth.

Did she have no idea who he was, of where he'd been?

She was fresh air after a millennium in filth, clear water and sunshine to his tarnished senses. He wanted to touch her, to taste her, to discover every inch of her white body. He wanted to inhale the fragrance of her skin and bury his face in the clean golden lights of her hair.

She was so young and fresh and shining, he could devour her.

She dared to step closer. "If I might have a word with you, Your Grace?"

Her recklessness confounded him. He had seen himself in the mirror. She should be running, hiding, shrieking out her disgust. Instead she stood in his unfamiliar chamber, her face set with determination, calling his brother's title like a command.

Weariness assailed him, rushing over him in waves. He had been alone in the midst of raving madness for so long he could not contain all the fragrant beauty of a sane world. The girl's chatter was pretty as birdsong but unnerving to decode. He needed rest and quiet and time to shore up his defenses. He needed her gone from his presence with a fierceness that made his hands go clammy. With a curt warning glance, he dismissed her and moved toward the hearth, where heat radiated like a blessing and held the chill of centuries at bay. Stretching out his hands, he reached for the flames.

They both heard it at once. The small *click* of the panel closing, a bolt locking.

Stunned, Annalise could only stare at the wall, expecting a door where there was none, looking for the gaping entrance back to safety. She finally spotted the brass knob set into polished wood and walked toward it, dismissing what she already suspected, refusing to believe that anything but the wind had just blown the panel closed.

And locked it.

Grabbing the knob, she turned it slowly at first, then rattled it as if it might need loosening. Her shallow breaths came faster as she turned it again with more wrenching force, then again and again. All to no avail.

"Oh," she said softly, a lost little quiver in her voice. She turned back to Bryson, that same lost quality in her eyes. "We've been locked in together. I can hardly credit it, but the duchess has locked us in."

He processed the words slowly, their clear meaning escaping him. Having been jailed for an eternity, he found nothing unusual in that, save that he was imprisoned at home now in a room free from fleas and lice, free from unbearable cold and filth, free from the lunatic rantings of Delphi and Mindless Mara and other demented souls. For whatever reason his mother feared him or hated him or accused him, he would take prison with this pretty girl over the priory and be grateful, at least until he found his equilibrium and determined his rights.

If Eleanor sent him back now he would die.

Frustration marred the delicate planes of the girl's face and put an edge in her demanding voice. "What are we going to do?"

Do? She was madder than he, if she thought there was anything to be done. He crouched down by the open fire and felt the heat bake his back and shoulders, chase the endless French winters from his bones. He thought he could stay that way for an eternity, but the girl approached him then, talking too rapidly in that frustrated tone for him to understand. She began to grind on his nerves, like a pesky gnat. She'd better watch that he didn't swat her away like one.

"I will be ruined!" she cried. "Don't you see? She has

every intention of leaving us together the entire night. You must do something!"

Her eyes were huge, round saucers of dismay, but he'd lived around a greater despair than she would ever know. Vacant eyes, deranged chants, maniacal ravings: All had been his companion for years without end. He could not command the energy or compassion to ease this distraught girl in her fresh clothing and healthy skin. He was exhausted to his bones, his patience fading too quickly to mind his behavior.

He must be careful now, one false move, one incorrect transit, and they would be on him like vultures ready to pick apart his bones.

His gaze scanned the room but he could find no place where the watchers might be hidden, where the doctors and scientists might observe his behavior from some secret alcove. The girl was a test, that much he understood, but to what extent he was uncertain. He did not dare hope that he had simply been abandoned to this room of comfort and warmth.

She spoke again, and Bryson's fist slammed down once upon a side table, startling her so that she jumped and scooted back. All color drained from her face, but she never lost the stubborn look in her eyes.

"But we've been locked in," she articulated slowly, as one would to an imbecile.

His fist came down on the table again, harder, shattering the fragile vase resting there.

"As you please!" Annalise shot back in a soft, furious voice more potent than her fear. "I shall see to this myself."

Pompous and pretty, she went to the hall door, rattling it until its hinges groaned, then to the paneled one and did the same. She found the windows next and flung them open, one after the other, as if the ground below would miraculously rise up to meet her simply because she worked at it. To Bryson's dismay, she began to repeat the whole process again with a sort of fanatical conviction. Door to window to door, like a pup fruitlessly chasing its tail. When she finally came to realize her efforts were futile, she did the one thing Bryson could not abide.

She opened her mouth and began screaming for help in a voice loud enough to summon the dead.

In one great lunge, he flew from his place by the hearth and grabbed her, slapping one hand over her mouth. He stumbled back, his shoulder slamming into the stones of the fireplace, but his feet found purchase at the bunched edge of the silk carpet. He held her tightly against him, crushing the sound from her small body. Her eyes widened above his hand, and her cries dwindled to nothing but muted puffs of alarm in each quick breath. Her anger and fear were tangible in the rapid rise and fall of her chest beneath his forearm, but he would not let go and have her screaming again. He could not tolerate it.

She was small against him, her body nothing but soft angles and round curves. She weighed less than a mite for all that she wiggled and squirmed as if she could overpower him. He waited for them to come, to burst in upon him for the violence. He planned to use the girl as leverage if they tried to take him again. He could not go back. He would not.

Her fragrance wafted up, a scent so clean it bathed him in its essence. Breathing heavily from exertion and fear, he lowered his face to the mass of her sunshine hair and inhaled its perfume, rubbed his skin into the silkiness of it. Holding panic at bay by a thin thread, he waited.

She went stiff and cried something sharp and enraged against his palm. He pulled his head back and shifted her enough to lift her face back and up to his. Her eyes were glassy above his hand, but there was life there amid the fury and plenty of fight left. She tried to jerk away, and her hairpins scattered like raindrops, plinking one after the other upon the hearthstones. Her hair tumbled down over his arms and hands like a waterfall of bright sunshine, smooth and shiny where it tangled with his fingertips.

His blood thickened and ran hot to his extremities, leaving him shaken and aggressive. He shoved her at arm's length, the distance necessary, but kept his hand firmly over her mouth.

Abashment scored her cheeks. She tried to turn her face away but he held her fast, the warning in his eyes colder, sharper now. His fingers slid from her mouth with caution, but she did not scream again. He lingered, stroking the embarrassed flush on her flesh, absorbing the wonder of her incredible skin.

Annalise bit the inside of her lip to keep from crying out as his palm slid from her mouth to her neck. Though gentle and restrained in his gestures, the expression on his face was fierce and undeniably direct. Her knees trembled suddenly, violently, and he gripped her upper arms so tightly that she need not try to stand on her own.

"Please," she said weakly.

She could not think what to do, what else she could say. She was clutched up tighter than a baby in bunting by a madman with demon eyes. Physically, she was unhurt, but her feelings had suffered a great blow and her nerves were twisted into knots of fear. There was no doubt he could snap her neck like a twig, or crush the breath from her lungs, or . . . do any manner of unseemly things to her person of which she was suddenly, too keenly, aware.

His eyes were a brutal combination of blazing suspicion and icy contempt, alternately burning and chilling her with the intensity of his gaze. She felt maligned and accused, as if he actually thought her responsible for their sudden incarceration. Indignation flared briefly in her own eyes.

"Unhand me," she demanded in a ridiculously meek voice. Her intentions were strong but fear had left her too breathless to lend any strength to her tone.

Annalise swallowed hard but dared not move. He was less than a breath away, his posture alert and defensive. His fingers reached out toward the scooped neckline of her gown where it lay against her breast bone. Though the style was modest, the sudden touch of his flesh against hers was not. She gasped on impulse and slapped his hand away, then froze when his expression turned brittle. His hand went back to her throat, fingers spread, so softly threatening she was uncertain whether he intended to caress or strangle. She grabbed his wrist and made a pleading sound of his title.

"Your Grace . . ."

He seemed not to care. His other hand went down over hers, hard, pinning the hand pinning him, as if he would not be mastered even the slightest bit. His eyes left hers to follow the path of his fingers over the delicate edging on her gown, an indecorous exploration whose purpose she could not determine as anything but intimidating or worse.

"Oh, please," she tried once more, but he only bent his head to her hair again.

His forehead pressed against her temple, the rest of him so close she could feel the embroidery on his clothing through her own gown and smell the bland soap in which he had bathed. His breath penetrated her hair and touched her neck. Moist and warm, it sent shivers down to her knees and alarm rising strong enough to dispel all fear.

"Your Grace!" she cried sharply.

He jerked back, his expression darkly agitated, but Annalise had had enough of feeling manipulated and afraid.

"I . . . I realize that you've not been . . . out. Among decent folk, I mean, for quite some time. You may be forgiven slight transgressions, but this is highly improper!"

Her eyes flashed with healthy outrage, compelling to a man who had seen naught but death and dementia for the past six years. He reached out and stroked her skin with the tip of one finger, then ran the back of his knuckles down her cheek and along her jaw. When he reached the pulse in her throat, he stopped to absorb the quick flutter of her anxious heartbeat. His gaze lifted, away from the heat staining her chest and neck, to the refreshing beauty of her face.

Untainted, unscarred—it had been so long since he'd had the opportunity to indulge even a glance. A touch was something of forbidden dreams.

And forbidden to him now. With one final warning look, his expression closed over, dark and hooded as the night, as impenetrable as his thoughts. His arms fell away and he stepped back, then returned to the fire.

Annalise watched him go, stricken by his actions, suspended by his silent retreat. She did not understand the threat in his eyes, or the sudden distance that removed him as effectively as a wall between them. She crossed her arms over her middle and clung tight but the uneasiness inside her did not abate.

She moved back silently and sat upon an embroidered settee to support her quivering legs. Her stomach was rolling in fits and starts, and her heart seemed to thud with the same uneven tempo. She could not fathom what to do. There was no way to leave the room, no way to bring help. By the rise of a new dawn, her reputation would be in shreds, her father's good name endangered, as well.

An aching hush filled the room, a thick shadow of unasked questions and pungent fear. Minutes ticked away, tormenting intervals stretching into quarter hours, then halves, then wholes. Neither did anything but regard the other furtively from time to time. Bryson with his dark, unreadable expression, content to stay near the hearth. Annalise holding on to more hope than was reasonable in the midst of her fading optimism.

She was used to the soft silence of day's end, quiet hours of stitching or darning or reading to Aunt Mellie, the natural flow of evening into night. This silence screamed at her, a crushing weight that pressed in from all sides. Bryson seemed oblivious, staring into the flames, rubbing his wrists absently from time to time. She remembered the rough feel of them, ridged over with scars, and wondered what Hell he had been through to receive such punishment. When she could no longer bear the suffocating stillness, she rose from the settee and began to pace, praying for a plan, some sort of strategy that would deliver her from this waking nightmare.

Bryson caught the girl's motion and turned slightly to watch her. She glided about the room with useless repetition, the sway of her hips graceful, an unconscious allure undiminished by her agitation. The prim press of her arms across her middle pushed her breasts up into high relief, creating a diverting silhouette against the hearth flames. Despite her bouts of restlessness, he found her remarkably composed given her situation.

He wondered why she had been locked in with him, what devious scheme his mother brewed? He gazed around the room, his calmness a contradiction to the riot inside him. Eleanor's betrayal ate at him, eroding his hard-won composure, but he would not give himself over to the chaos of malice. He still had not come to grips with the fact that she was alive, that Marchfield stood intact, when he had been left to rot in France. There was no reason good enough, no mistake wrong enough to explain his having been abandoned in that Hell.

And no forgiveness for the woman who had abandoned him.

He hated her now, a staggering sentiment when he had once loved her so well. His heartbeat shivered with a moment of terror, and he took slow even breaths until the feeling subsided. What had he done, what crime did he not remember committing that had doomed him so? Still, he could not forgive Eleanor for sending him away. But he would obey her, whatever dictates she imposed he would obey until he regained his strength of mind and body. Being sent back would put him squarely among the insane.

He only straddled that edge now, uncertain of his own competence. There were too many black spaces, too many missing years.

The fire hissed and crackled. He dissolved into the burnished heat until sweat beaded his brow and his clothing became clammy on his skin. The cold had been his constant enemy for so long, it took Bryson a moment to realize the chamber had grown overwarm. He stood and removed his coat, running the fabric through his fingers as if he must memorize the texture.

It was a singularly simple act that suddenly frightened Annalise speechless. She stopped pacing and stared at him, transfixed by the fact that he seemed to have accepted his fate and settled in to the reality of being held prisoner. He was making himself as comfortable as possible, without regard for the protocol or decorum that dictated that he should not be standing in his shirt-sleeves in front of a lady. But then what propriety was there to be concerned with when his own mother's goal was to ruin the both of them anyway? He only hastened the downfall with his cavalier attitude.

His shirt was of finest lawn and did little to conceal the wide breadth of his shoulders and carved muscles of his arms and back. His flesh rippled with each movement, sleek cords stretching taut over perfect bone structure.

Annalise wondered how anyone as ill as he must have been could have come away so physically superior. She found herself staring, mesmerized by the play of light through fabric, the construction of bone and tissue and muscle. Never, in all of eighteen years, had she studied a man's anatomy so thoroughly. Appalled, she excused the gesture as scientifically necessary. She must know how strong and able-bodied he was in the event that she was forced to do battle with him again. But her skin flushed just the same, not at all clinically studious, at the thought of his arms pinning her close to that fearfully solid physique again.

A small, distressed sound escaped her and she turned away to the window, needing solace. She thought of the cobbler's son, Nial, an overgrown man with the mind of a child. Naught in Nial's lumbering ways and slow speech reminded her of Bryson, naught in his physical appearance came close. She leaned against the windowsill and looked out but found only servants rushing off to their own hearths in the gentle gloom of twilight. She thought of calling out to them but didn't dare risk the wrath of the crazy Duke of Marchfield. She cast a surreptitious glance over her shoulder.

But he wasn't crazy, and she knew it, at least not in the way she understood the word or others defined it. She might not be certain of anything else in this troubled situation, but she knew Bryson le Fort, Duke of Marchfield, wasn't a candidate for Bedlam.

That ignoble institute would be reserved for her if she couldn't extract herself from this nightmarish situation.

She leaned on the heels of her palms and tried to catch the eye of someone below. A young maid hurried off, basket on her arm, bearing a slight resemblance to Mary Greer. Annalise's heart squeezed. As upset as she was in this unthinkable situation, Greer must be frightened out of her wits. She should have listened to her cousin and left for the village when they still had the chance.

She should have listened to her father and never come.

Her vision blurred and she wiped away a hot tear with the back of her hand. She shot Bryson an accusing look, but he only glared back, his expression unchanged save for the slight narrowing of his eyes. Annalise couldn't escape, couldn't call for help. And she most certainly could not spend the entire night locked in this room with *him*.

Helpless, she watched the trail of servants thin as they headed for their own cottages. Too soon they all would be gone. Desperate, she slipped a kerchief from her bodice and leaned out the window, waving it at the last of the stragglers below.

No one seemed to notice a village girl frantically

flapping a square of linen, save a stupid-looking boy who waved back with a lewd glint in his eye. With a growl of frustration she sent him a mean look and waved harder. He retaliated by thumbing his nose and turning away.

"Imbecile!" she huffed, and flung herself back against the wall, only to meet the chilly direct gaze of the Duke of Marchfield. "I didn't mean you!" she defended.

Chapter 8

DAWN CREPT IN WITH A WHISPER. THIN FOG COVered the land in soft gray mists that hovered dreamlike over the ground below. Beyond the fields and forest, the sun rose, shading the grays with pinks and golds. Bryson watched the early-morning rays spill across the girl's hair and skin in soft, muted colors. Even in sleep her brow was troubled, unreconciled to her fate.

He had not yet discerned exactly why they had been put together, but he had his suspicions.

Her lashes fluttered, dark against her fair cheeks, deepest midnight despite the color of her hair. Her brows were dark, as well, small shiny wings that arched delicately over her large eyes, lending her a perpetual look of astonished wonder. He thought for a moment she might wake, but she only murmured something disgruntled and continued sleeping, curled up like a child in the chair with her cheek tucked into the crook of her elbow.

She had not given in to the night or her incarceration, merely exhaustion. Like a warrior, she had fought a watchful, silent battle over the long, still hours, pacing with restless agitation of one confined against her will. He knew the agony and helplessness she felt at being imprisoned, but he was hardly the knight gallant to rescue her when his own fate hung tenuously in the balance. From time to time, she had pleaded with him, anger and resentment in her soulful eyes. But she had not screamed again.

When the candles had burned down to nothing but charred wick and the hearth embers to ash, her eyes had finally closed.

His had not.

For the longest time, Bryson had watched her sleep, listening to the small sounds of her breathing, reveling in the softly scented luxury of the moon-washed room. Simple things turned grand when denied for so long.

He had only dozed fitfully, awakening often to the warm, unfamiliar silence of the chamber and the freshness of his bedding. He had not minded the long hours of wakefulness, save the occasional tremor of fear, the whispered taunt that it would all end soon, that his leave from St. Bertram's was a hideous and temporary hoax to drive him closer to madness. It was that fear that kept startling him awake, cold and clammy in his own sweat.

He moved away from the window and closer to the girl, drawn to the pure lines of her face, the piquant stubbornness of her chin. One thick lock of hair draped over her shoulder, a fair golden ribbon hiding the fullness of her breast. She had grown chilled during the night, and her pale arms hugged her body close.

He wanted to touch her.

Her skin was soft, as velvety as the rose petals he remembered from childhood. The faintest floral scent seemed to linger in the air about her, a garden after a rain shower. His pulse hammered darkly, compelling him to reach for her, warning him to move away. Things were different here. There were rules that took precedence over animal instinct, a definitive morality to govern every action.

His memory was vague, the earlier things fresher than the later. he remembered the endless lessons in deportment, though not the tutor's name. The older ones had hated the lessons. He had not been equally subjected to them. His sisters were to be bartered like chattel, his older brothers would secure the dukedom. Bryson, William, and Richard had been free to tease and taunt, held only to the most ordinary behavior that they didn't embarrass the family name. He remembered that clearly yet . . . not. It was as if he viewed it from a distance far more removed than time, a mirror of images that looked real but were only a reflection of reality.

His head pounded with convoluted fragments of recall that taunted him. The girl's freshness beckoned him, a silken thread that tugged like steel. He obeyed a more circumspect self-discipline and stole to the window, distancing himself from a temptation he'd not had to endure around women of mindless intelligence and sour bodies.

For six years loneliness had been his only trustworthy companion, survival his greatest need. The luxury of this room softened him, made him weak and yearning. He wondered if they would take him back if he touched the girl. He wondered if the guards would come crashing through the door and put him back in chains. Pressing his palm against the glass, he allowed the early-morning coolness to temper the heat in his body.

Marchfield stretched out in every direction as far as he could see. Through swamp and glade, forest and field, the crops had been harvested, the woodland teemed with wildlife. A tributary of the river wound through the hills, a shiny thread that pooled into a lake, then trickled off into heavily foliaged marshlands. He stared until his eyes burned, light-headed with relief at being home again.

Below, the world began to stir. A boy in coarse homespun cupped small hands to his mouth and called out a request. A stablemaster answered, leading a striking Thoroughbred that pranced upon the cobbled drive in anticipation of a run. Bryson had reveled in the hunt when young, the exhilaration of the chase, the triumph of capture. He remembered the feeling of it clearly, but not the time or place or persons involved.

He didn't think he would ever feel that way again, but he was content to watch the sleek, powerful play of muscle as the horse sidestepped and tossed its sable head.

In the distance, the heather had begun to bloom, spreading over the hillside in a blanket of misty blue-violet so like the girl's eyes. Bryson stared at the bounty until his breath fogged the pane of glass and he could see nothing but the gruesome, hazy reflection of himself.

He slashed his forearm over the window, obliterating what he had become. His breath came faster, fogging up the pane more quickly than before. He forced himself to calm, not to care what he was, just that he was home, that he might perchance make another life for himself, one free from degradation and filth and lunacy. Without forethought, he trailed one finger down the beaded condensation, then traced his name.

"You can read."

He turned sharply to find the girl staring at him, a startled, sleepy look in her eyes. Her cheek was pink where it had lain against her arm, her clothing rumpled. Her hair, a mass of spilled sunshine, fell over her shoulders and down her back.

Bryson turned back to the window, away from her too-pretty face and vulnerability. He suspected they'd been put together to see how he might behave without shackles. He could not afford to fail—would not—and resented her for inadvertently making it difficult for him.

"I fell asleep," she said in a sad, resigned voice. "I meant not to."

She came up behind him, both curious and cautious in her fuddled state. Even as she approached, she kept her distance, alert and fearless yet full of trepidation. A night's sleep had not afforded her any more ammunition in this war of wills. Just as it had stripped her of reputation, it seemed also to have stolen her fight. She paused well back, then seemed to struggle with her thoughts.

He caught the telltale glimmer of tears in her eyes,

but she tightened her mouth as if controlling them would somehow manage the wreckage her life had become. He was not so impaired that he didn't realize a night spent with him had just ruined her. The fact that he also didn't care in this harder struggle for sanity left a bitter taste in his mouth.

She tried to bring order to her clothing but only achieved a look of tousled confection. Failing to smooth the wrinkles, she went to work on her hair. After pulling it over one shoulder, she began weaving it into a long tidy braid.

A pity. With a few flicks of her wrists and the nimble swiftness of her fingers, she subdued radiant sunlight into orderly layers.

She turned aside modestly, but Bryson saw more than she intended. The mirror he so dreaded became an object of vulgar pleasure when she lifted her hem, revealing slender calves and the dainty turn of an ankle. She stripped a length of ribbon from her shift and used it to secure the ends of her hair.

Having exhausted the means for any further toilette, she sent Bryson a hesitant look, then strolled closer. She reached out and wrote letters beneath his name on the glass.

"Annalise," she said, and touched her palm to the center of her chest.

Her intent hit him suddenly, insanely funny. He eyed her narrowly, his brow drawn in severe concentration. Looking pointedly at her name, then at Annalise, he reached out and flattened his own hand into the center of her breasts. With a small squeal, she colored hotly and backed up. Like a startled rabbit, her pulse pounded in her throat. A mixture of emotions crossed her face, from shock to embarrassment to anger, but the one that struck Bryson was the hidden inkling of feminine wonder. After a moment she collected herself and nodded as if commending him.

"Annalise," she said again.

He shouldn't toy with her. It was cruel at worst, unseemly at best. But she was so ripe with her guileless innocence and fearful trust. He moved forward, closing in, invading the defensive air surrounding her. She went still and alert, poised to flee. He lifted a finger and traced her lips, hoping she'd repeat her name for him, let him feel the sound of it on her flesh. But her bottom lip tightened and he withdrew, leaving her to her concern.

And her assumptions that he had no more mental capability than a schoolboy.

His memory was grossly defective but his intellect was intact. He could read, cipher numbers, quote Shakespeare. He knew but didn't know how he knew. He escaped back to the hearth where he could stoke the embers to life and take the early-morning chill from the room.

"The duchess says we are as good as married."

He spun back quickly in shock, then realized he'd given himself away.

Her eyes flashed. "You can understand me!"

Clever little baggage. Her statement wasn't entirely true. Having not heard English in so many years, he had trouble processing long strings of words spoken too quickly. He shrugged in semiacknowledgment, then looked away, distancing himself from her damnable curiosity and new awareness.

His meticulously erected defenses had just been penetrated effortlessly by this winsome, tenacious girl.

She approached him then, bright as the dawn, absurdly unwary in her wrath. "Do you speak?"

Curse her. He hadn't in a very long time.

He turned away from her demanding ire and fixed his gaze on the small flame leaping to life in the hearth. Crouching down, he placed kindling carefully atop the fire and waited patiently for it to catch.

"I must know," she entreated. "Do you speak? Can you communicate with me at all?"

He sent her a searing glance that stopped her cold. His muteness, his lunacy—they had been his only protection for too long now. He would not hand over in one thoughtless second what had been his means of survival for years.

Fear welled up within him, an overpowering call to action. Caution fled. With a snarl, he stormed to the door and grabbed the knob, rattling it like a maniac, then pounded his fists against the wood.

Annalise stared, afraid to move. His eyes were wild, his jaw fierce. The tendons in his arms stood out with the force of his blows. He did seem crazed, but no more than she, the both of them captured like rats in a cage to be exterminated. His frustration transmuted itself to her and she felt his anger and pain, his helplessness. His palm had begun to bleed and she knew she had to stop the self-destruction.

"Your Grace," she pleaded softly. She went forward

and grabbed his arm. "Please, they won't come. You hurt yourself for naught."

On reflex he slung her aside and she stumbled back. Horrified, he dove to help her, to right the wrong, then froze at her voice, so kind and soothing, without reprimand.

"It's all right. I'm fine." She crawled back to her feet, staying well away. Fear was there still, hidden in her eyes, but it was buried beneath compassion. "You're hurt."

He stared at his hand and swore silently. It was a scratch, nothing, less than that. He lay his forehead against the door, feeling his spinning world slow to a manageable pace. He had not meant to be overcome, had thought he could endure, but his small taste of freedom on the carriage ride home had expanded inside him until he was frantic to be outdoors, away from floors and walls and locked portals.

Careful not to startle her further, he moved away from the door, then crossed to the window and flung it open. The cold air blew in, cooling his temper, filling his soul with the fresh scent of morning. He stared at the fields in the distance, longing for them, yearning deep to the point of pain.

Annalise was not troubled by his silence, but the hunger on his face did concern her. There was savagery in his eyes and a fitful need in his intense concentration. To want something so badly did not make him mad, she reminded herself, but desperation was there, just beneath the surface, a tempered wildness hidden and ready to spring. She did not want to be near when it did.

But his hand was bleeding, and she could not ignore that no matter how hard she tried. "Your Grace." When he did not turn, she walked over to the basin and wet a cloth. "Will you tend your hand?" When he ignored her, she crept closer and held the cloth at arm's length. "Please, take it." Still he did not acknowledge her. She moved closer, concern for herself as well as him making a jumble of her emotions.

"I just want to clean it," she warned. She reached out and lifted his wrist, pausing to see if he would protest. Her own hands were shaking but his remained calm. Tentatively she touched his flesh with the cloth. When he remained still, she bathed the blood from his knuckles. Only raw patches remained where he'd scraped the skin off. "There," she whispered, "it's not bad, just a bit of . . ." Her words faded. His eyes were closed, his brow relaxed. It almost looked as if he were enjoying it.

Eleanor had the power to frighten him.

Bryson realized that repulsive fact at half-past eight, when the duchess opened his chamber door. Accompanied by Max and several servants who guarded the doorway, she marched regally inside.

She eyed Annalise with approval. "I see you have survived the night with your person—if not your reputation—very nicely intact."

Annalise's voice barely contained her fury. "Where is Greer?"

"That depends upon your disposition this fine morning."

Alarm trickled along Annalise's nerves. She knew perfectly well that she wielded no power here save her wits. A fit of temper would avail naught, and all the bravado in the world would be useless until she was free of this place. She knew the duchess now as a ruthless, conniving woman who would stop at nothing to get her way. Annalise would never underestimate her again or be deceived by her false kindness.

"I should like to see Greer," she said calmly.

"In good time." The duchess looked Bryson over from head to toe, no hint of emotion showing beyond slight irritation. "His clothing is an abomination. Get someone up here who can size him properly and have a wardrobe fit for a duke made with as much haste as my good name will behest."

Bryson's blood chilled in his veins. Dread stiffened his spine and made breathing a chore. Where were Luke and William, next in line after Stephen? Why did everyone persist in using the incorrect form of address with him? His fist began to clench and unclench by his side, but he could not stop the terror sweeping him. It roiled in his bloodstream, dimmed the edges of his vision.

He knew, of course, had suspected since last evening when no one came to greet him. But he had put suspicions aside in favor of the fledgling prospect that they were merely away, that his brothers didn't yet know he had returned. His pulse beat harder as he stood in abject pain, his heart thundering in his chest. He prayed even now that he was wrong when he knew better.

Eleanor glanced over at Annalise. "Well, my dear?

Shall I commission your ensemble, as well? Or will you go back to the village in disgrace, shaming your father and your aunt, ruined of any chance for a decent future?"

She would not cry. Annalise vowed she would not, but the exhausting night was taking its toll. She gritted her teeth against the hopelessness that washed over her and held back every fearful, angry emotion swirling through her like fouled water.

No matter how trapped, she must not show cowardice in front of the dowager. Eleanor would only use it against her. Annalise glanced at the Duke of Marchfield and knew she could not possibly spend the rest of her life with this speechless, unfathomable man, even to save herself and her family. Her father would neither ask it of her nor allow it. His love went far beyond the superficial commitment to bloodline, property, and power Annalise had found in this house. His love was simple, true devotion, and he would never want his daughter unhappy.

But if Annalise refused the marriage, she would drag her father's good name down into the mire with her own, and she could never be that selfish.

She felt like a climber who had reached the very pinnacle of the highest mountain peak, then found herself with no way to get down. She must stay and make a place for herself or crash to her doom. A mantel clock ticked incessantly, a mocking irony that time had run out and she must make a decision when she had been given no acceptable choices from which to decide.

She glanced at Bryson. Her dreams of a husband,

grand for a village girl, had still been puny things. He was more handsome and much wealthier than her fantasies had allowed. But he had none of the gentleness and adoration for her that she had imagined. She had seen the ugly violence that lay beneath the beautiful outer shell and knew she could not marry him. Too many miserable years stretched before her in a house of hatred and unanswered secrets.

Though she might live the rest of her life as an outcast, she would not live it in fear. And behind it all was the small glimmer of hope that she would eventually find someone who could ignore the unfair rumors and love her.

In this house, that chance was dashed before it even had an opportunity to blossom. As the Duchess of Marchfield, she would never be free to find the real love and companionship she had been raised to expect in marriage.

"What about His Grace?" she asked, stalling. "What does he want?"

Eleanor smiled. "Bryson," she said with silken poison, "you will wed this impertinent girl or be sent back to the priory. Is that understood?"

He did nothing more than look at his mother with loathing.

"Max," she said softly, "have the carriage prepared."

Bryson's world teetered dangerously on the brink. All of them were gone, everyone he had loved and respected and yearned for all these years. He could not credit it, could not accept it. In the far places of his mind, he'd harbored a small shiny hope: He would find his brothers and sisters, rescue them from whatever heinous place she'd sent them, and bring them home.

His chest felt crushed beneath unbearable anguish. Whatever particle of goodness left in him after six years in Hell went cold as death. He fixed a glacial stare on the angry, terrified girl. What did he care whether he wed a village girl or a king's daughter? Either would be used for one purpose only. His eyes narrowed cruelly and he nodded once, then turned away.

Annalise wanted to weep. His agreement had been cast in stony contempt. How could she wed a man who looked at her with indifference and at his mother with pure hatred?

"I need time," she temporized.

Eleanor laughed. "Not even a quarter hour will I give you, my dear." She cut a scornful glance at Bryson before piercing Annalise with the same glare. "Speech isn't necessary, as you can see. You need only nod your acceptance."

What she needed was a weapon, the means to rise above the trickery done to her and preserve her dignity. If Eleanor got the better of her now, Annalise would forever be in her grasp. Above all, she must get free of this place. She needed time to think and plan. An error made in haste now could doom her for the rest of her life.

She would find a way to escape and speak to her father, get his counsel before doing anything rash in either direction. And she must find a way to leave before bedtime.

In the boldest move of her life, she stared at Bryson, a silent plea in every ounce of her being. She promised much in that glance, if he would but grant this one small request. Taking a deep breath, she crossed the short distance that separated them and paused no more than a breath away. Heart thrumming furiously, she stretched up on tiptoe and whispered in his ear.

He stared down at her for long taciturn seconds, his face a mask. Annalise had no idea if he understood, if he had even heard. She raised upon tiptoe again and repeated her desperate request. After what seemed an interminable length of time, he leaned down and put his mouth to her ear.

Annalise nodded vigorously and turned back to the dowager. "You may have my wardrobe made, as well, but I alone will choose the date for the wedding ceremony."

Satisfaction gleamed in Eleanor's eyes. "Very well, as long as the time is reasonable." She then added with the most idle indifference. "What did he say?"

Annalise noted the duchess's covetous curiosity and smiled softly. "Nothing much."

Mary Greer hesitated in the doorway until Annalise beckoned with outstretched hands. She rushed over and knelt at Annalise's chair, a stricken look on her face. Grabbing her cousin's hands in her own, she lamented in a low pitiful voice, "She says you have agreed to wed him!"

Annalise nodded and tugged Greer to her feet. "I've no choice for now. She locked us in this room together for the entire night."

"But we will tell them—"

Annalise shook her head slowly, fighting to keep the seething resentment from her voice. "It won't matter, Greer. Even if we are believed, it won't matter. Come, sit beside me; we must plan."

She had been brought a basin with fresh water and change of clothes. Her embroidered gown was less extravagant than the one worn the day before, a simple fitted bodice, wide sash, and flowing skirt. The only concession to her modesty had been the arrival of a dressing screen. Set up in front of the hearth, it held the heat while she changed, but she never forgot that Bryson was only steps away. She had never washed and dressed so fast in her life.

She led her cousin to a narrow, cushioned window seat overlooking the courtyard. The window stood open, the breeze heavy with the smell of rain. Annalise watched the clouds gather in the distance, ugly blots against the azure sky, an ominous premonition, she was certain, of the black days ahead. She sighed and took her cousin's hands. "I fear the duchess will not allow us much time together, so we must speak quickly."

Near despair, Mary Greer hovered beside Annalise, but her gaze kept darting to the man by the fireplace. Tall and well formed, he dominated the small space in which he stood yet remained completely isolated. With the entire room at his disposal, he stayed by the fire, a man unto himself guarding his corner of forbidden ground. Mary Greer sensed that only the bravest or most foolish would venture near.

She was not at all brave but her curiosity won out and she studied him closely while he looked elsewhere. His shoulders were wide, his hair a rich golden reflection of the fire. Standing there, he appeared to bear the anguish and regret of an archangel fallen from grace.

Content to study the flames, he paid her no mind whatsoever, which was good. If the Duke of Marchfield so much as looked her way, Mary Greer was quite certain she would faint. She could not fathom how Annalise had spent an entire night in this room with him.

"Is he deaf and mute?" she whispered.

"He is not deaf," Annalise said with a hint of accusation.

"Did he converse with you at all?"

Annalise shook her head.

"Did he . . . do anything?"

"Greer, no!"

She burst into tears. "Oh, Annalise, I'm so sorry. Your papa will be devastated."

Annalise took her friend's hands and pressed firmly. "I have no intention of marrying him, Greer, but I need time to plan an escape. Papa must not know the true way of things until I can explain in person. It would leave him too worried and unprotected. Promise me you'll not tell, Greer. Not only would it hurt him terribly, but I fear it would put him in danger." She looked away, ashamed. "He warned me not to do this, but I was too headstrong to listen. Now look what I've done."

Mary Greer's eyes welled up again. She leaned in close and her words tumbled out in a whispered rush. "Is . . . is he horrid?"

Annalise cast a quick glance toward the hearth, then shook her head. "Oh, Greer, I don't know. There is something both terrible and compelling about him. I am completely frightened of him one moment and moved to compassion the next."

She hugged her knees to her chest, her expression far removed. "I have naught to liken it to, save the winter Papa found the wolf pup. Do you remember? It had been caught in a hunter's snare and was wounded near death. The entire time I nursed the beast back to health, I never quite knew if he wanted to bite me or lick me." She shivered suddenly. "I get that same feeling around His Grace. Like he might befriend me or devour me in one gulp."

"But he's a man, not a beast," Mary Greer cried softly.

"Are you certain?" Annalise whispered. Staring at him now with his wild hair and unearthly beauty, she wondered. "I am not sure when we'll be allowed to leave here," she added. "If we can, we will escape, but I know the duchess will watch us closely at first. I am going to see if she will allow you to return. If she does, go to Papa's study and find out what you can about illnesses of the mind and their treatments."

Mary Greer pressed white knuckles to her mouth. "But he'll find out."

"Go when he's working, converse with Aunt Mellie. You can do this, Greer, you must! I don't know how long I'll be here!"

Their time was even shorter than Annalise had anticipated. In only minutes Max was back, his two henchmen in tow. Annalise cut him a resentful glance but turned a reassuring smile on her cousin.

"Come." She rose from the settee and kissed Mary Greer's cheek. "You should return home. Tell my father that I am well but spread about the village that His Grace has been ill. That should strangle any wild speculation about his appearance."

"Oh, Annalise," Greer whispered desperately. "Are you certain?"

She was certain of nothing, but showing insecurity would reap naught but trouble in the days to come. "Tell Papa," she repeated.

The duchess appeared, satisfaction dripping from an otherwise sterile smile. Annalise regarded her coolly. "You should allow Greer to return and stop the gossip-mongers before they start."

"Perhaps," the duchess said, but her tone was noncommittal.

Annalise took a slow, deep breath and tried to appear casual as she committed her first blatant lie. "His Grace has requested a walk in the garden."

"Has he?" Eleanor eyed her son narrowly. "How do you know?"

"I'm not given to reading minds," Annalise evaded, smoothing the wrinkled folds of her gown to avoid looking the duchess in the eye. She might have just smudged her soul a bit with the lie, but she had no intention of blackening it beyond repair by adding more.

"Cheeky girl. Why hasn't he spoken to me?"

Something inside Annalise snapped—suddenly, irreversibly.

Perhaps it was the trauma of being held against her will or the fact that her reputation was ruined, her dreams shattered, her future forfeited over the course of one innocent night. But for whatever reason, the scales tipped and she lashed out with all the venom in her heart.

"Perhaps he has nothing to say to the woman who left him locked away in an asylum for six years!"

Lady Eleanor's rejoinder was so swift, Annalise never saw the woman's palm strike out. But the slap stung her cheek with staggering force. She stumbled back a step and put a hand to her burning face, fighting tears with every ounce of misbegotten pride left in her.

Without warning, Bryson lunged from his place by the fire, grabbed his mother's wrist violently, and twisted it up behind her back, while his other arm locked around her neck. The hold was incapacitating, potentially lethal, and had served him well over the grisly years. Eleanor's minions ran forward at once but were not fast enough. Their duchess lay in the clutches of a madman and there would be hell to pay.

Annalise cried out, pressing a trembling hand to her mouth. Violence seethed from Bryson and charged the air with electrifying force. Six years of anger and resentment and horror corded the muscles in his strong arms. Six years of isolation left a chilled vacancy in his eyes. It was obvious that he could snap his mother's neck without an ounce of regret.

"Oh, please," Annalise whispered.

Bryson eyed her narrowly. Panic made his pulse clumsy and irregular; hatred made it cold. In a reflex too quick to control, he had defended this silly girl, and it would doom him. He had failed the test. He would be cast back into the bowels of Hades for his behavior, never to resurface. His eyes burned into Annalise's with the bitter knowledge. He'd just lost everything on one thoughtless, useless moment of valor. He half wanted to release his mother and strangle the girl.

Tears slid down her cheeks. She bit down on her bottom lip to control its quiver, but her chest heaved from the effort to suppress a bout of weeping. She had never been struck before, not even as a child, and her emotions were tangled all out of reason. She felt humiliated and angry and confused.

The expectation of further violence hung thick in the room, choking her. Bryson seethed with it, so definitive she was shocked naught else had occurred. Eleanor's gaze remained cool, almost daring, and promised vengeance. Amos and Perkin were frozen where they stood, their livelihood teetering in the balance.

Greer stood well back, sobbing quietly, but Annalise dared not turn to comfort her. She pressed her hand to her mouth and tried to find the means to reconciliation. "Please . . ." she demanded. "I am responsible. No matter my opinion, I should have held my tongue in this house."

No one moved. Annalise wondered if they even breathed. The tension was volatile, expanding to the point of explosion. Her own emotions were swaying so wildly she was afraid to speak again. Each person standing before her looked as if he might do murder without a second's thought.

She backed away slowly, out of arm's reach, and focused on Lady Eleanor. Her voice trembled, but not nearly so badly as her knees. "My insult was thoughtless and unforgivable. However, you will *never* strike me again. I will tender my words with more consideration and respect in the future, but you must vow that you will never use any type of force, be it physical or otherwise, to restrain either me or your son again."

She took a deep breath for composure before sealing her bargain. "To save myself and my family, I have no choice but to marry him, but I will not live beneath constraints and fear the rest of my life. I would rather be ruined and free than become the Prisoner Duchess of Marchfield."

Eleanor stared coldly at Annalise, reluctantly admiring her pluck, little good it would do her. She should never have struck the girl. It was foolish and untimely this early in her plans. She needed an ally in the chit, not an enemy. She felt the strength of her son's hatred across her throat and in the grip on her arm, and knew her real battle lay there.

"On the contrary," Eleanor said smoothly. "I was completely overtaken by my emotions. It has been such a trying time for me. I do beg your forgiveness, dear Annalise, and assure you I will never strike you again."

Bryson's arm tightened on his mother's lying throat. He cared nothing for her plea for clemency, he wanted the vow of freedom. To be bathed in the sun's rays, to inhale the fragrance of earth and flora—he could hardly remember the gift. But neither could he abide being strung along on false hopes or taken out in ropes and chains. If he must be bound, he would take it within the secure, tidy elements of his room until he regained his strength and formulated a plan. He could not endure it elsewhere.

He watched Annalise for signs of weakening. She had stood up to his mother, but she would not last much longer. Her face was death-white beneath the shocking red print of his mother's palm, her hands trembling.

There was nothing he could do to help her. If he survived this outburst, he would never risk his freedom again. Snares awaited him at every turn—the woman beneath his hold, the men standing impotently at guard. And Annalise herself—the bright, frightened girl—was the foremost snare of all.

She looked at him in pleading silence, but she saw only cruel violence banked in his eyes, ready to erupt. Though it was his mother beneath his powerful arm, she knew to whom he directed his malevolent gaze. She swallowed hard and backed up another step. He might have defended her seconds ago, but she regretted it now.

She struggled for something to say that would ease the tension, but every word that ran through her mind was false and unconvincing. Finally she said the only thing that offered her a chance at escape.

"His Grace needs fresh air and vigorous exercise. He will never take his place as duke competently until his health is recovered."

Eleanor's eyes glittered with warning. She knew what the girl was up to and wished this stalemate done with as fervently as Annalise.

"Very well, but you will escort him and stay with him at all times. I pray he does not abandon you and run off like he did with my coachman . . . or do worse. It would

look very bad in the village, Annalise, very bad indeed
for you to be seduced by a madman then abandoned."

Annalise faced the duchess with steadfast calm but
inside she quaked with uncertainty. There was no possible way for her to stop Bryson from running off if he
took the notion. After all she had done for the wounded
wolf those many years ago, all the risks she had taken to
help the beast, the animal had snarled and snapped savagely at her when he was healed, then disappeared at the
first opportunity.

In truth, it did not matter. Annalise had her own
escape in mind, especially now when she knew what
Bryson le Fort was capable of. If she stayed she was
doomed; if she fled she was ruined. What difference did
it make which path she took? Taking a deep breath for
courage, she looked at Bryson. "Would you care for that
walk now?"

Tensions cramped the muscles between his shoulder
blades and turmoil hovered near, a tormenting demon
worse than the ones he'd left at the priory. He sensed he
would be taken the instant he released his mother, but
continuing was useless unless he was prepared to slaughter
everyone in the room, then attempt to take his place as
the duke without an ally. He was not foolish enough to
think he could accomplish that at this stage. He also knew
he could not stand forever at check. He gave a clipped
nod but could not force himself to loosen his hold.

Eleanor sensed his hesitation and ordered Amos and
Perkin out of the room. As soon as they were gone, the
arm at her throat lifted the slightest measure.

"You will not be locked up again, as long as you do

my bidding," she said. The fury of concession rang clearly in her voice. "But if you run off, I will not only have you officially declared a lunatic but a criminal, as well, and you will be hunted down as one." She pushed his arms aside, daring him to restrain her, and turned to face the last of her offspring. "On the other hand, if you do right by this family and produce an heir, you will have everything your title entails. Do you understand?"

Annalise blushed crimson and wondered if Bryson knew what was being demanded of him . . . and her. Nothing showed on his face, even less in his eyes. His mask was complete, the unemotional facade of a man gone too long without feeling.

"Do you understand?" Eleanor repeated.

Bryson's eyes narrowed dangerously. One corner of his mouth tipped up in ridicule. Yes, he understood now why he had been returned. He was the last of the line, the only one left to breed more fated March-field heirs. Something inside him shivered, then sealed shut. The darkness encroached like nightfall, shrouding his mind.

He turned toward Annalise and waited. He saw the confusion in her gaze, the hesitation in her step, but, finally, she moved forward and placed her arm on his. He felt the small tremors in her body, but there was little he could do to waylay her concerns or soften the blow. With a cutting glance at his mother, he pulled her around and delivered a brutal kiss that lasted only seconds.

Too shocked for words, all Annalise could do was gape.

Bryston noted the satisfied look in his mother's eyes, then released Annalise. He glanced over his shoulder at the sniveling girl in the corner and was at least grateful Eleanor hadn't chosen her. One so weak would be destroyed within a fortnight. He gave the girl a pointed glance and nudged Annalise.

"Greer," she forced past a dry throat. "Would you care to accompany us?"

Mary Greer rushed to Annalise's side, her soaked linen clutched to her mouth to stifle further sobs. She was scared out of her wits by the Duke of Marchfield but no less afraid of his mother. She grabbed Annalise by the arm and clung tight.

Chapter 9

THE SUN SHONE BRILLIANTLY OVERHEAD. GRAY clouds threatened on the horizon, but they had not yet moved in to steal the pristine perfection of the azure day.

Wild, long-stemmed Michaelmas daisies dotted the hillside like frolicking children, undulating skirts of green beneath lacy white caps. Hollyhock and larkspur ran along the streambeds and moist hollows, lush and verdant in the green countryside. Bryson turned his face up to catch the sun. Diamond-bright rays burned his eyelids, a cleansing of sorts, but the years of lack could not be quenched in one tiring stroll.

They made a motley troop, two frightened girls and a Bedlamite, as they passed the low-walled manicured grounds where boxed flowers, trimmed hedges, and fruit trees were laid out in predesigned precision. To the left of the pleasure garden lay the newly harvested fields, naked-looking. To the far right was a man-dug stone pond with marble steps leading in and Greek statues and fountains that bubbled refreshing water in graceful arches. The stables stood between, a favorite place, Bryson remembered, but could not piece together why. It seemed important to recall but he could not make the dim years clear.

He seemed to remember constant things, the lay of the land, the running of the household, the history of England. But secular incidences filtered through only in bits, tantalizing morsels to which he clung in the hope of putting the puzzle of his life back together piece by piece. He'd given up the hope that it would simply come to him someday all in one picture.

He inhaled the pungent smell of fresh hay and manure, and closed his eyes to relish the old familiarity.

The stablemaster stood just inside the main stall, staring as if he had seen a ghost. "Milord? It is you? Could it be after all these years?"

A boy nudged the old man in the ribs, then whispered in his ear. The color left the stablemaster's face. He looked back at Bryson and pulled his forelock. "Beg pardon. It's Your Grace, now, ain't it? Welcome home just the same."

Bryson offered a clipped nod then turned away. His gaze shot to Annalise, but she was taken with the young colt being led around the pen. Her face was animated, her eyes bright as she spoke with the boy working the rope.

Bryson avoided the stablemaster's eye and began walking past the crossed-fence corals, past these men and their recollections, past the simple courtesy of being expected to converse with them. He recognized Thomas Grimes but could not tell him of the past six years or ask about his favorite steed whose name he could not recall. He could only yearn to collect it all and put it back into place. He could go forward then, a whole man, a sane one.

Annalise turned and caught sight of Bryson rushing past the corral. She bade the stableboy farewell, then grabbed Mary Greer and hurried to catch up. She'd seen the hurt and confusion on the stablemaster's face. Bryson could not avoid the people of Marchfield forever. It was home to over a hundred hardworking souls: postilions, cellarmen, footmen, seamstresses, grooms, maids, and cooks. The older ones who had known him from birth would expect to be greeted. She could not fathom what the duchess had told them.

Bryson walked faster, beyond the conversation in which he could not indulge and the claws of insecurity. The girls caught up and followed him through the fenced pasture and into the open hills.

Amid long grass and wildflowers, he breathed easier. The land sloped upward, a gentle incline but taxing to one who had been confined to pacing a hard-packed dirt floor and an occasional march in a walled pen. Those infrequent walks had been the worst brand of torture. Chained to others, his hungry eyes had only been able to stare at the freedom just beyond the high wall, close enough to touch, a lifetime away.

He absently rubbed his scarred wrists. The girl beside him, who had been so animated at the corral, had that same trapped look in her eyes now. Fear controlled, a hungry craving for escape. But there were no chains or walls to hold her, and he knew she would leave as soon as she was able. He wondered if she noted the guards, his mother's inept fools trying to keep pace while remaining hidden. If wise, the girl would go as fast and as far as possible. His mother's vengeful reach was long.

The scent of grass and earth filled him. It had an essence, a taste he could absorb into his lungs. A balm to salve his wounds. But it was not enough. He knew what he must do, what he must put behind him before he could go forward. Dread weighted his steps as he headed for the small steepled church that had seen the christening, marriage, and burial of Marchfield sons for centuries.

It sat in the valley, pretty as a painting amid the gold and brown of fall. The perfect illustration of the ambiguity of the Flamboyant style of architecture, it showed strict simplicity in its elevation of two tiers. A high bare wall stood between the nave arcades and the clerestory. The piers, which merged into ribs, lent movement to the nave without disturbing the flat character of the wall.

Annalise was disappointed when Bryson did not attempt to enter but went around the side.

A graveyard lay at the back, a macabre place of cold stone vaults and lofty sloe-eyed angels. Intricately carved by master stonecutters, each noted how fickle and merciless life could be.

The churchyard gate squeaked obscenely when Bryson opened it. He should order it repaired. His time would come if he waited, he would make certain of it, but everything was still too new, too frightening, too easily corruptible. His defenses, strengths, and strategies would take time to shore up. He must first simply manage being home again, finding the way to be well and strong.

Ah, but this part was hard.

He forced himself to move through the ancient vaults, each step a contradiction. Pain flooded him, a physical force that staggered his breathing like a blow. He tried to ignore it but his chest tightened with each step. He reached the newest stones, those less weathered by wind and rain and time, and held on to composure with dull, iron fortitude. If he gave into the despair gripping him, he would break apart.

They were all there, from oldest to youngest, the heavy formality of their full names inscribed. Charles Stephen Elbert . . . Mary Eleanor Madaline . . . Joclyn Gabrielle, Gwendolyn Justine . . . Luke, William, Richard, even the unchristened stillborn twins.

A thousand rapier-sharp points stabbed his heart and made concentration difficult. He moved among the stones, a sleepwalker in a living nightmare, a place even worse than St. Bertram's where he had at least had hope of seeing them again. He felt the blackness creeping in, a murky chasm of bottomless cruelties that would pull him down into its vortex if he didn't resist. A muscle clenched repeatedly in his jaw, but his eyes were dry and cold. He kept his breathing even, his vision focused on the one harsh reality before him.

Everything was gone but Marchfield.

He turned away violently and began a slow jog out of the graveyard and into the hills.

Annalise watched him leave, tortured by the lack of expression on his face. If he was grieving, he gave no sign of it. There were no tears or prayers for the departed, nothing at all but the ice-cold vacancy in his eyes. But she sensed what he would not convey, what he would not even allow himself to feel, and it hurt to the marrow of her bones. She cast a helpless glance at Mary Greer and took off after him.

Bryson pushed himself to the very edge of physical limitation, then beyond. His feet pounded out the rhythm of sorrow, a crushing clockwork cadence that tore the memories from his heart and beat them into the earth—another burial. His mad trek did not stop the pain, only replaced it with something he could manage, a physical hurt he could later heal with liniment and rest.

He felt the burn in his muscles going to cramp long before his will collapsed. Too soon his body no longer cooperated and he was forced to slow, then finally stop. His breathing was labored, sweat rolled down his sides. Palms braced atop his knees, his entire body trembled in the aftermath. Only minutes of crossing the rolling section of land where he had romped for endless hours as a child had left him winded.

But he had another destination, one he'd had for six years, and he would not allow his worthless shell of a body to stop him. He must make it to the lake. His salvation lay there, proof that he was home.

Annalise paused beside him, her breath catchy from trying to keep up with his relentless pace. Her gaze darted to the strain on his face and the wildly determined look in his eyes. His long disorderly locks whipped about in the wind like spun gold, catching sunlight, covering his eyes and mouth. He pushed them back with an impatient hand but took little more notice. She had the terrible urge to do it for him.

His expression was severe, fixed on some point distant and obscure. Several times she suspected he was trying to escape but realized his harsh march was more than that. He seemed obsessed with getting to some place known only to him.

Mary Greer was bent at the waist, breathing hard. Annalise knew they should have left back at the church when they were nearer the village road and Bryson was consumed by grief. But she hadn't been able to leave him in that comfortless state, surrounded by the death of those he had known. Following this far, she would stay with him a little longer.

"Your Grace," she breathed.

He gave her a startled look, just now realizing she had followed. Her face was flushed, her hair coming undone in untidy clumps that reminded him of the young, impoverished French widow who had come to the priory after her husband's death. Addled, the widow walked around in constant disrepair, humming to herself, easy prey for the more deranged inmates. Unable to bear the resemblance, Bryson reached out and snatched the rest of Annalise's hairpins, freeing her locks to fall to her waist in more comely disarray.

With a startled squeal she backed up more than a long arm's reach. She exchanged bewildered looks with Mary Greer, then stared back at Bryson. "I . . . I need those."

Her cheeks were flushed, the musky scent of heat rose from her skin. She looked ready to bolt if he took one step closer. He curled his fingers over the hairpins and, for whatever twisted reason, tucked them into his waistcoat pocket.

Annalise's ire rose. "Those are mine. Return them to me, please!"

She would not reach for them, he knew, unless her anger grew stronger than her fear. He turned away and began walking.

"Those are mine!" she repeated with more vigor. She sounded childish but didn't care. Her nerves were already strung tight, and the simplest gesture seemed a huge affront. "Give them back to me at once."

He continued walking.

Her chin set, Annalise followed. The breeze whipped her hair into her eyes, insulting her further. "Where are you going with my hairpins?" she demanded.

He pointed to a rise in the distance and quickened his steps.

"Oh, most excellent!" She stared at the far hilltop, at least a quarter hour away. She and Mary Greer would have apoplexy in half that space if he kept up the grueling pace.

"Your Grace!" She pushed her hair out of her face and cajoled in a more civil tone. "Perhaps we should slow down a bit." The wind whipped up again, sending the hem of her skirt flying and whirling her hair back into her eyes and mouth. With a huff, she flung the heavy mass over her shoulder. "Your Grace!"

For ten minutes she managed to keep pace while he ignored her, but each step grew harder, each small slope a potential mountain. Mary Greer had stopped crying back at the church, but she was unnaturally quiet, her face still red and puffy. She continued trudging behind them, dull as a shadow pulled along in their wake. Annalise's vexation rose with her fatigue, as did the vehemence in her voice.

"The hill will still be there when we reach it, whether it be noontime or dusk. I have not known one yet that simply got up and moved away!"

Bryson halted abruptly and turned, stopping Annalise's scolding cold. Her skin was flushed, her breathing as fast as his own. She was slender but sturdy enough to traverse the grounds at a comfortable stride. Truly, he must have set a relentless pace for them all to end up so depleted.

Guards stood watch in the distance, frantic to keep him in their line of vision, despite what his mother had promised. His steady gait had been meant to give them a scare and test their mettle, but the gesture had reversed on him. Rebellion had cost him precious energy.

He stared at the hill with longing but did not begin the trek again. He would reach the lake given time. It lay there, just over the rise, waiting for him like a lost companion. On some ridiculous and inexplicable level of reasoning, he needed to see it, to be near it. But he could not get there at this rate. He looked at Annalise and grudgingly inclined his head in acquiescence of the needed delay.

She drew in a silent breath of thanks and moved to a shady spot beneath a broad oak. After pulling the fichu from her bodice, she dabbed at the perspiration on her brow.

"Come, Greer."

Mary Greer moved to Annalise's side and used the hem of her dress to wipe away the dirt on her cousins's face, then began to braid her hair.

"He'll return the pins," she whispered in a soothing tone. "It's only a boy's prank. My brothers do it all the time. You mustn't show you care."

"I *don't* care about the pins," Annalise returned. "It's just that he's so . . . unpredictable, so frightening. He looks at us as if he loathes us."

"No." Mary Greer shook her head. "He is as frightened as we are."

Bryson moved beside them, close but not touching, studying the intricacies of friendship as the two girls whispered. He could not remember his own acquaintances in a personal way, just snatches of things from time to time. A place, a party, a horserace. The younger girl's fingers moved dexterously through Annalise's tangled locks, putting them to rights with an order he found oddly staid and unappealing.

The cool shade provided nice respite but already he could feel the urge to go pulling at him. While they all must have rest, he begrudged even a small delay. He stripped the long-tailed coat from his back and hung it on the lowest branch, then removed his waistcoat, as well.

Color rose to Annalise's cheeks, a delicate pink that had nothing to do with the mad dash. His lawn shirt clung to him, made sheer by the perspiration soaking his chest and back, and his breeches were snug and revealing without the concealment of his outerwear. His musculature was impressive for one who had been confined so long. She looked away and pulled Mary Greer down to sit beside her.

Wide-eyed, Mary Greer tucked her skirts around her ankles. "He has removed his coat," she whispered in shock. "He's got more muscles than Charlie Blacksmith.

Amazed, Annalise swung toward her friend. "When did you see Charlie's muscles?"

Mary Greer blushed profusely. "At the fair, but I wasn't looking apurpose. He and Walter got into a tussle behind the bakery tent and both stripped to the waist for a round of fisticuffs. I couldn't help but see when he came rolling in right at my feet."

"What numbskulls," Annalise said, then suddenly wanted to cry. "I should have married Walter, Greer. I shouldn't gotten ahead of myself with such lofty ideas and done what any normal girl would do."

"Bother," Mary Greer said, shocking Annalise. "You would have been bored with Walter in a day."

Annalise pressed a linen kerchief to her mouth. "Oh, and I shan't be bored married to a lunatic! Is that supposed to console me?"

Mary Greer dropped her eyes.

"Forgive me," Annalise whispered. She folded her hands primly in her lap and stole a glance at Bryson's profile. Leaning back against the tree trunk, his posture held the perfect, casual indolence of a bored nobleman at leisure. But his gaze took in everything. Not hill nor valley nor boulder escaped his sharp consideration, and she realized suddenly that she would not escape him either if he chose not to let her go. Dread shivered through her. She had not counted on the Duke of Marchfield himself as an obstacle to her plan.

Her very first impressions of him were suddenly and unmistakably reaffirmed: The idiot duke was frighteningly intelligent.

Though she was no longer quite certain how sane.

"Why don't you talk?" she blurted out on impulse.

Mary Greer made a strangled sound.

Bryson's gaze seared her, but Annalise decided she was quite done with the tension and trauma of the day.

"Yes, I am aware of the ridiculousness of expecting you to answer such a question," she said. "What I mean to say is, *can* you talk? Have you a tongue and teeth and whatever mechanisms necessary for speech?"

His brow relaxed. He would like to show this pert girl his tongue and teeth and all the mechanisms necessary for things other than speech. But intimidating her into silence seemed more prudent. He crouched down only inches away and sat upon one hip, his knee raised. Picking a wildflower, he brought it to his nose and inhaled.

The fragrance replenished him, a delight taken for granted in his younger years but never again. He picked a cluster, then extended one to Annalise, another to the frightened little ghost beside her.

"Thank you," Annalise said, sounding inane and insincere. Stiff-backed, she stared at the flower in her lap, not at all certain she liked being courted by a mute lunatic whom she was about to abandon. Taking a deep breath for courage, she looked at him. "You are purposefully ignoring my question."

He was, of course, the persistent little chit.

She tilted her chin up. "I can only assume one thing by your obtrusiveness: It isn't that you *can't* talk but that you *won't*."

Her perceptiveness shook him for a moment. She was searching, as any bright girl would. He admired the intelligence of her quest, though he would not give up his secrets. He lay back on the fecund grass and let the sun beat down upon his closed eyelids. Bright patterns burst against black, heat like a benediction. He could have stayed forever beneath the sun's warmth had he not had another destination, a life to reclaim. His eyes opened suddenly and caught Annalise watching.

When he relaxed, she noted the way his face transformed into the stunning attributes of legends—archangels, demigods, heroes. It took no effort at all to see who he had been before: the golden son, the favored child. A father's pride lay in the strength of his body, a mother's joy in his startling beauty.

She thought for a moment he might smile, but the instant passed, leaving behind the unsettling impressions of horror and brilliance.

She shivered unaccountably and looked away. Whatever external beauty he possessed could not transcend what lay beneath. She had seen his violence firsthand. Just how much further he was capable of taking it, she did not want to imagine. She pulled away as far as she dared and slid Mary Greer a warning glance beneath hooded lashes to be ready.

Chapter 10

Bryson watched the sky through dappled leaves overhead. Shadows mingled with varicolored greens, shades as soothing to his senses as the cool breeze on his heated flesh. The ground was hard and uninviting beneath him, but high above a hawk soared, gliding on the wind with breathtaking and graceful majesty. He wanted to be that bird, to fly over forest and field on the wings of perfect freedom, then come to rest in his own good time upon the rich Marchfield soil of his memories.

Everything he loved had been stripped from him. All that was left was a title he held by default, and that only by the thinnest thread and his mother's cunning. If he could not adapt, if he could not go on in this world he remembered only in fits and starts, he could be proven incompetent. The king could revert his title and lands, and Bryson would be left with nothing, not even the Hades-hole from whence he had come. He knew he must do something to ensure the lands remained in his possession.

He glanced at Annalise. Her brows were drawn in vexation, her mouth set in sullen lines. Stalwart and stubborn in every inch of her petite body, she was still the prettiest thing. He wondered if this comeliness was his mother's concession for marrying him off so far beneath his station. Even an unattractive, impoverished earl's daughter would be more acceptable than a commoner. But there was little more he could expect with his very sanity on the line. A beautiful, spirited village girl was hardly punishment considering what he might have been saddled with.

Eleanor would need to claim a love match if she hoped to pull it off with believability among the ton. Even then, he would be silently condemned for sullying the bloodlines, and it was unlikely the girl would ever be accepted. He plucked another wildflower, a peace offering, and laid it in her lap.

"What a charmer," she whispered, blushing in spite of herself. "You only do this to confound me."

He did it to make amends for everything he lacked, for everything he would never be to this comely girl whom his mother had tricked and manipulated. This girl who would lie beneath him with or without her own consent and bear him a child to ensure the Marchfield line.

He was sane enough to know that much had to be done.

They headed for the rise at a much more normal stride. When Bryson reached the top, he paused to absorb the astonishing beauty below. The lake lay nestled in the verdant green countryside, as deep blue as the sky it reflected, surrounded by a thick copse of trees. Its glassy surface shimmered in the sunlight, a spark of Heaven to his decayed soul.

He took a shuddering breath and held it, then released his anxiety slowly. He'd had a terrible fear that the lake would be gone somehow, vanished like his former life. But there it lay, shining like liquid jewels to welcome him home.

He descended the hill at a comfortable run. Near the bottom the forest thickened, and he slowed his pace to move through the hawthorn and oak and clusters of prickly briars. When he emerged into the clearing, he stopped, his entire being suspended.

A fish jumped, a flash of sunlight reflected off its scales. Tiny insects skimmed the surface of the water, riding windswept ripples to the shore. Faint mist hovered along the edge in patches left from the early-morning fog.

Bryson walked to the very border and lay down, heedless of his clothing or the cool damp earth. Like the boy he had left behind, he took one deep breath and plunged his head fully into the water.

"Mercy," Mary Greer gasped, "he has completely lost the remainder of his wits!"

Annalise gave a strange, small smile. To her way of thinking, it was the most ordinary thing he had done so far. She stared at the water with longing, wishing she could join him, even to the point of stripping off stockings and shoes to wade in the shallow depths. The thought of a full dunking was too bold for her to consider, but secretly she would have liked nothing better than to swim like the slippery trout darting beneath the cool, shiny surface.

Bryson reared back, gasped for air, and shook his head like a wet mongrel. Flinging himself on his back, he stared up at the sky, his wet locks spreading out around him like whiskey-colored water weeds.

Annalise felt his soul-deep longing like an ache in her own chest. How many years had he thought of this? How many endless hours had he yearned? She started to say something, but her throat was too full, her emotions drawn too tight. Then suddenly, breaking the silence like church bells at noon, came a deep, masculine sound of contentment from his throat.

Annalise exchanged looks with Mary Greer, then came to an immediate and impulsive decision. Here among thick forest and hills, away from prying eyes, she could be every bit as preposterous as the Duke of Marchfield. He had a great title to protect, while she had only her reputation to concern her.

She sat down quickly before good judgment stole her chance and pulled off stockings and shoes, then stood and hiked her skirts to her knees. Ignoring Mary Greer's strangled gasp, she took a deep breath and tiptoed into the edge of the water.

The first shallow steps were warm, the water swirling around her ankles and calves with the most delicious sensations. Only when she pressed deeper did the water have a chilly bite, so she stayed near the shore, dodging slippery patches of greenish-brown algae and delighting in the feel of the sun beating down upon her shoulders, while the earth squished soft and wet between her toes. She smiled at her friend, wonder in her eyes.

"Come, you must try this!"

Mary Greer shook her head, looking appalled. "You will ruin your hem."

Annalise's face clouded over. "But it's such a small adventure, no one will ever know. Come join me."

"But you are half naked!" Greer whispered. Her anxious gaze darted to the duke, then back. "I can see two inches of your chemise, not to mention your ankles and calves—"

"Oh, don't spoil it," Annalise pleaded. Her voice dropped to a whisper. "Come enjoy the chance while you can."

But Annalise knew that Mary Greer had no notion of how to defy propriety and enjoy herself at the same time. She watched as Greer shook her head vigorously and remained on the bank.

Bryson listened to the wind carry the whispered discussion like a tattletale. Adventure and impish rebellion lay beneath Annalise's tone, reserve beneath Mary Greer's. The sun poured over him and he breathed deeply, an attempt to inhale its light, to abolish the darkness of his soul. An attempt to ignore what was going on in his peripheral vision.

Slender legs, clean and unscarred, pristine white beneath the clear spray of water. A flash of knee as she stepped up to balance on a rock. One drop of water rolling slowly down her calf to her ankle, sleek and trackless as the sun rays shining through her hair.

What a naughty girl to show so much skin and terrorize the sensibilities of her companion. He closed his eyes. Ah, but what did that make him, when he would have liked to catch that drop with his tongue?

The watcher stood on the rise, concealed by heavy forest. The scene before him was surreal—a girl frolicking in the shallows, another resting upon the bank, a Marchfield son surveying his holdings with the indolence of his entitlement. Add a luncheon basket and a couple of lapdogs, and Gainsborough could not have captured it more prettily.

One of the girls turned his way and he slid more deeply into the shadows. The lord resting on the bank was decidedly Marchfield, with his fair hair and strong, elegant physique. It was unimaginable that the only legal heir left to the vast fortune was an idiot—a nasty bit of fouled work, that one. But he could be easily disposed of again.

The watcher shifted his gaze around the countryside, noting Eleanor's guards but little else. He should have joined the *Roseti*, with their harmless devotion to poetry and wine. He could, at this moment, be sitting upon the bank of the lake beside two pretty girls, sipping a fine Merlot.

Instead he had joined the *Illuminati*, inspired by their rhetoric for equality. Bastard born, he had all the privileges of education a noble son could want but none of the birthright to inherit. He had gotten in with a secret sect that put down the right of blood over mankind.

Once in, he had wanted deeper. Beneath the layers of enlightenment, he found smart, sinister, and completely ruthless men operating under the guise of perfect reason. Half the leaders of the French revolution belonged to their elite group. Little by little, house by house, the same would soon be true in England.

Their strength was spreading, like an invisible blood-stain, throughout the civilized world. The power that had enticed him should have been enough to hold him, but now he wanted out, away from the malignant heart-beat within where governments were forged or failed. Internal decay was the best way to weaken a country before allowing foreign armies in to finish the job. House by house, England would crumble, then France would take her.

He had wanted to be among the elite when it happened, had wanted to be first in line to see his betters bested. Now he was not so certain. There seemed to be no end to their corrosive need for power, no end to senseless death.

He stared at the group lolling about the lake bank. "The small nation" was on the verge of collapse. Not financially but internally. The others had chipped away at it for years. Marchfield's back was broken, and he was being offered the opportunity to finish it, to be responsible for the greatest single downfall among the icons of English ancestry. He could not disappoint them; if he did, it would mean his own life. After slipping from the trees, he mounted his horse.

Sunset on the lake was magnificent. Gold and red mingled, creating brilliant shades of orange that faded into subdued hues of peach, pink, and apricot. But deep purple encroached upon the horizon. Dark would be upon them soon.

If Annalise wanted to make good an escape, she needed to move quickly. Bryson was asleep in the grass, an almost boyishness to his relaxed features. She had a moment's regret coupled with an enormous twinge of guilt for what she was about to do, but the feeling did not outweigh her need to flee. She needed to seek her father's council. She caught Mary Greer's eye and rose silently, motioning toward the woods.

Her guilt did not abate as she tiptoed toward the cover of trees, but neither did her purpose. Every step, every twig snap seemed magnified a thousand times. Even the breeze was overloud, whistling evening chill through the treetops. But her heartbeat was the loudest of all, thumping in her chest like a runaway horse. Annalise pressed her hand to her breast and continued sneaking toward thicker cover.

Bryson might have let her go. Who was she but one of a hundred village girls from whom he could have his pick, given time? But time was a luxury he could not afford to indulge right now. Annalise was pretty and industrious and quick-witted. She knew where he had come from and had managed the afternoon well enough. Another girl might go screaming off in terror as the mouse, Mary Greer, wanted to do every moment she was in his presence. He needed Annalise until he found his balance again and felt secure enough to function on his own. And Marchfield must have the child she would produce.

His mother's guards had moved in nearer as sunset approached and were less than fifty yards away. They had already noted Annalise leaving and would be on her as soon as they realized she had more than a bit of exercise in mind. There would be hell to pay when Eleanor found out the girl had tried to escape.

The guards were closer now, thrashing through the trees with the too-loud quiet of inept stealth. Bryson rolled quickly to his feet and chased after the girls, as if it were a game. He heard a muffled curse, then the rustle of leaves and dry twigs behind him.

He came upon Annalise just before the forest ended and caught her up in a lover's hold. Spinning her around quickly, he stole the scream hovering in her throat. His eyes fierce with warning, he lowered her roughly against a tree and began kissing her with all the passion of an impulsive lover. Or a man who had been held prisoner too long.

The guards crashed through the underbrush. Amos drew up short and Perkin stumbled into him like a drunken reveler. Mary Greer was too stricken to do much more than gape. Bryson drew out the kiss a moment longer, holding Annalise too tightly for her to move. Her muffled sounds of outrage could easily be mistaken for desire. Bryson gentled the kiss as a passionate suitor would, but his eyes held a warning she had better respect.

Annalise finally caught sight of Eleanor's men and her

startled lips quivered beneath Bryson's, then parted on a grateful gasp. Her entire body went weak against the tree, so malleable beneath him that Bryson was wont to forget the ruse. Her body melted into his, each curve molding to his shape, each soft inch finding its own complementary niche.

His blood thickened at the contact. He didn't know whether to shove her away or wrap her tighter. Stunned by the impact of her softening, he had to distance himself before he forgot who he was, where he was. He released her quickly, as if embarrassed at being caught.

Perkin tripped over himself with excuses and apologies, then skittered away. Amos stayed a moment longer, stumbling for words and settled on something obvious.

"Cook says dinner will be served in an hour." He bowed and backed away. "That's all. Just delivering a message."

Annalise had no words to express her mortification and relief. Though Bryson had caught her trying to escape, he had also rescued her. But his methods had been so disarming she couldn't find her balance. Anger mingled with relief, shock with fear, and over it all lay a layer of unsettling tension she had never experienced before.

With speech beyond her, she spun around and marched back to the lake. Her cheeks were flaming and her chest felt strange and tight. She'd never been held by a man other than her father, and certainly not one who had squeezed the breath from her. Kneeling on the bank, she plunged her hands into the cool water, then brought them to her burning cheeks.

Embarrassment throbbed with the heat of indignation in her pulse, but a strange lethargy stilled the anger
in her heart. Eleanor would have had her head on a plat-
ter if the guards had caught her in flight. Yet she could
not be completely thankful. She was still trapped as
before, and the winds of change moving over her life
were forbidding.

Mary Greer inched beside Annalise and put her arm
around her for comfort but said nothing. What was
there to say? They were caught like badgers in traps with
no way out.

Twilight fell with a chilled hush. Night creatures
began their inharmonious chatter, creating an eerie
cloak of sound. Annalise dared not try to leave again,
not with her limbs so trembly and riders just barely
visible in the distance. The temperature was quickly
dropping but still Bryson made no effort to return to the
castle.

It was rebellion, pure and simple. Annalise noted it in
every glance he made around the dimming countryside,
in every chilled shiver he did not answer with a warming walk back home. He waited to see if someone
would come and seize him, force him to return.

Mary Greer huddled beside Annalise to keep warm.
The girls exchanged perplexed glances from time to
time but mostly kept their own council over the matter.
Neither wanted to chance incurring his wrath. Annalise
pulled the edges of her gown away from her body. She
had indeed soaked the hem, as Mary Greer had warned,
and everywhere it touched chilled her to the bone.

Evening shadows blended, deep purple to gray to

black, creating depthless spaces in the land. Footing would be nigh to impossible on the trek back now. The off-key chorus, pleasant-sounding from the safety of her bedchamber window, grew louder, more threatening in the midst of falling darkness. Annalise felt another shiver seize her and stood abruptly, deciding she'd rather brave Bryson's anger than the frigid night.

"It is time to return to the castle," she said with more bravado than she felt. "Greer is like to catch her death if it gets much colder."

Bryse eyed Annalise coolly and extended his arm, an invitation for the girls to depart. Annalise blushed crimson.

"I am to stay with you," she said. "Your mother's orders."

One eyebrow arched with insinuation, and she had no doubt he referred to her earlier attempt at escape. She had no answer for that and merely repeated her earlier statement.

"It is time to return."

He shrugged. *Her decision,* the implication said. He was not keeping her there.

Annalise pursed her lips, chagrined by his lack of compassion, then tilted her chin to a considerable angle. "You only test your mother's patience with this . . . this sedition. You wait to see if she will force you to return, if you are really free to move about at will. But you are not free at all, not as long as you stay locked inside your own silence!"

With matching hauteur, she turned and helped her friend up. "Come along, Greer. His Grace may freeze to death if he wishes, in which case I shall not have to marry him and put up with such nonsense the rest of my life."

Impertinent, insightful little witch. Bryson watched the sassy turn of her hips as she spun to go change to a much more circumspect and delicate manner when she found she must pick her way through the darkness. He found her fetching in the deepening twilight, a bit of light in the encroaching blackness. The shadows grew and surrounded both girls, swallowed them in nothingness.

Bryson stared up at the stars. It was just as well that she was gone with her angel's face, comely shape, and shrew's tongue.

He wanted her. Fiercely. As he had not wanted a woman since long before St. Bertram's. He had run Annalise off for that very reason, a terrible complication at this point. His need was painfully obvious, which was to be expected after so many years of unnatural confinement, he supposed, but still uncomfortable to endure. He could feel her still, every angle and curve and soft round edge, pressed between him and the tree. The scent of her lingered, bathing his senses with a hint of jasmine and something else he could not remember.

There had been others who had inspired the same painful lust in him, but they were long ago. Girls of his own class, privileged daughters of noble fathers, flirtatious dalliances that had come to naught but wishful fantasies beneath the watchful eyes of their chaperones. He could not remember their faces or their names or even their importance, just that he'd not been given to noticing the lower class, save a kitchen maid once who had tried openly to seduce him behind the buttery when he was eighteen.

He didn't understand why that memory was so clear, save that it was the last before St. Bertram's. She was a buxom maid named Clara, and she had smiled a coy invitation that he had not noticed at first until she grew bolder to make certain he did. Untried and so ripe for her flirtation, he had followed her behind the out-building like an eager pup. There she had bared her breasts and offered them to him, a succulent feast for fledgling desires.

The memory sent a shock of heat flooding him. Though he'd never forgotten the incident, he had not dwelled upon it over the years. The members of the priory had their own brand of forbidden liaisons—savage and mindless rutting, rape, and self-mutilation—all of which Bryson had never partaken. To sully himself with the likes of Delphi or Mara or even the delicate but unstable Contessa had been unthinkable.

The incident with Clara had happened a lifetime ago, and the details were vague, but the feelings came back strong and disquieting, stirring him up to thoughts better left in the past with the present approaching him this very moment in the form of a half-frightened, wholly stubborn girl.

Annalise reemerged from the darkness, fists on her slender hips, ethereal-looking in the glow of a rising moon.

"I cannot find my way in the dark."

Resentment underscored her words, though to her credit, she kept her tone civil. Her huge eyes glistened suspiciously, but he sensed she'd rather take a beating than cry at this moment.

Cannot find her way? With a sigh, Bryson reached for his coat and rose. What a ridiculous chit to credit him with the ability to do any better.

Eleanor's eyes burned with resentment when the tired group walked into the castle. Annalise glared back, unwilling to accept blame for the lateness of the hour.

She thought the duchess should be grateful Bryson had returned at all. Had she been a daughter of this hall, she would have sought asylum in a nunnery. Had she been the duke, she would have sent Eleanor packing with a dowager's share and the order to never return.

The cruelty of Annalise's thoughts shocked her, but they did not fade rapidly. Life's tragedies had made Eleanor a cold, bitter woman, and Annalise should at least feel pity for the duchess. She was not convinced that she herself would be any different had she lost a husband and so many children, but charitable feelings did not come easily toward the woman who had lied to her and now held her prisoner.

The evening fire glowed with warmth in the massive hearth, chasing away the damp night air from that portion of the room. Shadows danced along the walls, secrets evading the light. A young man in elegant riding attire stood warming his hands. He had long dark hair and sharp, slender features. Annalise gazed at him with curiosity and at the flames with pure longing. She was chilled to the bone and in no mood to stay beneath Eleanor's glacial stare.

She motioned to Mary Greer, and they eased closer to the hearth. "Good evening," Annalise greeted.

"Good evening," he returned, and moved over to allow them room.

His accent was French, his face oddly familiar. Annalise regarded him more closely but was not impertinent enough to inquire about such things when they had not yet been introduced.

"Forgive me," he said, "but there seems to be no one to present me. I am Etienne de Chastenay, Maximilien's brother. I have escaped France and fallen upon the good graces of the duchess, who has been kind enough to take me in."

Annalise had an opinion or two about the "good graces" of the duchess but held her tongue. Britain was flooded with French émigrés who had lost everything but their dignity. "You must be relieved to have arrived safely." She introduced herself, then Mary Greer, who smiled shyly at the stranger.

"I hear it is quite perilous these days," Mary Greer said.

"It is impossible," Etienne returned. "France as I knew it is gone forever. A memory only, which we will mourn but never recapture."

"How dreadful for you."

"*Oui,*" he agreed, "but not as dreadful as those who lost their heads to Madame Guillotine." When the color drained from Mary Greer's face, he added hastily, "Forgive me. I forget that I am among gentle women who have not become hardened to the daily horror my countrymen have had to endure."

"No, do not apologize," Mary Greer said with compassion. "I only pray that your time here will be more bearable."

He nodded. "With such lovely young women about to share my woes, it will be more than sufferable, I assure you."

Mary Greer fell speechless at the compliment. His words brought home her predicament. She leaned toward Annalise. "When will you ask the duchess about allowing me to return home?"

Annalise's heart sank. She would be alone if Eleanor allowed Mary Greer to go back to the village, her future uncertain and no one to whom she could turn. But she could no more deny her friend a chance at freedom than she would deny herself. "I will ask tonight."

"Will she do it?"

Annalise shrugged. She had no doubt Eleanor wouldn't allow her to get much beyond the range of a fast-moving servant, but she didn't know about Mary Greer.

Etienne de Chastenay leaned closer. "You seem a bit distressed, mademoiselle. May I be of service?"

Mary Greer blushed from head to toe, then shook her head.

"Thank you, but no," Annalise answered for her. "It is a private matter."

He nodded graciously. "I will leave you then, but the offer will remain."

Mary Greer watched him walk away, a soft look on her face. "What trials he has been through."

Annalise nodded. "His eyes bear the ravages of it." They were cold eyes, dead eyes, even when he smiled. She shivered and brought her attention back to the present dilemma. "If the duchess allows you to leave, go to Father. Reassure him about my welfare."

Mary Greer frowned. "I would rather send help."

Annalise shook her head. "Not yet. I've Papa and Aunt Mellie to consider." She watched Eleanor berate Bryson. The duchess's tone was too low to carry across the room, but her eyes spoke volumes. He stood by in silence, his expression flat. Annalise realized he had completely removed himself from the tirade. He stood not two feet from his mother's vehemence, but he was as distant as the stars. Nothing touched him in this state, nothing moved him. He might as well have not been in the room. But beneath the safety of his guarded withdrawal, he simmered. Annalise sensed it in the tightening of his fist at his side, in the tensing of his jaw. That volatile part of him frightened her.

She sighed deeply. "It is all such a tangle now, Greer." And the web seemed to be drawing tighter and tighter with each hour. Annalise could see no way out and no way forward.

When Eleanor turned her attention to Max and Etienne, Bryson moved nearer the hearth, giving Annalise only the briefest glance. He seemed oblivious to everything but the flames leaping and hissing in the huge logs. But he heard every word, absorbed every spoken and hidden meaning in their muted conversation, and

Annalise knew it. He gave nothing away with his posture or expression, but she saw it in his eyes, watched their expression change from blank endurance to subtle, sharp awareness. It was unsettling to see the transformation, chilling to know that nothing went undetected by him.

Annalise moved away and turned to her cousin. Mary Greer was the finest friend and confidante, but she had a delicate constitution. If this escapade had shocked Annalise's iron sensibilities, it had devastated Mary Greer's. "I will go ask now."

Mary Greer nodded.

With a sigh, Annalise left the fire and returned to the duchess. "Greer would like to return home."

Eleanor smiled with feigned innocence. "Return? But she is your chaperone."

Annalise's stomach contracted. Too many things had gone awry for her to bemoan the fact that Eleanor had made that a farce. "It is unnecessary now."

The duchess's elegant brow arched. "Yes, but is it wise?"

"She will tell no one the real truth here," Annalise responded stiffly. "She can be trusted far better than I can."

"In truth?" Eleanor's smile turned intimidating. "Perhaps I should wed *her* to my son."

The blood drained from Annalise's face. "You jest, I pray."

Eleanor laughed humorlessly. "She hasn't the stomach for it." Almost gently, she reached out and pushed back a wayward curl from Annalise's temple. "But you, my dear, are as brave as one of my own." Her eyes clouded over. Ugly black bitterness seeped through in both her countenance and her voice. "Be glad you were not born to this cursed hall!"

Foreboding ran through Annalise at the bleakness of the duchess's words. She could not fathom the pain this woman had suffered or the fortitude it had taken simply to survive it. "Let her return," she bade evenly.

"You plead for her so well. What of you? Do you wish to return, also?"

Annalise was careful not to let the fierce longing show on her face. "Only to make arrangements."

Eleanor's eyes narrowed shrewdly but she never lost her benevolent tone. "But it would give me such pleasure to help you. The banns must be posted, and there are dressmakers, wine makers, gardeners, bakers . . . the list is endless, my dear."

And more elaborate than Annalise had funds or experience for. "A wedding for a duke," she said dully.

"And his future duchess."

Her dream of a small, elegant service in the village church with friends and loved ones present faded to a misty fantasy. The impossible was reality now, but reality had an ugliness Annalise had never before known. Caution was new to her, but she sensed she must embrace it fully until such time as she was certain of her escape.

"I will stay, then, if you think it is judicious," she conceded.

"What a bright child," the duchess crooned, but her eyes were a sharp disparity to her tone. She would never let Annalise go and risk spoiling her plans. They both knew it.

Eleanor strolled over to Mary Greer. "You will give your mother my utmost regard for the lovely sweet buns, and pass along the message that I shall look forward to discussing plans for the wedding feast with her."

Mary Greer nodded, fear constricting her throat. She could not have spoken if her life depended upon it.

"Gather your things. Max will see you safely home."

"As will I," Etienne offered, "if you will allow me."

Annalise stood on the cobbled drive and felt a rush of anxiety when the carriage pulled away from the castle. Though a dozen people milled about performing various duties, she felt alone, isolated by the choice she had made. In the course of one day, her entire life had veered off from any ordinary or acceptable path, and she didn't know how to acclimate herself to the drastic changes.

Like Bryson's flight from the cemetery, she wanted to run into the hills, heedless of the danger of pitfalls and stones and wild animals. She wanted to run until her breath rasped in her throat, until the tears stopped burning in her eyes. She wanted to run until she outran the course her life had taken.

She stared up at the stars with blurred vision and tried hard to be thankful that her future would not remain on the staid, predictable course of a simple chemist's daughter. She would be a duchess, a woman of means and stature. The elusive Heavens had lowered within her grasp. Grandeur and possibility were her future.

But a man would stand by her side, a stranger of unpredictable thoughts and manner, in a home where death had stolen the joy of life for twenty years.

Annalise shivered and hurried back into the castle. Sarah met her in the main hall, bobbing a quick curtsey. "Her Grace says dinner will be served in a quarter hour, if you please."

Annalise smiled at the girl from a neighboring village whom she had known most of her life. "Sarah, it's me, Annalise Weatherly. You needn't curtsey to me."

"Of course she must." Eleanor's commanding voice echoed throughout the large room for all to hear. "If she wants to keep her position, she will treat you with the deference due the future Duchess of Marchfield."

Beneath her lashes, Sarah flashed Annalise a brief but undeniable look of disdain, then rushed off to escape further scolding.

Annalise watched her go, adrift now in a way she had not anticipated days ago, dreams ago. She saw clearly what she had never anticipated in her wishful flights of fancy. She would not step easily from one world to the next but would be caught in between—accepted by neither, resented by both. The staggering impact of her mistake struck her then, the absolute and irreversible folly of her dreams.

Turning slowly, she faced Eleanor with all the hauteur of the duchess she would never really become. "I find my appetite quite diminished. If it would not be remiss of me, I shall decline dinner and request a light repast in my room."

Eleanor's eyes glowed with approval. "I will have a tray sent up."

Each step Annalise took up the wide staircase felt weighted by lead. She could not go back, but the future loomed ahead as a black swirling eddy of broken dreams and uncertainty. She had no one to blame but herself for her silly Cinderella fantasies. To imagine that a chemist's daughter could rise above her station to marry a duke was a bedtime fable. Given life, it became a nightmare. She dashed away a tear with the back of her hand and ran the remainder of the way to her room.

Slamming the door behind her, she flung herself on a silk brocade chaise and let the hurt flow. She would allow herself this one small moment of weakness, then be done with regrets and self-pity and wishes for what might have been.

Finally spent, she rose to find a cool cloth but drew up short. Bryson stood inside the door frame, leaning negligently against the jamb. His eyes were dark and unreadable, his expression solemn. Embarrassed by her weeping, Annalise looked away, hoping he would leave.

But he stayed, a silent watchful nobleman with an unseemly look in his eyes. He waited until she looked fully at him again, then lifted one hand out to her, palm up.

Whether beckons or summons, Annalise was uncertain. His eyes compelled and demanded and held her in a way more frightening than physical bonds. But he did not offer comfort. There was neither compassion nor pity in his look. She shook her head, denying him, unsure of what she struggled against, only that she must.

But his intention was set and he would not release her.

"No!" she cried, stomping her foot like a child, feeling utterly foolish when he had not made a single verbal demand.

He gave her a searching look, then nodded once and drifted back into his room. The panel closed softly behind him.

For one heartbeat she stood still, then bolted after him. Sliding the door open, she stood, her posture stiff and angry, her course less certain.

"What do you want?" she demanded.

Her eyes still glistened from tears, but her skin had lost much of its redness, save high on her cheekbones where indignation glowed.

Bryson turned toward the window.

She had been effectively dismissed—like a servant or a shrewish wife. Annalise's ire rose with her embarrassment. "You cannot summon me in one breath, then dismiss me in the next like . . . like chattel."

He glanced back over one shoulder, and for a fleeting moment, almost imperceptible, she saw the consummate duke in the lift of one eyebrow, in the arrogant curve of his jaw. But the madman remained, lurking beneath the surface, dangerous and unpredictable in his cornered state.

He turned back and waited for her artless rebellion to unveil itself. He was not disappointed. Within seconds, Annalise had forgotten her trepidation and crossed the room. Though he had not yet deigned to turn back, he knew she was there, hands balled into delicate fists, resentment and determination on her face.

It would ever be this way between them. Forced together by marriage, they would always struggle for self-possession, for that one small bit of independence that proclaimed each had not been manipulated and coerced, when in truth both had.

He turned suddenly, throwing her bravery so far off balance she floundered in the face of his nearness. He took a step toward her and watched alarm creep into her expression. It was not panic full blown yet, but it hovered just on the fringes. He thought he would help it along a bit.

Too quickly for her to see it coming, he reached out and caught her wrist, then jerked her forward.

Too late, her heels dug in, but she was already within the circle of his arms, staring up into his terrifyingly handsome face. His look was dangerous and inflexible, more animal than lunatic. She thought for a moment he might crush her. Instead, he spun her half circle until her back was to the wall, as it had been at the tree, and he was to her front.

His head lowered.

❖
Chapter 11

His mouth hovered just above hers, less than a breath away, the heat and scent of him invading her senses like potent wine. She felt him everywhere: in the thunder of her heartbeat, in the accelerated rhythm of her pulse, in the fluttering pit of her stomach. Her own breath came fast, mingling with his, making her light-headed with anxiety and something more.

Something indefinable.

She made a sound. Protest or fear or that same in-definable something. Not a sound she had heard from her own lips before, not a feeling she had ever felt. It was heat and dread, awe and aversion. She half wanted to push him aside, half wanted to pull him closer. She twisted instead, brushing him from chest to thigh, mak-ing the feelings keener, sharper, bright and expansive inside her.

He leaned into her, his body heavy and warm,

disarming in its comfort. She felt almost as if he shielded her in the same instant he ravished her.

"What are you doing?" she accused, but the words were less than forceful, full of breathless anticipation.

His own breaths grew faster, as quick as hers, his eyes darker. The comfort twisted.

His head lowered fully and his mouth captured hers, drowning out her startled cry. Harsh and warm, he smothered her, taking what she would not willingly give, devouring her like a ravenous beast. His arms tightened possessively, frightening her even more with the strength of purpose in the corded muscles and tendons confining her movements.

His body pinned her to the wall from breast to thigh, heavy and solid, a smothering warmth he had wanted to repeat since the early evening. She was soft and fragrant to his impoverished senses, the sweetest fruit, the richest confection. He could devour every morsel.

His palm rose and cupped her face. Her skin was silk against his roughness, sweet, so sweet. Her throat was warm, flushed with heat as his palm slid down.

She stood paralyzed, quivering in frozen silence like a forest creature caught in the predator's stare. His strength was like nothing she had experienced, his purpose too complex to unravel. She had heard stories of maidens being attacked by evil strangers, servants abused by their masters, but she had never thought it could happen to her. She twisted against him, unleashing an even greater strength. He moved with her, into her, sparking a maelstrom of convoluted feelings.

Bryson's thumb caressed the pulse at her throat, felt

her moan of protest. It penetrated the heavy mist of lust consuming him but had little effect on his conscience. He would force her to find a way to escape or stay and know him. There could be no middle ground for them. Their association had not been founded on gentleness, and it would not be consummated as such. A war raged, of neither of their making, but both were caught up in it. Survival was the only thing.

He meant to establish mastery in at least one area of his conflicted life. Perhaps on some deeper level, he meant to prove to himself that he was still a man. But with every twist and turn of her shapely body, he dissolved a little more, became both weak and unruly, an uncontrollable thing he despised.

He sensed immediately that he would never have power over Annalise. With greater strength he might subdue her, with charm he might woo her, but the ultimate mastery was hers alone.

She was not awed by his position or the influence of his title. She was only a little afraid of his insanity. Brute strength was the only thing that really frightened her.

The monster rose within him, screaming want, a driven anger, beastly and without conscience. He tried to force it away by softening the kiss, but Annalise's writhing had grown frantic and nothing gentle would hold her.

He pressed deeper into her, his full weight bearing her into the wall. His palms cupped her face and held her still for the marauding of his mouth.

Her breathing was hoarse and rapid, sounds of panic vibrated in her throat. A spill of golden hair tumbled from its braid, covering his hands and wrists, framing huge blue eyes glittering with fright and outrage. Every jerk and twist of her body sent lust pouring harder through him.

Twist, turn, writhe, buck—an endless sweet torture that lasted eons. Whether to prolong it or end it was a torment of indecision. Every place her body grazed, his blood coursed hot, pounding out the tempo of her struggles, the rhythm of his need.

He drew a breath and pressed deeper, unraveling a little more, becoming the crazed beast he had feared being for so long. She was warm and sweet and soft, fragrant as a spring breeze. So delicate and unprotected, she was no match for his strength. His body rocked against her, a mockery of what he wanted, a lascivious affront to her innocence.

Dangerous thoughts flooded his mind, the uncontrolled yearnings of an impassioned lunatic.

He could have her; there was no one to stop him but Annalise herself and she didn't have the strength. She would hate him if he forced her, but more likely than not, she would hate him anyway. With only the dire need for self-preservation to guide him, he lacked the conscience and compassion that would stop him. Whatever guilt lingered from childhood tutoring had little bearing on the grown man.

Annalise watched the look in his eyes change from passion to purpose. With an angry sob, she fought harder, using her knees and elbows to best advantage. When she renounced him, he covered her mouth, smothering her rebukes and pleas. When she fought him, he pressed deeper, pinning her more firmly to the wall. Eventually her strength waned and her struggling became a useless fight that drained her but seemed to make no impact on Bryson at all.

Finally, in utter desperation and outrage, she kissed him back. Returning to him all the fierceness and brutal aggression of his own assault, her mouth clashed with his. Her arms went around his shoulders and she grabbed his hair at the nape, digging her fingers in, pulling him to her. She restrained him as he had her in an imprisoning hold, ravishing his mouth as if she were the hungry brute, he the helpless victim. Her teeth scraped his bottom lip; she tasted blood.

He responded with a shocked jolt, then went still as stone, suspended in a surreal world of dark passion and suspicion. He allowed her daring assault, then slowly deepened the kiss, partaking little by little of her angry aggression, until they were both adrift in black, swirling emotions that threatened to swallow them.

His hands found her waist, so small within his palms that he could circle her with both hands. His fingers slid up her narrow rib cage to the underside of her breasts.

She cried out against their bruised lips, then kissed him deeper, received his touch as if starved. His hands were warm on her, possessive, as his thumbs stroked her ribs and his fingers dug into her sides. She felt breathless, spinning, as if she could not get enough air and must take it from him. Her body was on a violent spiral, going down a dark path to the center of forbidden desire.

"Why are you doing this?"

The desperation in her voice reached him far faster than her struggles had. He tried to ignore it, to cast it aside, but he had known that same torturous anguish before, the helplessness and confusion, the ferocious need for answers that would not come. He pulled back roughly, he breathing labored, and was horrified to find blood at the corner of her mouth.

"Please, I don't under—"

He made a sound, pressing two fingers to her lips.

Be still, be quiet.

She gave up and collapsed against the wall.

He caught her chin and tilted her face up. It was only a small wound where she'd bitten her lip—or he had. Anger washed over him at his animal lack of control, but he was nothing if not that after six years in a cage. He dropped his head into the hollow of her neck and shoulder, depleted by his assault, frightened by it. His thumb stroked her cheek, catching a tear that he brushed back and forth across her bottom lip.

When their breathing finally slowed, he pulled back and rested his forehead against hers.

Annalise felt his breath, cool on her wet mouth, hot on the skin of her jaw. His touch was unexpectedly tender and her knees suddenly went weak. She felt drained yet edgy, her stomach throbbing with an odd, inexplicable anticipation. She drew a sharp, confused breath and looked at him.

"Your Grace . . ."

He pulled back at the sound and caught the barely perceptible glimmer of heat in her innocent eyes. Impatience flared in his own. He caught a handful of her golden hair and pulled it to his face, inhaled the fragrance of flowers and woman and unfulfilled passion.

She made a small, needy sound and his mouth captured hers again, quickly, absorbing the offended gasp that followed, pressing harder and gentler than anything she had imagined possible. There was no force now, no take. Just an offering too hard to refuse. His mouth was soft and knowing against hers, a sublime mixture of caress and command, sweeping her past fear to a nether world of tantalizing curiosity and exploration. It held her transfixed, a far stronger confinement than his physical strength had been.

It was hardly his first kiss.

It was decidedly hers.

Both found the truth hidden beneath the cloudy layers of resentment and desire. She stood rapt and appalled by the knowledge that he was experienced at this; he found himself intrigued that she was not. Was she so young that she had never dallied, even innocently, behind her parents' watchful gaze?

He pulled back slowly, regretfully, afraid his mother had gone too far and found for him not only a commoner but a child.

Her eyes bore out that fact vividly as his fingers turned her face up to his, but when his hand slid lower, past throat and shoulder and propriety, he found a figure slender and ripe with womanhood.

Her eyes widened instantly in embarrassment, and her hands flew up to protect herself, but he easily deflected them by leaning more deeply into her with a body twice her size, thrice her readiness for battle. His control was slipping; she felt it in the tremble of his fingers, the shiver that ran the entire length of his body. His gaze was hot and intense. It never left hers as his palm boldly caressed her breast, sending fire into her cheeks and ice into her eyes. Her breathing caught, her lips gaped open. The affront was so great there were no words at her command, only strangled sounds of fear and heat and bafflement.

It took more strength than Bryson possessed to pull away. Annalise's face glowed with abashment, so fresh and guileless, too innocent for what he needed at this moment. But he was lost in the heat they created.

He wanted her. Against the wall, upon the floor, any-where a mindless rutting beast would take a maiden. He had never, not in all the time he was caged, allowed himself to be reduced to such base animal instinct. But he was driven by something greater than reflex, stronger than lust. It surrounded him, filled him, choked the life from him, then sent it shooting back like lightening.

He closed his eyes on a deep breath and shoved back, releasing her while he was still able.

Annalise's arms curled up protectively. Her breathing was shallow and uneven, her fury boundless. Still she had no words to berate him, nothing strong enough or vile enough to rail against his trespass. And beneath the feelings of resentment and invasion, her body hummed discordant music, a lute strummed in a pagan rhythm that frightened her even more than his touch.

There was heat inside her, new and terrifying, a shim-mering bright hot ember of mystifying need.

Anger was her only weapon, and she lashed out full of

insult. "How could you?" she condemned. "How do you dare to touch me that way?"

His eyes flashed a warning, but she did not heed it. She had lived a nice protected life, beloved and respected by the villagers. If someone bullied her, she fought back. Nothing in her past had prepared her to know when to retreat.

She hugged her arms tighter to her chest. "You must never touch me like that again! Never." Her cheeks flamed but she persisted. "Do you understand?"

His look changed suddenly. One eyebrow lifted in raw challenge. *Silly girl. She would be his wife soon. He would touch her any way he chose and in many more places than she tried to protect with her piddling efforts at this moment.*

His gaze made a burning sweep over her entire body, leaving no place sacred, no inch untouched. His hand struck out without warning, and he grabbed the fabric between her breasts, twisting until it pulled tight and revealing across her flesh.

Her eyes widened in shock.

Now who understood?

Annalise lunged away from the wall. Free of his hold, she darted past him and raced for her room. Slamming the panel door shut behind her, she leaned back against it, her heart hammering. She must escape now. She couldn't bear to think what would happen if she stayed. She had been kissed and touched by a man, a duke, and not at all in a chaste manner. Her pulse raced still, her swollen lips stung. She felt weak and silly and confused.

Bryson leaned back against the wall. She would go

now, or she would try. He would stop her, of course.
He could do no less, but he almost hoped she succeeded,
hoped one of them won and bested the duchess.

The first hint of daylight touched the horizon, warm
hazy colors more than light. Annalise stole to the hall
door, leaving behind what little she had brought with
her. No one was about so she walked out casually, as if
she only meant to take the dawn air.

Bryson stood at the bedchamber window and
watched Annalise sneak from the castle like a thief with
a pocketful of silver. She had made it past the servants
and his mother, but he doubted she would get much
past the outer gate. Her very stealth shouted guilt, a
beacon for the dawn watchmen patrolling the walls. If
she wasn't making things more difficult for him, he
could almost applaud her effort.

He slipped from the castle, craving the fleet-footed
swiftness of a good stead, but he was not confident of his
seat. Neither was he able to command a mount from the
stablemaster, so he set out to capture Annalise afoot. If
less certain of the land after so many years, he was faster
than she and found the exercise a challenge that almost
invigorated him.

She was only a quarter of the way to the village when
she heard someone approach. She darted for cover in the
woods, far enough back to be concealed, close enough
to see if the noise being made was a farmer, a peddler's
wagon, or a castle guard. Walking parallel with the lane,
she finally caught sight of a lone traveler out for an

early-morning stroll. She took cover behind a fallen tree and waited for him to pass, then followed as quickly as she dared.

Almost a third of the way home and still she had not encountered any of Eleanor's men. She was feeling more confident, almost light-hearted when she reached the bridge over Stony Creek.

Chapter 12

IT HAPPENED SO FAST, ANNALISE DIDN'T HAVE A chance to scream. One moment she was hurrying toward the wooden bridge, the next she was being dragged back into the cover of the forest, a hand slapped over her mouth.

She recognized him at once. His scent, his strength, the sheer magnitude of his presence left no doubt about who had captured her. With her back pinioned to his solid chest, there was no way to free herself, so she relaxed and waited for Bryson to make the next move.

His hand slid cautiously from her mouth and rested at her throat, light but threatening.

She swallowed angrily. "Go on, choke me if you like, then you will have no one to marry you!"

His chest expanded, and his hand slid from her throat to the slender space beneath her breasts. Her rib cage hollowed as her breath caught. He pressed her firmly back against him, his fingers splayed to encompass her whole midriff.

Her knees quivered from the heat of his touch. "I want to go home!"

He heard the tears in her voice and an underlying fear she tried to conceal, but it was impossible to indulge her. She knew him. And though she was afraid, it was his strength, not his weakness, that was daunting to her. He could not let her go.

He dropped his chin to the fragrant crown of her head and wished he had enough chivalry left in him to charm rather than ravish her in the days to come.

But her entrapment would build a wall between them, unbreachable except by force. He only hoped that time would provoke a compromise. His mother's demand of the night before still rang in his ears.

"A civilized union, polite socialites, enough ardor to make begetting children bearable, if not remarkable. It is not a lot to expect when many noble marriages are built on less. At least you are not strangers, and she is not uncomely."

No, Bryson agreed, Annalise was not uncomely.

As nitwitted as it seemed, he felt they were connected, each by his own struggle for freedom and self-possession.

He turned her slowly and cupped her cheeks in his hands, a fierce, almost desperate look in his eyes.

"Oh, please don't," she whispered, undone by the look on his face. "I can't do this; I must go home. I must see my father and aunt . . . I—"

The words were lost in a tangle of emotion as he

lowered his head and brushed her lips lightly, so softly she sensed it was not a real kiss, or not what they had shared the night before. Instead it was an attempt at communion and communication, a petition for understanding. He pressed more firmly, gentle urgency in his touch, a demand she was unwilling to answer. If she weakened toward him, it would be her undoing.

His hand cupped her shoulder, then slid down, a consoling gesture that turned possessive when his fingers curled in to hold her more tightly to him.

She made a sound of protest, but she felt herself slipping into his gentleness, a frayed silken cord untangling thread by shiny thread beneath the subtle power of his caress.

Bryson's lips were soft, his touch tender, yet the subtle strength of him invaded every pore of Annalise's body. She was melting beneath the onslaught of his kiss, sinking faster and faster into that blinding world of white heat and dark longing she had only tasted once. She braced her hands on his chest to push him away, but the sound of his harsh gasp when she touched him unraveled her even more. Her nails dug into the fine fabric of his shirt as her legs went watery beneath her.

His palms caressed her back slowly through the safety of her gown, but his fingertips ached to dip beneath and explore riper treasure. He pulled lightly and brought her against him, feeling her alternately tense and give as her mind warred with her body's natural longing. His arms tightened, reveled in the feel of having her near him, against him.

He understood that he needed to go slowly, to overcome her innocent defenses before he could taste the burgeoning responses buried beneath her inexperience and willfulness. But it would be difficult, perhaps more difficult than he could manage.

Trapped for six years, unwilling to sully himself with those who operated on grotesque reflex alone, his own desires were giving way to the innate beast within. A creature of the asylum, after all, conditioned by the rude containment, cut off from genteel behavior for too many years. He could not tolerate being reduced to the deranged inmates who had pawed at him for half a decade; but he didn't know how to stop it.

In those dark hours of incarceration, he had imagined just this. Perfumed skin, clean and white as snow, hair like silk wrapped around his throat. Warm, fragrant lips beneath his own. He wanted the sensory exploration, the willingness of wholesome flesh, but not now, not here along a village road as if he were naught but a plowboy and she a milkmaid, not where someone might discover them.

Privacy was as necessary to him as air. After six years of extremes—cold and heat, shrill screams and deathly silence, common rooms and solitary confinement—he craved the quiet and noncommitment of his own privacy.

Tonight, perhaps. Tonight in his locked chamber, if she could abide him again like this, he would take full advantange of the feel of her breasts crushed against his chest, the soft and round readiness of her unconscious movements.

But first, he must get her back to the castle. He withdrew slowly, reluctantly, savoring the last touch, last

breath of the kiss. Her unconscious sigh of disappoint-
ment almost pushed him over the edge. She didn't
know how dangerously close she trod to being taken in
the woods. He took her hand and began leading her
toward the road.

Fighting to regain her senses, Annalise dug her heels
in until Bryson stopped. She felt drugged and disoriented by what had just happened, not at all herself. It
was a kiss, nothing more, but her body felt as if a
firestorm had rushed through it, obliterating all that was
rational, reducing everything to a core of burning ash.
But for all that her mind was awash with bright images,
her body with burning sensation, she knew one thing
clearly: She could not go back. She would not put herself at the mercy of Bryson or Lady Eleanor again.

"I must go home," she said. "Please understand, I
cannot be held prisoner. It would destroy me."

He understood only too well, but there was naught
he could do for her when his own existence was at stake.
Though brought up as a lord and now risen to duke, he
was not noble enough to let her go. His sense of self-
preservation was stronger than his guilt, as unyielding as
the original castle stones that formed the foundation of
Marchfield. He prayed as enduring. His hand tightened
on hers.

She felt the immediate ownership in his touch. All
gentleness was gone from his hand, all tenderness from
his eyes. They were cold and fierce and determined.
Fear made her mouth go dry.

"You can drag me back," she whispered, "but you
can't force me to marry you."

He controlled the panic beginning to thud with his heartbeat and turned her face up. He ran his thumb across her lips, the question obvious.

What about this? What about the kiss?

Annalise began to tremble. "I need time to think, to decide for myself—"

His look changed, and she realized suddenly, horribly, that she would not be given time for anything but what he wanted. Like Lady Eleanor, he thought himself entitled to his own wants and desires over others. She was merely a pawn moved at their whimsy.

She took a step, then jerked her hand free and began to run.

The creek lay just ahead. She couldn't waste precious time getting back to the road and would have to brave the water. Footing would be slippery but Bryson would be just as disadvantaged. She dashed down a small embankment and raced into the shallow depths.

Her attempt at escape was useless. He was on her before she had taken three steps, his strong arms capturing and lifting her free. She twisted violently and they both went crashing into the water. She landed on her back, atop a small, sharp rock. Bryson landed on her.

Water poured over them in a gush, filling her mouth and nose, producing a fit of coughing. Cold as ice, it seeped into her gown and hair, stockings and slippers. Rocks bit into her back as Bryson's heavy weight bore her into the boggy bottom.

"Get off!" she demanded.

His face was only inches away, his eyes stormy with anger and impatience. There was no compassion there now, nothing but savage resoluteness. Annalise realized that the scene in the woods had been just that—a ruse, a courtier's seduction to woo her, not true affection or even longing. She felt humiliated by her own naïveté and furious with him for playing her false.

"Let me up, you . . . you deceiver!"

He pressed his body deeper into hers, a warning.

Her nerves twisted at the intensity of his gaze, the unholy purpose beneath his barbarous look. Anger welled up within her, driven higher by fear. "Don't you dare!" she demanded, though she hadn't a clue what he intended. His head lowered, his beautiful face only inches from hers. Her throat tightened and she repeated more frantically, "Please, don't."

She would come undone if he kissed like before, with gentle sadness and compassion for her feelings. But the mouth that met hers was punishing, a kiss full of desire and retribution and possession. Annalise jerked to the side but he only followed, proving his strength and her helplessness. His lips were hard and sterile, they took everything, gave nothing in return. She jerked to the side again and he moved to her throat. His teeth scraped the slender column of her neck, down to the tiny hollow where her pulse beat rapidly. His lips tugged at her pale flesh, and she felt the consumption of it, the sharp small pain, and knew he had marked her.

Bryson drew back and lifted slightly, just enough to stare at her water-soaked gown. It lay plastered to her chest and waist and thighs, the outline of her shape perfectly revealed. Her arms flew up to cover herself, and he grabbed both wrists in one hand and pinned them over her head.

There was no warmth in the gaze that traveled over her, but there was fire. Open and burning, his look seared every inch, leaving her no modesty. And not an ounce of kindness lay in the fingers that dropped to explore her slender, generous curves.

Annalise gasped out a protest and tried to twist away but he lay half on her, pinning her gown to the soggy creek bottom. Water filled her nose and mouth with each twist as she attempted free herself.

He traced her collar bone, over the hill of one breast, then the other. His eyes sought hers, and he watched her face with frigid intensity as his finger drifted down the hollow between. Annalise cried out in outrage and twisted violently but he only continued his indelicate exploration to the underside of her breasts.

His look frightened her, the cold and calculated determination that said he would do as he pleased. The promise of more. The heat in him was tangible through her soaked gown, burning her as his finger dared to glide up to touch the tight bud of her chilled flesh.

She made a terrible sound, fear and fury strangled in her throat. It was unconscionable that he would touch her so, even more unthinkable that the impious gesture would send heat spiraling thought her. She writhed away from him again, but she was completely trapped. "Stop! You mustn't—"

His mouth lowered, stripping the words from her as his hot breath covered her, *there* where her sensitive flesh stood tight against her bodice, where every nerve ending in her body seemed to coalesce. Frustration coiled tight within her, an ache low in her belly, a wash of heat through her bloodstream. Tears of confusion gathered in her eyes, but she blinked them back and tried to jerk away from him.

His mouth followed the movement, a gentle, scorching pressure that seemed to make her blood pool heavy and needy in the nether parts of her body. She made a terrible sound, embarrassment and wanting and confusion. Never had she been so affected or so frightened.

His head lifted slowly. There was nothing in his expression but cold perusal. Though he did not hurt her physically, there was nothing in his touch but the foulest intentions, no love, no adoration, no courtship to salvage her wounded pride. His hand covered her, his palm rotating lightly to bring the bud back to full readiness. Color seared Annalise's cheeks but heat and heaviness were still inside her, a taunting ache that sent a terrible burn to her extremities. His thumb brushed her nipple, then his fingers curled in to stroke and knead, sending fire into the center of her being. Astonishment flared in her eyes as her body arched up against him.

"This is immoral," she cried, "and depraved and . . . and—"

His head lowered again and he nipped the tight nub with his teeth, only the lightest brush, but the shock of it sent a wash of heat the entire length of her body. A grainy cry followed.

His look changed, no longer cold and detached but burning, more dangerous. His own emotions were being overcome by her impassioned innocence, moved along on a tide of needy wanting. His mouth lowered to her other breast and covered her in moist heat, taking the taste of starchy fabric onto his tongue, the taste of new-formed passion. She arched again, into him, panicked and yearning, at the very edge of chaos. She emitted a low cry of wanting, and he began pushing at her wet clothing, shoving it up from her legs and thighs.

Cold air hit her exposed flesh, bringing with it a frigid slap of reality. On a gasp, she rolled suddenly, her knees biting into rocks and mud as she scrambled to her feet.

Bryson lunged after her but caught only the tail of her gown, impeding her flight. Threads ripped until the waist gaped from the bodice. Annalise clutched at the fabric but could not move without losing her skirt.

Panicked and angry, she stared at him, breathing hard, the pale flesh of her midriff exposed. The wet fabric clung to every inch of her frame, outlining the puckered tips of her breasts, her narrow hips, the juncture of her thighs. Her eyes burned with resentment, but her body, defined so perfectly, provided a tempting feast for a famished man.

She was wild and fey with her unbound hair hanging wet and disheveled to her waist, her bodice gaping to reveal the imprint of his lips on her neck, her skirt gripped up tight in her fist, exposing her ankles. A chill wracked her body and she shivered violently. Though the heat in her eyes burned him with accusation, her lips were turning blue from exposure.

Bryson knew he must get her back to Marchfield before she caught her death in the drenched garments.

He twisted her skirt in his fist and rose, pulling her closer until his hand manacled her wrist.

Annalise fought a strange lethargy. The heat of her anger was waning in the frigid air, her strength consumed by shivering. She felt betrayed, attacked, and ravished. She fought against his hold but realized quickly that the struggle was useless. He was stronger and had the advantage in height and weight.

And he had more to lose than she did. No one realized that fact more strongly than he. The future of the dukedom rested on his shoulders. If he could not procure it, he was no use to anyone. The base facts provided a great impetous to continue the fight. Amid a cry of protest, Bryson hoisted Annalise over his shoulder and began the trek back to Marchfield.

She made every step of the way a test of his endurance and patience, but in the end the victory was his. Defeat was bitter, for she feared she would not get another chance at escape.

Eleanor watched Bryson's approach with a mixture of pride and dread. She never expected he would go after the girl himself. It shed new light on the situation and took a tremendous burden from her shoulders. He understood that the girl must be made to marry him at any cost.

Eleanor breathed deeply and turned to Max, her eyes alight with calculated mischief. "By the look of them, there has been a small mishap. Have a hot bath sent up to Annalise's chamber, and a breakfast with a soothing herbal tea."

His pulse quickened.

"Are my instructions not clear?"

"Quite clear, I fear."

"Dear moral Max. What a burden it must be to have your conscience. I only hasten things along." Her gaze slid over him in a way it had not for years. "After you are done, attend me in my chamber."

Black lust flooded him, both stirring and demeaning. He'd never been able to deny her, though she bore him so little affection he was naught but a churl at her service. He could refuse, he'd thought of it time and again, but he wanted what she demanded much more than he cared for preserving his pride. And she needed him even more, whether she knew it or not. She badly needed what little affection they shared in those rare, impassioned moments.

He had grown up resenting his mother's weakness only to find he had inherited it, as well. She had never wed her lover because he was already married. His and Etienne's father had provided well for his boys, but money did not wash away shame. It only softened the indigity and opened doors otherwise closed. He would do Eleanor's bidding and hate himself for it. But he would do it just the same.

Bryson hauled Annalise through the castle door, then set her on her feet. He was past exhaustion, every muscle crying agony.

Rebellion flashed in her tearful eyes as she spun to face him. "I will return home," she warned. "You can bring me back a thousand times and one thousand more will I try to leave. One day I will succeed."

Bryson believed her, and he could not risk having to go after her again. She had nearly made it to the village. Next time she would be more cunning. Had she crossed the bridge today, he would not have had the courage to go after her and chance fighting a crowd. God forbid that he run into someone he had known from before.

He steered Annalise through the entry hall and common room. Although reluctant every step of the way, she did not have to be trussed up and carried. She would save her energy for plotting and planning.

At the head of the stairs, she jerked her arm free. Fuming, she ran into her room and slammed the door, then threw herself onto the chaise near the window. The anger inside her was worse than anything she had felt since her mother's death, almost more than she could tolerate. It pulsed in her temples, filling her so full that she feared she might explode into a million brittle pieces.

Bryson was close behind, shutting her door more gently but loud enough that she understood he was in the room.

"Go away!"

Instead, he silently locked the door and slipped the key into his wet coat pocket.

Annalise glanced up. "Go away!" she repeated. "If you come near me, I'll scream this bloody castle down."

His eyes narrowed in warning but she was past caring. She crossed her arms over her chest in a show of belligerence and turned toward the window to ignore him.

In very little time, she heard the panel open, then close with a distinct *click*.

She had been locked in again. She tried hard not to cry but her fortitude was crumbling and she didn't know how much longer she could hold up. Chilled to the bone in her wet gown and shivering from head to toe, she began to pace in an effort to bring some warmth to her body. The exercise was futile.

The silence grew oppressive, smothering her. She went to his door and began beating on it, hoping it drove him to distraction, hoping he would come and at least fight with her.

Finally, the panel opened. But on the other side stood a maid, a stack of linens in her arms and a food cart beside her. "Miss, your bath is ready."

Annalise peered inside. Two men were pulling a tub closer to the hearth, but Bryson was nowhere in sight. "Where is His Grace?"

The maid look perplexed. "I don't know, miss. Shall I attend you?"

Annalise watched the steam rise from the bath with longing. "May we drag it in here?"

"Certainly, miss, but there's no fire lit. Let's get that done first so you don't get chilled worse than you already are." With the aplomb of an excellent servant, the girl acted as if it were not a bit out of the ordinary for Annalise to be standing around in a water-soaked gown.

Annalise stood by while the fire was stoked and the bath dragged into her chamber. The attention was a luxury she had never experienced, but she was too self-conscious in her drenched attire to enjoy it. When the maid stayed to help her bathe, her modesty would not allow it.

"Thank you," Annalise said, "I will be **fine** on my own."

"As you like," the maid answered. She placed the tray and linens beside the tub. "I'll return when you ring."

After the maid left, Annalise removed her wet garments. She stepped into the bath with an audible sigh of relief. The heat was soothing to her chilled flesh, the scented water a comfort to her frayed nerves. She reached for the tea on the side table and sipped slowly. It had a warm, fruity flavor that was pleasant and unusual. She found the combined effect of the hot bath and tea to be euphoric on her tired body.

Drowsy, she leaned her head back and against the tub and began to plan her next escape. Eleanor had already agreed to let her choose the wedding date. Annalise would bide her time carefully, draw it out as long as possible while everyone around her relaxed their vigil. Her next attempt would not fail.

As bleakly silent as the falling night, Bryson stood in the doorway, shaken by the vision of her nudity, unable to turn away from the sight of her pink flesh bathed in firelight.

He had just been told his presence was requested in her chamber. Had he truly gone mad?

Chapter 13

BRYSON HAD NEVER SEEN ANYTHING AS STIRRING AS the undefiled perfection of Annalise's fair skin. The fire burned low. Shadows leaped like dancers to the silent hum of a primordial song. The early morning's events must have unsettled her, but by the way she lounged in her bath, so relaxed and unguarded, she seemed to have given in to the heat of the bath and the warm room. She looked like she'd lost her desire to fight this battle.

And he suspected his mother knew that.

Everything inside him went cold. Damn Eleanor her machinations. He slipped back into his own chamber and softly closed the door behind him.

Annalise strolled the garden to the gentle warbling of birdsong. She had awoken early, her mind thick and slug-gish. She had thought at first that she was taking ill, but the feeling had passed soon enough. After donning a simple India-gauze gown, she had come here to sort through the confusion in her head and try to make a plan.

Men watched her. She'd given up counting how many. Her first maneuver would be to disarm them, get them to relax their vigil. Once she proved that she was not trying to escape, escape would be that much easier.

She sensed Bryson the moment he entered the garden. It was as if a stillness settled over her, a waiting. The reaction was puzzling, and a memory stirred of her mother coming to her rescue once when she'd gotten herself into a bind while tree climbing. Her mother had known she was in trouble, just known. Not second sight or premonition or fortune telling. Merely a bond that went deeper than intellect. The fact that she and Bryson now seemed connected did nothing to soothe Annalise's worries.

She shook off the odd feeling and turned to him. "Your mother wishes a word with us in the gallery."

An instant of dread crossed his face, and she felt her ire slip a small measure. There would be portraits there, vivid reminders of those loved ones he had lost. She realized that for all her resentment of him and the situation thrust upon her, she did not want him hurt. He had suffered too much the past six years to be bombarded with more now. But she could not protect him, and found it ironic that she should have even the slightest urge to do so given his strength.

"Do you know the way?" she asked.

He nodded and watched her approach. Her gown was simplicity itself and it suited her. Suited him. Sunlight streamed though the gauzy fabric, showing her shape in silhouette. Though velvet and jewels would line her wardrobe when she became a duchess, he preferred her like this, as fresh and unpretentious as a May morning.

He would rather go to the lake, watch sunlight dapple the leaves and shimmer on the water. Watch a village girl hike her skirts to her knees to dance in the shallows.

He turned sharply and led the way to the gallery, where he found his mother standing in front of the portrait of his father. Bryson's hatred of her was palpable, a bitter rancid taste in his mouth, but it shook him to the core to see the look in her eyes, a look he recalled from childhood.

Eleanor glanced over at Annalise and noted nothing out of the ordinary in her countenance. No blushing or horrified guilt from the night past, no uneasy shame. The tea had not done its job, then, or Bryson hadn't. She would use something stronger next time.

She turned her attention back to the portrait. "Do you remember him?"

Bryson stared. The artist had captured the duke perfectly but not the man. There was no humor in the eyes, no enthusiasm in the unsmiling mouth. It was an inflated portrait of a moderate man. He looked at his mother and noted that her hands were trembling.

She turned on him suddenly. "Do you remember any of them?"

Bryson's gaze followed the line of paintings. Some were as familiar as his own face, others completely foreign. He could make no sense of the garbled images that came with certain memories. Like flashes of lightning they came and went, illuminating short segments of time. A horserace, a concert, a ball. He finally gave up the taxing need to try. Later he would sort it out. Later, when his mother was not demanding that he remember with that awful look in her eyes and telling quiver in her hands.

"He had another child," she finally said with bitterness. There was an irrational and underlying tone in her voice that accused Bryson, that said he was somehow to blame for it all coming to this point.

"A bastard child," she added. "I thought it inconsequential, but I have received word that the man is here to pay his respects over Richard's death." She looked at her son, abject fear in her eyes. "He is a barrister, a man of law. Do you understand?" She began to pace, her steps short and agitated. "Elbert left provision for him, though he never legitimized the boy. If he realizes you are incompetent, he may have grounds—"

"He is not incompetent!" Annalise said.

All eyes flashed to her, and her cheeks flushed a dull red. She didn't know why she had defended Bryson, but she would not recall the words.

Eleanor's brows lifted regally. "Can you prove that, my dear?"

Annalise sent Bryson a condemning look. "Not as long as he will not speak."

At that moment, had he been capable of it, had his heart and emotions not been stripped from him long ago in a dark cell, Bryson would have fallen in love with her.

Would have fallen head over heels for this girl who did not pity him, or fear his madness, or excuse away his condition as an illness. Instead, she accused him and condemned him and expected things from him that any normal man could give.

But there was no love in him, no capacity for it. Like a stripped carcass, the elements of life were gone, leaving only dry bone.

"Well, he does not speak," Eleanor said. "And as long as he does not, it will be hard to prove that he is sane. Without an heir, he can be displaced."

Annalise flushed a dull red. "I will not set a wedding date. You promised you would give me time."

"I do not know," Eleanor ground out, "if we can afford the luxury of time."

Lawrence McGovern was a young man, though gray hair streaked his temples, lending him a distinguished look. His manner was polished and straightforward. Annalise noted a striking resemblance between him and the portrait of Stephen she had seen earlier.

Eleanor poured tea but there was no welcome in her eyes. She handed the lawyer a cup, then went straight to the heart. "Are you thinking to claim Elbert's estate now that Richard is gone?"

He flinched. "No, Your Grace. You have another son, or so I have been told, recently returned from a monastery."

"I do. What else have you been told?"

"That he ill, perhaps incapable of serving in the capacity of duke. I came to see for myself."

"He was ill for some time," Eleanor admitted, "but he is recovering nicely now." Her gaze was sharp as she turned to Annalise. "In fact, he is to be married to Miss Weatherly shortly."

Lawrence nodded at Annalise. "My congratulations." He rose from his seat to face the duchess. "I did not come here to cause you embarrassment, Your Grace, and I do not expect to be welcome. You are aware that I have children. Should the way become clear, and only then, will I fight for their right to inherit."

The duchess rose with him. "Is that a threat, sir?"

"Not in the least," he said easily, smugly. "However, I like to keep my affairs in order. I find that loose ends leave untidy messes. I would not want Marchfield to revert back to the Crown, when I have healthy sons whom I believe have a legitimate claim."

"You mean an illegitimate one."

Annalise gasped at the duchess's cruelty.

Mr. McGovern took it with grace, however, and bowed. "I will see myself out. Miss Weatherly."

Annalise tried to smile but Eleanor's cut to the man still stung. "Thank you, Mr. McGovern." As soon as he was gone, she turned to Eleanor. "You are a cruel, unfeeling woman."

Eleanor smiled. "And you, my dear, are naive. He is a vulture, but he will not pick my bones if I can stop it. However, you will have the power to set me aside once you are wed to my son. Think on that when you are trying to escape again."

Annalise turned on her heel and fled the room. She would not spar with Eleanor. It left her too shaken and unsettled. She turned the corner to find Etienne and Mr. McGovern in low-voiced conversation. They looked up when she approached and fell awkwardly silent. The tension was tangible, a suspended moment of strange confidences that thickened the air and made breathing an overloud embarrassment.

Etienne recovered first and smiled, the brilliant smile of a courtier. "Miss Weatherly, a fine morning."

"Mr. de Chastenay," she acknowledged, "Mr. Mc-Govern, I bid you both good day."

She noticed they did not resume talking until she was out of hearing range.

She retired to her chamber and penned an innocuous note to her father. She knew Eleanor would read the letter before allowing it to go out, so she made certain it was a simple, unremarkable message of her visit.

After plying her undeserving father with weak lies, she found herself too restless to sit any longer. She roamed the castle instead and found it a veritable treasure of old architecture and fine craftsmanship. The library held fascinating books, not only old and rare editions, but also the most current issues publishers had to offer. She would like to bring her father here, just to see the vast collection.

No one seemed to require her presence, so she roamed the lower floors. Finally exhausting their inventory, she ventured up to the third. Most of the chambers she peered in were not used, the furniture covered in dustcloths. She recognized Etienne's room by the pair of riding boots sitting in a corner and quickly shut his door.

She opened another and found a nursery. It was a long room, with a table for lessons and an open space for playing. A wooden rocking horse sat next to an empty hearth. A doll house with tiny furniture stood near the window. The beds were small, with a longer one for a nurse. There was no cradle. Annalise wondered if Eleanor had, at one time, been human enough to want her babies close to her.

There should have been laughter and tears coming from the room, arguments and scoldings, sweet whispers and daring secrets. Instead, it was grotesquely silent. A place for ghosts. Annalise knew the loneliness of being an only child. It was obscene that all the Marchfield children were gone, no grandchildren to take their proper place here. Unnatural that Bryson, having had so many siblings, should now have none.

Annalise pulled the door closed with a sadness she had not felt before, a sense of loss not even present at the churchyard. Being an only child had been her fate, but not his. That state had been thrust upon him, cruelly, viciously. A burden no man should have to bear. She walked quietly down the hall and was surprised to hear a sound in the corner room.

She pushed open the door and peered in. Bryson stood near a table, his fingers fisted around a carved chess piece. His clothing was exquisite and fit him to perfection. Buff-colored riding breeches, an unbleached lawn shirt, a darker velvet coat. Of a commanding height, he dominated the room with his presence, yet he seemed lost, as if he didn't know why he was there. Annalise sensed his struggle in the white-knuckled grip of his fingers.

"Was this your room?" she asked.

He looked up suddenly, then away. He had no recollection of this place but had come here by rote, so sure of his steps he'd not faltered once on his journey. He had opened the door expecting something, anything. But the room was as vague as his dreams. A place of nothingness for him—no memory, no understanding, no answers.

He had searched every inch. Naught but the chess board had sent any shock of awareness through him. And now he clung to it, like an idiot, as if some worthless piece of wood would bring his life back to him. In a sudden, hopeless rage, he flung the pawn across the room. It hit the wall and fell to the floor, spinning like a top.

Annalise cringed. The anguish in his eyes was unbearable, the dark vanquished look of a man beset by more armies than he can fight. His jaw clenched and unclenched, like his empty fist. A fight against nothing. At war with God or Satan or self. His arm flew out and swept the rest of the chessmen to the floor. They clacked like spilled stones. When he had nothing else tangible to destroy, he hung his head, exhausted.

When he did nothing more, Annalise walked over, retrieved a pawn, then held it up for his inspection. "Do you play?"

Even for a moment, she wouldn't let him wallow in self-pity. He didn't know whether to laugh or cry or howl. He wanted to kiss her and shake her and pull her into his arms and bury his face in her hair. He remembered it down, reflecting firelight, flowing over the creamy flesh of her throat and breasts. He ran one hand over his face in aggravation and thought her the most beautiful, frustrating woman alive. He pointed to the window, a question in his eyes.

She looked out at the clear day and nodded. "Yes, I would like a walk, if you promise to keep a reasonable pace."

Anger still boiled inside him as they walked from the castle, boiled to the point that, if he were not already mad, the feelings would have made him so. But he found peace in her presence, an odd comforting serenity as they passed through the garden. She talked to the plants and that soothed him, as well, her gentle voice, the nonsense of her words. A restlessness was inside him, but it was of a different sort, lust and longing and masculine awareness. With her, the darker evil stayed back, snarling only on the fringes. Her presence slayed them, the knight-reversed, chasing his dragons to the hinterlands.

Side by side, they left the garden, he willing, she resigned. He offered his hand when they reached a wide puddle near the stableyard. He did not let go even after she jumped clear. She tugged slightly but did not protest too much when he hung on and led her to a place he'd been earlier in the day. One he thought she'd enjoy.

He liked the feel of her skin against his as they crossed the stableyard, the excitement in her step as they entered the barn, the soft dewy look in her eyes when she spotted the new foal.

"Oh!" The word was a puff of wonder, a child's delight at seeing it try to walk on wobbly legs. Without a thought for her gown, she knelt in the scattered hay and put her palm out to feel its velvet nose. The foal butted her hand, then latched onto her finger, seeking nourishment, and Annalise laughed at his frustrated efforts. "Isn't he beautiful?" she whispered.

Yes, beautiful. The foal, as well. Bryson knelt beside her and stroked the baby's coat, but his eyes stayed on Annalise.

"I could see a new one everyday," she said, "and never tire of it, never grow accustomed to the wonder of new birth." She glanced back over her shoulder at him, a wry smile in her eyes. "I visit all the puppies and kittens and piglets born in the village."

He could see her that way, eyes alight, all pink and white innocence. She didn't belong here in this loveless house of black nightmares, with a crazed man and a spiteful duchess. She didn't deserve it.

A horse neighed loudly in the next stable, and Bryson's senses went on alert. He knew the sound, the familiar call. He pulled Annalise to her feet and hurried out of one building into the next. Thomas Grimes was trying to soothe the beast but it kept kicking at the stall door. He looked up when Bryson entered.

"He's wantin' to see you, Your Grace. Been like this since you got back. Picked up yer scent, I imagine."

Bryson walked to the horse and opened the stall door. It was the most handsome creature, tall and well formed, strong but sleek. He held out his hand. The horse tossed his head with a maddened cry and pawed at the dirt, then trotted right over and put his nose in Bryson's palm.

Annalise watched as Bryson laid his forehead against the horse's mane. Her heart melted at the communion. It was what she had seen at the lake, a homecoming, a place where he was not forgotten.

She moved closer to Thomas Grimes. She knew him from the village and his wife, Martha, too, though both lived and worked at the castle. "What's his name?" she asked.

"Balmoral," he answered softly. He motioned Annalise off to the side and spoke quietly. "The beasty was His Grace's favorite. Can't even be rode by no one else. Horse like to went crazy when His Grace took ill. It was Balmoral, if fact, that showed us where he was that day. Came galloping in here like a wild thing. Wouldn't rest until we followed him back to where His Grace lay unconscious in the woods behind the buttery."

Grimes shook his head. "It were a sad day, that. Something seemed to snap in the duchess. She ain't been the same since, nothing round here has." He tilted his head toward Bryson. "I know he ain't right"—he tapped his noggin—"up here, I mean, but I'm glad he's back."

Annalise sent him a stern glare. "There is nothing wrong with His Grace 'up here,' " she mimicked. "He's been ill, true, but he is recovering now. You and the others would do well to remember it."

Grimes nodded but looked unconvinced. "Some say he can't even speak."

"He *won't* speak," she corrected. "At least to them he won't. That is not the same as not speaking at all."

His eyes narrowed, half playful, half suspicious. "He speaks to you?"

She thought of the tales that would spread to the village, of the look on Eleanor's face when Mr. McGovern arrived. She lifted her chin at a lofty angle. "I would hardly have agreed to marry him otherwise, now would I?"

"Guess not," Grimes answered. "Don't know why he'd converse with an uppity chemist's daughter over his own loyal staff, though."

Annalise's mouth pursed in a pout. "Is that what you think I am, Thomas Grimes?"

He smiled. "You'll be my duchess soon. I'd best be keeping my opinions to myself."

"And the others, too," she pleaded. "Don't let them think ill of him, Thomas. He's not mad, just a bit confused right now. He was gone so long, you see, and . . ." She had no more words to defend him, no reason to believe them herself. She swung toward Bryson. "Are you ready to resume our walk, Your Grace?"

Bryson left Balmoral in a calmer state than he'd found the horse, but an unresolved guilt rested heavy inside him. The horse needed a good long run, but he could not manage it yet. He eyed Annalise curiously as they climbed the hill beyond the pasture.

She had refused to look at him since leaving the stables. He continued to stare until she was forced to acknowledge him.

"I can't believe I lied for you!" she said finally, and with such disgust he wondered why she had done it. "I

just can't let them all think you really are a madman."
Her chin lifted. "Though you certainly test my sanity."

He wished she could convince him of his sanity as
rigorously as she tried to convince herself. He put a hand
on her shoulder to stop her progress, then sat in the grass
atop the hill. The world fanned out below them, neatly
plowed fields, thick forests, and untidy marshes. The
grass was sweet and cool, the sun warm.

In a gesture of unabashed youth, Annalise lay back
and watched the clouds drift, making lazy patterns in the
sky. "A ship," she exclaimed. "Do you see it, riding the
high seas?"

Bryson saw clouds floating overhead.

"There." She pointed, making him look. "See the tall
mast, the billowing sails?"

He saw sunlight on golden hair, the fresh beauty of
unpowdered skin, a sprinkle of freckles across an impudent nose.

"Did you travel?" she asked. "Before the illness?"

He could not remember. There were things he knew,
but he could not say whether he had seen them with his
own eyes or learned them in a history lesson.

She rolled her face toward him. "Did you?"

He shrugged, and looked away from the innocent
intensity of her blue gaze.

"I always wanted to travel," she continued. "To Rome,
to Greece, to Paris. I've never even been to London."

London he remembered. The theater, the opera, the
gardens. He reached over and plucked a long-stemmed
wildflower, then rose to one elbow. He leaned over

Annalise and shredded it above her, watching the petals fall upon her bodice.

She glanced down to see what he was doing and blushed. She rolled quickly to her belly. "You are an evil man and I will not defend your sanity again!"

He took the denuded bud and stroked her ear, then the side of her cheek. She rolled back suddenly and grabbed his hand in both of hers. "Please let me return home," she pleaded. "Please, help me escape."

His lids dropped, shielding his eyes. His head lowered and his lips lightly touched hers, but there was no threat in the kiss. Only a terrible regret.

She reached up and cupped his face as fiercely as she had his hands. "Please! You don't love me; I don't think you bear me much affection at all. The duchess will find you another girl, a more willing one. What difference if you let me go?"

He needed her, her lack of fear, her defense of him, her strength. Her certainty that he was not mad even as she felt free and unafraid to call him insane when angry. He would never let her go. He would love her as a husband did a wife, if not with his emotions then with his body. And he would provide for her with things of monetary worth that she would never have with a village boy.

He closed his eyes to block out her desperate face and pressed his lips to hers to stop her pleading.

Her courage had failed her on the hill. When Bryson's lips had touched hers, all thoughts of escape had fled. It was not only unconventional for them to be alone, she found, it was dangerous. There must be an evil wanton inside her, because she could have lain on that hill for hours and let him kiss her in that soft way, and caress her face and tease her with the flower stem. He'd done nothing more untoward, and her defenses and anger had crumbled into nothing, to be swept away on the wind.

It seemed a dream now that she was back in the castle, an odd misty fantasy she had conjured in her mind. Bryson had been as cold and remote as ever during dinner, sparking her fear once again with the chilly intensity of his gaze, the sober severity of his unsmiling face. He was so removed in that state, so unreachable. She could not see him, feel him, understand him. He made her afraid.

She excused herself as soon as the meal was over and fetched the chess pieces. She brought them to the drawing room and placed them on a small table. She had decided that if she befriended Bryson, he might be more receptive to helping her. At the very least, it might ease some of the dark violence in his eyes.

Etienne stood warming himself by the fire. He'd been out the entire day and still wore his riding clothes. "I saw you cousin today," he said.

Annalise paused. "Mary Greer?"

"She is well. I stopped by the bakery to see how she fares."

Annalise longed for the same freedom; it must have shone in her eyes.

"I promised her I would return tomorrow, if you care to accompany me."

Eleanor swept into the room. "The dressmaker comes tomorrow," she interrupted. "Your fittings begin at ten."

Annalise knew the duchess had been eavesdropping and was relieved she had not tried to solicit Etienne's help. "Have you seen His Grace?" she asked.

"He's in the library. Max has gone to see if he cares to join us."

"I would rather join him there," Annalise replied. She rose, taking the chess set with her. When she found Bryson, he was poring over a rare volume on herbs and their uses. "My father would be in awe," she said. "He has coveted that text since he first saw it years ago."

Bryson closed it slowly. He had found little to address his symptoms.

Annalise placed the chess board before him and lined up the men. "Would you like to see if you can play?"

Of course he could play. He made the first move, quickly, angrily.

Annalise regarded him dryly. "I didn't mean to insult you."

He relaxed then and allowed that she had not. It was his own sense of inadequacy that spurred him, his own fear of failure. And the unnerving sensation that his life was spinning faster than he could catch up. For too long he had been on a stagnant course with no future, just the hellish present. It was difficult now to acclimate himself to the idea of possibility and promise.

"I am not very good," Annalise admitted with a sly twinkle, "but I should at least be able to beat a lunatic."

He captured her queen in four moves.

She received a summons at breakfast. It was from her father and demanded that she return home immediately, adding he never intended her to stay without Mary Greer. She showed the note to the duchess.

"How do you propose I answer him? Dear Papa, I am being held prisoner and cannot come home just now."

Eleanor's eyes flared. "Impudent girl! Go, then. Ruin him. No one will stop you."

Her appetite fled. She placed her fork down and rose. "I will tell him the dressmaker comes this morning."

She penned a reply that sounded trivial and just a bit spoiled, and was undeserving of her father and his love. If tears would have helped, she would have wept a bucket full, but she was dry-eyed with the half-truths, embittered with her betrayal, even as she did it to protect him.

Bryson watched her struggle with the letter, then left the room. He sought her out moments later, the rare book of herbs in his hands. He offered it to her with a nod at the note to her father still gripped in her hands. She looked as him, perplexed when he pressed her to take it.

"For me?"

He shook his head and tapped the note again. Her eyes widened.

"For my father?"

He nodded, then turned on his heel and departed, leaving her standing alone and awash with warm, uncertain feelings over his generosity. It wasn't just the book, he could afford a hundred. It was the fact that he had taken her comment about its importance to her father to heart. She pressed the volume to her bodice and stared off into the empty space left by his departure.

By the time she had spent two hours being poked and prodded and pinned, she never wanted to see another dressmaker. Ah, but the fabrics were fabulous! Muslins and lawns, velvets and satins. An endless array of patterns and gewgaws to complement each.

She was stiff from standing still on a stool so long and hurried for the outdoors as soon as the dressmaker left. She headed straight for the stables and the new foal.

She found Bryson in a pen, leading Balmoral around on a rope. The sounds emitted from his throat were soothing sounds, hums of patience and reward for achievement. The stableboys watched him with awe. No one could get near the stallion without taking his life in his hands. And the horse had suffered for it over the past six years. He was fed a healthy diet but lacked the rigorous exercise to which he'd been accustomed.

His superb condition had atrophied some, and Bryson was determined to bring Balmoral back to peak strength and performance. He'd raced him once at the Oaks; he remembered it clearly, or the idea of it. He could not remember who was there, who rode, or who won. He worked Balmoral around the pen. The memory filled him, the noise and excitement, the colorful tents and cheering viewers, the foam-flecked racers pushing toward the finish.

He felt alive with the recollection, excitement pulsing in his veins. The thrill of it, accompanied by the quickening of desire, flashed in his eyes when he turned to find Annalise watching him.

She approached him, his enthusiasm contagious. She could see that he'd experienced something, felt something strong and vital to him. She held a note in her hand and a dreamy look in her eyes. "My father thanks you—effusively!" She looked down, shy suddenly with the newer, more tender emotions. "I thank you, as well. It made him so happy. He forgot all about summoning me home—" She stopped suddenly, the thought just entering her mind, the hideous possibility of so profound a betrayal. She looked up, her eyes hot and glassy. "You didn't—"

He shook his head, slashed his hand through the air, an adamant refusal of her accusation, though in truth he would have done it to exact such a response from her had he known it would work.

Relief poured through her, heightening the color of her cheeks, the clarity of her eyes. "Oh, I'm so glad." She touched his sleeve. "So very glad."

Pink and white innocence. The book was nothing to him, less than nothing. He'd done it to win her favor and soothe her feelings, a gesture just as manipulative as the other. So, why did he feel guilty for accomplishing what he set out to do?

He handed the reins over to Grimes, then took Annalise's hand and led her away from the stables.

They were going to the lake, she knew. It was the look on his face, the longing. She felt an answering compulsion and went willingly, yearning for the crystal glimmer of water and its peace in the midst of such underlying turbulence.

Eleanor paced the solar. "We circumvented her father today but it won't last long. He'll summon her again, or he'll come here himself to fetch her."

Max couldn't read her mind but he saw it churning and knew it would not bode well for Annalise.

"We must move faster, do something now, tonight." Her lashes lowered and she tilted her head to the side with relish. "You know, Max. You know what you must do."

Annalise stretched languidly in her bath, a dreamy smile on her face. It had been waiting for her when she returned from her walk. Outside, twilight faded to dark, a gentle settling. Inside, candles had been lit, offering a warm golden glow. She relaxed back, resting her head on the padding, and let her hair fall to the rose-patterned carpet beneath the tub. Her wineglass was empty and she wished she had another to ease the oddly bitter taste in her mouth.

She wallowed in euphoria, a sublime floating she had never before experienced. She was light as air, buoyant as a cloud. She drifted in luxury, pampered and enriched and stirred by the warm caress of scented water over her naked flesh.

Bryson stood in shadow. The firelight did not reach the corner and he watched her from the darkness, his pulse running fast and thick. Like the week earlier, he had been told his presence was requested in her chamber. In his own bath when the message reached him, he'd climbed out and donned a velvet robe, had come at once.

He stole closer to the tub, ignoring traces of guilt. She had not sent for him; the servant was mistaken. He should leave, but lust was a more powerful advocate, and he had plenty to override the remorse flaying him for watching her like a voyeur. Too soon it would change, her placid manner would shift. Appalled in her sweet innocence, she would rail at him to leave.

And he would go, because he could not abide the unrest. His nerves were already strung too taut, his senses bombarded by the fragrance drifting up from the heated water, the glimmer of firelight on her exposed flesh.

Until the moment she sent him away, he would enjoy the rare beauty of her perfumed skin, her docile disposition in repose. Drawing closer, he watched the water lap against her collarbone. Small drops clung, pearlescent in the firelight, then trickled back into the pool.

He watched for an eternity, it seemed, his muscles tensing, his blood heating. A log collapsed, exploding in a burst of shimmering ash. He flinched at the sudden, stark illumination, yet she did not, just lolled her head back upon the headrest and yawned. Suspicious, he reached out and touched Annalise's hair.

She didn't jerk or cower. Instead, she murmured and rolled her face to the side, exposing her pale throat to his view. His heart began to hammer darkly in warning. He touched her again, more strongly, but she only smiled, a soft bemused look on her face.

"Bryson?" she whispered.

The use of his name should have warned him. He swallowed hard, ran the back of his knuckles down her cheek and neck, caught the faintly floral scent rising from the steam. He inhaled deeply.

She tilted her chin up to regard him with an abstracted look. "Your Grace," she chided gently, "you may not share my fire while I am in such dishabille."

He was uncertain what was happening but incapable of pulling away. He was caught in her trap, the net tightening. His hand drifted down, a test, over the pale pink flesh of her throat. She murmured contentment, shocking him, and he dared to go lower over the hill of her breast. Her flesh was slick and hot from the water, the sensitive peaks hidden just beneath the surface. His palm brushed her, only the lightest ripple of water and man.

Her breath caught. She moaned deeply and arched into him, a cat stretching to be petted. Water rushed over her as she rose, unveiling her fair beauty and the ripe dark tips of her breasts. Bryson's pulse quickened. He steeled a response and continued stroking her lightly, drowning in the slick feel of her warm skin beneath his callused fingers.

She curled away for a lazy moment, then made a distressed sound and twisted her body back against his hand.

Going down to one knee behind her, he buried his face in her hair, wondering how long she would allow the sensuous exploration, knowing even as he did it she must be plotting some scheme against him. He went willingly into the possibility. His arms surrounded her and he cupped handfuls of bathwater and dribbled them over her neck and chest, watching the drops fall in sparkling crystals to her flesh. The fire hissed as another log fell, and a flare of heat and light moved over them in radiant illumination, then sighed back to a shadowy glow.

His fingertips dipped beneath the surface of the water and touched her, wringing a hot confused sound from her throat—sigh, moan, mew—indistinguishable but stirring. His hands trembled with the urge to grasp her harder, enfold her completely.

He moved to a better position, his face alongside hers, his mouth at the tender hollow of her shoulder. He reached around and cupped her breasts in both hands. She made another sound of contentment and desire, rising into him, arching her head back for his lips. His mouth took hers and she gave in return, a demanding hungry exchange, a ravenous dueling of tongues and groans and desire.

He was lost, then, awash in heat and greed and her. He moved to take more of what she offered, and his knee hit the discarded wineglass.

It rolled, shooting prisms of light. A faint residue lined the empty sides.

A rush of cold flooded him. He closed his eyes briefly

against the treachery and his hands went still. Her skin glistened in the firelight, pink and gold, sweet naïveté, completely oblivious to the trap that had been laid for her.

He could not be a part of this, would not fall prey to his mother's diabolical machinations. But his hands were full of her, overflowing with the bounty of her beauty, her mouth seeking his even now. She twisted toward him, and his lips met her demand and his fingers traced up, then back down, over the shimmering rivulets trickling down her chest. He wanted one more touch, needed just one more breath of her willingness.

She smiled then, a whimsical, drug-induced euphoria. "Naughty, you mustn't share my bath, either."

He closed his eyes, his body tightening, aching like torture. His hands dipped beneath the surface of the water again to find her slick breasts, while his lips met the tender underside of her ear. Just one last touch, one kiss while she drifted in dreamy acceptance.

But she rose into him, uttering a soft, sultry sound of contentment. Then rose again with a breathless demand.

His hands slicked over her, breasts and rib cage and abdomen, testing to see if she would shy away, but she only undulated with the movement of the water, a graceful dancer whose music was the rhythm of her own inner longing. Rise and fall and rise again, she arched delicately into his palms, unconsciously reaching for his touch when he lightened it, sighing in deep-throated contentment when the pressure grew heavier. Water glistened on his forearms, burnished gold in the firelight.

Questing, his palms filled themselves with her fullness,

then his fingers stretched over her narrow waist, absorbing the pale luxury of her wet skin. Her arms lifted, offering him even greater access, and his hands went back to her breasts. Lightly he cupped her buoyant flesh, then gave her the edge of his callused thumbs.

Her movements changed.

Her back bowed, stretching high and exacting into his hands. His thumbs stroked her again, bringing her nipples to hard, aching peaks. Small sounds of passion thrummed in her throat, a tight accompaniment to the rapid cadence of her breathing. He was sent hurdling past rational thought then, past conscience. Moving on desire alone, he slid one hand lower, drifting over her flat belly to the nest of golden curls at her thighs.

Sweat beaded his brow as he dared what he had only imagined since first seeing her. He threaded his fingers through her, cupping and pressing her wet flesh.

On a distressed sound, she shied away, but he followed, pressing lightly, swirling water about her until she calmed and began to accept him again. He let the weight of his hand drop, pressing her more firmly, and she rose into him on a grainy cry, then again and again, agitated now, unconsciously offering what he realized he would take soon. He could not retreat. He was not strong enough to resist the very thing his life demanded of him.

He must have an heir.

The excuse was lame and fell away almost before it formed. Had she been barren, he could not have turned away from her now.

He continued to tease and torment her flesh, bringing

the cadence of her breathing to a shattering pitch. Her movements became anxious and grasping as she strove into him, searching, searching, finding naught but a coarse clamor inside her that begged release.

He rubbed his cheek against her neck and she turned into him, finding his mouth, ravenous in her desire. He touched her where he wanted, how he wanted, and she began to twist and turn as if she would get away. But never did she stray far from his questing fingers. On a moan that reeked of desperation, she arched high, exposing most of her to his hungry gaze.

Slick and flushed, her skin shone iridescent in the firelight, like the precious underbelly of a shell. In one quick movement, Bryson slid his arms beneath her neck and knees and brought her from the water, then carried her through the connecting door to his own chamber. To his bed.

The cold air hit Annalise like a betrayal. Dazed, she cried out and curled inward, but Bryson soothed her with gentle strokes and murmured sounds of comfort. He lay her down in a cascade of unbound hair, sunshine spilling over his coverlet. Her flesh puckered from the chilled air and he covered her with himself, sharing his warmth, the heat of his raw passion.

Confused, she stirred at his weight, but he captured her mouth quickly, urgently, chasing her protests back into euphoric insensibility. He wore only the velvet robe, tied at the waist with corded silk. The fabric caressed her, a luxurious lover, and she stroked it with long sweeping movements, dissolving in the exquisite feel of it against her bare flesh.

Bryson closed his eyes and breathed deeply as she touched him, inhaling the scent of her into his body. Her own stroking drove him past patience, and his hands ran over her silken flesh with loosely held discipline, restraining the tormented urges as long as he could bear it. He moved with her, imitating the ebb and swell of the mating dance, finding his own urgency dangerous to control. He tugged at the silk sash. The robe fell open, and they became a tangle of velvet and flesh, warm wet passion and dry raw desire.

She began to utter small disturbed sounds, gasping impatience, and he felt an answering hunger inside him. Too raw for delicacy, too far gone to care, he pressed his face into her breasts and breathed in her essence, luxuriated in the silk of her skin. She writhed beneath him and his lips captured one ripe breast, then suckled as if famished.

She drew a sharp, keening breath and lifted into him, imperious now in her demands. Her look changed from opulent sensuality to greedy craving. Her arms reached for him, grasping, her nails biting into his shoulders.

On a growl, he pressed her thighs apart, then moved between them, lost to her neediness, to his own. He found her slick and ready, and positioned himself to enter.

The breaching was difficult.

He cursed violently, silently. There would be no gentle taking to salve an unprincipled conscience. And it was too late to consider anything but having her. His mouth lowered and he captured one nipple and drew deep, igniting a fire to burn hotter than her discomfort.

He rocked into her, testing, his way barred by the tight restriction of her innocence.

She made an impatient sound and twisted, then grew confused by the sudden, heavy burn. She pulled away and he followed, a blunt pressure she could not avoid. He slid his hand between them and stroked her as he had in the bath, stroked until her cries started low, then grew high and stretched, a distressed need for completion that brought her hips lifting into him, against him. On a deep-throated groan, he thrust hard, forcing her open, savaging her like a beast.

Annalise's eyes flared suddenly. Heat exploded inside her, then vanished. Like a drench of icy rain, her blood chilled and her body contracted as if to protect itself. A rending pain replaced passion and she made a sound of wounded confusion, then began pulling away, twisting her lower torso until Bryson almost lost purchase. He grabbed her buttocks to still her evasion, but she turned fitfully to avoid him, increasing the friction, impaling him in her further. On a growl, he pulled her to him, closed his eyes, and plunged again, ripping away the last vestiges of trust and innocence with the brutal thrust.

She cried out, her sharp nails digging into his shoulders, her body shrinking away. He held her tight, forcing her to accept him, thrusting again and again as his climax overruled any sort of control and hurled him over the jagged border into oblivion.

He returned to her slowly, his face buried in her neck as his body throbbed out the last tremors of completion. The maddening drum of his heartbeat faded, his breathing calmed. Had he been a poet, he would have proclaimed he'd waited a lifetime for that moment, but **he** was only a man, an impaired one at that, pulsing with raw-edged completion.

When he had breath and feeble sanity again, he lifted and found Annalise staring off into nothingness. A vague stare of confusion. She pushed against his shoulders and chest. When she could not budge him, she covered her face with her slender forearms as if she must hide.

Bryson flinched, then dropped his head back into the hollow of her neck. He knew she would struggle and curse him when she came to her senses. He also feared she would be even more determined to leave.

Annalise fretted until she dozed, exhausted from struggling with him and trying to understand what was happening. Not a word had he spoken, but sounds of passion had echoed from his throat during the worst of it, as betraying to her as his force. She knew he could speak, if he chose, and hated him for making sounds in the throes of dark passion that he would not offer her in the light of day.

When she awoke an hour later, her head was throbbing, her mouth thick as lint. Though her mind felt cloudy, her situation was all too clear.

Trembling, she stared at Bryson's sleeping form, then slipped from the bed and returned to the cold bath. Stepping in, she recoiled from the impact but lowered herself and began bathing vigorously, as if she could wash away the shame of what they had done as easily as she did the evidence. But no amount of cleansing could repair the damage.

She had been despoiled. He had made certain that more than just her reputation had been shattered. And somehow, for some horrifying reason, she had helped him. She remembered the clamor inside her, the unconscionable way she had reached for him, urged him until the last when the pain began. How she could have been so brazen was beyond her comprehension.

She could never go to another man now. If she did not marry Bryson, she would never have a husband and children.

Dry sobs erupted suddenly and racked her body, but she refused to give into them or the melancholy smothering her. She covered her mouth with her palm, as if she could stop the storm, but it swelled within her until she was choking against her own hand from the outpouring.

Finally, she stumbled from the bath, dried off, then donned a simple linen gown. Her fingers trembled when she tied the laces but it could not be helped. She turned to find her slippers and her foot hit something cold. She bent to find her empty wineglass on the floor. A powdery substance clung to its side. Her father was a chemist; she'd seen similar substances a hundred times.

The realization hit her. She closed her eyes briefly but did not cling to the treason. She wanted nothing to sap her strength. There would be time later for the resentment and hatred rampaging her.

Night was thick, the moon a pale orb shadowed in heavy clouds. Not a star shone. It was as if the Heavens knew of her disgrace and would not offer a light to guide her steps home. Annalise finally found the road, staying to the dust and cobbles by feel. Every step brought a twinge of pain, a harsh reminder, and rooted bitterness even deeper into her heart.

She could not fathom how she had escaped the guards, but she did not slow down to contemplate it. She walked faster, her body aching. She might be ruined for another man, but she would not marry Bryson, either. He thought to force her hand by forcing her body, but she would never have him now. Never.

She slid into the bushes as soon as she heard the cart. A lantern swayed, casting eerie, inconsistent light along the bumpy roadway. Only when the wagon was upon her did she recognize the horse and driver.

"Papa," she whispered, scrambling from the shrubs like a flushed quail. "Papa, wait!"

"Whoa!" he called, sawing on the reins with the sudden strength of two men. "Annalise, God in Heaven! What are you doing out here?"

She climbed aboard and flung herself against him, her arms stealing around his waist, her face burrowing into his chest. She had aged a decade over the past few weeks, but she desperately needed to be his child again, the girl whose entire world he could soothe and repair with hugs and gentle words.

"I am sneaking home," she murmured into his vest. "You were right, I never should have gone to the castle. Take me home, Papa."

He stroked her hair, a terrible suspicion washing over him. "Did someone hurt you, child?"

"No, Papa," she lied. "What are you doing here?"

"I had an elixir to deliver. Annalise, what . . . ?"

"Just take me home, Papa."

Bryson stood upon the parapet and surveyed his holdings. Sunrise teased the horizon, a golden promise spreading over the hills. He had slept through the entire night, the first dreamless slumber he'd had in six years. Annalise was gone when he awoke.

He was foolish to have believed that she would stay after such ignoble violence. She was made of sterner stuff than that.

Eleanor strolled to his side, as regal as the dawn in an apricot velvet dressing gown. "Where is the village girl?"

He ignored her. He had come up here to be alone, to sort through the man he had become and reckon whether any part of himself could be salvaged.

"She has flown," Eleanor accused. "We cannot find her anywhere. How could you let her leave?"

Bryson closed his eyes and tried to dissolve into the rising sun, to be lifted to a place higher and warmer than the cold stone parapet and his sins.

"There is blood on your sheets," Eleanor said with

relish. "Did you bed her? Have you secured the dukedom?"

Bryson glanced over his shoulder and gave her a look that would shatter stone.

Eleanor paused only a moment, then slashed her hand through the air in disgust. "I will send someone to fetch her back. I only pray she has not spread too much poison through the village."

He spun suddenly, his hand lashing out to catch her at the throat and pin her to the wall.

Eleanor was staggered by his strength and vehemence. His eyes blazed into hers, an obvious warning. Though not easily intimidated, she knew the value of waiting out the seizure with intelligence rather than rash compulsion. She could not be certain at this point just how stable he was or how equipped to maintain his balance. But she knew without reservation that she never should have sent him away to France all those years ago.

"I have wronged you," she said coldly, "leaving you at the priory. Why was I not informed of your progress?"

He glanced over his shoulder at the long distance between the parapet and ground, his eyes dark as death itself. The implication was all too easily understood.

Chilled by the viciousness in his gaze, she responded in kind. "Do what you want with the girl then, but remember Marchfield is not secure without an heir."

He eased his hand from her throat, but the murderous promise remained in his eyes. She had nearly destroyed him, then brought him back at her convenience. It would take no effort at all to snap her neck or hurl her over the stone edge.

Eleanor regarded him with haughty disdain. "You will do your duty to this family, then you may proceed however you like. If you do not, you are of no use to me. I will have you returned to St. Bertram's without a moment's pause." She strolled to the very edge of the parapet and glanced over, as if daring him to follow through. "My lawyers have their orders," she said in arrogance. "If anything happens to me, they are to proceed immediately at having you declared mentally inconstant."

Bryson bowed to her brilliant foresight. Nothing provided more inspiration for him than the thought of returning to the priory. He would never chance it and they both knew it.

Eleanor pulled a shawl more tightly about her shoulders and looked toward the village. "Ungrateful baggage. Why did she leave? She had everything here."

Annalise had been brought to Marchfield under false pretenses, held prisoner once she arrived, then compromised by force.

And Eleanor thought *him* demented?

✦
Chapter 14

EVEREST WATCHED ANNALISE CONSTANTLY.

She knew it and tried to make each moment excruciatingly normal, approach every chore as if it were the same mundane experience she had left behind. But she was changed. She no longer trusted easily. She cried in a blink. Small tasks became gargantuan undertakings, yet huge endeavors were the simplest things imaginable to accomplish.

She had been home no more than a month but it seemed an eternity. Each day dragged out in suspended agony, as if precariously balanced on a needle point, about to topple either way. Other than a visit by the duchess, which had left her father pale and grim-lipped, Annalise had heard nothing from the castle or its inhabitants. Neither had her father told her what the dowager had spoken to him about, and she did not press.

Bryson did not come.

The small, dull ache in her heart became a constant agony. She wanted him to show up at her door, plead forgiveness, promise her anything if only she would return. She pictured a thousand times slamming the door in his face or giving him a sound verbal thrashing or ignoring him completely. She wanted to wound him as he had her, to shame and humiliate him, to betray him.

But he did not come.

Against her will, she worried about him. Though she tried most heartily to convince herself that she did not care if he fell into a bog and never resurfaced, it was a lie. She did care, which was why his betrayal hurt so badly. She worried that Eleanor was not being fair with him, that the servants did not understand what he needed. She worried that he was not working with Balmoral or climbing the hillside. That he was locked in his silence and withering away unnoticed.

She wanted revenge and retribution, but only from herself. For some reason more insane than he was, she wanted the rest of the world to leave him be. She resented him and missed him, hated him and longed for him. She wanted to curse him as badly as she wanted to make him smile.

She'd never seen him smile.

Strain kept her nerves edgy and raw. She rarely strayed far from the cottage. She couldn't bare to run into the townsfolk and have to pass an amiable quarter hour trying to explain why she had not been about this past month. She no longer had patience for the Widow Rukin or even her own friends. She couldn't look Mary Greer in the eye, afraid her cousin would see her dark secret.

Only with Silva was she comfortable. She spent hours at the pasture, stroking his velvet nose and talking to him of things she dared not admit to others.

It was Aunt Mellie who finally broke the silence—dear, intuitive Mellie whom Annalise had written off as too old and senile to pay much notice.

"What happened to you up at the castle?" she asked one evening at dinner.

Annalise's silverware clattered to the tabletop. For over a month she had been braced for the questions from her father. When none had come, she had relaxed her vigil. Aunt Mellie caught her unprepared. She trembled at the reminder and did not attempt to retrieve her fork for fear they would see her fingers shake.

She folded her hands in her lap, clutching tightly beneath the linen tablecloth. "My visit was unbelievable," she said calmly. "The castle is grand, the food superb. There are more servants than I can count."

"Yet you returned," Mellie intoned, "in the dark of night with the look of death about you."

Annalise's stomach churned. She feared in another breath she would be ill. Her hands grew clammy and she wiped them on her skirts, stalling for time, praying for answers that would not come.

"Things were not as she expected," Everest interjected calmly.

"You may cover for her," Mellie said sternly. "It is a father's duty and you have ever been the most excellent father, Everest. I am proud of the way you took the raising of your daughter upon yourself when your dear

Olivia died. So many others would have sent their only girl child off to a female relative to raise."

Mellie paused to regard Everest, her toothless mouth pinched to a fine, fragile line. "I am not a dithering old fool, merely old. Something has happened to our Annalise, and I can no longer ignore it."

Everest placed his fork carefully beside his plate. "It has been my wish to give her time." He looked over at Annalise. "You understand that the situation has not been resolved or swept under the carpet. I merely thought to give you time."

Indeed, she had hoped for just that. That the situation would be forgotten for all time and she would not have to give an accounting of her disastrous fall from grace. Tears welled in her eyes. She knew in another moment she wouldn't be able to control them.

She swallowed hard on the excuse. "The Duke of Marchfield was not at all as Maximilien de Chastenay represented him. He had been in a monastery, aye, but he had been there due to an illness, not because he was committed to the Lord." She rose from her seat. "I could not stay under false pretenses."

When Annalise rushed from the room, Mellie tinkered with her fork a moment, then turned her wise old gaze on Everest. "Is she with child?"

He sighed, the weight of the universe sitting squarely on his heart. "It is too soon to tell."

"And if she is? What will you do?"

He smiled ruefully, though he wanted badly to weep. "Call the Duke of Marchfield out upon the dueling field and demand restitution?"

Mellie chuckled dryly. "Olivia would have loved such valor."

"She would have abhorred it!" he returned.

"As your wife, yes, but not deep down in the woman's heart of her. She would have found you most gallant, as she always did."

His expression dimmed. "I have failed her, Mellie, and my daughter, as well."

"Bother!" With age came a certain acceptance of some things, a better tolerance for others. Impending death had a way of changing how one viewed life. "Think on the reality, Everest. Annalise would not be the first maid to find herself compromised before vows were spoken. Nor would she be the last."

"It grieves me to think I may have made her vulnerable to such depravity. She left here with high hopes and her head full of lofty dreams, determined to become the Duchess of Marchfield. She returned looking sickly pale and vowing she will never marry."

"Ah, but she will," Mellie said with the utmost and undeniable authority that came with respected age. "You have always given the child her head, and I have been grateful to see it in a time where a man's word is law. But if she is compromised, Everest, she will marry. There must be no discussion to the contrary. For her sake and the child's."

Annalise ran until her breath rasped in her throat, until her trembling knees gave way beneath her. The green behind her cottage belonged to the town, and she had grown up playing for endless hours along the sloping meadow. Panting, she knelt beside a well and drew the bucket. She dipped a cupful and drank but her stomach churned after only two swallows and she used the rest to bathe her face and neck.

She had not been well since her return. Memories plagued her. Bryson's haunted past, her feverish reaction to his seduction, the shame of her defilement. And with them the churning in her stomach.

Her mind swirled constantly with images of him as he had looked that first day when he arrived, shackled, betrayed, hurting. At the cemetery when he had seen the velvet-draped vaults. At the pond when he first tasted freedom.

And later, much later, how he had looked when he took her. There had been pain on his face but not regret, nothing to stop him from doing the unthinkable. She knew that a powder had been put in her wine. There was no other explanation for her reaction to his touch, no reason for the way her body burned and craved. No excuse for why she had not fought harder.

Her stomach pitched and she groaned. What was her excuse now? There were nights she lay awake on her bed, a maelstrom of feelings running through her. Heat and longing, shame and despair. He had betrayed her and she wanted him. What manner of woman was she to hate him and yearn for him in the same breath?

She dropped her face into her hands. If she could not get herself to rights again, she didn't know how she would go on. She felt listless and melancholy, always on the verge of weeping. She was losing weight.

But much worse, she was afraid she was losing herself.

She left the well and went to the pasture. Leaning against the fence post, she watched Silva canter around the field. She gave a low whistle and saw his ears perk. He ignored her as she knew he would, an untamable beast too long abused by his previous master. He would never be broken for a man's pleasure, but that did not make him useless. He would make a fine stud for generations to come.

Heat suffused her cheeks. It was an ugly parallel but she could not mistake it. Eleanor had taken Bryson from the priory, an abused, untamable beast, and would use him for stud service. Annalise propped her arms on the fence rail and lay her head down. He was being used like a dumb animal to propagate heirs for Marchfield.

But Bryson was not dumb. He was a highly intelligent man with an impaired mind. A whole man, like any one of the village men she knew, who had been injured. His injury was not visible like a game leg or crooked back, but he was not a lesser person for it.

Her anger resurfaced and she seethed. He was smart enough and manipulative enough to put something in her wine. And he had been whole enough to follow through with his evil intentions.

Although her anger was useless, it helped suppress the hurting parts of her, made the pain more bearable. She held out her hand for Silva, then waited patiently for his rebellion to settle. He finally trotted over and let her stroke him, as if gifting her with his presence.

"Oh, Silva," she whispered, her stomach churning. "What am I to do?"

❦

Annalise never expected to see the Duke of Marchfield ride through the middle of Marchfield Glen as if it were a common occurrence. She was astonished and dismayed and wholly frightened. She recognized the magnificent horse from his stables first, then realized it was Bryson who rode him. She scrambled back into the shop from which she had emerged, her pulse racing with a horrible anticipation and dread.

"Did you forget something?" Mary Greer asked, then stopped at the grand sight in the street. The villagers were gathering in wide-eyed awe around a prancing steed. The Duke of Marchfield sat with suitable ease, dressed out in full regalia. He nodded coolly at the villagers, his attention distant and reserved—a look that kept them perfectly in their place and loathe to ask questions. The squire came forward, his chest puffed out importantly.

"Your Grace! We heard rumors that you had returned. May I be the first to welcome you home!"

Bryson nodded regally.

"If I may be of assistance," the squire continued, "you have only to ask. The entire village is at your disposal, of course. Seeing as how you have been away for so long, would you like a tour?"

Annalise quivered at the words. Of course Bryson would not answer. Her heart squeezed for him and his predicament. She wanted to rush out and tell everyone to give him room, to make no demands on him, to require no answers. Instead she hung back, cowering behind the bakery curtains like a child caught in mischief. She would not risk seeing him face to face. She feared retribution for leaving the castle, but mostly she feared being overcome by the frightening, tumultuous feelings he evoked in her.

She turned to Mary Greer. "I will go out the back. Thank your mother for bread. Aunt Mellie will be delighted."

Mary Greer nodded, grieved in her heart. She didn't know Annalise anymore, and she longed to have the companionship back that she had thought unshakable. Etienne came to visit almost daily, with one excuse after another for baked goods. His presence soothed the hurt inside Mary Greer inflicted by Annalise's absence. She knew a delight she had never experienced before and she longed to share it with her friend, to whisper the secrets of her heart.

Mary Greer now felt for a man what Annalise had wanted to feel for Bryson the day they had traveled to the castle. It was awesome and inspiring and wondrous. And she despaired that things had gone awry for her cousin.

"Has His Grace come for you?" she asked.

Annalise shivered visibly. "No. Surely not after this much time has passed." It had been nearly two months, two long agonizing months fraught with uncertainty and guilt. She had expected such conduct of Eleanor but never Bryson, and certainly not now. Annalise was sure after the first few weeks had passed that she had been forgotten as easily as a pair of ill-fitting shoes.

She left through the rear door and rushed home along the back alley where cats mewed for scraps and dogs

tried to pull damp wash from the lines of the shop-
keepers who lived where they worked. She reached her
own cottage and slipped through the back door, panting
from exertion. Her father was waiting for her.

"Has he come for you?"

She jumped and threw her hand to her breast to still
her racing heart. "Surely not."

He did not look directly at her, but there was in his
voice a hint of dogged determination to which she was
unaccustomed. "I think that he has. I . . . am certain that
he has."

The color drained from Annalise's face. "Why would
you think such?" When he did not answer immediately,
tears filled her eyes. "Papa! Why do you think such?"

He looked up at her, his own eyes filled with sorrow.
"I sent for him."

Shocked, she could only stare at him, feeling stunned
and betrayed. "Why?"

"Are you with child, Annalise?"

Her chin dropped, color rushed to her face. "No!
Papa, how could you think it?"

"How could I not? You rush home in the dead of
night, stricken and silent. You act as if nothing has happened yet you won't discuss it. For more than a month
you have moped around like you are ill, you barely
touch your food and are sluggish and preoccupied.
There has been no laundry to suggest . . . you have not
bled." He took her face in his hands so she could not
turn away. "Can you tell me that you are not?"

Her shame was unbearable before this man she loved
and respected more than any other person in the world.

She bit the inside of her lip to keep it from trembling. "I can't be," she whispered.

"Can't be?" he asked just as quietly. "Or mustn't be?"

She looked away, devastated, every secret fear she'd held for weeks crashing open for him to see.

She hadn't let herself think of it, not once. To be with child would be the greatest joy of her life. But not now, not in this dishonorable way. Now it would be the greatest tragedy. She gathered courage where none existed and looked her father straight in the eye.

"I *will not* be."

"Annalise." He shook his head in regret. "You cannot wish such a thing done or not. I have sorely neglected your education if you think that." He touched her face, his eyes a reflection of pain. "I love you, child, no matter what. And I will not let the rake go unscathed, if what I suspect is true. Nor will I allow him to abandon you and the child to disgrace."

Annalise flinched and looked at the floor. It was not Bryson who had abandoned her but the reverse.

Chapter 15

COMMOTION FILLED THE DUSTY ROAD LEADING through Marchfield Glen. Mongrel dogs yapped like bloodhounds spotting a fox, and children squealed as if Saint Nick himself had come. Both ran alongside the elaborate carriage, baying and shrieking, until it stopped in front of the village apothecary shop.

Annalise cringed and turned to her father. The accompanying vehicle following behind the Duke of Marchfield could only mean one thing. "I will not go back with him. He cannot make me."

Everest's brows rose. "Perhaps he has only come for a visit."

Annalise blushed and fumbled with her apron string. "I will not grant him that, either."

"I think you should," Everest suggested quietly. He was completely lost along this avenue of parenting. He had failed at keeping her safe. Now he must try to correct and salvage what remained. "Walk out with him, Annalise; allow him a moment of your time."

She regarded her father flatly. "He does not talk."

"Does not talk? You mean he is a quiet man?"

"No, I mean he is mute."

"Mute?" He was startled but it explained many things. "Is it because of an infirmity or an affliction?"

"It is because he is mad, a lunatic . . . a *cad*—" She stopped before she revealed too much. Bryson was no more crazed than she, though he was definitely tilted in strange ways. Of a certain, he was a rogue, and a scoundrel, and a despoiler of women.

Everest eyed his daughter curiously. "You have never been one to prejudice yourself against those less fortunate."

"He is the duke, Papa. He could be deaf and blind and peg-legged and not be less fortunate than most."

His curiosity quickened. "I am shocked, Annalise. This talk is not like you at all. Have you no sympathy whatsoever for his plight?"

She was getting herself all tangled up in resentment and forgetting to whom she spoke. Her father had always striven to serve the needy and afflicted in whatever small way he could. "He is mute," she said, "but not much impaired by it." She turned to face her father fully, a distressed plea in her voice. "I cannot walk out with him. He will not say a single word, but he will look at me as if he knows every secret I have ever possessed. He will walk, I will do all the talking, then he will have his way—" She stumbled over the words, blushing furiously. "—I mean, he will force me back to

Marchfield Castle, and I will be held there until I consent to marry him."

Everest took her hand. "But, Annalise, you went there to marry him."

"I know but . . . I didn't know he was coming from an asylum, I didn't know he was mute, I . . ." She hadn't known that fantasy dreams were not reality, that she would be so scared of him one moment and so affected by him the next. "He is not a pious man, Papa!"

"I know," he said softly. He squeezed her fingers in compassion. "So few are these days. We are flooded with despots. King George has urged virtue and piety, but men and customs do not change with a king's wishes, at least not quickly. That is why I didn't want you to go, Annalise. Remember?"

"I'm sorry, Papa, truly I am."

" 'Tis too late now for sorry. Now is the time for doing."

She swallowed hard on a terrible feeling of foreboding. "Doing what?"

Everest shrugged. "Whatever is necessary." He slipped an arm through hers and urged her toward the door. "He is here. I think you must talk to him."

Indeed Bryson had arrived, in all the pomp and power of his office. His horse pranced with restless energy as the carriage pulled up behind it. Marchfield's head coachman stood, his rank displayed by the six capes of his greatcoat and the curled whip in his gloved right hand. His voice rang like thunder.

"His Grace, the Duke of Marchfield. Viscount Ridgestone, Earl of Shelfolk, Lord Anglin."

Bryson le Fort dismounted from his impressive steed onto the cobbles and dust of a common street and nearly stole Annalise's breath. He looked like a prince in his coat of sapphire velvet over an ivory brocade waistcoat and matching satin breeches. The banner of his office fell across his chest in military fashion, beautifully done but intimidating. His long hair was pulled back and tied with a sapphire ribbon, rugged and masculine-looking without the fashionable *toupets* at the sides.

Although sedately bound, Annalise remembered it another way. Vividly, destroyingly, she remembered his hair wild and unbound, flowing over her naked breasts like heavy silken threads. And his hands upon her—sleek as satin, strong as steel—bearing her down into comfort of a lush feather mattress. She grew flushed and tore her eyes away, afraid her father would see the terrible confusion Bryson's presence wrought in her.

Yet it was not Everest but Bryson himself who caught the telltale blush in her cheeks and the sultry embarrassment in her eyes.

Through the open window, their gazes met and clashed. Heat trickled through him, slow as hot honey, a lingering burn much worse than the fiery rush of simple lust. This was desire inside him, deep and hollow and achey. It was tangled and complex; it was as simple as nature. One inept coupling with her was not enough. Would never be enough. He had taken her innocence; she had taken his soul.

No matter how contemptible she would find the sentiment, he wanted to own her, to possess her like a rare *objêt d'art*. He wanted back the part of himself that she had stolen, and he wanted her with it. It was as base as that. He had no poetic thoughts or courtly musings at all, only an animal drive to lay siege to her small cottage and take her away like a conquering medieval knight.

She must have seen it in his eyes, for her own flared briefly with awareness and fear, before lacy curtains billowed out in the breeze and hid her from sight. When the drapes settled back, she was gone.

Everest opened the door, struggling not to hate the duke outside with every ounce of a father's protective instincts. But as he watched the young man step forward, his healer's heart secretly twinged. Bryson le Fort was handsome for a knave, so much more presentable than Everest had anticipated, not dissipated or overfed like so many of that ilk. But there was more than noble looks to his bearing, something harsh yet compelling beneath the aristocratic bone structure.

He had come in full power, omniscient and intimidating, but there lurked within him a hint of disquietude and overwhelmed chaos. Darkness and destruction lay beneath his gaze, a black place unattended and lurking. It was worse than madness.

It was mistrust.

Suspicion, misgiving, wariness—all shone from his haunted eyes. This man had purchased every particle of courage inside himself to come here this day, and the cost was high. His face was pale beneath his laconic pride, his hand clenching and unclenching at his side. On the exterior he was a beautiful, feral lion among lambs, but deep inside he was himself the slaughtered prey.

Even for a man of medicine, what Everest saw in

Bryson's eyes was almost indescribable. Instead of calling him out, he had the incomprehensible urge to rescue him. If he had instilled in his daughter an inkling of compassion, she would at least be solicitous of this man.

But Annalise had moved away from the window. Her face bore a stony cast, and her mouth was set in a firm line. She had folded her arms over her middle, a protective brace, he suspected, against whatever ill or embarrassment she imagined was about to befall her.

The duke reached the stoop.

Annalise ran for another room.

Everest sighed. "Your Grace."

Bryson acknowledged the greeting with a nod. The crowd was growing thicker, a cloying press that made his palms break out in a cold sweat. He gave the older man a narrowed look, hoping he would step aside.

Everest returned the stare. Instincts warred for dominance in his heart—resentment, fear, pity, curiosity. In the end, he put all personal assessment aside and merely stated the obvious. "Analise is here, but she has no desire to see you."

Bryson stood his ground, his fist clenching and unclenching at his side. Several in the crowd called his title, throwing out welcomes, asking inane questions. He finally gave the older man a desperate look and made as if to proceed into the cottage uninvited.

Everest stepped aside. "No need for a show of brutishness. It means nothing here."

The coachman stepped forward. "Now see here. You can't talk to yer betters—"

"Betters?" Everest said quietly. "God created each of

us, flesh and blood alike. His Grace just happened to be born on a different piece of property."

Bryson paused. Similar words filled his mind, words spoken long ago in a strong, masculine voice.

It ain't the blood what makes you better, my boy. Your name and coffer may count with men but not with the Almighty.

They were his father's words, spoken to Stephen one day in the garden. He remembered the smile on his father's face, his brother's perplexity.

God don't look at your birthplace, my boy, He knows where you came from. But what you do with the wealth and talent He gives you . . . ah, now there's the rub. You'll be accountable to that, mark my words.

Bryson looked at Everest Weatherly. He could see where Annalise got her sharp tongue, but the older man's was tempered with a quieter nature and hard-won wisdom.

Everest motioned for Bryson to enter the cottage, then calmly shut out the gawking village. "My daughter can be difficult," he said. "I hope you are made of sterner stuff than the local blokes, who dash out like whipped pups with their tail tucked betwixt their legs."

Slowly the stiffness in Bryson's shoulders dissolved. He offered the older man a noncommittal nod.

"Come then, I'll lead you to her."

Annalise stood by the window in a gown of simple muslin, a warm contrast to finery she had worn to the castle. Her hair was swept up into loose curls, bright as morning in the halo of golden sunlight. She looked angelic and innocent from a distance.

But her expression was that of a shrew.

Her lips were pursed, her expression stalwart. No doubt, she wanted to trounce him to a bloody pulp. He, on the other hand, wanted to throw himself at her feet and beg her forgiveness until he erased the contempt on her face, until she opened herself to him and he could bury himself in her heat, until he forgot everything, until the hot pulse of blood in his veins vanquished the chilling nightmares.

He stepped forward and offered her a small gift wrapped in silver-threaded tissue and tied with a velvet bow.

She glanced at it, startled, then shook her head. "I cannot accept it."

He took her hand and pressed the gift into her palm. She was forced to hold it or let it fall to the floor. With her father looking on, she closed her fingers over the pretty package, then placed it on a side table.

Bryson looked healthier than when she had last seen him. There was more color in his skin and the sharper edges of his face had filled out. He was handsome in his formal clothing, dynamic and powerful-looking. But strength was something he had never lacked. She remembered too well the force of his arms around her, pinning her, the heavy weight of his man's body pressing her into the soft luxury of his bed. A *frisson* of fear trickled through her, made worse by the underlying desire.

He was worse than a rogue. He was a charlatan, a conniving trickster and seducer of women. He had turned something sacred into something contaminated.

"You drugged me!" she accused.

Everest gasped, and Annalise spun toward him, her

eyes wide. She hadn't meant to say the words aloud. They had just risen up inside her, then spewed forth in anger and censure. Her hand flew to her mouth but the words could not be recalled.

Everest turned to Bryson, both condemnation and confusion in his gaze. "Is this true, Your Grace?"

Who had actually done the deed was unimportant when Bryson had taken full advantage of the results. He nodded once.

"For . . ." Everest could hardly say the words, they were so painful to admit aloud. "For impious purpose?"

Bryson nodded again.

"No!" Annalise cried, but she had trapped herself with her own words, and she could see her father knew the truth no matter what she might deny. "Father, no! Don't listen to him."

Everest's eyes were sad. "He hasn't said a word, Annalise. You give yourself away." He looked at the duke, and for the first time in her life, Annalise saw a formidable man rather than a gentle father. "Do you intend to do right by her?" Everest asked. "Will you sanctify this wrong with vows?"

Bryson nodded again.

Annalise grabbed her father's sleeve. "I will not marry him!"

He turned to her, a father's love and pain in his eyes. "You must," he said simply.

"No!" She glanced at Bryson, then back at her father, torn. She could not explain why. It was not a thing she could put into words, more a feeling that she must not be manipulated, that if she allowed others to tyrannize and coerce her, she would lose something of herself.

Her father's voice was stern, almost accusing. "Why, Annalise? You were determined to go to the castle for that very reason."

"I know but . . . he does not love me."

"You knew that when you left here against my wishes."

"Yes, but I thought love might grow, I thought . . . I had imagined . . ."

The truth was that she had not thought at all beyond the childish fantasy of an imaginary prince rather than the reality of a flesh-and-blood duke. She recognized the feebleness of her words and began to back away.

"I cannot marry him," she said. "I won't live like lesser chattel, always under his rule or the dowager's. I won't be confined like an animal!" she finished, and fled the room.

Bryson made to go after her, but Everest grabbed his sleeve. "Stay." The older man sighed and motioned the younger to sit. "She is a good and dutiful daughter, no matter how it looks at this moment."

A small, very cryptic look entered the Duke of Marchfield's eyes.

Everest saw it and wondered if Bryson le Fort, in spite of his great rank and physical limitations, would do for his sweet, strong-willed daughter. He looked down at his hands, struggling to get past the uncomfortable subject he must approach. "She may not go willingly to the altar." He looked up then, his expression severe. "Nonetheless, she must. You have done this wrong and I will see it made right. Do you understand?"

Bryson eyed him narrowly.

Everest's voice lowered; the wind seemed to have left his sails. "I believe, Your Grace, that Annalise is with child."

Bryson closed his eyes briefly and exhaled. Though he was truly insane to think God had taken his reprehensible act and turned it to his favor, it felt that way at this moment. As if he had been gifted with the very thing he needed most.

He stood, nodded to Everest, and went in search of Annalise.

He found her out behind the cottage in the midst of a pitifully sad garden. She sat on her heels, plucking weeds as if her life depended on it. He bent to one knee beside her.

"Go away." She went about her task with more enthusiasm but soon there were no weeds left. She rose to her feet, crossed the lane behind her cottage, and went to the neighbor's fence to watch the horses graze. Silva threw up its head and sniffed the wind, then kicked his heels to show off and dashed around the pasture.

The field was newly plowed and wet from the previous night's rain. Mud flew in clumps behind the horse's hooves, stirring up the strong scents of earth, manure, and trampled grass. Annalise leaned against the wooden rail and picked at the bark as obsessively as she had the weeds.

Bryson followed only to be ignored until he took her hand to still her nervous action. She tugged to get it back but he held firm.

She turned and sent him a searing look, her eyes glistening suspiciously. "I won't marry you. You nor my father can make me."

He expression darkened and he looked down at the slender lines of her simple gown. A muscle in his jaw twitched as he reached out and pressed his palm to her abdomen. She gasped, paralyzed by his audacity. His eyes were dark and fierce, a burning torch in a black cavern. With a twist, she tried to shift away. She knew she must leave, must get as far from him as possible, but when she tried to escape, he grabbed her skirt, holding fast. His eyes grew more intense as he bunched the fabric in his fist, drawing her closer until she was only inches away. His hand went back to her stomach.

She blushed hotly and turned her face aside. His touch burned. His intensity made her head reel. She tried not to consider her father's suspicion at all, as if thinking about a child might make it real.

It seemed all too real now. Her belly churned beneath his touch, her entire body felt edgy and oversensitive. She blinked back tears of fear and anger to face him fully.

"You can take me back to Marchfield by force. You can lock me up for eternity. You can drug me until I am senseless. But you can *never* make me marry you! I'll bear a babe in shame before I'll submit to you again!"

He pulled her even closer and pressed her against him, into him, as if he would force her to reason the same way he had forced her innocence. He ran the back of his hand down her cheek, so softly it felt like a caress, but his eyes were cold and unforgiving. His fingers splayed wide, possessively, over her belly.

"*My child,*" he said dangerously.

Annalise stood transfixed by the fierceness in his eyes,

the dark timbre of his voice. The words had rolled easily from his tongue, not halting or scrambled or even strained.

"Deceiver!" she rasped. She tried to speak further, but her own ability had evaporated. Her knees trembled so badly, she could barely stand. He had spoken finally, clear and unbroken speech, a few polished words that held the most dire threat. When she managed to find her own voice, her words were vapor thin. "My child! You do not own me."

"Then you do not deny it." He caught her hair at the nape and pulled her forward. Brutally, softly, his mouth lowered to hers and lingered there, a moist controlling touch.

She gasped in outrage, but his lips were gentle, a gifted promise that moved over her with unmerciful certainty. Their mingled breaths frosted the air and he tasted of coming winter, crisp and spicy against her cold lips. The heat of him penetrated cloak and gown to burn her.

Annalise was left with no doubt that if she weakened, she would be a prisoner beneath his hands. He surrounded her, overwhelmed her. His scent, his touch, the very essence of his existence filled her with an unsettling domination. She jerked to break free of the power of his presence, but there was no way to overcome his superior strength.

His tongue touched her bottom lip, a shocking wet warmth that made her gasp. He took greater liberty then, touching her deeper, his tongue a sweet saber dueling with hers. His hand slid from her stomach to her lower back, and he pulled her into him. From breast to thigh, he merged them, heat against resistance, a friction that promised to burn out of control.

"Oh, please . . ." she begged, but her words were lost beneath the pressure of his lips, the onslaught of another disarming caress.

Then, without warning, he released her.

Annalise stumbled back into the fence and pressed her palms tightly against the rough bark for support. Her breathing was shallow and fast, her mind churning as badly as her stomach. Her body felt abandoned as he stepped away. Cold seeped into each pore, chilling her until she trembled. "Go," she demanded.

He reached into his coat and pulled out an engraved invitation stamped with the Marchfield seal. With one last burning look, he pressed it into her palm, then turned on his heel and left.

She watched him cross the lane and garden with quick, confident strides, the movements of a man who knew his worth and power. On the exterior, he no longer looked ravaged by the years spent incarcerated, but his eyes still held that hellish vacancy. When he disappeared into the cottage, she pressed a trembling hand to her mouth.

Long moments passed. She could not move, she could hardly think. *My child. My child. My child.* How she had longed for him to speak, to prove what she had suspected all along. Now he had done so and the words rolled in her mind, the reality in her belly. Her goose was well and truly cooked. Fingers trembling, she finally opened the note in her hand. Gold-embossed and of finest linen, it was an invitation to the Marchfield Winter Ball.

❧

From cottage to shop, Marchfield Glen was abuzz with the news. There had not been a winter ball since the old duke's death. Most of the younger adults couldn't even remember the days when Marchfield Castle hosted the grand affair. Rumors had it that the castle staff was already drawing straws to see who had to work and who got to play.

Annalise slipped under the wooden fence and whistled softly to Silvaticus. His nostrils flared and he took off at a dead run. She waited while he pranced and strutted and tried to intimidate her with his pompous display, then she held out her palm. He loped over and paused out of reach, eyeing the hardened clump of sugar.

"You must take it from my hand," she said. "Or I will keep it."

He shook his mane, then made a dash across the pasture. She smiled at his rebellion, understanding too well that he wanted the treat but would not be mastered. Giving in, she tossed the lump a few yards ahead of her. He approached immediately and snagged it from the ground.

Within seconds, he walked up and nuzzled her hand. He had done it only once before, and then only for a few seconds. She stroked him gently, wishing she had another treat to make him stay. "That's all I could pilfer today," she said. "Aunt Constance needs every pinch for her contribution of pastries to the festivities."

She ran her hand over his neck, admiring the sleek, shiny coat, loving the ripple of muscle beneath. "You are so beautiful," she whispered. She laid her head against his neck and inhaled the scent of horse and wind and the morning's run. "Do you think," she added, "that you could take me far away? To another kingdom where my fantasies stay in my dreams and don't come true?"

Mary Greer stood in the distance, watching Annalise converse with an animal as she never conversed with her anymore. Her heart hurt for her friend and for the relationship that had somehow grown cloudy over the past months. She didn't think her news at this moment would bridge the widening gap, but she didn't want Annalise to find out from someone else.

She crossed the lane and called out.

Annalise turned, surprised to see Mary Greer picking her way through the mud. She gave the horse a final pat, then met her friend halfway. Things had changed between them. She knew it was her own fault but could not seem to find the energy to repair what should never have gone wrong in the first place. She found a smile she did not feel and felt her heart twist when Mary Greer did not return it.

"Something is amiss," she stated. Fear began to pound with her heartbeat. "Father . . . Aunt Mellie—"

"No! They are well. I didn't mean to frighten you. I've just come from the church," Mary Greer said softly. "I thought you should know that banns have been posted."

Annalise smiled wryly, relief uppermost in her mind. "For whom?"

"For you."

Annalise's face lost all color. "Come," she urged, and took her cousin by the hand.

They raced the back way through the village and were winded by the time they crossed the boggy field beside the church. Mud caked the bottom of their shoes and spattered their gowns and aprons almost to the waist. Like urchins, they were ragged and dirty by the time they reached the entrance.

Tacked to the wooden frame of the small church was an announcement of Annalise's forthcoming marriage to the Duke of Marchfield. Mary Greer stood by her side, a stiff comrade in outrage at the audacity of such being done without her friend's prior knowledge.

A crowd was gathering, closing in around both girls. From dearest friend to mildest acquaintance, the con-gratulations and wellwishes began. Faces beamed, eyes grew misty. Even the most querulous knew better than to ruin the moment for the rest of the village.

Annalise saw the truth in their eyes. She had given them hope, a future for their own secret fantasies. She had not the heart or energy to dash their enthusiasm.

Her hand slid down absently over her thickening waist. She had finally come to admit the truth when her second monthly cycle had passed without any sign of her flow. For all her bold words to Bryson, she was not brave enough or foolish enough to doom her child by bringing him into the world alone.

Love was lost to her. No man would want a woman and her bastard child. In truth, the banns were a relief. She would not have to go to him, her hat in her hands, begging forgiveness for her rash statement to save the future of her child.

Shouts had started behind her, both jovial disbelief and heartfelt compliments. Composing herself, she put on a brilliant smile and turned to face them.

"Is it true?" Sam Blacksmith called. "Is my Willie going to have to find himself another?"

"It's true," Annalise called back. "But tell Willie he can still come courting at my door anytime he likes."

Laughter erupted in the crowd. Willie, being just turned two years old, waved his arms wildly with the rest of the group. More questions were thrown out, the obvious and the badly veiled alike. Annalise answered them as best she was able, then retreated behind a secret smile. "I've plans to make," she finished. "Would you have me stand here idle all day?"

"But three weeks!" The butcher chimed in with a hint of dismay. "How will you will prepare so fast? That's the same day as the ball."

Annalise whipped back around to stare at the date. She had been so preoccupied with the announcement, she hadn't even noticed when the wedding was to take place or where. Three weeks it was. The churning in her belly reminded her that she could not stretch it out much longer with any hope of dignity.

When she turned back, her face shone. "The winter ball is the wedding celebration. The service itself shall be a small private affair in the Marchfield chapel. But I so wanted my nearest and dearest friends to share in my happiness after the vows are spoken."

Chapter 16

Etienne de Chastenay strolled to the entrance of Rosalie's Alehouse. He'd had no choice but to come to London after what he had discovered in the gallery. With the Marchfield ancestors staring down at him, timeless and superior in their posterity, he'd overheard the news that Bryson was to be married posthaste. Socially speaking, the marriage of a duke was tantamount to the coronation of a king. The fact that the vows were to be private and without fanfare spoke loudly of a rushed affair, possibly an enciente bride. He cursed vilely beneath his breath.

The night was cold and damp, a miserable English night thick with fog and secrets. His greatcoat held out the wind but not the chill, and he stamped his feet in the frost-coated rubbish of the street to keep them from going numb.

He reached the stoop only to find his admittance

barred. With excruciating politeness, a doorman the size of an enormous tree trunk asked for his credentials.

Etienne merely smiled and pulled a small thin cigar from his coat. "Have you a light, *m'sieu?*"

"Of course, sir." The guard produced one immediately but stayed squarely in front of the door.

Etienne inhaled the Spanish tobacco deeply, then lifted his eyes to the night sky. Stars glittered overhead, diamond bright in clear black. "Ah"—he sighed—"it will be a good day tomorrow. A perfect day for freedom. To see the sun rather than the inside of a French prison . . . well, you can imagine my gratitude."

The doorman nodded. "Quite right. If you are ready, sir?"

The great wooden doors were opened then, and Etienne moved through with the unhurried stride of a man who could have stayed outside all night in conversation and star-gazing. He found a clean, well-turned-out establishment done in the atmosphere of a posh gentleman's club. He realized soon enough that Rosalie offered much more than good English ale to her moneyed patrons.

The tables were linen-draped, the silver polished to a high gloss. Scented candles burned discreetly, giving light but not exposure. The fare was succulent, the servants whisper-quiet as they brought platters to each occupied table. Etienne was adequately if soberly dressed in his ordinary clothes, but he was waited upon with as much generosity and aplomb as the powdered and bewigged noblemen conversing over cigars and port.

A few played chess, others cards. Still others rose from

their seats and exited through an obscure door that, due to its placement in the room, lead neither to the front street nor the back alley.

Etienne ordered food and waited to be approached. He had been given no instructions, save to come here if he had pertinent information, and was loath to announce his presence too soon. He was operating blind and knew the men in power relished the unnerving cat-and-mouse game they played to establish authority over anyone with whom they had dealings. He hid a cynical smile. Let them enjoy. He needed neither power nor great prestige, just the chance to live a life of intellectual elegance again. He sipped an excellent Burgundy and savored its rich flavor. He had all night to enjoy the luxury of Rosalie's.

When the last course was removed, a woman approached him. She was dressed in a respectful, genteel fashion, her hair expertly coiffed, her smile demure, but there was that quality about her eyes that hinted she was no innocent.

"*M'sieu* de Chastaney?" she asked politely but did not wait for an answer. "Come with me please."

She led him through the mysterious interior door, down a short hallway and up a set of narrow, carpeted stairs. The sway of her hips was subtle but seductive, her perfume a mystical floral scent that teased him as he followed. Her dark hair was swept up and over to one side, exposing the fair skin of her neck.

Etienne made no comment, asked no questions, but his pulse began to hammer as the silence drew out. He suspected the many rooms they passed were occupied by gentlemen and their demiladies, but not a peep was heard from behind the closed doors. Even his own boots made no sound on the thickly padded stairway.

Finally, the woman paused and took a ring of keys from a hidden pocket in her skirt. She unlocked the door and opened it, then gestured for Etienne to precede her into the room.

The chamber was larger than he had expected and richly furnished. It was a gentleman's quarters with masculine colors and accoutrements. A fireplace burned off the damp English air and offered subtle light. To one side sat a gaming table with room for four and a side table with several choices of spirits. Dominating one wall was a large bedstead, draped with gold-tasseled, green velvet bed hangings. They were pulled back to reveal a seductively plush silk-covered mattress. Beside the bed, on a dark mahogany side table, lay a copy of *Histoire de dom B*, a collector's piece of illustrated French pornography.

Etienne felt a spark of lust at the rich accommodations and the woman handing him a snifter of smuggled French brandy. She smiled, such a knowing smile, and his pulse leaped.

"Come, *mon ami*," she said softly. "You must be tired from your travels. Her accent was softly French, utterly polished, and not at all perfected. It reminded him of the beautiful, peaceful days before the carnage, when the streets ran with the fever of bold ideas rather than blood. When a straw luncheon hamper in the mountains took precedence over a woven basket of aristo heads. This woman had come from that time, a noble daughter or wife, sold now into slavery to preserve her pale white neck.

She led him to the bed and began to unbutton his coat. After pushing it from his shoulders, she worked at his shirt. She had him remove his own boots and stockings, then she helped with his trousers. Her hands lingered, a lazy stroking that said she had endless hours to pleasure him.

Before he lost all rational thought, he grabbed her wrists and brought the back of her hands to his mouth. "Why are you doing this?"

She looked up in polite inquiry. "Do you wish me to stop?"

He smiled. "Hardly. Who is paying you?"

She smiled delicately and returned her dexterous fingers to the business at hand. "You are."

He inhaled sharply as she cupped him. "Perhaps not."

She only laughed and continued.

His hands rose and shaped her breasts, lifting and molding them to his satisfaction beneath her muslin gown. She cooed encouragement and contentment, which he recognized as practiced, and it became a game to him suddenly, a challenge to see if he could truly make her respond and want him as he did her.

He slipped her laces free, as casual as she, and delighted in her beauty without the hastening rush of raw desire. He slid her gown to her waist, then did the same with the delicate lawn chemise. Her skin was pale and sleek, a noblewoman's pampered flesh. She was Juliana, but older and more experienced, willing to pay for escaping the French guillotine with the high price of servitude on English shores. Etienne was curious to know just which leader had enough money and power to smuggle her out and set her up in such an obviously profitable venture.

The woman's eyes narrowed briefly when she realized the sexual control had turned. She was used to men who allowed themselves to be pleasured at whatever pace she set, men who rarely needed more than her false passion in return.

Etienne saw her flicker of irritation. He wanted to lose himself in the throes of ecstasy as badly as she wanted him to be done, but he needed answers first. He cupped her naked breasts and spoke to her in French, not words of seduction but pointed little cruelties, of places and things she would have left behind, of people she would have known. He felt her shudder, and he continued seducing her mind and emotions with the painfully familiar things of her past.

She understood too late what he was doing and gave him the sharp edge of her nails. He flinched but did not pull away. With a hissed obscenity, he spoke again of old France, a witty sarcasm about a feckless king, a gay recitation of inane poetry. She smiled painfully and continued alternately to caress and to sting him, a subtle threatening seduction that moved toward a dangerous edge. She had been with men both aggressive and lazy, gentle and cruel. Out of self-preservation, she had learned to work the mean ones before they damaged her for the easy ones.

But this man was different. Gentle in his aggression, giving in his assault. He was French, a well-versed lover, an intelligent conversationalist. She despised him for his polished callousness, for making her feel again. She raised on tiptoe and pressed her mouth to his to stop the words that shook her to the core, that made her remember, made her yearn as she had not since before they took her husband and child away. She rubbed herself against him, uttering a stream of filthy innuendo, then knelt to perform what no man could deny.

Etienne exhaled sharply and grabbed her beneath the arms before his knees buckled. He pulled her up and into him. "Who are you?"

Her eyes flashed with icy resentment. "No one, *m'sieu*. Do you wish me to continue?"

More than anything, he wished her to continue. As much as she, he wanted to forget, to put the old days behind him. "Of course."

"You have news."

"*Oui*, are you the contact?"

"Only one of many," she replied, "who will send your message along."

He smiled. "I hope I discover many more things to bring to you."

She felt him relax, felt her power return. Her hand slid down to stroke him, while her teeth caught his ear. "What news have you, *m'sieu*?"

He drew a sharp breath. "Later. I want no politics in my bed." He turned her suddenly, pushed her face into the mattress so he could not see her, as he pushed her skirts up over her backside. He thought of Mary Greer as he entered the whore, pictured how he would one

day do this to her, how he would take her innocence
brutally, thoroughly, while she cried out in passion.

Sated, he left near midnight. The woman climbed
from the bed and walked across the room. She pushed a
curtain aside to reveal a door. She knocked twice and it
opened.

A man stepped out, disgust on his face. "You could
have hurried him along!"

She said nothing. The man before her was more
brutish than the one who had just left. She dared not
cross him. And he was English, which made him even
more loathsome in her eyes.

"He had news," she said.

A dance instructor had been summoned. He pre-
sented himself to Annalise as Master Horacio Divine
who, by orders of the duchess, had come to teach her
the rudiments of the waltz, the minuet, and the quadrille. Annalise gaped at the effeminate little man who
moved through the front door of her cottage with the
grace of an angel and the pushiness of a general. Bryson
followed, an unreadable expression on his face.

"But there isn't room here—" Annalise began.

"Of course there isn't," the little man snapped, "but I
was told that you refused to come to the castle until the
wedding, so we must do what we can here."

Annalise had received a summons, badly cloaked as a
request, two days earlier. With a lifetime of Marchfield
ahead of her, she had chosen to ignore the invitation.

She was uncertain now if her decision had been a bit hasty.

Despite the poor conditions, there was no stopping the dance instructor. Within seconds, he had furniture pushed aside and Annalise and Bryson standing face to face in the middle the parlor.

"Very good, now hold hands just so." He positioned them to his own satisfaction, cooing when delighted and grumbling when irritated. He had no patience for their obvious discomfort with each other, and rode them like a tyrant until Annalise's ire switched from Bryson to Master Horacio Divine.

"No, no, no," he groused for the hundredth time. He moved Bryson's arm lower on Annalise's back. "Hold her as if you cannot live without her, as if you will not let another man close enough to steal her away."

Bryson's hand twitched and Annalise gave him a scathing look. She was all too aware of the strength of his fingers, of his entire body. His heat touched her, his masculine presence invaded her. Would that he had true feelings for her rather than the heir she carried. The notion came from nowhere and was so unsettling it shook her composure and she stumbled on the first step.

"Preserve us!" the instructor swore. "This is a dance! It is art in physical form. It is an eloquent expression of the soul's inner desires. It is *not* a grape-stomping contest at a winery."

Annalise blushed and gave him her full attention. She did not want to disgrace herself at the ball, but more important, the sooner she learned the steps, the sooner Bryson would be out of her cottage. Her reaction to him confused her, his strength frightened her. She could not imagine spending the rest of her life fending off his male urges or enduring his painful invasion of her body.

Yet there was a part of her that wanted to be with him, inside him, as if the two could be merged. But she remembered the pain well, the overwhelming sense of loss. If there was one redeeming issue in an otherwise untenable situation, it was the fact that she was already with child. There would be no need to suffer his advances anytime soon.

"Now, look him in the eye," Horacio ordered. "He is your betrothed, your lover. The dance will reveal to all what you feel for one another."

Annalise glared coldly at Bryson.

❧ Chapter 17

T HEY HAD ALL COME WITH ANNALISE, AN ENTOU-
rage of village commoners in the wagon Everest used on
shopping day. Refusing the Marchfield carriage was
decidedly a foolish rebellion, but one that made Annalise
feel superior and in control of her own actions, until she
realized how hard the trip was proving to be for Aunt
Mellie. The elderly woman had not said a word of com-
plaint, but Annalise noticed the exhausted look in her
eyes and the frail droop to her shoulders.

Also piled into the cart like gypsies were Papa, Aunt
Constance, Uncle Nathaniel, and Mary Greer. With the
protection of her family around her, Annalise felt less
afraid as they bounced along the lane to Marchfield
castle.

The air had turned wintry overnight. Frost covered
the ground and glittered in the sunlight, making the land
look clean and bright. Annalise's nose and cheeks stung

with rosy color, and she huddled deeper within her
woolen cape and rubbed Aunt Mellie's gloved hands
briskly to keep some warmth flowing.

The elderly woman smiled. " 'Tis a beautiful day for a
winter wedding. You should have a snowy white cloak
with a fur collar and boots to match."

Annalise's stomach contracted but she smiled. "I
would look like the bride of a Russian czar rather than
an English lord."

"A duke," Aunt Mellie reminded softly. "Your
mother would be astonished and so pleased, Annalise.
You are about to fulfill every mother's dream for her
daughter. Try to remember that in the difficult days
ahead."

She was about to fulfill her own dreams, as well, save
they were turned nightmarish in the reality. "Will there be
difficult days ahead?" she asked quietly. "*Must* there be?"

"Aye, I think there must. It is so with every marriage,
no matter how well suited the couple." She squeezed
her niece's hand. "You can choose to grow together or
grow apart. Either is hard work."

The duchess awaited them under the portico and had
the wagon removed at once. But otherwise she greeted
Annalise's family with all graciousness of a proper
hostess.

Annalise could hardly look at this woman who had so
easily manipulated her. Especially shaming was the fact
that she had been foolish enough become Eleanor's prey.

In the room that would be hers from this day forth,
Annalise dressed with care for the small ceremony. It
would be her only marriage. She wanted it to be perfect

no matter what the circumstances. She closed her eyes and tried to picture her imaginary prince awaiting her at the altar, but Bryson's face kept intruding, a sinister twist to his mouth, a hot look in his eyes. She shivered and focused on her own face in the dressing mirror, keeping the unsettling thoughts at bay.

She heard the sound of water splashing in the next chamber. He was there, tending to his own ablutions. She wondered what he thought, what he felt. Did he dread this as much as her, did he resent his free will being bartered in favor of the heir she carried? She moved toward the connecting door, of a mind to ask, when the hall door opened.

Sally brought in a wreath made of pale white flowers and deep green laurel leaves. "Look, my lady, ain't it pretty?" She placed it on Annalise's head, cooing all the while. The sounds in the next room were forgotten beneath the onslaught of Sally's ministrations.

For the wedding ceremony, Annalise's hair would hang free to her waist, simple and unadorned save for the garland. Her gown was similar in intent. Simplicity itself, it was of white lawn, fitted at the high waist and embroidered at the hem. The fabric was so sheer and delicate, Annalise wore a colorless silk chemise beneath to preserve her modesty.

"Ohhh." Sally beamed. "You look like a winter fairy, m'lady, so beautiful you are."

Annalise smiled but disagreed. She looked like a chemist's daughter all dressed up in the best the dowager's coin could purchase. "Have you seen Greer?" she asked.

"Yes, m'lady, she's being attended by Bess. Shall I fetch her?"

"Only when she's done. My aunts and my father?"

"Your aunts are having tea with the duchess. I ain't for certain about your pop, but I'll check."

Annalise almost resented the duchess's grand generosity, yet hoped it would continue after the ceremony. She prayed her family would be welcome here, not just tolerated, in the years to come.

A face, stark and without color, stared back at her from the mirror. Not her face, a likeness, but not the heart of her. This girl stood ashamed on her wedding day, afraid to walk away from a ceremony that would protect her reputation and that of her child.

And not the face of a duchess, though that's what she would be after this day. The title was huge and burdensome for one of her narrow upbringing. If she could not take her place in a manner befitting the office, she would become an outcast, belonging nowhere, despised by the very ones who should support her. The thought was terrifying.

Her palm slid over her waist. For this child, she must learn. For his future she must endure. Nothing else mattered now. Neither her own misgivings nor Bryson's rough ways. Nothing but the life they had created, the future of Marchfield.

Ah, but it was easy to do this when she thought of the innocent child and the advantages this marriage would bring to him.

She rose from her seat and turned. "Are they ready for me, Sally?"

"Yes, my lady," the maid answered, and held up a white woolen cloak with matching fur at the collar.

"Oh." Annalise laughed lightly. "Aunt Mellie will love it."

Every effort had been made to get the old chapel warm, but still Annalise shivered as she stood at the rear, awaiting her father's escort to Bryson's side. The Duke of Marchfield was magnificent in formal attire, a small dress sword at his side. His jaw was stern and unsmiling, his eyes piercing as they gazed upon her. He seemed to take her measure with calculating efficiency, then withdraw.

She sensed he wanted nothing more to do with this charade than she and felt somehow diminished by the revelation. She looked away, seeing not the handsome bridegroom but the empty years ahead of her. Silent, lonely years.

Nay, not silent, she vowed. Let him glower and retreat in silence. There would be his child to fill her days, his child upon which to lavish love, his child to keep the loneliness at bay.

She smiled for her father's sake and took his arm. She had always thought she would marry in springtime, with fresh blooms filling the village church, the many voices of the town choir rising to Heaven in celebration. Instead, she walked the aisle of a ancient chapel, the haunting wail of the dead rising in protest to the very eaves. She shook off the disturbing impression and listened to the wind howl in the drafty rafters and the

sweet high voice of the single choirboy who had been
brought in from London.

The stroll down the aisle was the hardest walk she'd
ever made. With each step her anxiety grew, until she
was pale and shaken when she reached the reverend. He
smiled encouragement but she could only stare, feeling
as if her life's blood was flowing out.

He had not been required to say a word! While
Annalise had repeated wedding vows in a trembling
voice, Bryson had only been required to nod his acceptance of the mandates to love and honor and protect,
forsaking all others until death.

My child.

Annalise sent him a glaring look. He had certainly
had a voice to say those words. She felt betrayed that he
had not used it now, when it was so important to her.
The service was not worthy of a duke. It felt furtive and
clandestine, a marriage of duty.

The reverend demanded she hold out her hand.

She felt the smooth dry touch of Bryson's gloves as he
slipped the ring onto her finger. The gold shone dully in
the candlelit church, a shackle of finest quality, binding
her to him forever.

Then the reverend pronounced them man and wife,
the Duke and Duchess of Marchfield. She turned to find
tears on her aunts' faces, satisfaction on Eleanor's.

Suddenly the church doors were thrown open. Sunlight poured in and she saw servants lined up like soldiers, happiness on their faces, petals in their hands. She

smiled for them, these people she knew and understood better than the one she had just married. She felt tears forming as they began to cheer. On her husband's arm, she passed out of the church and through the assemblage of Marchfield servants, petals falling like raindrops, vivid pinks and reds against her white gown.

She swallowed hard against the knot of gratitude in her throat. They smiled so hugely, with hope and gladness in their eyes. Several she knew from the village winked audaciously and made her laugh. Her heart lifted as their smiles filled her and the petals swirled and danced on the crisp air, a sweet kaleidoscope blurring color on the wind.

At the end of the long welcome, a carriage awaited them. The head coachman nodded. "Congratulations, Your Grace."

Annalise's heart pounded. He was looking at her, addressing her. In less than an hour she had gone from being the apothecary's daughter to the Duchess of Marchfield. She nodded back out of duty and gave him a shaky smile. "Thank you."

Bryson handed her up into the carriage, then settled beside her. He looked neither right nor left, just stared off into nowhere, his profile strong and stern in the bright morning sun.

A soon as the door closed, she spoke. "You could have said the vows."

He glanced at her briefly, then away, his shoulders stiff and unyielding. The carriage jerked, then moved forward at a comfortable pace.

"The marriage may not even be legal because of it."

She was purposefully goading him, but couldn't seem to help it. "If someone were to question the validity—"

He turned suddenly, grabbed her behind the neck, and pulled her forward. His mouth met hers, a punishing kiss that lasted only seconds but stole her breath and effectively silenced her for the rest of the ride back. The euphoric tide of happiness she'd felt moments ago was dashed, and she felt reality settle within her like a stone.

The day was bright and cold. The frost had begun to melt and dew clung to everything. The remaining servants awaited them at the castle, and the couple walked through another shower of flowers and well wishes. Again Annalise smiled and nodded, but with less enthusiasm, wondering if the rest of her days would be spent in this sort of false happiness, pacifying those who were not at fault, resenting those who were. Once inside the castle, she jerked her arm free of Bryson's escort and went to the hearth.

A huge log burned and she stood in its warmth, hoping to dispel the chill of her uncertainty. Bryson followed and stood next to her, an unreadable man, frightening because Annalise did not know what he expected of her, of a wife, now that the vows had been made.

Asking would be fruitless, so she ignored him, praying that this night would not be a repeat of the one two months earlier. Though the memory of it was hazy, an almost surreal dream, she knew she could not bear it again. She remembered the tortured look on Bryson's face, the burning pain in her body.

She was with child. Surely there would be no need to repeat the act that got her that way.

The day sped away with a sort of frantic bustling about of servants and workmen. The castle staff had more than they could manage with the evening's preparations and Eleanor's demands. Bryson had disappeared, and Annalise's father and uncle were engrossed in the library. She passed the time with her aunts and Mary Greer in a small parlor that caught the afternoon sun. Too soon, the evening approached and it was time to prepare for the winter ball.

Annalise retired to her room and found her things already laid out. Her gown was colored Pekings, the silk brilliant. Eleanor must have ordered it when she did the wedding gown. The connecting door stood open and she approached it slowly, hesitant to know if Bryson was on the other side.

He stood by the fire absently warming his hands. He wore a dressing gown of emerald velvet, and the memory of it against her bare flesh sent heat speeding into Annalise's cheeks.

Glancing up, Bryson found her standing in the doorway, staring. He stared back, a probing look that seemed to pierce, then connect them in a way Annalise did not understand. Her nerves twisted and she backed away, pulling the door shut. Protected by the barrier, she let out the breath she'd been holding and drooped against the wall.

His presence had the strangest, most disarming effect

on her. He filled her with heat. He drained her like a sickness. She never knew what to expect anymore, save that she would be left trembling.

Sally hurried in, slippers in her hands. "I'd almost misplaced these." She grinned. "Now, wouldn't that have been the thing. The new duchess dancing in her bare feet."

The maid's gaiety was infectious, and Annalise felt herself settle down over the next hour while Sally dressed and coiffed her for the evening ahead.

Patting the gown in place, Sally spun Annalise toward the looking glass. "As pretty a duchess as has ever been!"

The gown was very French and along the same simple lines as her wedding dress. The neck was low, the waist high, and the colors shimmered when she moved, giving her an ethereal appearance. Silk gloves reached to her elbows and her hair had been piled high, secured by a jeweled comb and crowned with ostrich feathers. She looked older, more mature. Married.

When the last curl was patted into place, she glanced back over her shoulder at Sally and took a deep breath. "I am ready, I suppose."

Sally nodded and opened a box on the dressing table. Inside, on a bed of black velvet, lay a necklace. With awe, the servant lifted it and placed it around Annalise's neck. "It is so beautiful, m'lady, it hurts my eyes."

Against her pale breast lay the jewels of Marchfield. They would, the servant told her, effect a certain acceptance among the ton. Indeed, they were stunning, affording her a modicum of presence and prestige. But

Annalise had more faith in mankind's ability to form its own opinion without the aid of props.

She smoothed the folds of her exquisite gown and lifted her chin. She did not dress for Bryson or even for herself but for her father and the villagers dearest to her who would be present. If the charade would be played out, she would play it well. Let them delight in her grand accomplishment; she would not spoil their fantasy. She knew only too well what it meant to have one's dreams dashed.

A knock sent Sally scurrying to the door. She returned in less than a minute, beaming. "It is time."

Annalise's heart skipped a beat. "Will you get to come, as well?"

Sally made a face. "I got the short end of the straw but no matter. I'll have my day at the next one. My man is working, too, so we'll get an extra stipend and days off to celebrate later." She gave Annalise a tiny push. "Go now." In a whisper she added, "Go for us all."

Annalise arrived at the head of the stairs and found little comfort in the grand ballroom decorated to elaborate perfection or the impressive guest list. On one hand it seemed a sacrilege that she should not enjoy what she had wished for all these years, but on the other it appeared ridiculous to delight in her own downfall.

Rebellion was a bitter herb, but no one else need bear the bad taste of it. Annalise had no wish to spoil the lavish preparations or hurt the feelings of those who had worked so hard. She determined to set her resentment aside and pretend, at least for this one night, that she was the little cinder girl of Charles Perrault's *Tales of Past Times* being courted by the handsome prince.

In truth, she found it an easy fantasy when she reached the head of the stairs and saw her father in his dapper new clothes, conversing with the Duchess of Wakelawn. He caught sight of his daughter at almost the same moment and a smile transformed his serious face into one of absolute pride.

Guests mingled everywhere, bedecked in the finest ensembles of linen, wool, and lace. Silks and satins mixed with simple homespun; porcelain skin shone fair and privileged next to ruddy, wind-chapped cheeks. Only Eleanor could have pulled off a coming together of the classes and have it work so effortlessly. Though the lines were obviously, if subtly, drawn, there seemed no contention in the air. Every chair was taken, and valuable standing space was guarded by sly, sharp elbows or lost.

The great doors had been thrown open to accommodate the crowd. The overflow spilled out into the courtyard and pleasure garden where flambeaux burned brightly along the walking paths and paper lanterns hung from tree limbs and swayed dreamily in the breeze.

Constance and Mary Greer clustered together in one corner, in awe of their surroundings. Their gowns, along with Aunt Mellie's, were the latest fashion sewn by a London modiste. Annalise knew Eleanor's gesture was not an act of kindness, merely an assurance that the family members closest to Annalise would not stand out as the commoners they were and embarrass Marchfield.

Reaching the landing, Everest took her hands. "You are a beautiful sight, Annalise!"

She smiled. "Not nearly so handsome as you, Papa."

His returning smile was strained. "Your Aunt Mellie looks quite spry talking to that gentleman in the green silk coat."

Annalise nodded. The underlying concern in his voice was also etched in worry lines on his forehead. There was naught she could do to ease him when she had the same worries constricting her throat. By un-spoken pact, they would pretend that all was well and hope to make out of this something better than the worst mistake of her life.

"Well, here is your husband."

She saw Bryson in the next instant and found her breath stolen from her lungs. Though pale and some-what self-contained, as if bracing himself for the night, he was also magnificent. His coat was dark plum-chocolate velvet, his pants and shirt a creamy satin. His features were grim and hard, and Annalise found that in an odd way he needed the severity to offset his stunning beauty. Without the sharp derision in his eyes or the cold set of his lips, he would have been much too pretty and foppish for her interest.

Instead, tall and commanding and undeniably the Duke of Marchfield, he drew the attention of everyone in the room. Some, hearing the rumors, had come only to see the Mad Duke; others were not so ignoble and disdained such talk as rubbish. But all were curious about the heir who had been missing so long.

Glancing at him, Annalise felt her usual resentment

slip. His brow was knit, his mind scrambling to make sense of the clusters of guests that continued to stream into the castle. She could see by his expression that he knew some, thought he recognized others, and had no hope of recollection about the rest. She forcefully pushed aside a twinge of compassion. It was his own fault that they must all be here now, smiling false smiles and making fools of the few who truly wished them well.

After a time his expression grew fixed, and she knew he was retreating, giving up the taxing need to remember. How draining such a plight of confusion must be for him. She had to remind herself how detestable he was and that he deserved every second of discomfort, but in the end she only felt drained, as well.

Stiffly she murmured, "It can't last forever."

He gave a clipped nod and held on a bit longer.

Eleanor was nothing if not precise. She allowed ample opportunity for the onlookers to gawk and speculate, then swept forward and nodded to the orchestra.

Annalise knew she and Bryson would have to make their entrance and lead the first dance, but with the moment upon her, she felt a thousand butterflies start swarming in her belly. Everyone was watching, waiting to see if she could fill the slippers of a duchess. Waiting to see if she would fail.

She searched for the ones she knew and loved, those who would not judge but bless the union. The local gentry, the mayor of Marchfield, the rector, and the bishop. If there was envy among any of them, it was mild and sprang from joy. Misty-eyed, Aunt Constance stood with Tilly Hardwick, beaming with pride. Sam

Blacksmith nodded at the contentious Widow Rukin as if to say *See, Gerty, one of our own made good.*

Even Mary Greer seemed overwhelmed by the magic of the night. Her cheeks were flushed, her eyes dewy as she smiled shyly at Etienne beside her.

Annalise felt a twinge of concern, then a sudden foreboding that made no sense. Quick as a rain shower it swept in with drenching force and left her slightly chilled. She could not account for the feeling but it was there, ominous and portentous, making her heart pound with inexplicable menace.

Etienne was well traveled and accomplished, Mary Greer innocent in the extreme. Perhaps it was the unlikely combination, or the fact that she now knew what could happen to an incautious maiden. Or perhaps it was only the trauma and attention of a ballroom full of watchers. Whatever the cause, she felt a bit light-headed when a rap on the lid of the pianoforte signaled the orchestra.

Resplendent in wigs and livery, the musicians bent to their instruments and began a triumphant processional. Annalise accepted Bryson's arm and they began the descent to the ballroom floor.

Polite applause rippled through the room and swelled to surround the two. Bryson was the handsome, prodigal son returned to his rightful place, his bride dazzling and perfect to give him heirs.

Etienne watched from the shadows, wondering if this would be the last time the great castle would host such a ball. In months Marchfield would be stripped bare, its treasures sold to fund the bringing down of an even greater edifice, Britain itself. Bryson and the dowager duchess must be assassinated. Annalise could be allowed to live only as a pawn. If she accepted their ways and was willing to fund the movement, she would be a great advantage. Otherwise she must die and the estate would revert not to the Crown, as everyone suspected, but to Lawrence McGovern, Elbert's bastard son, who had been conveniently legitimized by a master forger and follower of Reason.

Etienne sighed. Marchfield's magnificence made him envious of its riches, something he had not felt since the fall of France. He now looked forward to the internal tearing down of more wealth than he would ever know in his lifetime.

He smiled down at Mary Greer, the light of conquest in his eyes, and asked for the first space on her dance card.

Bryson and Annalise reached the center of the floor, and the orchestra struck a minuet. Bryson's steps were sure if perfunctory, his arms secure as he guided Annalise through the small steps and glides, the hand movements and salutations. She felt some of her nervousness dissolve as she flowed to the fluid motion of the music. Others came slowly to the floor but kept their distance. For this first dance, the attention would be on the celebrated couple in the center.

When it was done, Annalise was slightly flushed but given no chance to worry if she had made a fool of herself. A succession of dances followed and always a gentleman was waiting to claim her hand. The quadrille, the pavane, the polonaise. One flowed into another to the beautiful accompaniment of the orchestra.

Chandelier light glittered off the jeweled guests and seemed to spin about her. Gold and silver, crystal and diamond. Sapphires, rubies, and emeralds sparkled with vibrant color at the pale throats of elegant women and at the cuffs of their gentlemen. Together their white gloves made intricate patterns as they gestured in the pleasing courtesies of the dance.

On the fringes of the room, gossip rustled like dry leaves. A hint of stale powder and body odor covered with perfume mingled in the more congested areas, and many took strolls in the garden to escape the cloying closeness.

Annalise was passed from partner to partner. First an earl who was quite handsome, then a duke who was not, albeit he was kind. Then a captain of the blues, who had known her father for some time. Her head reeled from the experience of being spun around the floor on the arms of such dashing gentlemen, and her heart felt light at their blatant flattery, even if frivolous and expected. She was finally returned, breathless and enlivened, to her husband.

The Duke of Marchfield gave her a sober look and slid his arm through hers, an almost proprietary gesture.

She gave him a bewildered look but allowed the small restriction, confident she could free herself at will. In truth, she needed a moment to rest and catch her breath. She would have loved a stroll in the garden but was afraid it would be inappropriate to leave the ballroom.

A short, rotund man approached, beaming with pleasure. "Bryson!" he said, pounding the duke on the back. "We'll be calling you Marchfield from now on, I suppose, along with Your Grace and other such noble flattery." He grinned hugely. "Peter ain't in town, but when he finds out you've returned from the grave, he'll swoon like a girl. Never did believe that church business. You a cleric? Had me laughing all the way to White's the night I heard it."

He sobered suddenly, and his eyes took on a bewildered, uncomfortable look. "Falkes is here though, trying to decide if he's speaking to you or not. Rather boorish of you never to send us word, you know. Bad form, Marchfield, us being your best friends and all."

Bryson stared at the man with absolute blankness. His palms grew clammy and his mind raced for a way around the awkwardness.

Annalise saw the hidden apprehension on Bryson's face, the dearth of understanding in his eyes, and realized it was more than muteness that caused it. She touched the lord's sleeve and whispered conspiratorially, "We thought you have heard."

He leaned forward, his brows raised. "Heard?"

"He's been ill, you know. Contagious. Had to stay away for the safety of his family and friends. Wouldn't let the dowager tell a single soul for fear they would try to come see him."

"Egad!" he said, straightening. "I never knew! Brave of you, Marchfield. I'd have whined until the world was at my feet and I infected them all." He stepped back, just realizing the full extent of what she'd said. "He ain't still got it, has he?"

She smiled softly. "What do you think?"

He smiled back, relieved. "Just a joke, mind you. I best go get Falkes. He'll want to know the truth."

As soon as the man was gone, Annalise glanced over at Bryson. "You don't remember him."

He shook his head, his mouth white at the edges.

"There's a lot you don't remember, isn't there?" she said quietly.

He nodded, then shrugged as if it were unimportant, but she noted his stark eyes and the deep even breaths he took to compose himself.

Compassion flooded her. It was not pity but a profound sadness for his confusion, for the years stolen from him. Most of his family had been destroyed, and he didn't even have his memories to comfort him. She slid her hand in his briefly and squeezed. There was nothing more she could do.

Bryson could not abide the sorrow on her face. He could live with the memory loss, but he did not want her dragged down into his pain. With an angry gesture, he shrugged her hand off.

She glanced up at him, startled, but saw nothing in his eyes to suggest a bad temper. His gaze was fixed on the open doors. Confused, she turned away to look for her father but found him engaged in what appeared to be a lengthy discussion with a viscount. Mary Greer danced with Etienne and Aunt Constance was nowhere in sight. That left Aunt Mellie, who was dozing lightly by the fire.

Annalise started toward her but was brought up short after only one step. She gave Bryson a searching look, but he only stared back and refused to release her arm.

"First you push me away, then you hold me," she

said in an exasperated whisper. "Make up your mind. I must check on my aunt."

The hand on hers squeezed tighter.

"Fine, if you will not release me, then you must accompany me."

She jerked on her arm as if to prove her words and almost stumbled when he took the first step with her. Composing herself for her family's sake, she strolled with her husband to the massive hearth. The fire was bright and soothing, holding just the right amount of warmth for those not involved in the dance.

Bending, she touched her aunt's sleeve. Mellie opened her eyes and smiled. "Child."

Annalise smiled back. "May I present to you the Duke of Marchfield."

Mellie eyed him shrewdly. "He's handsome," she stated. "Too bad. Been my experience that the handsome ones are not usually the faithful ones. Too many temptations."

Annalise opened her mouth, then closed it. Her aunt had always spoken her mind, but never had she said anything so inappropriate.

"I've shocked you, my dear. Forgive me." She pointed a slender, wrinkled finger at Bryson. "You're not shocked though, are you?"

He shook his head and didn't back down from her steely gaze.

"Well? Is it true or isn't it? I despise apathetic positions. Mark my words, indifference is the curse of humanity. France is a perfect example."

Bryson had the feeling she was right, though her reasoning behind comparing a revolution to an unfaithful lover escaped him.

Mellie smiled. "You mustn't mind me, I'm just a crazy old woman."

Hardly. A smooth termagant perhaps. He knew insanity and all its faces intimately. The old woman was as lucid as they came. He glanced over at Annalise, who still seemed a bit flustered by her aunt's boldness, and motioned to the open doors leading into the garden.

Annalise hesitated over walking out with him, especially into the dark.

Mellie rapped her cane on the floor. "Go ahead, child. The two of you must come to some acceptable agreement before tonight or your lives will be deplorable. Believe me, I know." She pointed the tip of her cane at Annalise. "If he can't speak, he can't order you about. It seems a perfect beginning to me."

Annalise blushed at her aunt's brashness but still made no move toward the door. Bryson did not need his voice to exact his power, and she would be at his mercy soon enough.

Mellie saw the stubbornness in her great-niece's eyes and the fear, as well. "Mingle with your betters, then. You'll have to get used to that, also."

Given the two choices, Annalise opted for the stroll. She searched for her father first but found him newly engaged in heated conversation with an earl over some scientific theory. The earl paid his respects to Bryson, then immediately turned back to the discussion at hand.

Annalise was surprised to find that Everest conversed with the nobility quite easily. Over the years he had

served many of the present guests with medicines to ease
their ills while visiting Marchfield, but she had not
known he could parley so competently on subjects as
varied as politics, music, and art.

Most of his animated discussions were with older
gentlemen and friends of the late duke, but younger
ones, too, remembered him from the years when
Marchfield rang with laughter and gaiety, when invita-
tions to its endless parties were the most coveted post—
when there were still marriageable daughters and sons
at home.

Annalise was startled to see this other, almost cos-
mopolitan side to her father, a man not only confident
in discussing any topic but as comfortable in collecting
humorous anecdotes as in routing malicious gossip.
Even Eleanor was not immune to his congenial wit.
After making her own rounds, she stood by his side, elegantly attired in deep purple velvet, and laughed at his
sage advice to a young viscount.

Outwardly the dowager duchess was the perfect, gracious hostess and on grand terms with the family of her
son's bride. She had put about in whispers that Bryson
had fallen madly in love with the country girl and who
was she to stand in the way of matters of the heart? The
romantic few believed it. Others waited to see what lay
beneath her scheme. But all, to Annalise's eternal shock,
had yet to notice that the Duke of Marchfield was mute.

He was adept at nodding or taking on expressions of
deep contemplation or boredom, and he was a master of
evasion. But still, she found it fascinating that people
were so preoccupied with their own conversations and

absorbed with their own wit that no one seemed to notice that Bryson had not yet answered a single question aloud.

Eleanor noticed, as well, but was not nearly as surprised as Annalise. She had long known that many of her acquaintances possessed little more than rudimentary intelligence and many were so obsessed with themselves that they took little notice of others, unless they needed an adversary or made an enemy. Those of keener wit and mental acumen were given the illness story and had enough upbringing not to attempt to converse overmuch with a man who had been convalescing for so long. If they wondered at his silence, they chalked it up either to weakness or to the entitled arrogance and eccentricity of being a duke.

Unerringly Eleanor made a mental note of each family present. The villagers invited were counted quickly, then disregarded. She had expected they would come to reap the benefits of her excellent kitchen and the chance to mingle with their betters. The blooded families were a different matter entirely.

Each house not present represented a snub of indifference or disapproval. Eleanor knew the game well. She could care less what they thought of the match, but they would pay their respects or suffer her displeasure in the years to come. To be deliberately snubbed by the House of Marchfield was dire indeed. They might set about malicious gossip in whispers, but a direct cut was unthinkable. None of the more powerful families had chosen that ill-fated path; they knew better. Either they were present, or they had sent perfectly acceptable excuses. Only those with more insolence than brains had set about to openly rebuke the new Duke of Marchfield for his choice in a bride, thinking others whispering behind the safety of their gloved hands would follow. If they did not know better before, they would after this night. A social death knell awaited their unfortunate stupidity.

The dowager duchess glanced briefly at Annalise, satisfied that the girl was enduring with aplomb. While she had not been certain how Annalise would hold up an entire night, she had been confident that if any untrained miss could handle herself in a crowd of perfumed and bejeweled vultures, it would be this one.

Having lost an earlier fight over hair powder, Eleanor secretly thrilled to the way Annalise's rebellion had worked in her favor. In a room of overly coiffed matrons and pretentious airs, Annalise shone like a rare bird, all bright color and healthy spirit.

Properly gowned and placed in the Marchfield setting, she appeared original rather than colloquial and would no doubt be gifted with a sobriquet by night's end. Her legend would make the rounds quickly. Those not present would regret most heartily that they had not shown up and were now *de trop* with the Dowager Duchess of Marchfield and hence the whole of England.

Success felt marvelous. Eleanor had not cared about it in years, but now she realized how much she had missed the surge of power through her veins, the reward of accomplishment. Her gaze glittered boldly at her secretary. "What do you think, my dear Maximilien?"

"Perfect, as you well know," he answered, but his

gaze kept going to Etienne. His fondness for his brother had not clouded his reason. There was something odd, something not quite right about Etienne's move to England. Although his suspicions seemed groundless, still Max could not shake the feeling that all was not as it should be.

"Perfect, yes," Eleanor purred. "And your brother. Is he getting on well enough?"

Max stiffened. She felt it, too. "In truth, I do not trust him, but with so many displaced counts and other Frenchmen floating around England these days, it seems ridiculous to suspect my own brother of nefarious schemes."

"Discount no one," she warned. "He could be Napoleon's best informant and we would not be the wiser."

It was not Napoleon he was concerned with. Whoever Etienne was in league with was much worse. There was something in his brother's eyes, something not quite alive. The man had become so used to death, it was a part of him now. He was like a handsome, polished apple rotting from the inside.

Chapter 18

Bryson tugged on Annalise's hand and motioned toward the garden. Finally she nodded and strolled with him from the glow of bright chandeliers into cold moonlit solitude. He breathed easier there, she noticed, apart from the throng of prying eyes and questioning conversation. His shoulders relaxed as he leaned against a large old oak and inhaled, seeming to take the night deep inside him.

Annalise was chilled and rubbed her arms briskly, trying to stir up some warmth. She should have brought her cloak, a stunning cherry velvet with an ermine collar and silk lining. The jeweled clasp at the throat was more expensive than any gown she had owned before now. Bryson removed his own coat, then wrapped her in it. Not from a sense of chivalry, she suspected, but because he did not want to be made to return.

The velvet was luxuriously soft against her skin and

carried his scent. Subtle and masculine, it did strange things to her composure. She realized that she would have taken comfort in such a gesture had he been a friend or a brother. But he was neither, and that fact was never borne out more fully than when he looked at her, his eyes piercing and intense, as if he could see straight through layers of velvet and silk and lawn to the flush suddenly covering her flesh.

Annalise shrugged the coat off and handed it back to him. "You'll catch your death. I'll just go—"

He raised his hand, a simple enough gesture, but it brought a servant running immediately.

"Your Grace?"

Bryson nodded at Annalise. Amazed, she requested her cloak and was further startled to watch the servant smile and dash off as if her wishes were the most important thing in the universe. It was amazing. For a brief moment she had felt so powerful and knew she must be careful to remember her humble beginnings. She never wanted to lose sight of the line she had crossed or the responsibility it carried.

When the servant returned with her cloak, she thanked him profusely. She turned to speak to Bryson but he had gone still as stone. His nostrils were flared, his gaze intense. It caused an unsettling disturbance in her pulse rate until she realized he did not look at her. Instead he was focused on a woman making her way closer.

She was beautiful, elegant, and poised. She strolled alongside a gentleman, her face rapt with interest at his every word.

Bryson's face was engrossed, as well, with recognition. Annalise felt an unfamiliar emotion surge through her. Though she had never met the woman, she resented her on sight and was appalled at the intensity of her feelings. Bryson continued to watch as she approached, an obscure expression on his face. When she was little more than a yard away, he stepped into the wavering light of a torch.

"Oh!" The woman's gloved hand went to her heart. "You startled me—" She peered closer, then recognition dawned. "Oh, Bryson," she whispered, "is it really you?"

He nodded once.

"I cannot believe it, my heart is racing away with me." She pulled her companion over. "Perry, come you must meet Lord Bry—" She laughed softly, sadly, at her blunder. "His Grace, the Duke of Marchfield." She took Bryson's hand, pressed it to her lips. "I cannot believe you are back. I have missed you so!"

Annalise saw his eyes close briefly with something akin to pain. Her heart thudded strangely. She felt their sadness, their longing, but had no idea from whence the feelings came. Were they friends, lovers, family? She felt it too impertinent to ask, so remained quiet, feeling like an outsider or, worse, an intruder.

Servants appeared, announcing fireworks by the stone pond, and a crowd emerged from the house, laughing gaily and pouring toward the bank of a small man-made lake.

The woman squeezed Bryson's hand once more.

"The Grecian garden and fireworks! It feels like old times. Will you come?"

He glanced at the faint marble pillars and moon-washed statues in the distance. Paper lanterns were strung along beech trees to light the way. He shook his head, regret in his expression.

She did not press. "I am so grateful you are recovered." Her eyes welled with tears. "Papa forbade me to visit you in that horrid place, and I worried so, but I can see that you are quite well. We must talk, later when there is more time and quiet."

He nodded. A melancholy look lingered in his eyes long after she was gone.

Annalise smoothed the folds of an unwrinkled gown, picked imaginary lint from her sleeve, and patted her perfectly coiffed hair. It was the grossest breach of etiquette that they had not been introduced, but she would never let him know how much it hurt her to be disregarded so completely. She considered him with idle disinterest. "Who is she?"

"Lady Claudia Pembroke."

She nearly jumped from her skin. Her head snapped around to him with a jolt. She had not expected him to answer, much less to speak with such deep yearning. Her chin dropped slightly, then heat flooded her skin.

"You will not speak wedding vows with me, yet you can say her name clearly!"

Overcome, she snapped her mouth shut, grabbed the hem of her cloak, and rushed blindly through the garden. She went in the direction opposite the crowd and lost herself in a maze of shrubbery and boxed hedges. She didn't know why she ran, just that her heart hurt as if she had been betrayed by her closest friend. Tears spilled and she dashed them away, furious that she was crying over that . . . that worthless, voiceless, conniving *scoundrel*!

She left the stone path and went deeper into the gardens, past the small benches and lighted walkways to the edge of a thorny barrier. She was so distracted that she almost fell into the ditch that separated the formal gardens from the park. It had a sheer face that no deer could climb and kept the gardens unravaged by the larger wildlife and the view unblemished by a fence.

She changed directions, hopped a low stone wall, and trespassed into the medicinal and kitchen plots where row upon row of herb and vegetable mounds striped the uneven ground. There was not much to tend this time of year and the smell of damp, barren earth rose beneath her slippers. She tripped over a spot of tilled dirt but kept running, with nowhere to go, no mission in mind except to flee from her own heartache. As she came up against a wall of greenery and spun about to go the other way, she plowed right into Bryson. He caught her by the upper arms to keep her from falling.

"Liar!" she accused, trying to wrest herself from his grasp. "I knew you could speak all this time. Your very silence was a lie."

He held tight until she calmed, then brushed her forehead with his lips.

"No!" she said as if he had spoken. "I will not be taken in by you ever again. I will not forgive you."

He sighed, stirring the wisps of hair at her temple. His

hands kneaded her upper arms, a consoling gesture. "My sister's friend," he whispered, "my brother's fiancée."

Something in Annalise went weak and trembly at the longing in his voice. She held onto her anger with determination and cursed her quivering lower lip. "That changes nothing. You can say 'My child' as if I were naught but the vessel holding it, and you speak another woman's name with such passion I expect you to chase after her, but you could not repeat your wedding vows to me?"

"Not in front of others," he said tightly.

It took a moment for her anger to simmer down enough for her to understand the full implication of his words. "You've spoken to no one else?"

He shook his head.

She was loath to believe him and make a ninny of herself but could not stop the soft, warm feeling moving through her. "No one at all?"

He gave her a look.

"Why?"

He shrugged, closed off again, and she knew by the fixed look on his face that he would not speak further. She stirred the dirt with her toe, wondering things that had not occurred to her before tonight.

"Did you have someone before?"

He lifted an eyebrow, suspecting where this was leading, not wanting to go there.

"A friend, a fiancée?"

In truth, he could not remember and had no desire just now to contemplate what his life had been like before. Trying to put back together the particles of the past that floated through his mind was vexing as well as exhausting. This was his wedding night. There were other things upon which he'd rather concentrate.

His hands slid down her arms and he laced his fingers through hers, then began to lead her from the kitchen garden.

Leery of the look on his face, she held back, but he dragged her along as if she were light as a feather. "Where are we going?" She stumbled on a rut and grabbed his arm for support. His muscles bunched beneath his coat sleeve, strong under her fingers, both appealing and frightening. "Your Grace!" she demanded. "Where—"

"Bryson," he said, but that was all.

She jerked again and felt that odd rush of amazement. She would never get used to hearing his voice, so dark and clear and unexpected. It did funny, shivery things to her composure. "Bryson," she tested, and though her voice held a note of resentment, she liked the sound of his name on her tongue.

She followed him more peaceably, not really caring where they were going as long as it wasn't back into the crowd or toward his bedchamber. There would be time later to worry about that last place, so she chose to enjoy the night. As she placed her hand willingly on his arm and lifted her chin, he gave her a strange look.

"I am pretending that I am being escorted along on the arm of a prince who loves me, rather than a mentally deranged duke who has settled for me."

He almost smiled. She was certain of it.

When they once again reached the pleasure garden,

he headed toward the stables. Delighted, Annalise followed. "I love to watch the horses," she said, "all animals, really. Did you know that?"

He knew but did not respond. He liked her chatter when she wasn't angry or afraid. It was sweet and innocent and full of the life he'd lost.

"Papa rescued a wolf once," she said in a distant voice. "It had nearly bitten its own legs off in a trap. I nursed it back to health but the ungrateful wretch ran away as soon as it was healed."

For the span of two heartbeats, she paused and stared at the moonlit path. "Will you do that to me?" she asked quietly. "When you regain your place here, will you leave me behind for those of your own class?" The breeze whispered through the trees, a mournful sound. Shadows danced along the path. "I have heard stories of wives being left comfortably situated at the country estate while their husbands pursue a mistress."

Only after begetting the required heir, Bryson thought, but said nothing. He was lost in terror and triumph at the idea of returning to his former self, his former life.

She took his silence as agreement and frowned. "I find such behavior appalling." Still he said nothing and her ire grew. "It doesn't signify, I suppose. You can set me aside like so much rubbish, if you choose, but I won't be turned out to some distant place. I will stay in the village near my father and friends." Not that her demand meant aught. He was the duke and her husband; he could do as he pleased and she would not have a thing to say about it. But she had two strong legs to carry her back home, if needs be.

Bryson gave her a peculiar look. She'd worked herself up into a fine snit over something that would never happen. He put a hand to her shoulder and moved her closer to the barn.

The stablehands were still busy attending Marchfield's horses and the visiting ones, as well. A guest might call for a carriage at any time, so they slept only in shifts. The boy called Martin bobbed a greeting. "Good even', Your Grace. Have you come for the new one?"

Bryson nodded and pushed Annalise forward.

In a thrice, Martin had the horse out of the stall and prancing in the stableyard. "Ain't he a beauty?"

"Silva!" Annalise exclaimed in wonder. "What are you doing here?" She turned to Bryson. "This is Silvaticus, the loveliest stallion in all of Britain."

"And the meanest," Martin said wryly. "He took a chunk of me arse." He flushed dull red. "Beggin' your pardon, Your Grace, but he goes for me ever' time I try leading him around the pen."

Annalise made a sympathetic sound. "I am sorry for your discomfort. He is a trying beast but simply misunderstood, I think." She gave young Martin an understanding look. "His first master was an ogre. Silva doesn't know yet that all men are not like that."

She approached the horse slowly, her hand extended. "I'm sure the blacksmith will bring him around in time."

Martin worked the rope gently but firmly. He couldn't let anything happen to the new Duchess of

Marchfield, or it would be his head. "Not too close, Your Grace, he's unpredictable."

Annalise looked around for Bryson, then realized Martin addressed her. The title sounded so strange and out of place, it took her a moment to grasp that it was her form of address now.

"Have you a treat?" she asked. Martin fished in his apron pocket and pulled out a half-eaten apple. Annalise took the fruit and spoke softly. "Silva, come." The horse perked his ears but pretended to ignore her. "Take the rope off, Martin. It makes him nervous."

The stableboy looked at her as if she were being silly-headed, then at the duke. Bryson nodded once. "If you're certain," he hedged, thinking of his poor backside. "Stop me anytime . . ." He did as he was told, but slowly, warning Annalise every step of the way.

She stretched out her palm. "Silva, come."

Moonlight scattered the night shadows and glowed on her intent face. The cloak covered her, but Bryson remembered her shape in candlelight, her flesh smooth and rich as cream. Her hair was neatly coiffed but tendrils had come loose and curled in the damp night air. They clung to her temples, wisps of windswept elegance. She was small but unafraid as she held out the apple.

Silva walked up arrogantly, took the apple, then tossed his head and pranced off. Annalise only laughed at his pompous show. "Haughty beast," she accused, but it sounded like an endearment on her lips. A bewildered look crossed her face suddenly. "What is he doing here? I have not seen the blacksmith."

Martin beamed. "For your bride gift."

"Silva?" Annalise gasped.

"Nay!" Martin looked appalled. "Not that mean beasty, but his offspring. His Grace's stables have some of the best mares around these parts. He had Silva brought here to sire a foal for you. Your bride gift."

Annalise turned to Bryson, awe and delight in her eyes. "Is it true? Am I to have a horse of my own, one of Silva's?" When he nodded, she clasped her hands together over her mouth. Her eyes sparkled as he had never seen them, and her face fairly glowed. "Oh, I can hardly believe it! I am beyond words of gratitude!"

Bryson could think of a few ways she might show her appreciation but doubted she would like any of them. The night was peaceful, if his thoughts were not, and he wished the winter wind would cool his errant desire. He was raw with yearning, burning to have her in his bed again. He found Silva to be a fine beast to add blood to his stables, but the gift was more than a business trans- action. It was a calculated effort to soften Annalise toward him.

He did not want a war in his chamber every night, and he could not abide the tears that would flow if he forced her or, worse, her cold hurt and rejection. He could hold with tradition and set her up in her own rooms, but he did not want to sleep separate from her.

The lack of privacy at St. Bertram's had been enough to drive him insane, but solitary punishment had been far worse. Even now he could not endure being alone too long. Though he liked a certain quiet and solemnity, he could not bear absolute isolation.

For an hour, Annalise stroked Silva's coat and spoke to him in the sweet melodious tones women use with children and animals. But their absence from the celebration could not last. By the time Eleanor sent a servant looking for them, they were already on their way back to the main house.

The hour was noticeably late. Music still played, dancers spun across the floor, and food continued to be plentiful. But it was time for the newly wedded couple to make their exit. Short of making a spectacle of herself, Annalise had to retire gracefully. It was her wedding night; it was expected. But all color left her cheeks as she quietly kissed her father and Aunt Mellie good night, then mounted the stairs to her chamber as if her feet were weighted with lead. It was humiliating to know that guests and servants alike knew where the bride was going and what the groom had in mind when he joined her.

Her chin lifted a notch when she reached the landing. Let their sordid little minds speculate. She had no intention of doing anything more than sleep.

Sally was waiting for her when she entered her chamber. The fire had been stoked to take the chill from the room, so there was no excuse for Annalise's shivering. Sally took her cloak, then helped her undress right down to nothing but bare skin. She then held up a nightrail as sheer as her wedding gown had been.

Annalise's eyes widened in shock as Sally slipped it over her head. There were no sleeves, just lace straps at her shoulders and a narrow ribbon beneath her breasts. The fabric was delicate but so transparent she might as well have been naked. And there was no chemise beneath it, as there had been with her wedding gown, nothing to hide her but a gossamer swath as insubstantial as a cloud.

Blood rushed to Annalise's cheeks when the servant commented upon the beauty of it.

"Beg pardon, Your Grace," Sally said, suddenly contrite. "I can see you're spooked by the whole thing. No need to worry. It ain't so bad, really. I'm sure His Grace will go easy on you the first time. After that, well, men are animals, I always say, but you'll get used to it in time."

Annalise's eyes grew rounder, her cheeks hotter. She would never get used to what Bryson had done to her. Since she already carried the Marchfield heir, there would be no need for her to endure another night of his attentions until years from now when he wanted more children.

"Sally?" she asked in a constricted voice.

"Your Grace?"

"Did you marry for love?"

"O'course. Our class don't marry for money, that's for certain."

"And your wedding night was . . . difficult. Even with love?"

Sally brushed out Annalise's hair as she talked. "Me Davie is a lusty fellow. We courted for a while and he was a perfect gentleman. But after I agreed to marry him, he acted like the vows were already spoken. I ain't sayin' I didn't like the attention, mind you, him being so handsome and all, but I still had my morals even if he seemed to have lost his.

"He caught me out by the lake one day and got me so worked up and agreeable, I let him have his way. I didn't like it one bit, that's for sure, but it was too late by the time I realized it weren't all kisses and sweet touches he was slipping beneath my skirts." She shrugged. "I guess my wedding night was easier for it, though not much. Davie ain't a patient man, but I got used to it. I boxed his ears a few times when he got too rough and he learnt. Now I like it most times, and I ain't ashamed to admit it like some are. It takes time, though."

"Time," Annalise echoed.

Sally noted the discomfort in her lady's eyes. "Once you're carrying his child, you'll have an excuse, I'm told. My Davie never let nothing stand in his way, but there's others what have used that reason." The new duchess's face seemed to have grown paler. "I guess you could look at it this way: It might be bad some in the beginning, but it's a lot worse when a man don't want to come to his wife's bed any more. When he's found something better elsewhere, if you get my meaning."

She spread the golden curls down Annalise's back. "I'll leave you now. Ring if you need me." She paused at the door. "Shall I have some wine sent up? To help your jitters?"

"No!" Annalise nearly shouted. "No wine!"

Stunned, Sally nodded and hurried from the room.

Annalise collapsed into the chaise, her knees trembling. She tried to prepare herself, to think of something convincing to say should Bryson come to her room, but there were no good ways to argue with a man who spoke only when he chose.

For an hour she watched the connecting door, tense with waiting, her nerves nearly jumping out of her skin every time she heard a sound, but it remained closed. Exhausted, she lay her head on her arm and finally drifted off to sleep. She awoke to the sensation of falling, and flailed her hands about. Strong arms tightened around her and she was pulled into a solid chest.

He had come.

Bryson had her under her knees and neck, and was carrying her like a child into his chamber. Her mind groggy from sleep, she muttered her discontent, but none of the scathing remarks she had practiced would surface. She was too tired and disoriented to rail at him just yet.

Bryson lowered his new bride slowly to her feet in front of the hearth and watched the flames turn her flesh golden, watched the outline of her body take shape through the sheer gown. Her hair was unbound, and he pushed the silken locks back over her shoulder. Her breasts stood high and chilled against the diaphanous fabric, and her arms came up quickly to hide herself from him.

As if she would ever be allowed that now.

They were wed, bound unto death. Rumor had it that the Duke of Marchfield, of one of England's most powerful families, had fallen head over heels for a village girl. Some were calling it tragically poetic.

He grabbed her wrists and pulled her arms out to her

sides, marveling at the perfection of her form, the beauty of her small waist and slender hips.

She tried to twist away but her gestures were sluggish from sleep, as he had planned. She was his wife and he would not spend another cold night alone, but neither would he have her screaming the castle down upon him and upsetting the guests. Her breathing grew shallow as panic crept in; her cheeks flushed with color. He had hoped to calm her by the fire first, but she had already set herself against him. He swept her up and went to the bed. With one arm, he stripped the covers back, then lay her in middle.

"No!" She rose up only to meet the flat of his hand on her chest. He wore a robe that gaped at the neck. She could see the taut muscles of his chest, the fine light hair that tapered down until it disappeared beneath the sash. "No!" she repeated. "I don't—"

He pushed her back down, then moved his hand to her mouth. "Shhhh," he commanded. He tugged the sash at his waist with one hand and shrugged out of the robe. It fell to the floor with a soft, ominous sound. He was naked beneath, and Annalise squeezed her eyes shut and made a terrible sound against his hand. He crawled in beside her, cradled her, and pressed his face into her hair.

His breath was warm, contrarily sending chills across her flesh. "Y-you mustn't," she stammered. "I'm with child and it could damage—"

His hand went back to her mouth, light but definite, and his eyes bored into hers with a severe, unreadable expression.

Annalise lay like a statue, her heart racing, waiting for
the struggle to begin. She could feel the heat and
strength of him pressed to her, the heavy weight of his
thigh covering her hip, the thick weight of his desire
against the side of her buttock. His hand covered her
mouth and his forearm lay solid against her breastbone.
He would ravish her now and, as before, she would be
helpless against his power and determination.

She swallowed back tears and pleaded against his
palm, "Think of the child. Think—"

He pressed harder, until naught but garbled sounds
came from her lips. He exhaled heavily and dropped his
face back into the hollow at her shoulder. His breath
sighed over her in a warm weary sound.

Within minutes, his arms relaxed and she realized
there would be no struggle. Her husband was asleep.

Relief flooded her. She could hardly believe her good
fortune. Perhaps he cared for the child after all and did
not want to see it endangered by such heathenish
behavior. Perhaps he only wanted her by his side, to
know that she was not trying to escape. Perhaps the
experience had been as horrible for him as it had been
for her and he never wanted to repeat it again.

A touch of insecurity crept into her relief. Perhaps
he'd found "something better elsewhere."

The awful sounds woke her, though the thrashing
should have. Inarticulate groans, deep-throated and agonizing, came from his very soul. He flung his arm out
and caught her across the chest, emitting an animal

growl of frustration that chilled her to the core. Annalise sat up in bed and pulled her knees to her chest, watching him struggle with night demons, hurting for him in spite of her resentment.

The hearth had burned low and the room was cold. What was left of the burning embers gave off only a feeble light that cast his tortured face in twisted misery. He writhed in the bed linens, naked and powerful, yet helpless in the grip of something stronger. Annalise reached out and stroked his brow, finding it hard to hold onto anger or fear in the face of his terror.

For minutes he wrestled with the night, twisting and thrashing and groaning. True memories, Annalise wondered, or figments of an unbalanced mind? He arched back, his hands fisted, his chest rising as if he would break the invisible bonds holding him. Frightened, she touched his shoulder, then said his name.

"Bryson!"

He calmed immediately. It took only that.

She looked down at her hand, so small and pale against his darker skin, and felt it was somehow significant.

His eyes opened slowly, ravaged and suspicious. He lay very still, as if any sudden movement would doom him. A sheen of perspiration covered his chest.

"You had a bad dream," she whispered.

No, he'd had a bad reality.

He reached up and touched her arm. Her flesh was chilled; it pebbled further when he stroked her. He rolled swiftly from the bed and went to the hearth, then stirred the coals back to life. Adding another log, he watched the flames lick their way over the wood, devouring it. Fire had always fascinated him, but it was a gift now, a treasure too long denied. It soothed him, chasing away the memories as her voice and touch had.

He glanced back over his shoulder and found her huddled in the coverlet, her eyes averted. He had forgotten he was naked. He should consider her sensibilities but he had no heart for it, not when he was neither modest nor ashamed—not when he wanted her naked, as well.

"Do you have bad dreams often?" she asked.

He nodded but didn't look at her. He would not ravish her, not like before. But he wanted to be inside her, a part of her, her heat surrounding him like fire. He wanted the forgetfulness she could give him, to move with her and in her until there was no past or future, only now. He could think of little else.

He went back to the bed and saw her flinch when he crawled in under the counterpane. He touched her arms, so gentle she could not take offense, but she was already afraid and every movement seemed a threat. He continued stroking, running his finger lightly down her arm over her hand.

Her fingers twitched but she remained quiet, hoping he would do nothing more if she did not acknowledge him, like a young child hiding her eyes behind her hands and thinking the world cannot see her.

He ran one finger over each of hers, one at a time, between each one and then her thumb. He then traced back up to her wrist, over her forearm to the crease in her elbow, then her shoulder.

She knew what he was about. Though he would

cloak it in gentle, leisurely touches, she knew and it frightened her.

Her neck was soft, the skin tight when she swallowed. The air took on the musky scent of passion and fear, a quivering heat that surrounded them. He breathed it, and touched her face, then slowly, slowly, moved down her throat to her breast. Her heartbeat pounded beneath his hand, her breathing grew catchy. The lightest sheen of sweat covered her temples and her face tensed with dreadful anticipation.

He covered her with his palm and felt the strangled cry of desperation in the vibration of her chest. His hand moved softly, the smallest pressure, and her nipple tightened against his hand. Her eyes flew open, shocked, but dewy with unaccountable heat. He watched her struggle to understand and continued to move his palm slowly, so carefully, a sensuous circle taking her farther from fear.

She felt as if heat were rising inside her, as if her bones were melting. His touch was nonthreatening but it made her quiver nonetheless. She remembered the feelings from before, the heat and desperation, the grasping hunger, then pain and shame. She felt like she had been drugged again but knew that was not possible.

"What is happening to me?"

Her impassioned cry was his undoing.

He rolled her beneath him and captured her mouth, cursing himself for his lack of discipline, his animal hunger. With her, he was reduced to instinct alone, driven and uncontrollable. He had no sense of himself, no restraint. He shoved her nightrail up and pressed her knees apart, knowing she would hate him, unable to change his course. He grabbed her face in his hands, a plea in his eyes. Her own were enraged, and he pressed his cheek to hers so he would not have to bear her censor when he took her body.

By law he had the right but there was something immoral in his aggression. He tried to temper it but he was so lost with her. His thighs pushed hers apart and he entered her slowly, determined he would not brutalize her. She gasped and tried to shy away, but he knew she was not hurt this time. Her muscles contracted protectively, surrounding him, and sweat broke out on his brow as he tried to hold himself in check. He would not ravish her; he must not. His arms quivered from holding himself aloft, and he pushed himself to the hilt and went still, surrounded by her scent, held captive in her tight warmth.

Annalise cringed at his possession but she did not cry out. There was no terrible burn or rending pain, only discomfort and a heavy stretching fullness that confused her. She waited for the motion, his thrust and retreat that would cause her such distress, but he went still as death and her body waited in tense quiet, then began to expand and accept him. She turned her face away as a single tear caught in her lashes.

"Do you do this to punish me?"

He made an anguished sound and shook his head. Cupping her face, he turned her back. He kissed her mouth, then her eyelids, small penitent touches that she did not understand.

"Then why?"

He could not explain with or without words why he

must have her, why he was so helpless to stop himself from taking her. He had lived among mindless beasts for so long. Why, after finally escaping, had he become one?

Using every ounce of strength and dignity within him, he slid from her body and rolled to sit on the side of the bed, his face in his hands.

Annalise grabbed the sheet and pulled it to her breasts. Her hands trembled but inside she was hollow and achy. Staring at his broad back, she felt relieved and abandoned and incredibly sad. She touched his back. "Bryson . . ."

He shrugged her off. Didn't she understand that he had no defenses against her, no shame or nobility? One more touch and he would sling her to her back again and take her completely. One more touch and he would not be able to stop himself.

"Go!" he demanded in a gruff voice.

Scrambling from the bed, she went.

Chapter 19

MORNING DAWNED COLD AND DREARY. GRAY clouds choked the leaden sky and made the chill in the room unbearable. Annalise had added too much wood to the fire and it burned overhot, yet the warmth would not stay. She alternated between freezing and perspiring as she moved near the hearth and away, trying to find a comfortable spot.

There was no comfort to be had.

She had left her husband's bed on their wedding night. It was ignoble and unkind, and she knew it.

She could hear her father's voice quoting Scripture: "Wives submit to your husbands . . ." She had tossed and turned in her own cold bed, lonely and guilty and resentful. "What about the one that says 'Husbands love your wives?' " she whispered. "Am I bound when he is not?"

Morning brought no relief, only the vision of Bryson's

tortured face as he had withdrawn from her body, the harshness of his voice as he commanded her to go.

Her front was well baked. She turned her chilly backside to the fire. Married only a day and already she was a wicked wife who didn't know her duty to her husband. She flung herself from the fire and marched to Bryson's room. Without so much as a knock, she walked right in and caught him at the washstand, scraping whiskers from his jaw. He was fully dressed in buff riding breeches, high boots, and lawn shirt, and was handsome enough to steal a maiden's heart. He made a hissing sound when he nicked his chin.

"I thought a valet was supposed to do that for you."

He turned and gave her a cold look.

Heat staining her cheeks, she twisted her fingers together and took a deep breath for courage. "I've come to tell you that I know my duty as your wife and am willing to perform it no matter how much it inconveniences me."

His eyes flared, a frigid ice that chilled her to the bone. Then they narrowed menacingly. He pointed to the bed, a dangerous challenge in his eyes.

"Now?" she squeaked. "I meant tonight, after dark, when . . . *decent* folk are abed."

He only kept his finger pointed, a dare for her to prove her words. The color left her face and she stomped her foot like a child.

"It's full day!"

He turned his back on her.

She wanted to hit him, pummel him like a bloody fishwife. She also wanted to rail foul words and throw things and pound his broad, arrogant back. She had just been dismissed as a spineless charlatan and knew it.

"But daylight! You cannot expect . . ."

He expected nothing, and that was the worst of it.

"Fine," she stated, as arrogant as he, and marched back to her own room. But it wasn't fine at all, and she didn't know how to make it right when she wanted no part of him or his daytime demand. She made her bed herself, not wanting Sally to know she had slept there. The embarrassment she felt when she had mounted the stairs on her wedding night was natural. What she felt now was not. When the light rap came at her chamber door, she tiptoed back into Bryson's room.

She ignored his strange look. Let him think what he would. She would not have the servants know that they were not behaving as man and wife.

"Your Grace?" It was Sally's voice, muffled through the adjoining door. "I've left you a breakfast cart. Ring when you want me to remove it."

"Thank you," Annalise called back, grateful she would not have to face the servant's experienced eyes.

Etienne filled his breakfast plate from the sideboard. Silver and crystal sparkled on starched white linen. Servants hovered, ever ready to please. Since his youth, he had been treated as a guest in this house. First because he had delighted the duchess with his wit, she had said. Later because his brother had become her lover. He hated the *Illuminati* for what they would do to this house and its treasures, but it could not be helped. He hated more the privilege that would never be his by accident of birth.

He sighed. This meal would be one of his last here. Under the cover of darkness, the elegant whore from Rosalie's had come to his room, her seductive body offered like a sacrifice upon the altar of his desire. The time had come, she had told him. They were ready to finish it here. His plan was in place, he had assured her, but it might take days to complete.

Bryson and Annalise moved through the next two days in a silent battle of wills, edgy and resentful when they happened upon each other in private, falsely cheerful when in the presence of others. Bryson spent hours at the stables where Annalise wanted to be, working with the horses, taming Silva with the silent care and companionship that Annalise had never had enough idle hours for.

Like children after a spat, they were lonely but too hard-headed to be the first to give in. Annalise finally got so bored with the castle, she went to the stable anyway, knowing she might encounter him there but beyond caring. She had never been so idle in her life and the inactivity was wearing.

She heard the ruckus when she neared the larger building. The scream of a horse rent the chilly air along with several shouts from the stablehands to each other. She picked up her skirts and ran the rest of the way, fearful of what she would find. Darkness hit her when she entered the long shelter. It took a moment for her eyes to adjust to the gloom. Dust motes floated in the streamers of sunlight pouring through the few windows, but the noise and shouts were not coming from this quiet hall. She dashed down the long corridor lined with stalls, looking for Silva, finding only a few restless mares and geldings. She raced for the back coral where even now she could hear the piercing cry of a horse in distress.

She burst into blinding sunlight and almost toppled Martin. "What is happening?" she cried, frantic. "What are you doing to Silva?"

Color rose in Martin's cheeks. "Oh . . . Your Grace," he hedged, shamefaced and tongue-tied.

But Annalise had finally recognized what was happening. A mare was in the small pen, roped so she couldn't get away, and Silva had mounted her from behind. Done, he pulled away, parts of him grotesquely huge and glistening in the sunlight. The mating was barbaric and natural, and if she had not been so embarrassed she would have stayed to stare. Instead, she turned away and dashed back inside the stable, her cheeks hot, tears of embarrassment stinging her eyes.

Bryson caught her near the entrance, but she had her face in her hands and would not look at him. He pulled her into his chest.

"Let me go," she said wretchedly. "What an ignorant, green girl they must think I am to carry on so!"

"Just innocent," he whispered into her hair.

She shook her head against him. "Nay, don't speak to me of innocence when it is merely stupidity. I carry your child, I know the way of things."

"Ah, but how well?"

She heard the dark challenge in his voice, and something newer—the faintest hint of humor. It was startling and stirring and set her heart fluttering. She peeked up at him beneath her lashes, a rosy stain on her cheeks. "Well enough to get me compromised."

His eyes grew sultry. "Not well at all if that one mistake is your judge."

"Mistake?" she said, offended. "Is that what you call drugging then ravishing me?"

He laid his palm along her jaw. His voice was whisper-quiet, for her ears only. "You were drugged but not by me. I take full responsibility for the ravishment though." He looked in her eyes, laid himself bare. "I could not help myself, Annalise. I am powerless in your arms."

His words, his admission, rolled over her like warm honey. She loved his voice, his meaning, the frightening heat in his eyes. She felt her heartbeat stumble, then race on. "You have never been powerless."

"I have. I am," he said, and lowered his mouth to hers. The kiss was rich with promise, potent with desire. "With you I am a boy, untried and fumbling."

She speared her fingers through his hair and clung, feeling the sharp new pangs of regret and something more, something deeper and more lasting. Stunned by his admission, she felt the answer within herself, the first awakening. She had hated him and pitied him and cared for him. But this was deeper and stronger, an everlasting bond that united them.

"Bryson," she said against his lips. She recognized his longing and need in the grip of his hands; they mirrored her own. When fear rose, she kissed him deeper, burying it beneath the wonder of desire. Her heart clamored for him, her flesh craved his touch. She could no more deny herself this physical union than she could deny herself air, water, or food. Everything necessary for life was suddenly in his touch.

When he pulled back, she was breathless. His own gaze was predatory as a wolf's. "Tonight then?"

Shy, she dropped her forehead to his chest and accepted the challenge. "Aye, tonight."

Annalise dressed with care for the evening meal. In scarlet velvet and black slippers, she looked like a duchess. But an impish smile took the seriousness from her attempt at refined elegance. Mary Greer had been invited to dine and surprised Annalise by being almost animated by the end of the meal. The fact that Etienne flirted outrageously with her had something to do with it, but Annalise was still shocked by the way Mary Greer blossomed under his attention.

The night was sweet with the crisp scent of evergreen and cold wind. Etienne suggested a stroll in the garden, and there seemed no reason to forgo such a pleasure when there were heavy cloaks to keep out the chill. Bryson chafed at the extended evening, when he would rather have gone to his chamber and coaxed Annalise to fulfill her earlier agreement. But Mary Greer could not walk out with Etienne alone, so Bryson and Annalise gathered cloaks and muffs and strolled arm in arm behind them, finding a peace unknown in their turbulent relationship before this moment.

The moon rose higher, a bright, sharp sickle in the dark sky, and they strolled farther from the castle. Bryson hung back as Etienne and Mary Greer strolled to the stone pond, pulling Annalise behind a tall hawthorn. He traced a ringlet from her crown, down her neck to the tip of her breast where it lay. She made a soft sound and he let his fingers linger and watched the heat rise in her cheeks, watched her eyes grow lazy-lidded with a mixture of confusion and desire. He put his face alongside hers and touched her temple with his lips. "Soon," he whispered. "I cannot wait much longer."

She took a heavy breath. "For what?"

"For you."

His lips traced the contour of her face to her mouth, his kiss light, airy as a fantasy, so tempting she was forced to lean into him to make it real. His breath mingled with hers, then his tongue, then the full devouring mouth. He groaned and pulled her against him, wishing they were alone in his room, without the restriction of clothing and inhibitions.

She said his name self-consciously and he pulled back, sliding his hand safely to her waist.

The first hint of foreboding struck, a small tingling up Bryson's spine, that fine edge between suspicion and knowledge. Etienne had returned with Mary Greer, though he'd been given leave to be alone with her. Mary Greer's eyes were humid and lovestruck, so Bryson knew it was not she who had demanded they come back.

He pulled Annalise tight against him.

"The night is chill, and a warm fire awaits," Etienne said loudly.

Something flashed in Etienne's eyes, triumph perhaps. Too late Bryson turned to look behind him.

The world went black.

❧ Chapter 20

France

Death had come to France. The air was still
and dry, too quiet for a city that had once prided itself
on the jocularity of its citizens. The sun shone red in the
west, red as the blood choking the fly-infested gutters.

Annalise pressed back against the carriage seat, her
stomach queasy. She had been taken by two men, while
Bryson lay bleeding at her feet and Mary Greer cried out
for help. Etienne had made as to run after the thieves
but, once away from the castle, she realized that he was
one of them and had planned the whole thing.

She pressed her hand to her abdomen, feeling nausea
roll in waves, with the turning of the carriage wheels.
She had always thought of Paris as a romantic city, one
she would have loved to stroll arm in arm with a gallant
suitor. Such important dreams, she had thought once.
They were silly and fanciful now in a city where the
smell of death curdled the very air. She tried breathing

through her mouth, but the taste of it was there, as well, sharp and coppery on her tongue.

Ahead, the infamous guillotine come into view, its blade ready. Baskets lined the base, smeared with the legacy of centuries—the heritage of France reduced to an ugly stain. The revolutionaries had certainly found equality. Noblemen bled the same bright red as commoners.

A crowd gathered, their faces so like the ones Annalise knew back home. A baker, a cobbler, a black-smith. But their eyes were different. Lit by the fires of insurrection, some blazed with unholy bloodlust. Others, the worst ones of all, shone with nothing. They had seen so many executions they were numb and unmoved.

Annalise understood the plight of the common man and his resentment of an arrogant gentry. But she would never understand this. Mr. Guillotine's machine should have been reserved for murderers, traitors, and men like the ones who now held her hostage. She looked at Eti-enne, bitter because he had answered none of her ques-tions, and confusion was like a rope growing tighter and tighter around her throat.

The carriage slowed to a crawl, and her breath purled out in shallow puffs. She didn't know if they had brought her here to watch or to die. She shuddered with a violent take when the vehicle stopped completely. Would she, who had so aspired to become an English lady, now die a French death because her dreams had come true?

The child within her fluttered, the faintest movement, but not her imagination. Heartsick at his uncertain future, she draped her arm across her middle as a shield, a comfort.

Etienne's face was cast in shadow, an unforgiving profile that let nothing touch him. She could never have imagined that the man who had laughed and teased so graciously over the past evening, the man who had wooed Mary Greer so sweetly, could be so diabolical.

Sensing her scrutiny, he turned. "Do not think to ask for help here," he warned. "No one in France has sympathy for an English aristocrat. Even if they did, they would not risk their own necks to show it."

Annalise looked at him with pity. "Where are your sympathies, Etienne?"

He shrugged elegantly. "With me, of course."

She shook her head. "You would have me think you coarse and without remorse, but I do not believe it."

His eyes grew hard, his smile brittle. "Believe what you like, madame. You may believe it all the way to the blade, if they so decide."

She cringed at his cruelty. "Who are 'they'? What could possibly be the reason behind all this?"

He smiled at her choice of words. " 'Reason' itself." He turned to face her fully, tired of her pitiable stares and gross confusion. "War will soon be declared between France and Britain. I am involved with the *Illuminati*. We work toward Britain's defeat. France will fight and win and take republicanism and reason into yet another country. But first the country must be weakened, rotted from within. A man waits in each of the great houses in England. Our sect will take their fortunes and Britain will crumble."

She understood then what he had not said. For years evil men who prided themselves on intellect had been working to bring about the downfall of Marchfield and other British dynasties. From Marchfield they had taken first its duke, then one by one the heirs who had not succumbed to natural illnesses. How many other suspicious deaths over the years had been disregarded? The absolute horror of it overwhelmed her, and she feared she would be sick.

"Etienne," she whispered, "how can you turn me over to such depraved people?"

"To save my own skin, of course. I feel no animosity toward you, Annalise. I have a job to do; that is all."

"And Greer? Will you let them have her, as well?"

He flinched slightly. "She has nothing to do with this. She will not be harmed."

How little he knew of true human nature, when he'd seen only the twisted side for so long. "Everything you do to me will affect her."

A large man robed in a monk's frock approached the carriage. He carried his heavy bulk with authority, but his presence did not inspire reverence in Annalise. He pulled open the door and glanced at her face, then her belly. He smiled at Etienne. "You have done well, Citizen."

Annalise's mouth went dry. "What do you want with me?"

"You? Nothing, my dear. Are you feeling well? Has Etienne treated you with consideration?"

Bewildered by his gracious demeanor, it took her a

moment to respond. "I have not been harmed but I do not understand what you want with me."

"Only to help you see reason," he said gently. "We have the utmost care for you in mind." He took her hand in his. "England will fall but you need not. You are common-born, like the rest of us. If you can understand our ways, the perfect sense of things, I am certain you will want to join us." He paused. "You are not with child, are you? We would not want to do anything to hurt—"

She seized the opportunity. "Yes, I am with child. I am feeling quite ill, in fact."

His eyes narrowed in satisfaction, and all congeniality left his voice. "How inconvenient."

By his look, his tone, she knew she had given him the information he had come seeking. She closed her eyes to keep from fainting.

The monk opened the door and called a destination to the driver as he hefted his bulk inside. Settling his robes around him, he smiled triumphantly. "It begins."

They traveled the length of the day, their conversation full of ideological rhetoric. Annalise nodded and listened as if interested. A brave or rebellious front was foolish in light of her disadvantage. If she could convince them that she welcomed their ideas and ways, she might spare her life and that of her child.

Near noon they stopped in a small village to make inquiries. A man in drab black clothing approached them within the hour. He was harried-looking and carried a surgeon's case. Thin and pale, he needed assistance climbing into the carriage. He glanced nervously at Annalise, his beaked nose and small eyes lending him the appearance of an anxious vulture. She wanted to scream at him for joining these horrid men. She wanted to beg his help, but she sensed there would be no aid from anyone associated with Etienne and the monk beside her.

Dusk fell upon the valley, creating mysterious vacant spaces between the forest trees. Disembodied night sounds began, lonely things that echoed from the grayness. The hours stretched into a sameness broken only by an occasional bump or curve in the road. The men with her spoke little now, and then only in French.

They descended a sharp hill and finally pulled up before a sprawling tomblike structure that looked old as time. Made of stone, the building spread out in several directions. It was an odd place, cold yet peaceful in the moonlight. The men alighting from the carriage seemed intrusive upon its serenity. A hooded figure slid from the shadows, a candle in his hand.

"This way please."

Annalise was ushered inside, then down a long dark corridor that lead to a stout wooden door. It was locked. The monk that greeted them at the entrance took a ring of keys from his waist and opened the lock. A set of narrow stone steps loomed before her, swallowed up by darkness. The monk gently pushed Annalise to take the stairway.

She put a hand out and grappled with the wall. "You must help me," she whispered. "Those men mean me harm."

He only gave her a kind smile and nudged again. She took the first stair to please him, then pleaded again. "If you truly are a man of God, you will help me—" The stench hit her then and she recoiled. "What . . . ?"

Strong hands banded her arms immediately, an unbreakable grip. He spoke pleasantly in French, as one would to a child, all the while forcing her down the steps. His voice was consoling but his hands were steel grips on her arms.

"Where are you taking me?" she cried, but he only continued moving her down the narrow staircase. Moans came next, hideous tortured sounds that seemed to swirl on the darkness. Annalise dug her heels in but the hooded man continued to press her forward, closer to the terrible groans.

She began to buck and twist but the downward descent was impossible to stop. "Where am I?" she cried. "I demand to know at once!"

"St. Bertram's," the man said in heavily accented English. "Never fear. We'll do what we can for you here."

But his voice, though kind, was despondent and un-convincing. The monks had come to expect that nothing but prayer could be done for the lunatics sent to them.

Mary Greer stood wringing her hands, her face pale as death. "This is it? This is the only thing they left?" She held up a note, cryptic in its message.

Bryson nodded. He was already stuffing a sack with a change of clothing and food.

"Etienne is behind this?" she whispered in tears.

Bryson nodded again, but did not look up. He could not bear to see the pain of betrayal on her face.

"I must go with you, then," she added quietly.

He swung around to glare at her.

"It must be a mistake, but if it is not, he will listen to me."

"Are you insane?" he snarled.

She jumped at his voice but did not shy away. "Annalise was right, then, you can speak when you choose."

He finished stuffing provisions into the cloth sack, then tied it closed.

She moved forward and touched his sleeve. "Annalise believes in you, so must I. Etienne is . . . misguided. I think I can help him see logic."

Bryson drew a harsh breath. "If he harms Annalise, I will kill him."

She cringed at the cold, calm fury in his eyes. "I need to try."

He threw the sack over his shoulder. "He will destroy you, as well."

"That may be," she replied, "but you cannot stop me from trying."

"I can."

"If I must make my own way, I am doomed from the outset."

"You are doomed either way." He sighed, beyond desperate worrying about Annalise. "This is not the time for the timid mouse to become a tiger, Greer."

Foreboding crept through her. "I feel no courage at

all and wish such histrionics were not necessary. But I must do this. It is like a calling from God, an instinct impossible to ignore." She smiled sadly, then touched his sleeve. "It is what Annalise felt when she first came to this castle to meet you."

His voice roughened with pain. "See where it led her?"

Eleanor swept into the room, a small valise in her hand. "I have summoned the carriage and an army of outriders. We will—"

Bryson gave her a murderous look. "I am beset with valiant females."

A breath hissed between her teeth. "Finally you speak. I gather you have been capable all along and only wished to torture me."

He said nothing, just looked at her with abhorrence.

"We caught one of them in the garden and know who they are now. Even your bastard half brother is involved." Her voice began to tremble. "They killed my family," she said bitterly. "Everyone but you is gone and they will make certain you are dead within the week." Her hand shook on the valise she carried, and for the first time he saw tears in her eyes. "I will see them in Hell before I'll let them take another child from me!"

Bryson ground his teeth against her fear and pain. "Stay and help me here, then. If I find Annalise, I will need a ship ready on French shores to bring me back to England. Take your coin and your connections, Mother, and see how many boats it will buy you."

She nodded, a chilling desperation in her eyes. "I will have a fleet waiting for you," she promised.

He shrugged into his coat, then threw the sack over his shoulder. "See that you do." He paused. "And make certain Greer does not follow."

Stale, sour bodies dashed for the four corners of the room when Annalise was dragged into their midst. They huddled there, watchful and afraid, some clinging to each other, some hiding within themselves.

"The time has come!" an old woman screeched, and lunged at Annalise.

She ducked and cried out, taking the impact of the hit on her shoulder. She spun around to see if the woman would attack again but the crone had already scurried into a corner, burying her head in her knees.

Annalise gulped and clasped her trembling hands together. She studied the room to get her bearings but could find no means of escape. It was dark and dank, the smell of urine and unwashed bodies suffocating. A torch burned high, out of reach, but kept the deeper corners in shadow. Creeping into a vacant spot near the stairs, Annalise sat and stared at the people surrounding her. Some stared back, others did not.

A woman in rags wandered aimlessly, another laughed for no reason at all. Another crouched against the cold stone wall and rocked to some internal humming. Muttering to herself, a middle-age woman began a graceful ballet across the straw-littered floor. A toothless man joined her until she screeched that he had no rhythm. Chastised, he crept back to his corner to cry like a berated child.

Annalise's heart fell. To her horror, she saw pieces of Bryson here, not in their madness but in their vacant desolate eyes, in their hopelessness, in their need for love and freedom. How had he endured six years in their midst? How had he come home stronger and more sane than many men she knew?

These desolate people needed sunshine and fresh air. Long walks to build body and spirit. It was no wonder Bryson craved trips to the lake and the stables, anything away from the four walls. Annalise cursed Eleanor for such depravity. To send her own child into this Hell was an abomination. There were hospitals in England, private retreats, as well, where Bryson could have maintained some semblance of dignity. What Eleanor had done to him was unforgivable.

Annalise didn't think she could ever look on the woman again without seeing these dazed faces, smelling their foul stench, feeling the sick hatred that coursed through her at this moment.

She only prayed she would be given the chance.

She understood why Bryson had given up speech. Here he would not have been heard. In silence, he was disregarded, and he could listen and absorb and remain separate. In silence, he could move about unnoticed and learn to survive.

Given voice, he would have died trying to plead his sanity to deaf ears.

Too late she wanted to hold him and shield him. Too late she wanted to tell him she understood. Too late she wanted to love him and care for him and give him solace for the stolen years. And she wanted to learn from his strength.

Cold and forsaken, she huddled in a corner and prayed for help.

They came for her within the hour. Two men in rough clothing, certainly not priests or monks. They dragged her to a small, spare room.

"What am I doing here?" she asked. "Please, tell me why you have brought me here."

The men only exchanged glances and moved her toward a table. There was something ominous about the scarred surface, something forbidding in the bare walls. It was a sterile place, not an office or bedchamber or dining room. One man pulled straps from his pocket, then nodded to the other.

He gripped her by both arms and picked her up, then sat her atop the table. His quick motion jarred the breath from her, and she doubled over in reaction. He pulled her back upright and she began to struggle. The motion sent pain streaking through her abdomen. She gritted her teeth against it and fought harder. But his hands were meaty shackles, his strength thrice her own. With a grunt, he pushed her down onto her back.

Her screams were nothing in this place of madness as they strapped her wrists down, her pleas for help falling on deaf ears as they shoved her legs apart and strapped her ankles to the corners of the table.

A sob congealed in her throat. They were large and foul-smelling, hired thugs with little intelligence behind their dull eyes. Even if she spoke French, she didn't think she could reason with them. Their loyalty was bought. The strap at her wrist gave a little when she tugged, the old leather cracking along the edge. But it was not enough to gain her even a particle of freedom.

"Please," she begged, bucking against her restraints.

They ignored her. Finishing their task, they stepped back and stared at their handiwork. She could not fathom that they wanted to ravish her. The men were brutish but they had not leered at her, or looked her way with anything other than their instructions in mind. In truth, they would not meet her eyes at all.

Spread upon the table, demoralized, she cried at them for cowards and knaves, then pleaded with them again to help her escape.

"My husband is a rich man," she cried, sobbing. "He will pay you handsomely."

It did no good, not her promises or threats or bribes. If they understood her, they gave no sign of it. They only made certain her bonds were secure, then left the room, taking the candle with them.

In the darkness the sounds were keener. The scurry of rats, the scratching of cockroaches. A long, low wail rolled in a distant corridor, then faded, followed by maniacal laugher. It was icy cold. She shivered, unable to wrap her arms around herself for warmth. She pulled at her bonds until her wrists were raw but it did no good. The leather was worn but held. Still she continued to tug until her hands grew slippery with her own blood.

Not the room nor the cries nor the darkness frightened her overmuch. It was the low cramps in her belly that made her mouth go dry and the sound of approaching footsteps that sent terror through her heart. The door opened with a grinding creak and in stepped the feeble surgeon.

He did not look at her, just lit the torches in the wall sconces with his candle. He laid his case upon a side table.

"What are you going to do to me?" Annalise asked. "Why are you here?"

He opened his case. Candlelight glimmered off metal instruments. He took several, then laid them between her legs on the table. Never looking at her face, he began shoving her skirts up.

Annalise screamed like a madwoman and kept on screaming until she was forced to draw breath. With every ounce of voice and energy, she yelled and twisted and fought against her bonds.

The doctor gave her an exasperated look, then shoved one hand inside her and felt her belly with the other. He then gave her a baleful look. "They will not let you bear the child," he said in broken English. He turned aside, then took a cloth and splashed liquid into it.

Annalise could smell the pungent aroma even before he turned back. "No!" she cried. She pulled on her wrist and heard the frayed leather rip. She jerked harder. The doctor ignored her struggles and advanced, the soaked cloth held aloft. Annalise knew if he got it over her nose and mouth she would be helpless. He spoke something in French, then lowered it toward her face.

With a scream of fury, she reared up. The leather broke loose from the table. Her fist caught him in the face, bloodying his nose. He staggered back, then fell, too stunned to catch himself. While he was struggling to stand she unhooked her other wrist, then pulled one foot free. Intimidated by her mad fury, he turned to the door to call for help.

Annalise freed her other foot and climbed from the table. She grabbed up the long, sharp instrument he had meant to use on her and hid it in the folds of her skirt.

He could not risk one of the monks coming, and called for one of the henchmen in a civil tone. When no one answered, he cursed softly and stepped out into the hall. Annalise slid around the end of the table and moved in behind him. When the doctor turned to close the door, she rushed him. With amazing speed, his arms rose to deflect the blow. They fought over the lethal metal, scrabbling like street brawlers. The doctor was surprisingly strong for such a frail-looking man, and Annalise knew she was loosing ground with each minute passed.

She swung her knee up hard and caught him in the groin. With a shocked look, he lost balance and lunged forward. She flung her hands up to protect herself, and the metal instrument pierced the base of his throat. His forward lurch sent it plunging right through to the other side. His eyes glazed over in bafflement before he keeled over into a heap.

The world receded. Annalise understood its existence only from a distance. She felt herself falling, drifting down toward the cold floor, her skirts billowing out over the doctor's inert figure. Her head hit the wall, then everything went black with pain.

For hours she lay in his blood, grieving.

The cramping pain was still in her body, but it was distant, naught compared to the anguish in her soul. Someone had found the doctor and her on the floor. A mad rush of whispered curses and accusations followed, then they simply dragged the old man away and locked her in a cell.

Her head pounded; her stomach rolled. She was afraid she was dying, not physically, but in her heart. She had killed a man to save her unborn child and felt no guilt. Yet the pain was there still, beating with the agony in her head, with the squeezing constrictions in her belly.

Bryson, I'm so sorry.

He would come for her. Into this hellish place he would come and be murdered. They waited for him like vultures, and there was nothing she could do to protect him. She lay upon the cold floor, dry-eyed and still, her soul crushed beneath the weight of an impossible suffering. She was losing the baby; she could feel it in the squeezing cramps, the lowering pain. She could not breathe, she could not think. She only existed in excruciating fear for her child and Bryson and wished for a numbness that would not come.

Sometime near midnight, a man entered the cell. She watched with dull eyes while he approached. He spoke in warning and censure but she did not understand his French. He moved in closer, cautious, smarter, and started pulling her skirt up.

His intent hit her, and she screeched suddenly, lashing

out at him with feet and fists and claws. Screaming, she curled in upon herself and wrapped her arms around her knees.

He backed away from her fury and shut the cell door behind him. "Blood's everywhere," he said to whomever waited in the darkness. "I think the doctor got to her before she got him."

Satisfied, the man in the shadows nodded. "Come then. Drag her down there, to the last cell."

The huge man reentered the cell with caution and caught her up in a suffocating hold, then carried her down the corridor. He shoved her into a dark room and locked the door behind him. They left her in blackness, shivering in the doctor's drying blood. When she realized they did not care whether she died in her own filth or lived to be executed later, she curled into a corner to rest. A bitter peace settled in her heart.

She would not die for their sake.

She would live to destroy them.

Chapter 21

Bryson knew where they had taken her. It was the one place they knew he could not go, the one place that would take his strength, sear his mind. In the deepest, most vulnerable parts of himself, he knew he could not survive another encounter with St. Bertram's. But he had no choice, and his entire being rebelled with a physical shaking as he rode the sandy hills that stretched inland, the moon his only light.

Spiky grass crunched beneath his horse's hooves. The sea crashed behind him, growing fainter and fainter still as he rode deeper into the hills. Land began to buffet the sound until only a stillness remained and the lingering scent of salt air on his clothing. Fog drifted in, hovering over like ghostly shadows, distorting the moon-washed path. Bryson continued through it, armed and alert, pressing forward on a prayer that he could endure.

He stopped several times during the night to rest and

get his bearings. His eyes were gritty from lack of sleep, and he dozed when he could but never for long. Fear for Annalise kept his mind racing, driving him forward even in the darkest part of night, when he and the horse could press forward only along a stretch of well-traveled road and the weak light of a half-moon.

Dawn spread over the horizon, revealing familiar terrain. His mind sharpened with hatred.

He entered the forest, pungent with smell of evergreen and winter decay, and sat still as death while puffs of condensation frosted the air with each rattling breath he took. His fists tightened on the reins. He could do this, he must, but his mind shied like a skittish stallion from the idea of drawing nearer.

The taste of bile clung to his throat, fear manifest. Sweat made his hands clammy inside his gloves. He hung back, immobile, a coward clinging to the cover of trees.

The forest brightened with the sun, revealing an outside world little known to him over the years of his incarceration. Through the trees, beyond a large field, stood the old stone priory. It was little changed in a few months' time, but it seemed as if years had passed. Safe at this distance, he saw it with clarity now and felt his chest constrict. It was nothing more than an old abandoned retreat. Like a bastard child the church had forgotten to support, the monks were old, its strength old, its usefulness a thing of the past. Prayer brought the sun up and saw it down each day, but the inhabitants of St. Bertram's were so far removed from the heartbeat of

France, their petitions went out by rote rather than for the needs of the people.

A shudder moved through him. He could have escaped this ill-guarded place. Had he not so succumbed to the horror of his confinement, he could have gained freedom long before he was removed. Ill for so long, then consumed in the darkness surrounding him, he had not seen how pitifully inept a prison it was, good for nothing but stretching out the years for its elderly monks. The reality sickened him, and he was forced to push the feelings aside. He needed his wits now as never before.

He concealed his horse deep within a copse of trees, then crossed the stubbled field toward the well and the priest who worked to draw water there.

"Father Armand."

The priest turned, an inquisitive smile on his face that changed rapidly to wonder. "*Sacre!* It cannot be!"

Bryson put a finger to his mouth. "Quiet, please." He moved in closer. "Did they bring someone in during the night?"

The father thought, then nodded. "*Oui*, a young woman suffering from delusions. She thinks she is British royalty. Obviously she is not safe in Paris spouting such nonsense, so she was brought here. I've not had a chance to see her yet." His hands folded together, prayerful and joyous. "You are a sight for these tired eyes! So healthy and recovered. God has surely answered my prayers."

Bryson nodded. "The woman is my wife, Father.

There is a terrible conspiracy going on within these walls."

Shock flooded the old priest's face. "How can this be? Such a thing here in God's house?"

"There is much you do not know, but it can wait. First I must find her."

"Come, then," Father Armand said. "I will see what I can do."

Bryson stopped at the priest's benevolent voice. He remembered it too well from before. "I am not mad, Father, you must believe me. I have not come on a foolish mission."

Pity softened the priest's gaze. "No, of course not. I daresay you would never return here if it were not a matter of life and death."

Bryson breathed easier. "I will need a place to hide. They are expecting me, I think."

Father Armand often helped take food down, so no one was suspicious when he gathered a basket of bread and cheese for the "poor souls" below. Accompanied by a tall, silent monk, he unlocked the door and descended the steep staircase. He knew none of the priests of his order were doing Satan's work within the priory walls, but someone was, if Bryson could be believed, and he meant to find out who had desecrated these halls.

Stepping into the common area sent nausea reeling though Bryson's belly. He took his breaths slowly, evenly, to keep from being overwhelmed by the memories. The stench wafted over him, a net drawing tighter.

The despair was pungent and tangible, thick as mist on the moors. Like a sickness, the hopelessness spread from the inmates, contaminating all it touched. Sweat broke out on his palms and he clenched his fists and kept reminding himself he was not one of them.

He searched the common area slowly, methodically, but a frantic pulse beat inside him. He must get Annalise away from here before the foulness touched her. Mindless Mara crept forward and plucked at his robe. He contained the old instinct to shove her away. She was naught but a lost soul, needy and desperate. With a hand that trembled, he reached out and stroked her filthy hair, offering what he had not been capable of giving when he was here, knowing it was not enough. She made a cooing sound and lay her head against his side.

He closed his eyes briefly and listened finally to her words. She sang a child's song in a woman's voice, her eyes blank. Why had he not heard her all those years, why had she been such a threat? He patted her shoulder and moved her away from the drafty area to a spot that kept more warmth.

An old man with a thin, frail body cackled from the corner, his toothless face skeletal-looking in the bad light. He muttered dire warnings in French, then something that sounded like German, and Bryson wondered if there was any truth to his words. Did this man have a story to tell, a warning to heed, or had he been disregarded so long his words were only disoriented ramblings indeed? The old man had taken off most of his clothes. His bony flesh looked ghostly in the bad light.

Father Armand found a threadbare woolen blanket

and covered him. The old man's hand lashed out and grabbed the priest's wrist in a surprisingly strong grip. "Have they infiltrated France yet? They are sly, you must beware."

Shaking his head, Father Armand disengaged his arm and left a goodly portion of the food, them motioned Bryson to his side. "There is no one new here."

A sense of foreboding washed over Bryson as they left the man behind and ventured out of the dingy, torchlit room to a corridor black as pitch. Making their way by the light of a lone candle and feel, they combed the cells where the more dangerous patients were kept.

Bryson kept his breathing even, but his pulse beat frantically. He had been locked away here too many times for his violence. Even now he could feel the walls closing in on him, stealing his breath and his thoughts, maddening him further. Even protected in his monk's disguise, he felt naked and vulnerable. He concentrated on each cell, forcing himself to look in, keeping Annalise's face ever before him.

Halfway down the corridor, the priest found a woman he did not recognize. "Come quickly," he whispered.

Bryson crept closer and almost recoiled. They had put Annalise in with Delphi, a keen diabolical decision. Pleas for help would never be heard over Delphi's screeching.

"Annalise," he said softly.

She came awake slowly, painfully. Her eyes were stark, her face pale as death, her gown covered in blood.

"*Mon Dieu,*" Father Armand hissed. "Can you walk, child?"

The compassion in his voice and eyes called to her, but the monk who had first taken her down the stairs had been kind, too. She pressed back against the wall, trembling.

"Please," he coaxed. "I mean you no harm. I have come with your husband, see?"

Bryson pushed back his hood, and Annalise cried out.

Hands trembling, she rose to her knees, then, using the wall as a lever, got to her feet. "Help me."

"*Oui,* please hurry if you can," Father Armand whispered as he unlocked the door. "I fear it is not safe here."

She struggled over, her gown dragging at her feet. She shivered from head to toe but barely felt the cold over the combined joy and desolation in her heart. Once in the corridor, Bryson swept her up in his arms and carried her back the way they had come. Delphi began screaming, an eerie, guttural cry that echoed down the hall and would soon alert those who had put Annalise there.

Bryson began to run. Passing through the common area, Annalise swallowed back her fear at the dull stares, the spittle and mindless noise. But all of that she could endure, if Bryson could.

He had come for her!

She wanted to weep and rejoice, to plead his forgiveness for bringing him to this place once again. But all she could do was cling to him and wonder how he could bear the torture.

The long halls and catacombs took an eternity. The emptiness resonated with each footstep, marking their passage. She expected Etienne and the obese monk to come upon them at any moment and finish what the surgeon had begun. Finally they reached a door, one not much different from the many they had passed, but more used. Its wooden surface was scarred but well polished, and heat sifted from its cracks like transparent smoke.

Father Armand opened it, then motioned Bryson to precede him. Once they were all inside, he barred it behind him.

Bryson placed Annalise on a cot, then shrugged out of the monk's robes. She stared up at him, her prince, her hero. He was tall and commanding, bright as the morning sun in this hellish place. How had she ever mistaken him for one of the pitiful lunatics? She buried her face in her hands and began to weep.

Bryson lunged forward and pulled her into his arms. His eyes burned into the priest's. "What have they done to her?"

Father Armand shook his head, troubled. "I fear the worst."

Bryson cradled her like a child. "I need to get her to a doctor, but I trust no one here."

"No," she cried. He looked down, terrified by the pallid cast of her skin. "I don't need a doctor. The blood is not my own." She began to ramble; she needed to get the words out before they were found. "We must escape, Bryson. They will kill you when they find you here. They killed your father and brothers. You and your mother are next. They have invaded Germany and destroyed France; England will follow."

"Shhh," he breathed, frightened by her frenetic words. She sounded as mad as the patients below.

"Please, you must listen," she cried. "I am not babbling. It is the work of the *Illuminati*. They are after Marchfield's wealth to fund their cause. They will take it if they can." Her words faltered. She knew she sounded crazed, but she had to make him see. "We must get away."

Father Armand wrung his hands. "What conspiracy is this? The *Illuminati*, more than a vicious rumor?"

Bryson looked up. "You have heard of them?"

The priest went to the shelves lining the walls, searching until he found the *Tractate* by the Abbé Mousseline. "I have heard of such but the Latin is so bad, and I found the idea so unreliable and lacking in authority." He pulled forth the large leather volume, then found another, Balthazar Hildebrand's *Disquisition*. He put on spectacles and began with the *Tractate*.

Mumbling the Latin first, he then translated in his own words. "The sect was founded by a man called Adam Weishaupt, of Ingolstadt. The movement was started in 1776. Was that not the same year as the American rebel, Washington, claimed independence from England? Well, nothing will come of that, I am certain. Ah, this Latin is so inept, I cannot be certain whether this is gossip or fact but I will continue."

He shifted his spectacles. "They aim to establish and propagate a new religion that is based on enlightened reason." His eyes grew bold and offended. "As if they know what such is! They aim to overthrow the existing church and governments of the world! How can this be?"

"I think it is," Annalise whispered. "If you had seen their eyes, their ruthlessness." Tears slid from her lashes at what they had tried to do to her, but she hid them in Bryson's chest.

Father Armand opened Hildebrand's book. "He concurs with Mousseline and also says they believe in an inner light and are very secret and highly organized. And they believe that the ends justify any means." He looked up, saddened. "I am astonished."

"Does it mention aught of England?" Bryson asked.

He studied a moment. "No, it only says that the movement started in Germany, was driven south, and found a home in France. Mousseline also says they are strong in Italy."

"But nothing of England."

The priest shook his head. "Still, it is not impossible."

"The old man," Bryson said, aghast, "the harmless one in the common room who speaks German. Where did he come from?"

Father Armand shrugged. "I am not certain, but there was another, a woman who was brought here years ago and tried to convince me of an international conspiracy. She perished within a few weeks." He cringed at the memory. "God forgive me, I did not listen to her, not to her words. How many others have we forsaken here? I think it is not impossible, Bryson. But who among us here has such wickedness in his heart that he would use St. Bertram's in so evil a manner?"

"A large man," Annalise whispered, "who wears a monk's costume but has not the calling."

"A man not of here," Bryson grated out, as the identity dawned on him. "One who has connections with the revolution and visits here too often. Fabien d'Eglantine."

Horrified, Father Armand pulled his spectacles from his head and softly closed the book. "I have so little with which to help you," he explained. "An old cart, a nag."

"I have a horse," Bryson said, "and a ship will be waiting if I make it back to the coast." He stroked the hair back from Annalise's face, his jaw clenched. He was more frightened than he had ever been in his life. "I don't think she can travel just yet."

"I must," she said through bloodless lips.

But he knew she could not. Her skin was pallid and he noted the way she winced from time to time and cradled her stomach as if she could protect it. He also knew that they had no choice but to get away. After d'Eglantine's men searched the priory, they would search along the coast. "We will need a hiding place."

The priest nodded. "Travel into the hills. The ground is treacherous but there are caves for hiding and ledges that look out over the valley, so that you can tell if someone approaches. I will see to your provisions, food, and a change of clothes and many prayers to speed you on your way." He searched the strength of Bryson's healthy skin, the intelligence in his eyes. "Forgive me for not knowing."

Bryson took the priest's hands and kissed the age-wrinkled backs. "It is of no import. I am eternally grateful for your help now." He squeezed the hands gently. "Never let them know you helped us or your own life is in danger."

The old priest smiled. "I have no fear for myself. What awaits me in the hereafter is much more inspiring that what will be waiting for d'Eglantine."

They left the priory garbed in monks' robes that covered them from head to toe. They walked the distance of the open ground casually, until they reached Bryson's horse tethered in the trees. He settled Annalise in front of him and cradled her close, offering warmth and a protection he feared had come too late. He kicked the horse into a slow trot and watched her face for signs of strain. He saw little beyond her wan skin and the grim set of her mouth.

They stayed within the cover of trees as they passed through the valley, then between small ricks of drying hay when they crossed fields. The air became colder as the day waned and pungent with the scent of pine, a prelude to what lay ahead. They reached a plank bridge over a small stream and Bryson stopped to let the horse drink. Annalise went listlessly into the trees for privacy, while Bryson refilled a skin with water for later.

"Are you well?" he asked when she returned.

Tears glazed her eyes, but she nodded. It would not do to tell him that she had begun to bleed.

The land sloped upward, too steep to travel by horseback. He worried about her health, the drain on her energy, as they climbed higher into the dark pine forest, but she seemed to rally when necessary. A thousand times he asked if she could go on, a thousand times she answered yes, but she was so pale and her breathing so shallow, he was not convinced.

"Annalise . . ." he whispered.

Eyes closed, head against his chest, she answered. "I like the sound of your voice."

"I'm glad it pleases you," he said, but his heart was crushed beneath the weight of worry. He rested his chin on her hair and let the horse find his own pace.

A colony of rooks circled overhead, noisy as harpies above their nests. Pine needles crunched beneath. The rocks increased as the land fell away, growing more prevalent than soil. The way was treacherous. They could no longer ride the horse, and Bryson feared they had gone as far as Annalise could travel. He helped her down but she would not stop to rest.

"If we stop, we die," she said simply. "I have not come this far to die." She looked up at him, her eyes fierce and feverish. "We must not let them win."

"But the child," he said finally, and watched her cringe.

"I think mostly of him," she returned.

Weighted down with their provisions, Bryson helped her over boulders and around slippery outcroppings of tumbled stone. They both became flushed with the climb, and the hint of color in Annalise's cheeks helped Bryson continue the trek to safer ground.

He found a cave close to the crest. It had a wide opening and plenty of brush to cover the entrance. There was the welcome sound of rushing water nearby. The sun peaked, then began to slip lower in the sky, approaching the tips of the highest hills. He led Annalise inside, then spread a blanket for her to sit upon. He unpacked bread and cheese, then bade her eat, but he could see she had no appetite.

She had been silent the entire day, as withdrawn as the women of St. Bertram's. He wanted her to rail at him, to blame him, to curse him. But she only watched with weary eyes as he gathered kindling and brush for a small fire later.

"Eat," he demanded. "You will need your strength."

She nibbled because he pressed, then packed the leftovers carefully away. Once done, she said absently, "Do you hear water?"

He looked up. "A waterfall, by the sound of it."

"Can I bathe there?" Her tone frightened him.

"It is so cold, Annalise."

She could not recall him having said her name before. The sound of it on his lips was rich and endearing, but there was also a strange desperation in his tone.

"I want to go there." She wanted the doctor's blood off her body.

"I don't think it wise."

She looked up at him. "Why?"

"It is so cold and you are not well."

She closed her eyes briefly. "I want to go there."

He could not tell her no. It was not within his power to deny her anything when whatever had happened to her was his fault. "Are you certain?"

For answer, she rose and gathered a change of clothes. He led her by sound to the rushing water. There was a pool carved from stone and a wide clearing that would be sweet and grassy in summer. Now it was barren, only a cold rock-strewn slab with a few hearty plants struggling to make it until spring. Water rushed into the pool, creating a rainbow halfway down its fall. Far below, where the water tumbled from this pool into another, was a wider clearing and a long, low hut made with pine branches and turf.

She stared at it with worry.

"It is only a summer shelter for shepherds," Bryson said, "a refuge from wolves and weather." His voice softened. "My brothers and I spent several nights in a similar one when we were young. We had come to visit some of my mother's family in France and thought it a grand adventure to live like peasants. We could sleep there tonight rather than the cave."

She shook her head. She wanted nothing to do with a place known to others. She climbed down until she reached the pool. The sun was setting but her mind was set on washing. She stripped bare behind a tangle of shrub and rock. She knew Bryson watched but her modesty had been cruelly stripped from her, and she had little care for preserving her dignity now. Taking a deep breath, she pinned her hair high on her head, then walked into the pool. A moan hissed between her teeth at the cold but she did not withdraw. She stayed only minutes in the shallow depths, cleansing her mind as well as her body. Although it was impossible to dissipate the cold or ignore it, she grew numb in seconds and did not feel it as keenly. Both invigorated and fatigued, she climbed out.

Bryson waited for her, wrapping her shivering body

in a blanket and pulling her close to him for warmth. With haste he led her back to the cave, then began building a fire.

"Is it safe?" she asked through chattering teeth.

"Shepherd fires will cover these hills after dark. If ours is seen, it will only be one of many."

She nodded and stared at the flames that began consuming the dry kindling. Warmth rose like steam and began to fill their small, confined space. Her blanket grew hot, then her skin. She bathed in the heat as she had the cold, letting it burn away the chill and restore what feelings it could.

She watched him work to make things comfortable. His hair had come loose from its ribbon and fell about his shoulders in a tangle of deep gold. He looked wild and windswept, like a Viking on raid. But his eyes were fierce and tired.

"When will we return?"

He looked up. "When we can travel fast and hard should we encounter trouble."

Tears stung her eyes suddenly. "They tried to kill the baby," she whispered.

"Oh." The word burst from him in anguish. He lunged forward, gathered her in his arms, and rocked her close while she wept. "I am so sorry, Annalise," he murmured to the wrenching sound of her agony, "so sorry."

"I stopped him." She wept. "I killed the doctor. His blood was all over me."

"Shhhh," he soothed, "it's over. Thank God you got away."

Her voice broke. "I may lose the child yet."

He closed his eyes and pulled her close, his heart breaking at the danger she had been in, the horror still pending. "No, you won't," he said to give her courage. "We'll rest as long as you need. We'll hide here until he is born if necessary."

She smiled at his attempt to encourage, but her heart hurt and her tears would not seem to stop. "I love you," she said. "I've been so afraid I would not get a chance to tell you." She buried her face in his chest. "You don't have to love me back; I just wanted you to know."

"How could I not?" he whispered, but worry weighted his words. "How could any man not love you?"

They slept fitfully through the night. He awoke often to stoke the fire or merely listen. Annalise felt ravaged, but there was safety in his arms, a comfort and security she had never felt before. She held him as tightly as he did her and took strength from his nearness.

When the sun rose, they ate in silence, but Annalise felt more herself. Her body was sore and shaken, but the twinges in her lower body had slowed to a dull ache in her back. Bryson watched her, noting the color in her cheeks and clarity in her eyes. She seemed more determined, though a coolness remained. He knew the look, the reserve and self-protection, and feared it would be with her forever.

But for the first time since his return, he understood something of his mother's demeanor. The threat of losing one unborn child had been enough to make him feel like a berserker toward those responsible. He could not fathom the fortitude it had taken for Eleanor simply to survive the loss of so many. If he could not forgive her cruel actions and manipulations, he at least now understood what drove her to them.

Annalise did not mention the baby. She was weepy and scared when she thought of him, so they talked of other things, and ate hard bread and cheese and pretended they were on holiday. The cave became a refuge, a sanctuary for shared ideas, a place for unfolding the years. Bryson found the more he talked of his murky past, the more he remembered. The fragments still came in fits and starts but some were clarifying now, scenes joining together to create whole episodes in his life.

It was a slow process, confusing and frustrating for Bryson, but Annalise was content to hide in the cave and rest, and learn of him. As each day passed she felt a bit stronger, less vulnerable, and she learned more of him than she would have at the castle. By the fourth day, she was fairly certain the child was safe. Her bleeding had stopped and she chafed at the meager diet and the cave's restriction. She was stronger, almost eager to be away.

Bryson knew they could not hide in the hills forever, but a part of him wanted to remain. He had felt a contentment and purpose here caring for Annalise that he had never felt before, and he was loath to put her into danger again. But they were low on food and they needed to get back to Marchfield and warn Eleanor—if Etienne had not already gotten to her first.

He gathered their few belongings and put out the fire. They dressed in peasant clothing, though Bryson's horse would give them away to a trained eye. He would stay well away from populated areas if he could but a chance encounter could not be foreseen. For the next few hours, they made their way down the hillside on foot. When the pine forest thickened and the ground grew less rocky, they mounted. They both knew the danger that lay ahead but neither spoke of it.

When the night grew too dark for Bryson to accurately assess Annalise's fatigue, he found a crude hut in a field. There could be no fire, so they lay together on a bed of hay, as closely fitted as their bodies could be without intimacy. Bryson covered them both with all the blankets and clothing provided by Father Armand.

Within the circle of his arms, with his heartbeat thumping steady against her cheek, Annalise felt safer than she had in months. It was a false security, she knew.

Chapter 22

Annalise awoke at sunrise to find several Gypsies staring down at her. The woman wore full skirts, a
low-scooped blouse, and a vest. Her head scarf glimmered in the early morning sun with shiny gold disks.
She had few teeth and a suspicious smile, but Bryson did
not seemed to be concerned.

"I heard them making camp in the field during the
night and did not want to wake you," he said. "There is
no danger."

Self-conscious, she crawled from their makeshift pal-
let and tried bringing order to her hair. The old woman
only cackled and fished a carved ebony comb from her
pocket. Annalise smiled tentatively and accepted it. After
creeping from the shelter, she found several wagons with
brightly painted roofs.

The old woman's face was thin and lined with age,
but she seemed strong and agile as she carried a bucket

of water to an open fire. She muttered something in Romany to the others, and Annalise knew by their sympathetic glances that Bryson had told them something of her plight. A younger woman came forward, offering hot food, and Annalise nodded in gratitude.

They were an easy people, pragmatic in some ways, capricious in others. She and Bryson were offered safe passage with them for a day or so, if they chose, and Bryson thought it wise to accept the offer. Strangers were suspect in France these days, but Gypsies were familiar and tolerated as they traveled from town to town.

Annalise was given their clothing to hide her identity and told to sit on the driving board of a wagon beside the old woman called Rawnie. She had always heard that Gypsies were dirty vagrants, but the wagons were scrupulously clean, as was their clothing. Rawnie made easy conversation as they traveled across the French countryside, but she also seemed just as content with long periods of silence. During those times she would smoke her pipe and contemplate the world around them.

The woman looked old as time but her thin, wiry strength made it hard for Annalise to guess even the decade in which Rawnie was born. "Can you tell the future?" she asked on impulse.

The old woman's lips thinned in a wise smile. "You have had recent tragedy in your life. You feel as if your heart is broken, but it will mend. You and your husband are afraid and in hiding, but you are innocent and it is the evil ones after you who are to blame."

Annalise's jaw went slack, and Rawnie's shoulders hunched with laughter. "You wear it all on your face, little girl. Anyone who keeps their eyes open can tell the future."

Annalise smiled, then settled back to listen to a hundred stories of the Rom. Some were delightful and believable. Other were so outrageous, Annalise could only laugh and try not to offend the ancient woman with her disbelief. Her smile faded when the old woman stiffened and fell silent.

Rawnie spat as a village came into view.

Annalise's heart rose to her throat. Two guards stood at the village entrance, but as soon as they saw the Gypsy caravan, other soldiers joined them. For her or Bryson to be caught in France was an instant death sentence. Bryson pulled up beside the wagon and handed his gelding's reins over to Rawnie's grandson, who was driving. He then leaped onto the driving board and disappeared into the back of the wagon.

"Keep you hair covered, Annalise," he whispered. He crawled back inside and lay down, wrapping an old blanket over his hair and covering his body with another.

"What?" She craned to look back at him, but the old woman snapped for her to face forward.

The wagons soon slowed. Villagers lined the road and stared. The superstitious crossed themselves and looked away lest they fall beneath a Gypsy's evil eye; the others just watched in suspicion, wondering how much of their livestock would be pilfered before the caravan left the area.

Soldiers carrying muskets and bayonets strolled toward the lead wagon. One stopped to stare at the old woman and Annalise, the others walked up and down the line of wagons, inspecting, lifting chickens and pots and whatever they wanted from the side hooks while the words "thieving gypsies" were still fresh on their tongues.

"Your papers," the soldier said in French.

Rawnie fished a wrinkled sheet from her pocket and handed it to him. He looked it over quickly, then glanced at Annalise. "And yours?"

Panic hit her. She could do nothing but sit there and stare at him, her heart racing. Rawnie scolded her in a language Annalise did not understand, then slapped at her pocket. Annalise slid her hand inside and found a folded sheet of paper. Her throat dry, she pulled it out and handed it to the soldier. Rawnie scolded her again and took her chin and jerked her face forward, then jabbered to the soldier in French.

His eyes lit up at the words and he gave Annalise an appreciative look. "I don't care if you're promised to another man. Look all you like, *chérie*. A *livre* for you, if you come join me for a while."

Annalise understood almost nothing of his words, but his suggestive tone was hard to misinterpret. She got an offended look and he began to crow like a cocky rooster.

"Think you are too good for a simple soldier?" he asked. He hooked the tip of his bayonet beneath the hem of he skirt and lifted it enough to reveal her ankles and calves. "What have you here?"

She gave a startled cry and glanced behind her without forethought, seeking Bryson's help.

The soldier's eyes narrowed and he moved forward, a greedy look on his face. "What have you in the back there?"

Rawnie screeched like a madwoman. "It is a lie! Whatever you heard about there being sickness in our camp is a lie!"

The soldier's face went white. He wrenched the door open and found a man covered in blankets and sweating profusely. He jerked back out of the way and yelled, "Be gone!" He signaled to his companions. "Quickly, let them pass." Then he looked back at Rawnie. "If you stop even once in town, I will have you all shot!"

She nodded and jabbed at her grandson to get the horses moving.

Trembling all over, Annalise gripped her fingers together until the knuckles turned white. Her throat was so dry she could not swallow. "I'm sorry."

Rawnie said nothing, just looked straight ahead until they had passed through the village and were deep into the countryside again.

"Tell your man he can come out now."

Annalise knocked on the wagon wall. Bryson emerged, looking less shaken than she still was. "I almost gave us away," she whispered miserably. "I'm so sorry."

"It was nothing," he reassured her. His eyes glittered coldly. "That French soldier who tried to lift your skirts was in much more danger."

Annalise blushed. "And he only offered me a *livre* for the privilege!"

Everyone chuckled, as she intended, lightening the mood from their narrow escape. But guilt clawed at her.

She knew the Gypsies would have been in danger also had they been caught hiding aristocrats.

Annalise looked over at Rawnie. "What did my paper say?"

"Scribble scrabble. The man could not read."

A shudder rolled through her. "How could you tell?"

"I handed him mine upside down as a test."

Annalise closed her eyes. "I am so sorry. I almost gave us away."

The old woman did not look at her. "Among the Rom, we have rules. A man and woman do not share a bed before marriage. We never wash the woman's clothes with the men's, for to do so is unclean. We never wear white, which is the color of death, or put our shoes on the table." She turned to Annalise. "But we do make mistakes. We just try not to make them twice."

Annalise nodded. She was ashamed but she had learned. Next time she would be stronger and smarter. Their survival depended upon it.

Having stopped so late the night before, the Gypsies made camp in plenty of time for Rawnie's grandsons to "go hunting," which Annalise found out later meant they were out stealing chickens from a farm several miles away.

Rawnie made her own fire and cooked her own food. Annalise helped when allowed but mostly the old woman seemed to want to coddle her.

"Sit," she scolded. "One day we will travel to England and camp on your lands. We will steal your chickens and use your hay for our horses, and you will not call the sheriff on us."

Annalise laughed. She sat and gathered her knees to her chest. "I will *give* you chickens and hay for your horses, and I will not call the sheriff on you. And I will cook your meal that night."

The old woman cackled heartily. "I hope it is good or I will have to put a curse on you."

Annalise sighed. There was peace here beneath the open sky, a freedom unknown to her before traveling in the caravan. The Gypsies called no place home but embraced each new land. The world was their home, yet it shunned them.

"Is it always this way for you?" she asked. "Your men are accused of thieving, your women are offered money like prostitutes."

"In many places."

"Then why do you wander?"

Rawnie shrugged. "It is in our blood," she said as if that explained all. "Look at your husband. He hauls wood, he tends the horses, he helps the men. But it does not change his birth or his destiny."

It was true, Annalise saw. No one would mistake Bryson for a farmer or blacksmith or blade-sharpener.

As if sensing their scrutiny, he dusted the wood chips from his hands, then looked up. He spoke something to the man beside him, then walked over and sat beside Annalise. "Tomorrow we will part company with the Gypsies and head for the coast," he said. He tugged on her head scarf until it fell to her shoulders, releasing her golden hair. "It is criminal to hide such beauty."

Rawnie gave him a look out of the corner of her eye,

then walked over to the next wagon and spoke with one of her grandsons. She did not return.

⁂

The night was dark, the stars brilliant. Somewhere in camp a man sang an old, sweet song, a tale of love and betrayal. A woman hushed a crying infant. A cloud drifted over the pale slice of moon.

Bryson ran his hand down Annalise's hair. Heat pooled in her eyes, and a sudden, terrible sadness. "I wish we were home and safe—"

He pressed two fingers to her mouth to stop the words. "We will be. I swear it."

She leaned her head into his chest. "Forgive me."

"For what?"

"For being mean-spirited, for not telling you sooner how much I love you. For not showing you."

Desire shook him but he kept his breathing even, his hands solicitous as he whispered, "Come," then helped Annalise climb inside the wagon. He situated her on a bed much more comfortable then what she had endured the past few nights.

His eyes were bold, seeking.

Self-conscious, Annalise played with her borrowed skirt. "Won't Rawnie be along?"

"No."

His voice was deep and husky. It held a note not unfamiliar to her now. She glanced up to see him light a candle before closing out the night completely.

"The *vardoes* are built so that not a single bit of light can filter in."

"Ah." Her mouth formed the word but little sound came out. Her eyes were locked on his, her pulse suspended. He was crawling forward, the candle in his hand, his eyes hotter than the flame.

"They reason that if no light can get in, then rain cannot, either."

Her breathing grew shallow. Light illuminated his handsome face and hair in a brilliant halo of white-gold, then it gently faded away as he put the candle on a ledge.

"Are you well, Annalise?"

"I . . . yes."

He crept forward, over her, on his hands and knees. He reached out and touched the scooped neck of her Gypsy blouse. "All day I wanted to do this. I had to stay away from the wagon or embarrass myself."

Her lips parted, her cheeks grew hot from his words. She sat very still, filled with both trepidation and wonder.

He pushed one sleeve down over her shoulder, then the other. A pulse throbbed in her throat. Candlelight bleached her skin of color, and he could not tell what she was feeling. When she did not protest, he pushed the blouse farther until it pooled at her waist. Her breasts were ripe, her skin flawless. His breath hissed out in a rush at her beauty. He leaned forward to taste the delicacy of her skin. His tongue touched her nipple and she flinched.

He pulled back to find her eyes wide and startled. "Did I hurt you?"

She shook her head but said nothing. Her throat was

too constricted. She gripped the covers to keep from pulling them up to hide behind.

He saw her dismay and dipped his head again to taste her, so lightly she could not take offense. There was no way to overcome her shyness except with time and experience, and he did not expect her to sprawl for him like a courtesan. His tongue laved her nipple and he did not draw back this time when she made a sound. Instead he spoke to her, his lips against her flesh.

"Are you certain you are well?"

"Yes." she gasped. "Very certain."

"I will stop if you insist. But you must tell me."

His breath was hot on her, his words a vibration that sent the heat straight into her loins. He circled her pink flesh, feeling the tip harden against him, then moved to the other one.

The cold air hit her moist flesh. Her breathing grew faster, deeper, and he pulled her nipple into his mouth and suckled until she moaned and dropped her head back, offering more. He moved in closer beside her and slid his hand into her skirt, then pushed it down over her ankles. She recoiled instinctively but he gently pushed her legs back down and spoke softly, looking only into her eyes.

"Do I stop now?"

"No," she answered. She would die if he did.

His hand flattened on her belly and stroked the rounded curve, the blessing that had brought them together. He dropped his lips to hers, felt her gasp when he touched the curls at the juncture of her thighs. He moved deeper.

She moaned, a little frantic, a little shy. He pulled back and slid his hand over her leg, then grasped her ankle and brought it up, parting her for greater access. She said his name on a whisper, lost to the way the candlelight shone in his hair, revealed the harsh cast of his impassioned features.

His hand cupped her. He watched her eyes widen, watched the color climb her cheeks. He began to rotate until her lips parted and her head arched back slightly. His mouth covered hers and their tongues dueled. The heat burning him worked its way through her body as well. Humid with desire now, she rose against him and he stroked her with one finger, lightly up and down until a burning madness was inside her. The chaos swirled, a high hot spiral in her blood.

She gripped his shoulders and pulled him to her, not even realizing she was doing it until he was between her legs and his sex was prodding her against the bunched fabric of his pants.

Alarm filled her eyes.

He paused.

"I'm afraid," she whispered.

His voice was gruff with restraint. "I'll be gentle, I promise."

She touched his face, cupped his jaw. "No, of tomorrow. I'm afraid that there won't be another night like this for us—"

His mouth crashed down on hers and his body shook as if from a fever. She kissed him back with all the desperation of her fears and the passion of her love. He pulled back when he could and stripped his shirt over his head. He was wild and pagan in the glow of a single candle. His eyes were fierce with purpose. Her eyes dropped to his pants, then shyness engulfed her and she looked away.

He reached for her hand and brought it to him, a gentle demand. Her fingers curled into the fabric of his pants, then began to tug. Her eyes flaring with determination, she grabbed the Gypsy trousers in both fists and pulled until they slipped over his hips. He kicked them free and knelt over her. Her palms grazed his buttocks, then his thighs. She wanted to touch all of him but did not know how, had no idea the limits allowed.

Her palms flattened on his chest and she reveled in the feel of sleek muscle, the crisp cover of hair. "What can I do?" she asked, shy but drifting on a haze of ardent curiosity. "Where . . . I want to touch you."

He growled an impassioned obscenity and grabbed her hand, kissing each finger. "Not now." There was a harsh smile in his voice. "I'm too close."

Her brow furrowed. "Close?"

He dropped his forehead to hers, his heart thundering in his chest. "You can touch me everywhere. Every night for the rest of our lives." His knee slid between hers and parted her, settling himself in the cradle of her thighs. "But I want to touch you first."

He entered her swiftly, rougher than he intended. She winced as she took him but did not shy away. He cupped her face in his hands. "I will try to go slow. Tell me if I hurt you."

She wanted to give him what comfort she could, but his heavy weight filled her, stretched her. She was

at Annalise could he even hold onto a belief in divine intervention.

With her he saw his future, a gifted promise. Sons and daughters born with strength of character, who knew little of social boundaries and bloodlines. Their coming together could have been inspired only by something higher than the erratic, mortal world trying to destroy them.

He carried a small arsenal to ensure better odds for their future. He wore a sword strapped to his own side, and pulled out a small jeweled dagger for Annalise.

"This belonged to the first Duchess of Marchfield," he said. "They say she was fierce and beautiful and a handful for the first duke, whose name I bear."

Annalise looked into Bryson's eyes and felt a sudden, indescribable quickening in her heart. It was not the explosive heat of the night past, when he had possessed her body with a force and gentleness that had transcended everything she'd ever known or even imagined of desire.

This was different, not something she had ever felt before, not something that would easily come again—a feeling that would take a lifetime to unravel and define.

Her heart quivered with uncertainty, but she had believed in the beauty of fairy tales and happy endings her entire life. She lay her hand along his strong jaw.

"And if I take the dagger, do I become fierce and beautiful and a handful for the duke who bears the name?"

He swallowed hard, than lay his hand atop hers. "You

are already braver and more beautiful than any duchess before you or any that will come after."

She made a small cry. He breathed her name and pulled her to him as he never had another woman, in love and desire, in fear for her well-being. Adversity had brought them together; love would make them stronger, *if* they could endure. They knew the evil now and they could fight it as his mother never could. He felt a consuming pity for Eleanor and a measure of forgiveness he had not thought possible.

He stroked Annalise's hair, while his heart beat heavy against her cheek. He could have stayed that way forever, but their future was forfeit if they did not get back to England. He pulled back and kissed her forehead, breathing in the scent of her to hold inside him.

"I love you," he whispered. "No matter what happens, remember that."

"And I you," she returned fiercely.

Dragging his sack over, he brought out two pistols and an ammunition pouch. After loading both, he handed one to Annalise.

"Can you use this?" he asked.

She thought of their child, and her eyes grew cold. "Aye, easily."

She wore an old apron with deep pockets. She slid the pistol inside and practiced putting her hand where it might be needed. Taking a deep breath for courage, she nodded at Bryson, then they rose as one and headed for the dinghy.

The beach was deserted, their escape too easy. Bryson searched the shoreline methodically as he positioned the oars and began to row toward the small ship anchored farther out beyond the cliffs. The air was still, the cry of gulls distant. He could not determine if they had gotten away undetected or if a trap awaited them aboard.

When the dinghy scraped alongside the vessel, he grabbed the rope thrown down to him by a sailor he did not recognize. "Where are you bound?" he asked.

"Marchfield, Your Grace," came the prearranged answer.

Bryson breathed a sigh of relief and helped Annalise aboard, then climbed up after her. They exited France in the same way they had come, stealthily and uncertainly and in danger.

Annalise turned her face up to catch the sun's rays. She felt Bryson's arm steal around her and she leaned into him, feeling drained and afraid. "How will we stop them?" she asked. "Who will believe us?"

He had no ready answer, only a hope for the future that had been absent from his life too long. And a future worth fighting for. "We will make them believe us or England will fall."

She smiled then, her heart lightened. "England will never fall, not with such a strong, handsome duke to see to its security."

He took her face in his hands and kissed her thoroughly, like a lover. Like a husband in love.

And she kissed him back the same way, with joy and sadness and their whole future awaiting them.

"How endearing."

They broke apart immediately and turned to find

Etienne standing on deck, holding a whey-faced young woman beside him.

"Oh, Greer," Annalise whispered.

Through lips that trembled, Mary Greer looked from Annalise to Bryson. "You were right. I cannot help him. He means to kill us all."

Etienne smiled. "Such drama, Greer." He ran his hand over her midriff, stopping just beneath her breasts. "Warm my bed as you warm my heart, my love, and we will set the new world on fire." His words turned cold. "I cannot alter their fates, but you will not be harmed."

She sent him a bitter look. "You foolish, pitiable man. You cannot hurt those I love and expect me to love you in return."

He only laughed and motioned to Bryson. "Put your weapons down carefully. The sword first, then the pistol." Bryson hesitated but Etienne grinned and nudged Mary Greer forward. He had the point of a gun tucked into her side. "Only if I must."

Annalise shivered and slid her hands into her pockets. "Etienne, please . . ."

Bryson slid his sword to the deck of the ship, his mind racing over options, finding precious few alternatives. He then crouched and laid the gun down carefully, so carefully, in fact, that the moment was drawn out beyond any rational caution. When he arose, he lunged straight at Mary Greer's knees and toppled her to the floor.

Two shots rang out.

Bryson rolled, coming to his feet to do battle, but Etienne lay facedown upon the deck, his body shaking in jerky spasms, in a spreading pool of blood. He looked at Annalise, but she was still as stone, the gun still pointed at the dead man.

Mary Greer's screams reverberated over and over.

Sailors were running, shouts of exclamation on their lips, disbelief in their eyes. Bryson grabbed up his gun and kept them all in his line of vision. "Stay back," he warned, not knowing who might be friend or foe.

As if from a distance, Annalise slowly lowered the gun. Her eyes were glassy, her skin pale as chalk. She began to tremble and gripped her hands tightly together. She heard Mary Greer's anguished cries but could not move. She was too numb, too terrified.

Bryson touched her carefully. "Annalise."

"Is he dead?" she whispered dryly.

Mary Greer looked up, tears streaming down her face. "He's not breathing."

"I am not sorry," Annalise rasped. "I'm not, Greer!" But she was breathing hard and shivering and trying not to cry.

Bryson pulled Annalise to him. "He would have killed us all, Greer, you included."

Mary Greer sobbed harder because she knew it was true. "I'm so sorry."

They had been in Lord Carline's office all morning, talking to his secretary first, then finally getting in to see the Lord himself. The government servant shifted aside a pile of papers purloined from the highest committee of the French government.

"Last week's meetings of the Committee for Public Safety," he said. "They sent a letter to the American president asking him to keep his treaty obligations and declare war on us."

He pushed up the spectacles on his nose and regarded Bryson. He had the small, flighty appearance of a hummingbird, harmless to the casual eye, but Bryson suspected that Geraint Carline was as sharp as a man needed to be whose very job consisted of evil, intrigue, strategy, and secrets.

"Ah, here it is." Carline held up another sheaf of papers. He had dismissed his secretary some time ago when the Duke of Marchfield began his unlikely tirade of suspicions and accusations about secret societies.

Alone now, he laid the papers before Bryson. "Your Grace, you will see that we have known, or suspected, for some time that they would try to bring their treason to England."

"And did you not think it prudent to warn people?" Bryson's voice was cold and cut quick.

"We needed proof."

Bryson's anger seethed. "I lost my father and siblings to these—"

Annalise put her hand on her husband's shoulder. "Now you have proof," she said calmly. "What will you do?"

"What we have always done." Carline sighed and shrugged. "Hang the traitors when we catch them. It seems you have spared Albion's Fatal Tree its justice with Etienne de Chastenay and done the job for us." He scowled. "I would have liked to question him first."

Annalise lunged to her feet, and now it was Bryson's turn to place a hand on her shoulder. "Pardon the inconvenience," he said sardonically. "The man had a gun pointed at us."

"Yes, well," Carline conceded, "pardons are all fine and good, but information is better."

Bryson handed him an envelope. "We have outlined everything we know, with what names we have. You may question Lawrence McGovern at length, then hang him if what we suspect is true. You will see to this?" Though posed as a question, no one doubted the demand.

Carline nodded. "We are closing in, I assure you."

Bryson rose. "I will make certain."

London teamed with life: hawkers calling, shoppers strolling, carriage wheels rolling. It was not a thing Bryson had missed until this moment. London had never been his favorite place. The endless round of balls and gaming and upholding a certain stuffy behavior for his parent's sake had held little appeal for a boy who still enjoyed riding and fishing better than teas and dancing.

After his father's death, his mother had not ventured often into the city, preferring to host soirees and balls at Marchfield to fulfill her social obligations.

But there were things he'd like to show Annalise now, places he wanted to take her. There were gardens and plays and operas. Museums and shops and restaurants. He would find the finest dressmakers and cobblers. Indulge her with the sweetest confections.

"What are you thinking, Your Grace?" Her face was turned up to him, the sun shining on her golden hair. "Your expression is quite forbidding."

He smiled to soften the look. "Actually, I was thinking of everyplace I wanted to take you in London."

"I would be happy with our room right now," she said. "I could hardly sleep last night for worrying that they wouldn't believe us."

"I would have made them," he assured, "or been called a madman for it."

She smiled in relief. That he could joke about such was a good sign that he was getting free of the past.

He led her to the carriage where his mother waited.

"Well?" The word was razor-sharp but she looked old and worn. After finally handing over the burden of trying to keep Marchfield safe, she seemed to have withered.

"They have known for some time," Bryson said. "They needed names and proof. We gave them that."

Tears glistened in her bitter eyes. "Bedamn their incompetence. Will they do something now?"

He could not hold back his pity for her. He wanted to hate her, but it was not within him to do so. Hate was a thing of his past, love the promise of his future. He would not retreat even for an instant into that black world of bitter hopelessness. Without waiting for the coachman, he opened the carriage door, helped Annalise in, then followed.

"We cannot forget what has happened, Mother. But we can put it behind us."

She pressed a linen kerchief to her thin lips. "I am retiring to the town house in London."

"It is not necessary."

"Yes, it is." She looked at Annalise. "I will not ask your forgiveness. You could never have done better on your own."

Bryson stiffened, but Annalise smiled. "Then I will thank you for tricking me and holding me prisoner and forcing me into marriage with your son."

Annalise gazed at her husband. "She is right, you know. It's just like the story. If it had not been for Cinderella's ugly old wicked stepmother, she might never have lived happily ever after with the prince."

He slid an arm around her waist and laughed so hard his eyes teared up. He found he could be thankful in his own way for his mother's manipulation and the vows that had bound Annalise to him long enough for love to grow.

He cupped her chin and looked deeply into her eyes. "It will take a lifetime for me to share with you everything I feel," he said.

"Good." She smiled. "Because it will take just as long for me to return it."

If you're looking for romance, adventure, excitement and suspense be sure to read these outstanding romances from Dell.

✳

Antoinette Stockenberg

EMILY'S GHOST	21002-X	$5.50
BELOVED	21330-4	$5.50
EMBERS	21673-7	$4.99

Rebecca Paisley

HEARTSTRINGS	21650-8	$4.99

Jill Gregory

CHERISHED	20620-0	$5.99
DAISIES IN THE WIND	21618-4	$5.99
FOREVER AFTER	21512-9	$5.99
WHEN THE HEART BECKONS	21857-8	$5.99
ALWAYS YOU	22183-8	$5.99

Christina Skye

THE BLACK ROSE	20929-3	$5.99
COME THE NIGHT	21644-3	$4.99
COME THE DAWN	21647-8	$5.50
DEFIANT CAPTIVE	20626-X	$5.50
EAST OF FOREVER	20865-3	$4.99
THE RUBY	20864-5	$5.99

At your local bookstore or use this handy page for ordering:

DELL READERS SERVICE, DEPT. DS
2451 S. Wolf Rd. , Des Plaines, IL . 60018

Please send me the above title(s). I am enclosing $ _____
(Please add $2.50 per order to cover shipping and handling.) Send check or money order—no cash or C.O.D.s please.

Dell

Ms./Mrs./Mr. _____

Address _____

City/State _____ Zip _____

DHR2-9/96

Prices and availability subject to change without notice. Please allow four to six weeks for delivery.